OUT
OF THE
DAWN

Also available by P. C. Cast

Sisters of Salem,
with Kristin Cast

Spells Trouble
Omens Bite

House of Night,
with Kristin Cast

Marked
Betrayed
Chosen
Untamed
Hunted
Tempted
Burned
Awakened
Dragon's Oath
Destined
Lenobia's Vow
Hidden
Neferet's Curse
Revealed
Kalona's Fall
Redeemed

House of Night Other World

Loved
Lost
Forgotten
Found

House of Night:
Legacy The Graphic Novel

Goddess Summoning

Goddess of the Sea
Goddess of Spring
Goddess of Light
Goddess of the Rose
Goddess of Love
Warrior Rising/Goddess of Troy

Partholon

Divine Beginnings
Divine by Mistake
Divine by Choice
Divine by Blood
Elphame's Choice
Brighid's Quest

Mysteria, with Maryjanice
Davidson, Susan Grant,
and Gena Showalter

Mysteria Nights
Mysteria Lane
Mysteria

Tales of A New World

Moon Chosen
Sun Warrior
Wind Rider

OUT OF THE DAWN

A NOVEL

P. C. CAST

CROOKED
LANE

NEW YORK

Published in the United States by Crooked Lane Books, an imprint of The Quick Brown Fox & Company LLC.

Crooked Lane Books and its logo are trademarks of The Quick Brown Fox & Company LLC.

Library of Congress Catalog-in-Publication data available upon request.

ISBN (hardcover): 978-1-63910-274-7
ISBN (paperback): 978-1-63910-856-5
ISBN (ebook): 978-1-63910-275-4

Cover design by Peter Strain

Printed in the United States.

www.crookedlanebooks.com

Crooked Lane Books
34 West 27th St., 10th Floor
New York, NY 10001

First Edition: August 2023

Trade Paperback Edition: August 2024

10 9 8 7 6 5 4 3 2 1

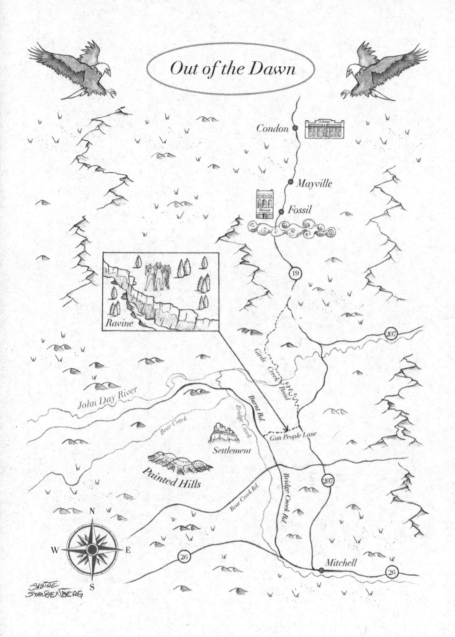

This book is dedicated to the other three members of the real Core Four: Teresa Miller, Kim Doner, and Robin Greentree Tilly. Y'all want to meet me at Timberline?

CHAPTER

1

THE DARKNESS WAS unrelenting. Blackness mixed with that damnable green fog blanketed him like a fucking shroud, which shouldn't have surprised him. *He was dead.* He was also filled with rage—rage about the way he'd died. Rage at the pain, at the absurdity of it, rage at the fact that the end had come too soon. *Too soon!* The new world needed him, whether they knew it or not. He belonged to it. He'd been strong and smart—a leader—and this world definitely needed strong, smart leaders. But all of that had been cut short. Fury roiled within him, tugging him away from his shroud of emerald darkness. His first breath burned. The sudden return of pain only fueled his wrath and he clung to the world of the living so tightly that he was able to take another breath. And then another.

It felt as if he was wrapped in the arms of the earth and through that embrace he could feel the strength of the land. He clutched that strength, pulling it from the shadows, gathering it to him—absorbing it, using it, making it his own.

Sensation washed through him. His body wasn't dead! It was awakening anew, just like the earth. The bombs had shaken the world. The mist had reformed it and the people who inhabited it into something different—something brutal, raw, and *real.* In this new world the strong would survive and the weak would either submit to them or perish. It's how it should have always been. He understood that with remarkable clarity.

It delighted him, and more than anything he wanted to be part of this brutal new world.

No, not just part of it. He wanted to lead. He wanted to control. He wanted to possess.

His skin blazed with heat, though it was difficult for him to tell where his skin ended and the earth around him began. Through the embrace of the earth he absorbed power with the focus of a predator tracking its prey. He absorbed cunning with the innate intelligence of a fungus that buries itself deep so that it can more easily spread. Then he absorbed a special, singular kind of knowledge—the understanding of things that lurked in shadow, that fed on darkness and reveled in the underbelly of the world.

He absorbed, observed, learned, and waited.

Through it all he continued to fight his way to consciousness. He fought to live again.

When he finally opened his eyes he could not remember his name—not yet. But he remembered *her*. The one who had caused his death. He would eternally remember *her*. She must be made to pay. He would be strong and cunning and smart. She could not possibly stand against him. Not now.

He flexed his arms. Their strength was impressive. He stood, stretched, and realized his body had changed. It was larger, more powerful, and there were other differences as well, differences that made him laugh. His laughter was not a merry sound. It was nails on a chalkboard, a ripping cloth, the death shriek after the strike of a predator.

Slowly, methodically, he began to formulate a plan.

2

"*BELLOTA!*"

Mercury came abruptly awake at the sound of her nickname.

"What? I'm here! Don't go!" She sat up and pushed hair back from her face as she looked around, wide-eyed, heart beating like a bird trapped in a small room. The pit bull that was curled at her feet lifted her head and tilted it in a doggie version of a question. Mercury drew a deep breath, held it, and then let it out slowly. "Sorry, Khaleesi. Did I wake you up?"

The blue pit bull's tail thumped against Mercury's sleeping bag.

Mercury leaned forward and stroked the dog's smooth, warm head. "So, I hate to ask," she whispered, though she could already see that no one else was in the cozy nook of the cave-like structure in which their little group had made their temporary bedroom. "But did you hear that, too? Did you hear *him*?"

Khaleesi's tail continued to thump as she licked Mercury's hand.

"Oh, good. I don't have to wake you."

Mercury turned to see that Imani had entered the cave and was striding purposefully toward her. She stopped just short of Mercury's sleeping bag, put her hand on the curve of her hip, and shook her head.

"You've been sleeping a lot, sis."

Mercury shrugged. "I've never been a morning person."

"Yeah, that's what Stella said, but there's a big difference between regular sleeping and depression sleeping. Which one is this?" Imani made a gesture that took in Mercury's disheveled bedhead, her sleeping bag, and the dog that had become her shadow.

Mercury opened her mouth to give Imani an auto-answer of *I'm fine, just tired*, but her friend's kind gaze had her swallowing the rote response and sighing instead. "I'm not sure."

"Well, it's something you should think about. You can drive that truck, right?" Imani said.

"Yeah, I can drive a stick. Why?" She glanced up sharply at Imani. "Has something happened to Stella?"

"No, no, no. Everything is fine. Stella's just down at the creek with the kids and Karen and Gemma. It's late enough in the morning that the mist has cleared from the creek, so they're fishing," Imani said. "I want to take the truck up into the hills and try to reach Jenny at Timberline. My gut tells me they need to know we found our place and where it is. Stella's intuition agrees."

"Oh, yeah, that makes sense." Mercury reached for her jeans, which were folded beside her sleeping pallet, and began pulling them on. "Wait, did you say the mist had cleared over the creek? Is that a thing now?"

Imani rolled her eyes. "Now? It's been a thing for days. It usually hangs over the creek until midmorning or so before the air gets hot enough that it blows away." Under her breath she muttered, "Depression sleeping." Then she raised her voice and continued. "Anyway, I told Stella I'd get you up and have you drive me into the hills, which is when she mentioned you're not a morning person." Imani's full lips tilted up. "I think she said it as a warning."

"Probably." Mercury made herself smile, though it felt strange. *Is it okay to smile? Isn't it too soon? He's only been gone for three days.*

"Well, I told her I'm not scared of you, so she should keep fishing with the kids while you and I trek into the hills. I made you a pbj sandwich and there's coffee ready. Pee, brush your teeth, and let's go." Imani's gaze went to the dog. "And I added some fish guts to Khaleesi's kibble."

Mercury stood and stretched. "What's the rush? What time is it?"

Imani met her gaze. "The rush is that it's almost noon."

Mercury felt a jolt of shock. She'd retreated to her sleeping bag just after dinner, about dusk, which meant she'd slept almost seventeen hours. *Shit, I'm definitely depression sleeping.* "Oh. Okay. I'll, um, hurry."

"Good. I'll feed your dog. Come on, Khaleesi! Time to eat!" Imani slapped her hand against her thigh, calling the dog, who whined and glanced at Mercury.

"Go on, pretty girl. You've gotta be hungry." Mercury made a shooing motion and Khaleesi padded quickly to Imani, who ruffled her floppy ears and led her out the front of the cave.

Mercury moved a lot slower. Her body felt stiff and sore and her mind was foggy. She poured coffee, black and strong, from the sturdy campfire coffeepot Stella had snagged from the general store in Mitchell.

Mitchell . . . that was where Ford had been killed.

Mercury had a sudden urge to throw the coffee pot across the cave and shout *This wasn't worth dying for!*

She didn't, though. She sat on one of the water-whitened stumps that had been rolled into the cave from Bridge Creek, a nearby offshoot of the John Day River. She didn't feel much like eating. Mercury hadn't felt much like eating since Ford had been killed, but she also felt hollow and weak and definitely not herself, so she chewed the peanut butter and jelly sandwich slowly and washed it down with the scalding coffee. She'd just finished and was sipping her second cup of coffee when Imani returned.

"Enjoy that. It won't be long before coffee will be as scarce as wine," said Imani.

Mercury looked into her cup at the black, aromatic liquid. "Huh? We should be able to figure out how to grow coffee here. I mean, if our blood can sprout potatoes and carrots, why not coffee beans?"

"Oh, please. Think about it. Coffee beans are roasted. Roasted seeds don't grow. Unless we can find some unroasted seeds we're screwed on the coffee front."

"Well, shit. Stella's gonna be pissed when she realizes that," said Mercury.

Imani's lips twitched up. "She knows. If you'd been yourself the past few days, I wouldn't have to tell you that."

Mercury didn't know how to respond to Imani, so she put the cup in the bucket of water they'd allocated for dirty dishes and shoved her feet into her cowboy boots. She knew Imani was right, and even though her friend's tone hadn't been admonishing, she felt her cheeks heat with shame. Each of them—Imani, Stella, Karen, Gemma, Georgie, Cayden, and Hayden—had *all* lost people. For most of them, including Mercury, their entire families were either definitely or more than likely dead, but she was the only one of them depression sleeping. *I have got to pull myself together.* She cleared her throat and gave Imani an apologetic look. "Yeah, you're right. I haven't been myself lately. Sorry. All I have to do is brush my teeth and pee and I'll be ready to go." She grabbed a bottle of water, her toothbrush and toothpaste, and started to hurry past Imani, but her friend's hand gripped her arm to stop her.

"It's okay to be sad," said Imani.

Mercury bit her lip and nodded jerkily. "I'll, um, be right back."

Imani squeezed Mercury's arm before releasing her. "I'll be waiting at the truck, 'kay?"

"'Kay." Mercury left the cave-like slash in the cliff. She blinked against the bright, midday sunlight. She couldn't see Stella and the rest of their group, but she could hear an occasional excited shout mixed with the distant liquid susurrus of the creek. She made her way around to the far side of the cliff and the area they'd dug for their latrine, and blinked in surprise. It was no longer just a rough, stinky ditch. There was an actual roof over it. The ditch had been expanded with fragrant, feathery pine boughs strapped to the framed outhouse as stall dividers. Someone had taken three of the camping chairs they'd scavenged in Mitchell, cut holes in the canvas seats, and made fairly comfortable side-by-side toilets that actually had some privacy. *When had they built that? How did I not know about it?*

Mercury brushed her teeth, used the facilities, and then cut through the cave, grabbing a scrunchie to pull back her hair after she put away her toothbrush. Khaleesi waited with Imani at the truck and greeted Mercury as if she hadn't seen her in days.

"Hey, who's my good girl? You are. That's right." Mercury kissed the pitty on her nose. "You should stay here with the kids. I'll bet they'll give you more fish guts."

"She's not going to leave you until you're better," said Imani in a matter-of-fact voice. "And it's no problem to take her with us." She opened the passenger door and told Khaleesi, "Let's go!"

Khaleesi wagged happily, but didn't jump into the cab until Mercury got behind the wheel.

Mercury started the truck, ground the stick into first, and before lifting the clutch she turned to Imani. "So, where to?"

"Well, we haven't had much luck getting the truck up into these hills." Imani made a gesture that took in their shelter as well as the surrounding butte-like mounds. "These cliffs are too sheer or rugged. We're going to have a hell of a time carrying the adobe bricks and such up there as we start building." Imani waved her hand dismissively. "No big deal, though. I'm already working on figuring out a pulley system to fix that, but it definitely won't help the truck get up there. Last night Gemma was talking about the Painted Hills and how she'd hiked them with her parents several times. She explained that people weren't allowed to walk on the actual hills because of how porous the clay is, *but* she described a viewing area where hikers and tourists parked at the start of the designated trails. She said she thought the area was pretty high up because she remembered looking down at a bunch of the hills. So let's backtrack along that road that brought us here."

Mercury nodded and released the clutch. "Bear Creek Road. I remember."

"Yeah, that's it. Gemma said we should look for a side road that'll be heading off to the north and then some kind of overlook or trailhead marking. She couldn't remember the name for sure," said Imani.

"Okay, sounds good. We'll find it."

Mercury drove in silence, bumping along the rough terrain of Bridge Creek—the tributary of the John Day River they'd followed to find their settlement—until she came to the raised area that was the little two-lane road that had brought them into the national park.

"Pull onto the road, but then stop," said Imani. "We're being really careful about covering our tracks."

Mercury nodded and swerved around a big pile of broken limbs and debris, and then climbed the ditch to the road, where she put the truck in neutral and stepped on the parking brake. By that time Imani was already out of the old Chevy and had begun to drag some of the pile of debris over the tracks they'd just made. She glanced up at Mercury.

"Grab some of those juniper branches and brush out the tracks between this pile of stuff and the road. I'll take care of our tracks from here to that clump of scrub. With our immediate tracks covered no one from the road should have any reason to look beyond here."

Mercury told Khaleesi to stay in the truck and headed to the pile of debris. It was sunny but only pleasantly warm, though it wasn't long before she was sweating. When they got back in the truck Mercury wiped her face with her sleeve, put the truck in gear, and took a right to backtrack along the road that had brought them there. "That's harder than it looks."

Imani turned in the bench seat to face her. "It's only hard because you've been sleeping for three days."

Mercury chewed the inside of her cheek as she tried to figure out what the hell she could say to her friend who had lost two small children and her husband, yet she'd continued to function. Mercury blew out a long breath and blurted, "I know. I'm sorry. I feel like an idiot."

"Why?"

Mercury glanced at Imani, but her friend wasn't being sarcastic. She was watching her with an open, listening expression. Her brown eyes were filled with compassion, and Mercury had to blink several times to keep tears that welled from spilling over. Khaleesi whined and licked her cheek. Mercury petted the sweet pitty, cleared her throat, and answered Imani honestly. "Because I only knew him for a few days. We weren't married. We weren't even lovers. But I feel like part of my heart is missing. I *have* been depression sleeping. I didn't even realize y'all had built a three-seater outhouse, or that you'd done all of that." She pointed her thumb behind them where her friends had so meticulously made sure anyone driving by wouldn't be drawn into the reserve by their tire tracks. "I let myself check out for three days because I lost a man I hadn't known much longer, and that's why I feel like an idiot."

"Mercury, the depth of love isn't judged by time. The depth of love shouldn't be judged at all. It should be felt, celebrated, and when it's gone, mourned. But the problem with grief is that it's seductive." Imani looked out the window, away from Mercury. "When I found out Jasmine and Austin and Curtis were dead I wanted to die too. There are times when I still want to die. Not because I don't find any joy in life without them. I do. Even though that's made me feel guilty."

"It shouldn't," Mercury interrupted.

Imani turned in the seat to look at her again. "Rationally I know that. Just like rationally you know that we're not judging you for grieving Ford. But I still feel guilty."

"You said you wanted to die too, but not because you don't find joy in life anymore. If not that, then why do you still sometimes want to die?" Mercury asked the question quietly, as if she was afraid of the answer.

"Because without them I don't feel whole. I don't think I ever will. So I understand exactly what you mean when you say that you feel like part of you is missing without Ford," said Imani.

"But they were your *kids*. Your babies. And Curtis was your husband. Ford was none of those things to me." Mercury felt hollow inside, like she hadn't eaten in weeks and hadn't laughed in years.

"Love shouldn't be quantified. You're not doing anything wrong by mourning Ford. And it's not pie. Your grief takes nothing away from mine or anyone else's. But, Mercury, we're surviving in an apocalypse. You're our warrior and we need you. So I say this with love and understanding—because this is *not* about how long you did or didn't know Ford. This is about timing and circumstance. You're going to have to figure out a way to compartmentalize your grief so you can move forward. 'Cause three days in an apocalypse passes like dog years." She ruffled Khaleesi's ears. "No offense, pretty girl."

"How do I do that? I've never felt like this before."

Imani lifted her shoulder. "Ultimately, you'll have to figure out what works for you and your grief. It helps to keep moving, keep busy, and keep talking. Holding all that sadness silently inside is destructive. It might help to know that we'll all keep Ford's memory alive. He saved Georgie. We wouldn't have escaped Madras without him. He was a big part of guiding us here. None of us will ever forget that."

Mercury wished her chest didn't feel so tight. Her whole body felt heavy and so damn tired. But it did help to know that her friends weren't judging her, and that they would remember Ford with her.

The road curved to the left and then gradually headed north. They'd found their settlement site deep in the John Day Fossil Beds National Monument, following Bridge Creek, which was east of where the Painted Hills began, but now they backtracked into the heart of the Painted Hills. The sun was at its apex and it lit the clay hills so that they were on magnificent display. The hills were layered with vibrant colors, like stripes on mounds of bright, happy quilts. What Mercury remembered as rust was now the red of fall maple leaves. The mild yellow had turned saffron, and there were even deep, imperial purple and moss green veins of tinted clay that made the hills blaze with exquisite color.

"Wow, it's so beautiful and more vivid than I remembered," said Mercury.

"Yeah, the colors change according to sunlight and the weather—or at least that's what I've figured out in a few days." She smiled at Mercury. "I'm glad you're coming back to yourself. I need another science person. The clay is fascinating. I think we're going to be able to make dye with it, and Stella says she's sure she can figure out how to use it as paint."

"Makes me wish we'd settled over here in the middle of all of this," Mercury said. Then she continued to study the rolling hills and shook her head. "But it's not safe enough. Our cliff is a better choice—farther away from any road and a hell of a lot higher up, so easier to defend. Plus, I don't see any water out here. No, it's really pretty, and I hope we can use this colorful clay to make our homes and paint and whatever, but it's definitely not safe enough," she repeated.

Imani nodded and grinned. "There you are. I knew our warrior would come back to us."

"You know I'm not really a warrior, right?" Mercury said.

Imani's grin widened. "Of course you are." She pointed at a narrow gravel road to their right that climbed up into the hills. "And I do believe that sign says Painted Hills Overlook. Take a right."

3

G EMMA'S MEMORY HADN'T let them down. There was, indeed, a gravel
parking lot high in the Painted Hills. A giant RV was parked in the
middle of the lot. Another smaller RV and a truck had been in an accident where it looked like they had collided head-on, but it was difficult
to tell exactly what had happened because both had been destroyed by
fire and one had been knocked on its side. There were no other vehicles
and no sign of living humans.

"Shit. I totally forgot to check and be sure we brought the .38," said
Mercury as she steered the truck past the silent vehicles, taking them
higher into the overlook. Carefully, she left the gravel lot and followed
a path just wide enough for the truck to an area that ended at a trailhead where the path narrowed so that she couldn't drive any farther and
parked.

Imani opened the glove box and brought out the holstered weapon.
"I didn't forget."

Mercury slid the gun into her pocket. She and Imani got out of the
Chevy and, with Khaleesi beside them, they turned their backs to the
stunning hills to look at the huge RV. Mercury let out a long breath.
"Those things are like moving houses, especially big ones like that. One
of my brothers dragged me to an RV show at the Tulsa fairgrounds a
few years ago. I don't know which was more shocking—their price, how
luxurious they were, or how much gas they guzzled."

"I don't think I've ever even been in one," said Imani.

"Hey, if there's nothing too gross inside it, maybe we should consider taking it back to our camp. Well, assuming it wasn't running when the bombs hit and it'll even start. It'd almost be like living in a house. Might be nice to have the shelter while we're working on our place in the cliffs," said Mercury as she stared at the RV.

"No."

Imani's voice was so firm that Mercury's gaze was drawn from the RV to her friend. She raised her brow.

Imani's shoulders moved restlessly. "I didn't mean to sound like that." She paused, cocked her head, and added, "Actually, I did mean to sound like that. I spoke from my heart and my heart tells me that we need to leave what belongs to our old world in the past."

Mercury nodded slowly. "Makes sense. If we want our world to be different we can't live in the past, literally or figuratively." Her gaze returned to the RV. "You can stay here. I'll check that RV so there will be no people surprises."

"No way. Khaleesi and I are coming with you." Imani punctuated her words by patting the pitty on her head. Khaleesi's whole butt wriggled as she wagged and smiled at Mercury. "See, your dog agrees with me."

"Outnumbered again," Mercury grumbled, but she also felt her spirit lightening. *It's going to get better. A little at a time it's going to get better.*

With Imani beside her and Khaleesi padding along with them, they approached the big RV.

"No sense in messing around," said Mercury. She squared her shoulders and went to the door. She'd raised her hand to knock on the bus-sized Winnebago when Imani touched her shoulder.

"No need to knock." She pointed through the window at the driver's seat, where there was the figure of what had been a man, now jellified in death. What was left of him, mostly bones and hair and clothes, slumped over the steering wheel. The window beside him was rolled down and as the wind whipped around the RV it brought them the fetid scent of decay. Imani gagged and took a step back. "No one alive is going to be in there with that."

Mercury grimaced. "True. But should we go in and see what we can scavenge? There might be coffee."

"Coffee and dead people. I do not like coffee that much." Imani shook her head and sighed. "But we'd better check. There might be other things we can use."

"I should say I'll go in there by myself," Mercury said. "But I seriously do not want to."

"I wouldn't let you do that alone." Imani sent her a side-eyed glance. "*Unless* you change your mind and *really* want to go in by yourself."

"Not a chance."

"Yep. That's what I figured. Okay, uh, hang on, let me go back to the truck and get a couple of the bags that you and Stella brought back from Mitchell. I shoved them behind the seat in case we found anything interesting." Imani jogged to the truck and Mercury took a few steps away from the RV, trying to get out of the death scent range.

Too soon, Imani returned with plastic shopping bags under her arm.

Mercury jerked her chin at the bags. "Those will outlive all of us."

"One good thing about an apocalypse is that it's stopped the production of single use plastic," Imani said sardonically.

"Agreed," said Mercury. Then she sighed. "Are we done procrastinating?"

"Sadly, almost. Wrap this around your nose and mouth. It might help." Imani gave her a strip of what looked like an old T-shirt. "It was Stella's idea."

"Of course it was. Okay, let's get this done. Khaleesi, stay." Mercury opened the door to the RV.

The stench was a tangible thing. Mercury gagged and coughed and averted her eyes from the slumped shape of the man. Instead, she looked to her left where there was a decent-sized sink, cabinets, and a refrigerator/freezer combo. Across from the kitchenette was a table with L-shaped bench seats. Mercury moved farther into the RV with Imani on her heels as she peered into the dimness of the bedroom area. She'd just wondered if the bedding could be aired out when her eyes adjusted enough to the wan light and she registered what was on the bed.

"Oh, no! That's just awful," said Imani softly as she peeked over Mercury's shoulder.

The woman lay on her back across the bed. All Mercury could see of her was one hand that was a strange, reddish green color and her distended abdomen. On the floor below the woman's hand was a gun that looked like a Glock. Not far from it was an open handgun lockbox. Rust stained the walls around her as well as the bed linens.

"She was all alone," Imani murmured. "She must have felt completely helpless."

"I hope she's found peace now," said Mercury, her voice muffled by the fabric. She glanced at Imani. "I'm going to get that gun."

Imani nodded. "I'll start going through the cabinets. Quickly." From the doorway the pit bull whined and sneezed as if to punctuate her words.

Do not look. Avert your eyes. Get the damn gun and the box, help Imani, and get out of here, Mercury told herself as she walked briskly down the short, tidy hall that led to the bedroom. She didn't look at the woman, but shifted her gaze to the left, where there was some blood spatter as she bent and grabbed the Glock and the gun box. There was a curtain that served as a privacy veil. Mercury ignored the dark stains on it and quickly closed it before she made her way back to Imani.

"Coffee, tea, and lots of canned salmon and beans, a bunch of bags of rice, and three bottles of red wine. That's good." Imani nodded at the well-stocked cabinets she'd opened.

"I'll hold the bags. You fill them." Mercury breathed shallowly through her nose. Imani nodded and did the same. They made quick work of it, but as Mercury turned to get the hell out of there, Imani pointed at a storage area below the bench seats. Mercury didn't take time to speak. She bent and pulled open one of the padded cabinet-like drawers while Imani opened another, and then the women blinked in surprise. "Huh. Let's take them."

"Definitely." They pulled a large drum from each of the nooks, as well as a beautifully crafted reed flute, and then they retreated from the RV, bags laden and arms completely full.

They staggered up the incline to the truck, breathing deeply to clear the stench of death from their noses. Mercury shuddered. "I'm gonna smell that for days." She sniffed at her shirt and grimaced. "I think we might reek."

"We might," Imani said, "but it was worth it. The flute is gorgeous, and I love the drums."

Mercury grinned. "Drumming around a campfire sounds good to me."

They put the instruments in the back of the truck, wrapping the flute carefully and then propping the laden bags around the drums so that they were held in place. Imani took a plastic bucket from the bed of the truck, and then they made their way to the edge of the overlook. Standing beside a wooden bench, they shielded their eyes with their hands as they gazed out at the Painted Hills. The colors were shocking in their brilliance—doubly so in the areas of the hills that had been split open by earthquakes. It reminded Mercury of a multilayer cake that had been randomly cut into.

"It's even more beautiful up here than what we saw from the road on our way in," said Mercury. She spotted wisps of emerald fog in the distance, moving with the wind and pooling in low spots between hills, and made a mental note to stay vigilant and away from the damn green mist. "The colors are incredible."

Mercury nodded. "What I remember reading is that the colors of the clay were made by different layers of volcanic ash millions of years ago. This used to be a riverbed with lush vegetation all around it, which is why there are all those green layers and even some purples—along with the reds and yellows and creams."

"I wonder if the dinosaurs were capable of hubris?" Imani murmured. Then she tossed back her dark, curly hair and held up the bucket she carried. "I'm gonna go collect some of that clay. I want to start experimenting with creating our bricks. I know I can use the sandy soil by the creek, but I'd like to mix some of this clay with it. Clay's great for bricks, but also—" Imani paused, and her full lips turned up in a soft smile. "It's beautiful. Can you imagine how our homes in the cliffs will look made with a variety of these colors?"

"It'll be lovely," Mercury agreed. "And I'll bet Stella can figure out a way to use the clay for paint, or at least dye. Hey, how about I fill a bucket of clay while you see if you can get the CB radio to reach Jenny?"

"Deal," said Imani.

Mercury headed toward the first of the hiking trails and then paused, calling to Imani over her shoulder. "Hey, I know we're high up here, but the wind is pretty crazy. If any of that green mist gets much closer, call out. I'd rather come back later than get caught in it."

"Agreed."

With Khaleesi beside her, Mercury climbed to the trails and quickly came to an area that was a raised, wooden walkway—or rather it had been a walkway before the earthquakes. Now it looked as if a giant dog had grabbed it in its jaws and shaken it before discarding it like a forgotten toy. Mercury picked her way carefully around the broken platform to the base of the first of the hills. This one was a rust color, so deeply scarlet that it reminded her of drying blood.

She shook off the unease the comparison caused and walked onto the clay, which easily gave way under her feet. Gemma had said that people had been forbidden to walk on the actual hills, and it was easy to understand why. Every step Mercury took dug into the soft, pebbled clay, leaving footprint-sized wounds in the hill.

She bent to scoop the clay into the bucket when her sense of unease intensified. The fine hairs on her forearms lifted and the back of her neck tingled.

Mercury felt as if someone was watching her.

She straightened and looked carefully around. There was little vegetation. The only large plant life in the actual hills was scrub junipers, and there were only a few of those within sight. Her gaze went to the clay. There were no footprints except her own. She glanced down at Khaleesi, who sat contentedly beside her. "Well, nothing's bothering you, and you can smell and hear a lot better than me." Khaleesi woofed softly, tongue lolling in her wide doggy smile. "I need to get a handle on my imagination," Mercury muttered as she finished filling up the bucket and headed back to Imani and the truck.

The feeling of being watched remained with her—almost as tangible as the scent of death in the RV.

4

THE STATIC OF the CB radio reached Mercury before she could make out Imani's words. Her friend had extended the long, aluminum antenna and was speaking into the handheld microphone. Mercury put the full bucket in the bed of the truck and joined Imani.

"Jenny, this is Imani, anybody there?" Imani lifted her finger from the button as they listened to the static and hoped for a response.

Over the radio noise Mercury asked, "Have you heard anything at all?"

"You mean like a douchey guy asking about our location? No. Thankfully. But I also haven't heard a peep from Jenny," said Imani before she keyed the mic again. "Jenny, it's Imani. Come in, please."

They waited and listened to the static. Mercury pointed out at the display of hills that went on as far as she could see. "I don't like that there's still so much green mist out there."

Imani nodded. "Yeah, there's definitely a lot of it around, which is another good reason to hurry up and get our cliff homes built. It's heavier than air, so the higher up we live, the better. I should be able to have our cliff homes finished enough that we're able to live there before it gets too hot here in the high desert. Up high in the cliffs we'll catch the breeze, which will cool us, and living in dwellings made of adobe will insulate us." She keyed the mic. "Jenny or anyone—this is Imani. Please answer."

"Yeah, I completely agree. What do you need to start making the bricks?" Mercury asked as she squinted out at the distant mist.

"The past couple days I've made some test bricks. I'm pretty happy with them, though the hotter the days get the quicker they'll dry. I wish I had some reference books about—"

"Imani! It's Jenny!" the CB interrupted. "Is everyone okay?"

"Jenny! Yes, we're good—really good. Here's Mercury." Grinning, Imani passed the mic to Mercury.

"Jenny! It's so great to hear your voice! How is it there?"

The static took out half of Jenny's reply. "—and that was bad. So we're worried."

"Wait, you cut out. What was bad?"

"I said, the mist is—" Her voice faded and then was suddenly back "—I think it must have something to do with our elevation and the thinness of the air."

"What? Repeat that," Mercury said.

Jenny's voice became audible again while she continued to speak. "And what's left of our part of the lodge is crumbling." More static crackled through the radio, drowning out her words. "—which means it's definitely not structurally sound. Did you find a place to—"

As static overpowered more of Jenny's words, Mercury keyed the mic and spoke quickly. "Can your people move?"

"Yes—" Her words cut out, and then, "It'll be slow going, but we're mostly healthy and since—there are enough to get us out of here—where we're going, though."

Mercury nodded as if Jenny stood in front of her, glad she'd thought about how she'd communicate their location to her friend without giving it away to anyone listening. "Yeah, we've got you. So, charades without any hand movements. Here's where you need to go. Two words. The first is Stella's favorite medium, past tense."

She waited for Jenny to think about it, and then her voice lifted above the static as she responded. "I think I've got that."

"Second word. In north Tulsa there's a neighborhood called Reservoir *blank*. The second word fills in the blank."

There was a short pause and then Jenny's voice returned, sounding excited. "Oooh! Hilary says she knows—" Static bisected her sentence. "—that is!"

"Tell Hilary that we're near there. Just get close and *we'll* find *you*."

Another pause, then Jenny responded. "Hilary says she understands. Mercury—soon. Looks like there's another spring storm—we've already had a few inches more since the—" Her voice faded away into nothing but static.

"Jenny? Are you still there? Jenny?" The only answer was static. Mercury sighed. "Well, at least we know they're going to head this way. Or I hope they understood my charade clues."

"Stella's favorite medium is paint?" Imani asked.

"It's actually acrylics."

"Good clue, though. And there's a place in Tulsa called Reservoir Hills?"

Mercury smiled. "Reservoir Hill, but they were the two references that I could think of that only someone from our group would know." Her smile faded and she ran her hands through her hair. "Are we really doing this? Can we handle thirty more people?"

Imani sighed. "I think we have to, don't you?"

Mercury lifted and lowered her shoulders. "It's going to make building a settlement in the cliffs more complex."

"Well, yes and no. We'll need a bigger group of cliff homes, but more people also means more hands to help build and plant. And some of those people could have experience we need. Like, I can guess at how to create a windmill, or even a waterwheel-type contraption to help us irrigate and shuttle supplies and bricks up to the clifftop, but it would be great if someone had real experience with those things," said Imani.

"That's a good point. I guess it just seems overwhelming. I mean, it's tough keeping seven people alive." Her gaze dropped. "When we were eight we couldn't keep all of us safe. But *thirty-seven*?" It's a little terrifying."

"It's also the right thing to do." Imani spoke softly, with no condemnation, but her words weighed heavily on Mercury's conscience.

"You're right. And I don't think I could, or even should, turn them away." She raised her gaze to Imani's. "That is if Jenny and Hilary can actually interpret my lame charades."

"I think you did a great job." Imani paused and added, "Did you hear that it sounded like the green mist is giving them trouble?"

"Yeah, weird. After the initial blast that sent the mist up into Mt. Hood it shouldn't have been a problem. It's heavier than air, so—"

A woman's voice, definitely not Jenny's, crackled through the radio, sounding much clearer and closer. "Hello? I'm Arianna! I need help!"

Mercury met Imani's gaze as she lifted the mic and answered. "What kind of help, Arianna?"

"Thank god you answered! I need help! So do my kids! Where are you?" asked the voice.

"What kind of help?" Mercury repeated.

There was a pause and then the woman said, "We're hurt. My kids are hurt. Help us, please! We can come to you. Where are you?"

Being careful the mic wasn't open, Mercury said, "I wish Stella was here."

Imani shook her head. "We don't need Stella. Even if we were sure the woman is telling the truth, which we are not, we can't give away our location over an open radio frequency like this. We already know others are listening in, and how dangerous they can be."

"Hello? Are you still there? Did you hear me? Where are you?" The woman's voice had taken on a pleading edge.

Mercury drew in a breath and let it out slowly before she responded. "Arianna, we'd rather come to you."

There was a longer pause before Arianna spoke. "Okay, sure, a town called Pine Grove. Are you from here? Do you know where that is?"

Mercury was quick to respond. "Yes, we're from here. That's a town off 216, correct?"

"That's right! Are you coming? Please hurry, we really need help and—"

Imani reached forward and turned off the radio. "Highway 216 is where that Mack asshole tried to take our truck."

"Yep," Mercury said.

"How'd you know that town was off 216?"

"I didn't," said Mercury as they began to take down the long antenna.

"I feel sorry for that woman, but we can't put our people in jeopardy to try and save someone who might not even actually want saving, especially since it looks like we're adding thirty to our group. And that's not callous or mean. That's just a fact." Imani spoke firmly.

"Let's get out of here. I have an itchy feeling at the back of my neck," said Mercury.

"Yeah, that just gave me the creeps."

Mercury backed to the parking lot and then quickly drove by the RV tomb. As she reached the road, the itchy feeling finally disappeared.

In the days since Ford's death, when Mercury had mostly just been sleeping, the rest of their small group had been busy transforming their shelter and beginning to work on preparing the clifftop for their permanent settlement. Just outside the entrance to the cave-like room two round grills had been assembled. Logs had been rolled in and placed in a circle around the inside fire to serve as seats and tables. Over that fire they'd built a strange-looking contraption from which hung their cooking pots.

"What is that?" asked Mercury around a mouthful of tasty salmon—a single big fish that had been a group effort to reel in that afternoon—and rice that Stella had plated over a mixture of dandelion greens, wild onion, and sage.

From the log seat beside her Stella raised a brow. "It's a cooking line I made. Like it?"

Mercury's lips twitched up as she studied the two metal posts and the taut cluster of barbed metal lines that ran over the fire from which two pots hung, one filled with rice and the other with water being boiled for drinking. "Yep, but it looks like a very strange miniature fence."

"That's because Stella built it from part of a fence!" Georgie added with a gap-toothed grin from across the fire.

Stella shrugged. "While you were sleeping Georgie and Gemma and I foraged out here in the wilderness. We followed the creek north and found a rickety barbed wire fence, which we confiscated. And after some pounding and finagling I managed to make a pretty good cooking line thingie."

"Pounding? I didn't hear any pounding," said Mercury.

From her seat between the young twin boys, Cayden and Hayden, Karen suddenly spoke. "You were in a place where outside noise couldn't reach you." Then she blinked, like she'd just awakened from a daydream, and her cheeks flushed pink. "I apologize. That was presumptuous of me to say."

"Don't apologize for telling the truth," Mercury said quickly. "You're right."

Karen met her gaze and nodded slightly. "But you're back now."

"I am," said Mercury. She cleared her throat and raised her voice. "I'm sorry about the past few days. It was self-indulgent."

"You were grieving," said Imani from her log seat beside Gemma.

Gemma nodded and added, "It's okay to be sad. We are all sad about Ford."

Stella's gaze found her best friend when she said, "But we're glad you're back with us."

"Me too," Mercury said softly.

"Ford wouldn't want us to be too sad too long," said Georgie.

Grief washed through Mercury at Georgie's words, but she forced herself to smile at the little girl. "You're right. He wouldn't. He also wouldn't want us to forget him. Can you help me remember Ford?"

Georgie's shiny brown hair bounced as she nodded enthusiastically. "Yes I can! I'll tell the story of how he saved me from drowning over and over and over."

Mercury's smile felt more natural then. "He'd like that."

"I'm so glad you reached Jenny today," said Karen. "Do you really think the group from Timberline is coming here?"

"From what I could gather from a very crappy connection, I do think so," said Mercury.

"Yeah, it sounded like they have structural problems at the lodge and need to get out between snowstorms," added Imani.

"Hello! That place reminded me too much of the *Titanic*," said Stella with a delicate shiver. "Half of it had already gone under in the quake. Just a matter of time before the other half joined it." She leaned over and butted Mercury with her shoulder. "Good job with the charades."

"Seriously," said Gemma as she picked a bone from her fish. "No way is anyone going to get that hills reference without Google."

"Do you really think people were listening in?" Karen asked.

"Yes, I do." Mercury answered as she and Imani shared a glance. They'd decided not to tell the group about Arianna until after the children were in bed—no point in making them feel any more fearful than they already were. The twin six-year-old boys still hadn't spoken since she and Stella had found them and their sister, freezing, terrified, and starving in their cabin, with their dead parents inside the burned husk of the SUV in their driveway. Imani, their expert on children, had said they'd talk when they felt safe enough. Mercury definitely wanted them to talk.

Cayden, the twin who sat beside Mercury and kept sending her worried but adoring glances, yawned magnificently. Imani stood and stretched before saying, "Okay, kids, let's go out to the wash barrel and clean up before you get into your pjs."

The twins glanced at their sister and Georgie nodded before asking Imani, "Hayden and Cayden want to know if you'll read us a chapter from that big Winnie-the-Pooh book."

Imani's face beamed with mom love as she said, "It would be my pleasure. I love Winnie-the-Pooh. I believe we're at the chapter where Pooh helps Tigger get his bounce back, and that's my favorite." The kids put their plates in a big bucket filled with boiled creek water and then, like baby ducks, followed Imani single file out of the cave.

"She's such a good mom." Gemma's voice sounded wistful.

Mercury turned to the teenager whose mother had abandoned her so that she could go after her husband—even though he was almost certainly killed in the initial blast. "You okay?"

Gemma drew in a deep breath before she nodded. "Yeah. I'm good. But now I want to hear what *really* happened today."

"Smart kid," muttered Stella.

Quickly, Mercury recapped the truth about the RV—they'd left out the dead bodies part when they'd told the story in front of the children earlier—as well as the CB conversation with Arianna.

"Good call not to give any hint of our location to her," said Stella.

"I'll pray for her," said Karen.

"So, we don't have much time before the Timberline group gets here," said Stella.

"Is that a *feeling* or just a reaction to what Jenny said today?" asked Mercury.

"Both."

Imani returned with the children, who disappeared into the rear of the cave, which was the area they'd sectioned off into little makeshift bedrooms. While they changed into their pjs, Imani took her fireside seat and motioned for Stella to refill her glass of wine. She glanced at Mercury. "You told them the rest?"

"Yep. Stella says Jenny and the group will be here soon."

"Well," Stella corrected, "by soon I mean a week or so."

Imani nodded. "And that means we need to get going on our cliff homes." Her gaze went to Stella. "I think I've got the bricks pretty much figured out."

"Did you decide if we need a kiln or not?" asked Stella.

"Thankfully not," said Imani. "Though it would be a good thing to build eventually. Right now I'm more concerned about engineering details of adobe cliff houses, which means that I'm worried about whether we have time for a bunch of try and fails."

Stella's answer came immediately. "No, we do not." She paused and added, "Shit."

"Right?" Gemma said. "We need the internet."

"We don't have that, but we may have something almost as good," said Mercury.

"A library," said Karen.

Mercury smiled at her. "Exactly." Her smile faded as she continued to speak. "Gemma, I don't remember seeing a library in Mitchell. Do you know if there's one there?"

"No. There isn't." Stella said quickly in a voice tight with tension. Mitchell was where Ford had been killed—where Stella and Mercury had almost died with him. "And I *know* that's the truth."

Mercury let loose the breath she hadn't known she'd been holding as Gemma chimed in. "I know that there're two libraries around here. Well, except for the bigger cities, which I think we should stay away from—right?"

"Right." The adults spoke together.

"So there's, like, a really tiny library in a town called Fossil. I only remember 'cause Mom and Dad and I were on a road trip last summer and we laughed when we drove past it. It's seriously in one little building they share with the city hall and the fire department."

"Doesn't sound like that would be big enough to have a decent reference section," said Imani.

"I doubt it. The only other library I know about is in Condon. I know 'cause they also had a little café there with really yummy breakfast served all day. When I was young, Mom and I used to go on Saturdays when Dad had to work." Gemma looked down at her feet and added, "It's by their library, and their library is definitely bigger than Fossil's."

Mercury's heart ached for the teenager who didn't feel young anymore. "That's excellent info, Gemma. Well done, you!" The teenager raised her chin, blinked through unshed tears, and smiled at Mercury.

"So, looks like we're taking a road trip tomorrow," said Imani.

"Mercury, Gemma, and I are going this time." Stella's voice was grim. Mercury glanced at her. Her face was expressionless except for her Caribbean blue eyes, which looked decades older than her forty-something years.

Conversation after that was sparse, especially after Imani joined the children to read to them. Gemma and Karen turned in early, leaving Stella and Mercury to bank the fire and tidy the dishes. They worked together companionably in silence until their chores were done, then Stella poured them each a glass of rich red wine, which they sipped before the fire.

"I'm really glad you're back," Stella finally said.

"Me too." Mercury breathed in the scents of the excellent cabernet, savoring each sip as if it was her last—because someday in the not too distant future it would be their last bottle. At least until they could plant and grow their own grapes. "I shouldn't have checked out like I did."

"It was understandable, Acorn."

"I had some really weird dreams," Mercury said hesitantly.

"Also understandable. Do you want to talk about them?" Stella asked.

"Maybe, but not right now. Now I just want to drink the rest of this glass and then sleep." She glanced at her best friend. "For a normal amount of time."

Stella smirked. "Well, Acorn, rest assured that if you try to sleep in tomorrow morning I will haul your butt right outta bed yelling *Time to shit, shower, and shave, hello!*"

Mercury grinned, glad that the horrible tightness of grief in her chest had loosened. "Your vulgarity is definitely part of your charm."

"Fuckin' A right it is."

Mercury lowered her voice and asked, "Did you include Gemma in our group tomorrow because someone is going to get hurt?"

"I hope not," Stella said. "I hope her name came to me because she knows her way around and it'll save us time to have her with us."

"But you don't know for sure?"

"No, I do not know for sure," Stella said slowly.

Mercury's stomach tightened. "Shit."

"Yep. Definitely shit."

CHAPTER

5

✦

IT WAS ONE of those spring days that was so sunny and bright that it might fool one into thinking it was also warm. It was not. The wind whipped from the north, lifting hair and gooseflesh as Mercury, Stella, and Gemma stood beside the truck getting last-minute instructions from Karen.

"Are you sure you don't want me to go with you?" Karen smoothed the map's flapping edges and held it down on the hood of the truck as she peered from it up at the small group. "These old roads are barely visible on the map and I'd hate for you to get lost."

Everyone looked at Stella, who shrugged. "I know you're really good at reading this map, but my gut keeps telling me just the three of us should go. No clue why."

"You've gone over the route with a pencil." Mercury traced the line with her finger. "We're just going down Bridge Creek Road until we see a gravel side road."

"That I remember camping off of with my parents, so I'll recognize it," said Gemma.

"Yeah, and then we follow that road until we get to 207, which we only stay on long enough to find Girds Creek Road, which is another of those little gravel cutoffs." Again, Mercury followed the slim gray line Karen had traced. "We keep going north on that road. Eventually it runs into highway 19, then we turn north. It goes through Condon, which isn't too far from where they intersect."

Karen nodded, even though her brow wrinkles furrowed deeply with worry. "I know it's going to take a lot longer to go on those rough gravel roads, but . . ."

"Karen, we agree," Stella said, putting her hand on the older woman's shoulder. "We're going to stay off highways as much as possible. The truck's gas tank is full, and we have both spare gas containers with us. They're also full—*and* we have the hose for siphoning."

"Plus, a ton of sammiches and water," added Gemma.

"And we put the shell on the truck and brought some sleeping bags. If for some reason we can't get back tonight we can stay in the camper. So don't get worried if we're not back until morning," said Mercury. "You figured that pre-apocalypse, using all highways, it would've taken us about an hour and a half to get to Condon from here. Double that using those windy side roads and then triple it for apocalypse travel."

Karen's gaze went to Stella. "Tell me you're all coming home."

Stella paused, cocked her head, and her fact lit with a smile. "My gut says we're definitely all coming home."

Karen released a long breath in relief and nodded. "Okay, Imani and I will keep the kids busy."

"It would be great if y'all could catch another salmon," said Mercury.

"For reals," said Gemma. "That fish was yummy last night."

Karen's severe face softened as she smiled at the teenager. "For you, honey, we'll definitely try to catch another fish."

"Okay, let's go. It's early, but that doesn't mean we should waste daylight," said Stella.

Khaleesi, who had been sitting quietly beside Mercury, stood and trotted to the passenger's side door of the truck. Mercury looked down at the pitty. "I think you should probably stay here today."

The instant Mercury spoke the word *stay* Khaleesi started to whine pitifully.

"Aww, let's take her. You know she doesn't like being separated from you," said Gemma as she ruffled the dog's floppy ears.

"She's almost person-sized," said Mercury. "It'll be a squeeze with the all of us in the cab."

"So? Bring her. If we get too crowded we can make like true Okies and tell her to ride in the back of the truck." Stella purposefully increased her Oklahoma twang as she walked around to the driver's side and got in the truck.

"Guess you're comin'." Mercury mimicked Stella's twang as she motioned for the dog to jump in the cab.

"Your accents are weird," said Gemma, laughing softly as she climbed in beside Mercury and closed the door.

"*You're* weird," Stella said playfully. Then she put the truck in gear and bumped along the hard-packed earth of the high desert.

Mercury noticed Stella didn't follow the tracks she and Imani had made the day before, even though they, also, were heading to Bridge Creek Road. They came to the road about a football field's length to the east of where she and Imani had emerged yesterday, but there, too, was an unassuming pile of scrub brush situated close enough to the road to be used to wipe away tracks—which they quickly did before continuing east along the little two-lane.

"How many of those hidey tracks places did y'all make while I was depression sleeping?" Mercury asked.

"Five," said Gemma. "I'll show you the others tomorrow if you want."

"I want," said Mercury. She glanced at her best friend. "That was smart."

Stella's lips quirked up. "Teachers are really good at figuring shit out."

"Indeed we are," said Mercury.

"I'm glad you're done depression sleeping," said Gemma as she petted the pitty, who'd squeezed between her and Mercury.

"Me too," said Mercury.

They crossed Bridge Creek and Stella said, "We need to figure out how to block that other bridge over the creek—the one that's north of here and entirely too close to our camp. Ford was right when he said it needed to be done."

Mercury was glad that they'd started mentioning Ford again, even though every time someone spoke his name something inside her chest tightened. She shook off the feeling and said, "I think it has to look unintentional, though. If people can tell it's been blocked then they'll know we're hiding something."

Stella snorted. "Hiding *from* something is more like it, but you're right."

"Hey, what if we took that broken tree that we were fishing off of yesterday and float it down to the bridge? Once we get it there I'll bet we could tie it to the truck and pull it up to the road. We could make it look like it'd fallen during one of the earthquakes," said Gemma. "Then all of us could sweep away the truck's tracks."

"Not a bad idea, kid. We can loosen up some earth at the side of the road and try to make it look like it fell over—or at least it'll look like that if no one studies it too much," said Stella as she drove around a GMC truck that was stalled in their lane.

Gemma looked out the passenger's window and grimaced. "Ugh, dead guy in the cab. I'll keep checking, though, everything we pass just to be sure."

"It's been ten days since the bombs. I can't believe anyone who survived the initial blast would be stupid enough to stay out here by a highway. Like they're waiting for first responders to show up?" Mercury said. She paused and added, "While I was out of it, did you reconnoiter anywhere? See or hear anyone else?"

"Nope," said Stella. She steered around a big sinkhole that had opened like a giant wormhole in the center of the road before continuing. "We stayed at our camp, made the latrine more bearable, created those hidey exits, and did a lot of talking about adobe brickmaking."

"Yeah, Imani even climbed up the cliff and chose some home sites," said Gemma. "Oh! There's that little road!" She pointed to a gravel road that was barely noticeable on their left.

Stella braked and slowly took the turn, muttering, "This is not going to be fun."

"But more fun than running into douchebags like the one I knee-capped back on the highway," said Gemma.

"Very true," said Mercury.

The road was awful. Even before the apocalypse and earthquake it would've been rough driving. Post-apocalypse it made the going slow and Stella's knuckles on the steering wheel were white. Often Stella had to steer completely off the road for long stretches to avoid sinkholes or fallen tree debris, though there wasn't a lot of the latter as the trees were mostly scraggly junipers.

They didn't talk much, allowing Stella to concentrate, and Mercury gazed out at the desolate land. She could tell the elevation was increasing by the change in the trees and other plants, and was just thinking that it had a barren kind of beauty when she realized what else she was seeing.

"Green mist over to our left," Mercury said and pointed.

Stella glanced to the left and nodded. "Yeah, none of it's come up to the campsite, but it hangs out in the low spots over the creek, and we've seen it in the distance, especially around dawn or dusk."

"We made a plan about it while you were depression sleeping," said Gemma.

"And?" Mercury prompted.

"Imani's using what she thinks is a deer trail to get up to the part of the cliff where we're gonna build our homes," Gemma explained while Stella nodded and made sounds of agreement. "If we see the mist getting close we grab Hayden and Cayden and head for that trail."

"Fast," added Stella. "The chances that the mist will lift all the way up to the top of the cliff are slim to none."

"Good plan," said Mercury. "I wish we knew how many exposures women can have to it and be safe." She looked at her best friend. "Have you had any specific gut feeling about that?"

Stella shook her head and her thick blonde waves bounced around her shoulders. "Nope. My spidey sense is conflicted about it. On one hand I feel sure that it's a positive thing that we were all exposed, but when I think specifically about re-exposure I get a crawly feeling inside. And remember the dead women we saw in Mitchell? Some of them had obvious injuries they'd died of, but definitely not all of them."

"Yeah, and we have no idea how many days Mitchell was covered in that green stuff," said Mercury.

"It makes me worry. It also makes me believe we need to avoid that damn mist."

"There it is! This is that awesome camping place my parents and I discovered. We were the only people out here for a whole weekend." The teenager's voice hitched on the last couple words and she bit her lip, obviously trying to keep from crying.

Mercury reached across Khaleesi and patted her leg. "I'm sorry, Gemma."

Stella released her iron grip on the steering wheel long enough to stretch her arm across the back of the bench seat and squeeze her shoulder. "I'm sorry too, kid."

Gemma nodded. "Thanks," she whispered and put her arm around Khaleesi, petting the big pitty gently.

Mercury studied the area more closely as Stella slowed to drive around huge potholes. At first the area looked like the rest of the rural high desert they'd been driving through. Starkly beautiful—raw and fierce with its severe hillocks, scraggly trees, and brown grasses—and also lovely where it was dotted with wildflowers. The sky was huge and brilliantly blue, and Mercury thought that they could've gone through a time portal and been transported back to the wild, wild west.

Until she saw the closest of the hillocks was inhabited. On top of it, a group of tents clustered around an old Airstream. The door of the Airstream banged open as a tall man with a long beard exited—rifle in hand. Several other men emerged from the cluster of tents; they were all armed. Mercury thought she glimpsed a couple of women through the open flaps of the tents. "Stella, people—to our left on top the closest hill. With guns."

Stella glanced to her left; her knuckles whitened again as she pushed the gas pedal, and the old Chevy fishtailed in the gravel and then shot down the road.

"We need to remember this on the way back," said Mercury.

Stella's sharp gaze took in the land on either side of the road. "I think on the way back I need to leave the road—on the opposite side from those campers—and not chance a roadblock or a warning shot."

"They definitely didn't look friendly," said Gemma.

"Kid, I think we have to assume no one is friendly, especially if that no one has a gun in his hand," said Stella.

When the side road finally ended at highway 207 and Stella turned north, she breathed a sigh of relief. "So, those campers are at about the midway point on that gravel road."

"I'll remember," Gemma spoke up, "and let you know when we get close so you can leave the road."

"We're lucky it hasn't rained recently," said Stella.

"Accident ahead!" Gemma alerted them to a pileup.

Stella guided the truck off the narrow two-lane onto a rocky shoulder as they passed what looked like a four truck and one car pileup. Half the vehicles were blackened.

"Dead folks." Gemma turned her head and averted her eyes. "Inside the trucks and out on the road."

As they drove by, buzzards lifted from the mounds that used to be people.

"So gross," Gemma whispered. "Makes me wish we could bury them."

"I'd stop if I thought it was safe," said Stella. "But it isn't. I know it looks deserted out there, but I can feel danger and I'm pretty sure danger means people. Or that." She jerked her chin to the left at what might be mistaken for moss hugging the low parts of the land—but moss wasn't a thing in the high desert, and it definitely didn't undulate in the morning breeze.

"Could also mean rattlesnakes," said Mercury.

"Do they have those here?" Stella asked. "Seems like a very Oklahoma thing."

"Yeah, we definitely have them up here in the high desert, and today is a total rattlesnake alert day," said Gemma.

Stella and Mercury looked at her and the teenager shrugged. "That's what my dad called it when it's been cold, but the sun's starting to warm things up. Snakes like to come out and find rocks to bake on."

"Maybe I was a snake in another life," Mercury mused. "I like to bake in the sun on a cool day, too."

Stella snorted. "Face it, Acorn, you like to bake in the sun on any day."

"True," said Mercury. Then she sent a brief, apologetic look to Gemma. "But don't do that. Your skin will thank you for not baking it."

"Sunscreen is important," said Gemma.

"Been trying to tell Mercury that for years."

"It's too late for me, but not for—shit!" Mercury swore and braced herself and Khaleesi as Stella braked then swerved around a panicked deer that had darted across the highway in front of them.

"I'm gonna concentrate now and stop talking." Stella wiped each of her palms, one at a time, on her jeans.

"We'll be quiet and be your lookouts," said Mercury.

"And navigators." Gemma lifted the paper map.

They were mostly silent until they came to a vehicle that was stopped in the middle of the lane facing them—another abandoned truck. It was undamaged.

"Two dead people in the cab," Gemma said as she squinted and shielded her eyes against the midmorning sun.

Stella slowed to a crawl and stopped when the two trucks' gas tanks were opposite one another.

"Pee break and gas siphon break?" Mercury asked.

Stella nodded slowly. "I don't feel anything too awful right here, but keep your eyes and ears open. Let's top off the tank."

"I'll unwrap three of those sandwiches." Gemma glanced at Khaleesi and said, "I mean four. Wanta take a break to eat them, or eat and drive?"

"Eat and drive. Definitely," said Stella.

"If you get me a bottle of water so I can rinse my mouth I'll siphon the gas," said Mercury.

"Gladly," said Stella. "It'll be my turn next time."

The three worked together well. Mercury siphoned gas while Stella and Gemma peed. Then Gemma got out the sandwiches and a big bag of chips, scavenged from the Mitchell general store, while Mercury rinsed her mouth, and then she and Khaleesi took their turn using the facilities. The wind was brisk, which kept the day from feeling too warm. Mercury was standing by the rear of the truck, trying to keep her hair out of her face as she did some quick yoga poses between bites of her sandwich when movement in the desert pulled her gaze. Her stomach lurched until she realized what she was seeing.

"Hey, check it out. Goats!" Mercury pointed as Stella and Gemma joined her. "Wonder if they'd let us catch them."

"Ohmygod, you're not going to eat them, are you?" Gemma asked, face twisted like she'd sucked a lemon.

"Oh, hell no," said Stella. "Mercury would never eat a pet, and she'd totally make them her pets. Hell, I wouldn't eat a pet. Not unless I was starving." She shrugged. "But my blood grows things, so starving is probably not going to happen. What are you thinking, Acorn? Goat cheese?"

"Actually, that's exactly what I was thinking. You can make it, right?"

"Hum . . . I need to remember how to collect rennet from plants, but yeah, probably," said Stella.

"I'll bet we can find a book on it in the library," said Gemma. "Oregon has, well *had* a lot of people who forage for food and stuff. Should be easy to find a book on that in a library out here in the—"

Gemma's words were interrupted by Khaleesi's low growl. Everyone turned to the pit bull, who faced away from them, staring into the northeast. Mercury followed her gaze and felt a chill crawl up her spine. "Green mist. Coming toward us with the wind. Looks fast."

"We're outta here! Now!"

They piled into the truck and Stella floored it. The mist was only a few yards ahead of them. It covered a good part of the road, which had taken a dip down as it snaked across the country.

"I'm going to speed through it," said Stella—and she did.

The truck parted it, though as Mercury turned to watch it through the window of the camper shell, it rippled and lapped strangely, reacting to the truck more like water than air.

"Rationally, I know it can't get us in here," Stella said as she wiped sweat from her brow with the back of her hand. "But every time I see it I flash back to Mack, and how it closed over him and killed him."

"And Ford," Mercury whispered.

"And how it almost got the twins," said Gemma, sounding very young.

"We avoid it. Big time," said Mercury as the other nodded.

Not much time passed before Gemma shouted, "Hey, that's it! I'm pretty sure the little sign we just passed says Girds Creek Road!"

Stella braked and backed to the sign.

"Yep! Found it!" Gemma said around a handful of chips she shoved victoriously in her mouth.

"Great. Another gravel road." Stella sighed as she took the left.

This road was a lot more twisty than 207. They saw five deer, but no people, for which Mercury was grateful, especially as they often glimpsed pockets of green moving almost gracefully with the constant north wind. The land was completely free of homes until they came to the John Day River. Near the bridge that spanned the beautiful, wide river were several homes, though they saw no one as they passed. A boat had run ashore on the north side of the river and was half capsized.

"More dead people down there," said Gemma quietly as she closed the chip bag.

"If we knew the river systems here, living on a big boat wouldn't be a terrible idea," said Mercury.

"Tough to grow crops on a boat," said Stella.

"Well, I did say a *big* boat. But I agree that it's not super practical."

Gemma cleared her throat and said, "It could be a good escape route, though."

"What do you mean?" Stella asked without taking her gaze from the narrow gravel road.

"Well, our creek flows to the John Day, right? And that's the big river back there. Could be an escape route if we ever need it."

Stella and Mercury shared a raised brow look before Mercury said, "Gemma, I like the way your mind works."

"Thanks! I do too." Gemma grinned.

They lapsed into companionable silence, together breathing a sigh of relief when their gravel road finally dumped into highway 19.

"Kid, look on that map and see if you can figure out how far it is from here to Condon," said Stella.

Gemma rustled the map around and traced the road with her finger before answering. "It's only about thirty miles. First we come to Fossil, which is just up the road. It's super tiny. You know, the town that I told you about that has their library, city hall, and fire station all together. Then about ten miles from that is Mayville—it's tiny too. *Then* Condon, which is also small, but has the biggest library in the area."

"And an excellent breakfast café," added Mercury.

"It definitely used to," said Gemma. This time the memory made her smile.

"So I'm not stopping in Fossil or Mayville. I'm going to drive straight through them as fast as possible. Keep your eyes open for people. And guns," said Stella.

There weren't people to worry about in Fossil. The little town was situated in a curve in the highway that dipped down just enough to capture and keep the green mist. Stella braked the truck on the edge of the fog. "Roll up your windows. I'm gonna race through this place," she said.

Stella steered the truck around wrecks like a pro. The green fog lurked close to the ground, and as they sped through it the emerald rippled and washed against the tires of the truck like the Chevy was a barge parting a shallow green river. Because the fog stayed low to the ground, she was able to maintain a decent speed and avoid obstacles— except for obstacles that were lying in the road. When the truck squished over the first of them, they shuddered and Khaleesi whined.

"More dead people," Gemma said. The healthy pink had drained from her cheeks, and she bit her lip as the truck bumped over another body.

"They can't feel it." Mercury spoke gently to her friend. "It's not your fault that you can't see them to avoid running over them."

Stella nodded, but her face, too, had lost all of its color. "I know, but that doesn't make it any less terrible."

Not knowing what to say, Mercury put her arm around Khaleesi and held the dog close.

In the heart of downtown the mist had dissipated enough that Stella was able to slow to avoid bodies, and the scent of decay seeped into the cab, causing them to gag.

"I see some women." Gemma's voice was hushed. "Like what you guys said you saw in Mitchell. I don't see any injuries. They're just dead."

"I think you should speed up," said Mercury. "Even if you run over some dead people."

"Agreed." The pickup shot out of downtown, leaving an eddying green river in its wake.

6

M AYVILLE WAS SMALLER than Fossil, but they saw no green mist as they sped through the silent town. Stella had to swerve around a group of deer that were trotting down Main Street, but other than that, nothing stirred.

"It looks like a ghost town." Mercury spoke softly, almost afraid of disturbing spirits.

Gemma shrugged. "It looked like that before the apocalypse."

"It is beautiful, though, with all these hills and canyons." Stella rolled her shoulders and opened and closed each hand, relaxing a little as their current section of highway 19 was sinkhole free with no vehicles in sight.

"It is, but I can see pockets of green higher up in canyons around here than it should be." Mercury gestured at a particular area off to their right where the emerald mist seemed to cling to the side of one of the canyons. "I wonder if its behavior is altered by elevation."

"The elevation of Mayville is almost exactly three thousand feet above sea level," said Gemma.

Mercury stared at her. "How the hell do you know that?"

Gemma smiled smugly. "I'm smart." Then she giggled and added, "Plus, I needed extra credit in my eighth grade geography class and the easiest way to get it was to memorize a bunch of towns and elevations in Oregon. Timberline is at—" She paused and tapped her chin as she thought. "I remember! Six thousand feet."

"Do you remember the elevation of the Painted Hills?" Mercury asked.

"Oh, yeah. That's easy. It and the fossil beds, which are really where our camp is, are at just a little over two thousand feet."

"Damn, kid," Stella said. "Good memory." Then she glanced at Mercury. "What were you saying about that green stuff and elevation?"

"Well, yesterday Jenny tried to tell me something about the green mist acting weird, but the connection was so bad she didn't make much sense and I just thought I'd misheard her. Our scholar here says Timberline is six thousand feet up. And now we're higher up in elevation than our camp, which means those"—she gestured at the distant canyons—"are even higher in elevation. It makes me wonder if elevation affects the behavior of the mist."

"How could that be?" Gemma asked.

Mercury shrugged. "It's hard for me to speculate because I have no idea of the chemical makeup of it, but it's a general truth that intermolecular attractions are affected by external circumstances."

"Speak English, not science," said Stella.

"Okay, the mist is a gas that is heavier than air. But think about cooking at a high altitude."

"You have to alter recipes for high-altitude cooking," said Stella.

"Yep. For instance, water boils faster at a high altitude. It takes less heat to get it to a gaseous state because the altitude affects the water molecules. Altitude pressure could cause the molecular makeup of the mist to behave in a more gas-like, chaotic manner," continued Mercury.

"Wait, I think I get it," interrupted Gemma. "That means that the mist could become lighter."

Mercury nodded. "Yeah, and its movements would be less easy to predict were it lighter. Think of it like those clouds you see that seem stuck on mountains. And now that I'm following this line of thought, the color of the mist could also be concerning."

"Why?" Gemma asked.

"Green could denote the presence of chlorophyll, and chlorophyll absorbs sunlight."

"Why would that be a problem with the mist?" asked Stella.

"Because heat is another variable that can affect intermolecular attractions. The hotter they are the less sticky, or heavy, they are—and that would make the mist more easily moved and its behavior harder to predict," said Mercury.

Stella sighed. "That sounds like a problem. A big problem."

"Yeah, but less big if we're clued in to the possibility that the mist can change under the right circumstances," said Mercury.

"Does that mean we can't make our new houses on the cliff?" Gemma asked.

Mercury shook her head. "No, I don't think so. Like you said, the elevation there is about a thousand feet less than here, and no mist has been trapped on the clifftop. But we do need to think about creating a fan-like system in case this summer the mist is heated up enough to float up to us."

"A fan system? You mean like a windmill?" Gemma asked.

Mercury grinned at her. "Yes. That's exactly what I mean, and I know a couple science teachers who can figure out how to do that without electricity."

"One's you, right?" Stella bumped her shoulder.

"Absolutely, but Imani's the engineer. I'll just be her semiskilled helper. Let's remember to grab reference books on wind turbines and water wheels. Things like that," said Mercury. She peered out the window, surprised at how flat and wide the land on either side of the road had become. "Farmland? What is that, wheat?"

Stella shrugged. "Don't know, but that looks like a town just up the road."

"That's definitely Condon," said Gemma.

"Okay, kid, do you have any clue where the library is?" Stella asked. "I'd like to get in—grab the books—and get the hell out. This talk about molecules and mist is freaking me out."

"I totally remember. The library is catty-corner from the Condon Café with the great breakfasts, and that's right on this main drag through town," said Gemma.

Mercury put her arm around Gemma and squeezed her shoulders. "You're excellent at this navigation and reconnoitering stuff. I'm so glad you're part of our family."

Gemma's smile was brighter than the high desert sunshine. "Me too!" Khaleesi woofed softly and licked her cheek.

Condon seemed to be about the same size as the last two towns they'd gone through, and as the highway fed directly into Main Street, Stella slowed to swerve around stalled vehicles.

"I don't see any green mist, do y'all?" Mercury asked as she peered out at the hushed town.

"Nope, I don't," said Gemma.

"Me either, but you know what else I don't see?" Stella paused.

"You don't see any dead people." Gemma whispered the answer.

Mercury felt a jolt of shock. Gemma and Stella were right. There was not one single body on or along Main Street. "This is fucking creepy. And I do realize how strange it is to say that *not* seeing dead bodies is creepy."

Stella cleared her throat before she said, "There are stains. I can see places where bodies *were*, but no bodies."

"It's like someone cleaned up Main Street," said Gemma. "I wonder if we'd see bodies if we took a side street."

"I'm gonna veto that idea," said Mercury.

"Agreed," said Stella.

Gemma tightened her ponytail and then nodded. "Good. I didn't actually want to."

They quickly got to the heart of Main Street, which had been lined with what probably had once been lovely old brick buildings. Currently, most of them were brick rubble. Stella had to drive up on the wide sidewalk three times to avoid huge tears in the street. Mercury was surprised that there weren't more vehicles stalled in the little town, but at least their lack gave Stella more room to maneuver the truck.

"There's the café." Gemma pointed to the left of the street at the rubble of what looked like it used to be a two-story brick building. "And there's the library. It's still standing!"

"Looks like it's one of the newer buildings in downtown," said Mercury as Stella stopped the truck in front of a one-story white stucco building. Its black awning had fallen to the wide sidewalk, the PUBLIC LIBRARY sign had come loose, and the big front windows were shattered, but it was definitely still in one piece.

"Good thing, because those older buildings were definitely not earthquake proof." Stella put the truck in neutral and engaged the parking brake. "Here's what I'm thinking. Mercury and I will go into the library. Gemma and Khaleesi stay out here."

Before Gemma could protest Mercury added, "Yeah, but not in the truck. Gemma, you and Khaleesi stay over by the sidewalk. Not so close that you get glass in your feet, but close enough that we can see you and you can see us—and more importantly, we can hear each other in case something wonky happens."

Gemma frowned. "Okay. I guess. But I hate it when you treat me like a kid."

"Well, you are technically a kid," said Stella. "Though an unusually old and cool kid, but we're actually treating you like our getaway driver."

"Oh. That's sorta better," said Gemma.

"What're your spidey senses telling you?" Mercury asked as Gemma opened the truck's door and got out, and she opened the glove box from which she retrieved the .38, holster and all, and shoved it into the waistband of her jeans.

"That we shouldn't, as my grandma would've said, dillydally—but that we're also not in immediate danger."

"Okay then. Let's do this." Mercury followed Gemma and Khaleesi out of the cab, with Stella making a detour to the back of the truck to grab the plastic bags and a few cardboard boxes they'd gotten from Mitchell.

"Leave the doors open in case we need to get the hell outta here fast," said Stella as she opened the hatch on the camper shell.

Mercury glanced over her shoulder at Stella. "I thought you said there was no immediate danger."

"It's the apocalypse; that could change."

The door to the library had been blocked by the fallen awning, so Mercury led them around it to one of the big, broken picture windows, where she stopped, feeling cold fingers walk their way up her spine. "There's no glass."

"Because the windows are broken," said Gemma.

"No." Stella had stopped beside Mercury. "She means there's no glass on the sidewalk."

"Or left in the window frame," added Mercury.

"It's been cleaned up. Like the people." Gemma spoke softly.

"You and Khaleesi stay out here, right by this window," Mercury said. "Stella and I are going to grab books fast."

Gemma bit her bottom lip and nodded.

"Khaleesi, stay with Gemma," Mercury said, and then she and Stella stepped over the low window ledge and entered the library.

Stella breathed deeply. "I love the way books smell."

"Me too, particularly when there is no underlying dead body smell," said Mercury. "Okay, we need books on adobe brickmaking and building construction. Windmill and waterwheel info would be helpful too."

"And books on cheese making as well as edible wild plants in the area and winemaking and beer brewing," said Stella, winking at Mercury. "You know, quality of life stuff."

"Agreed."

"It'd also be good to grab as many fiction books as we can, especially some for the kids on our way out," added Stella.

"Oh, shit! Check this out! It's an honest-to-god card catalogue." Mercury reverently touched the big square wooden box that held long sleeves of actual cards. "I haven't seen one of these in years and years."

"Is it just for show?" Stella peered over her shoulder as Mercury pulled out one of the drawers.

"Nope, it's a working Dewey Decimal catalogue!"

"I can't lie. That's making my little teacher heart happy," said Stella on a sigh.

"Ditto! And it's super helpful."

The women quickly located the different sections they needed, grabbed the little white cards, and headed to the stacks, most of which were still intact.

"Found the cheese making section! Hello!" Stella thumbed through a big hardback book. "That kid was right again. There're directions in here for gleaning rennet from local plants." She paused and they squealed happily before she added, "And a bunch of books on winemaking and beer brewing."

Mercury stepped over a mound of books that had fallen from an end display. "Here's the section on brickmaking. It's not big, but . . ." She went through several books and then shouted, "Yes! Adobe brickmaking!"

"Heading to find a section with how-to-make-a-windmill books," said Stella.

And that was when Khaleesi gave a little bark, jumped over the window ledge, and padded into the library, with Gemma close behind.

"Sorry! She was sniffing the air and her tail started to wag and then she wouldn't stay out there with me." Gemma said as she trotted after the pit bull.

"Khaleesi, it's okay. I'll be out in just a sec." Mercury had turned to face the dog, but the pitty wasn't coming to her. Instead she had stopped in front of a long aisle of floor-to-ceiling bookshelves that was in the darker, rear part of the library. Her tail and ears were up and she sniffed the air again, woofing softly.

Sighing, Mercury followed her. "Khaleesi, what are you doing?"

"Hey, Mercury, hold up," Stella changed direction and headed toward Mercury. "You don't know what might be—"

A *woof* interrupted Stella, and then an enormous German shepherd padded slowly from the shadows. He went directly to Khaleesi, greeting her with a wagging tail as the much smaller pitty wriggled happily.

"Oh, shit. He's huge," said Stella, stopping beside Mercury.

"I think he's beautiful," Gemma said breathily as she joined the two women and grinned at the big, sable dog.

"I agree, but does he bite?" Mercury asked, careful to keep her tone light and happy.

A deep voice rumbled as a mountain of a man holding a rifle limped from the depths of the library stacks. "Badger only bites bad guys. So the question is—are you bad guys?"

7

✦

MERCURY PULLED THE revolver from her waistband, letting the holster fall to the floor. She pointed it at the man. "Actually, the question is whether *you're* a bad guy or not."

At the appearance of Mercury's gun, the shepherd's friendly demeanor instantly changed. He didn't growl. He didn't lunge. He went very still as his focus shifted from Khaleesi to Mercury.

"Badge, platz," said the big man and the shepherd instantly went to a down position, though his attention remained riveted on Mercury. The man's gaze never left Mercury. "I can give him one command and Badger will take that weapon from you, but I don't want to do that as that would mean he'd also tear up your arm, and that's something I'd be sorry about if you're not bad guys."

Mercury kept the gun pointed at the man as she studied him in the thick, tense silence. He was huge—definitely well over six feet. His head was shaved. His beard was closely cropped, black flecked with a little gray. His skin was the ebony of a starless, moonless night sky. And his eyes were dark and expressive. They studied her right back.

"What were you doing back there?" Mercury asked.

The giant shrugged a shoulder. "I live here. Well," he added, "I used to live across the street. Now that building is a pile of rubble, so I took up residence here."

"Hey, I know you!" Gemma blurted.

The giant's gaze shifted to her and his brows lifted. "I believe I know you too. Are you a fan of eggs Benedict?"

Gemma grinned. "Absolutely! It's my fav." She turned to her two friends. "He's definitely not a bad guy! This is the cook from that awesome café I was telling you about."

The giant snorted. "Cook and owner." He tilted his head in a little bow. "Marcus Maples. Always nice to meet a customer."

"I'm Gemma."

"Put the gun down, Acorn," said Stella.

Mercury lowered the gun. "Sorry. We've had some really bad experiences since the bombs. In a normal world I would never point a weapon at anyone. My dad taught me better gun etiquette than that. Oh, I'm Mercury Rhodes." She bent and picked up the holster, put the .38 back in it, and returned it to the waistband of her jeans.

"And I'm Stella Carver. You did the cleanup out there, didn't you?" Stella jerked her chin toward the front of the library.

"The glass, yes. Couldn't leave it. Badger would cut his paws."

Stella cocked her head. "Yeah, that, but also the bodies. Or lack thereof. That was you too, wasn't it?"

Marcus nodded slowly, but said nothing.

"Where are the people?" Mercury asked.

"Buried them. Mass grave. Outside town."

"That was a nice thing to do," said Gemma.

"More practical than nice." Marcus's deep voice rumbled. "I'm no saint. I figured I'd be here for a while and rotting bodies make for bad living companions."

"I meant the living people," said Mercury.

The big man's eyes returned to her. "Gone or dead. My turn to ask questions. What are you three"—he paused and glanced at Khaleesi, who was curled up facing Badger—"four ladies doing here?"

"Research," said Stella.

"Research on what?" Marcus shifted his weight and grimaced, and Mercury realized that what she'd at first thought was a rifle was actually a big stick on which he was leaning heavily. Her gaze went to his right leg. His jeans had been ripped open and she glimpsed a crude splint covering the bottom half of his leg.

"You're hurt!" Gemma exclaimed and began to move toward Marcus. "You shouldn't be standing on that."

"Gemma, stay away from that dog!" Mercury snapped, her voice much harsher than she'd intended out of fear for the girl.

"It's okay," Stella said before Marcus could respond. "That dog isn't going to hurt Gemma." Her gaze lifted from the shepherd to the man. "And neither is Marcus."

"Come on over here closer to the windows so I can look at your leg." Gemma switched into her doctor mode, instantly gaining years and confidence. She stopped in front of Marcus. "Do you need to lean on me?"

Marcus's full lips tilted up. "Not unless you want to be crushed, baby girl."

Gemma grinned. "I'm stronger than I look."

Mercury sighed and went to Marcus. "So am I. Come on. I'll help you." Before Marcus could protest, Mercury slid an arm around his waist.

Stella moved quickly to his other side and looked down at Badger. "I'll help too, but I don't want to step on your werewolf."

Marcus's lips twitched up into a full-watt grin and his chuckle rumbled around them. "Werewolf! That's what I call him sometimes too. Badge, with me."

The shepherd got to his feet and stepped a little in front of Marcus, glancing over his furry shoulder while Stella took his place.

Gemma scurried behind a big wooden desk and rolled a large chair to the front of the library, calling, "I've got the librarian's chair!"

Together, the two women guided Marcus to the chair. Badger and Khaleesi followed, both sitting behind the chair into which he collapsed heavily, grunting in pain, brow beaded with sweat. Gemma knelt at his feet and pulled his torn jeans aside. She placed her hands on his leg gently. Marcus jolted at her touch, and then he sighed, his wide shoulders relaxing.

"It's broken and part of the bone is pushed against your skin." Gemma spoke more to herself than Marcus as she examined his shin. "It looks really painful. I wish Doc Hilary was here 'cause I think it needs to be pulled back into place, which sounds awful. This splint definitely needs to be redone. I wonder if I can figure out how to make a cast?" She stopped speaking as she pulled off his sock and checked his foot. "Foot's not too cold so your circulation is okay, which is really good because I do *not* want to amputate anything." She shuddered. "Anyway, you don't feel hot and your leg's not oozing pus." Gemma sniffed. "It also doesn't smell bad, so it's not infected."

Marcus nodded wearily. "That's only because I managed to limp my way to what's left of the pharmacy and get a bunch of antibiotics and pain meds *before* the, ur . . ." He paused and looked at Gemma before he continued. "Before the group of bad guys on motorcycles came through town." He blew out a long breath and added, "Been too worried about that green stuff and more bad guys to take much of the pain meds, though."

Gemma looked up at him. "You can cuss in front of me. I'm older inside than sixteen."

"I don't doubt that for one minute," said Marcus. As long as Gemma's hand touched his leg, his face was relaxed and the sweat stopped beading his forehead.

"How did you clean up all the bodies hurt like that?" Stella asked.

"I couldn't have. I just broke my leg a week ago. Damn stupid thing to do. I was trying to scavenge in the rubble of the Main Street buildings." He shook his head. "Shoulda known better. They're all unstable. A beam came down right across my leg. It was blind luck that I was able to push it off and get myself out of there. I've been next to no good since then." He stared out the broken front window at the silent town as he clenched his jaw before letting out a long, ragged breath. "Yeah, damn stupid thing to do and damn bad timing to be useless."

Gemma stood. Keeping her hand on Marcus's shoulder, she faced Stella and Mercury. "He needs me. And us. I can't do much for him here. Maybe just help his pain. I need to do some research so I know for sure what I should do about that bone trying to stick through his skin. I won't leave him here."

"He comes with us," said Stella. She wasn't looking at Gemma or Marcus. Instead, she unblinkingly met Mercury's gaze.

Mercury nodded once. "Okay. You come with us," she told Marcus.

"Do I get a say in this?" Marcus's voice was semi-amused as his gaze took in all three women.

"You're here alone, aren't you?" Stella asked.

Marcus's dark gaze halted on Stella. "I wasn't alone at first, but I am now."

"You said the people who were here are either gone or dead. Where did the living ones go?" Mercury repeated her earlier question.

"Most the people died. The men in that green stuff. The women either when the quake happened, or from injuries afterwards. The majority of the town was in church that morning, as usual. Every church was damaged. Two completely collapsed, killing almost everyone inside. The third musta had a gas leak because it exploded right after the first quake. No one survived. The last church did better. Only half of it collapsed. That's where most the survivors came from."

"Where were you?" Gemma asked.

"I was where I am every Sunday morning—my kind of church—in the kitchen of my café, feeding the early risers." His gaze softened and a smile lifted the corner of his lips. "I like to get there before my fry cook comes in for the church rush and listen to a little Motown while I serve up breakfast to my regulars."

"But the café is all smushed," said Gemma. "How'd you get out?"

"Well, baby girl, it wasn't smushed until the second quake."

"Did the green mist not get inside your café?" Gemma asked.

Marcus's shoulders slumped and he wiped a hand down his face, as if to erase the memory. "It did. I was in my walk-in refrigerator getting more eggs when the bombing started. The first quake happened right away, and the shaking knocked a jug of sweet tea off the refrigerator shelf. Hit me on the head." His hand lifted to a puckered scab over his left temple. "I fell and musta been out for a little while because when I stood and got to the door of the refrigerator I could see out into the café. It was filled with green mist." He looked down, shaking his head slowly. "It killed 'em. Every man who'd been sitting there, minding his own business, eating his breakfast. Nothing I could do but watch them dissolve. I woulda run out there—tried to help—but my mind was foggy and I couldn't make my legs move."

"Your foggy mind saved your life," said Stella softly.

His gaze lifted to hers. "I figured that out pretty fast. It was windy that Sunday and the mist blew away in minutes. I'd just left the fridge and was trying to help the womenfolk whose husbands were piles of guts and jelly when the second quake hit. I got 'em all out except Mrs. Lovelace. She wouldn't leave her husband's body."

"Your fridge had a window in it?" Gemma asked.

The question made the corners of Marcus's lips twitch up. "Yeah, I'd just had it installed six months ago. Business was good so I took a chance and splurged. It was one of those big metal walk-ins with a door that sealed it shut and a round captain's window.

"Anyway, the buildings along Main Street came down. Weren't hardly any people in them on an early Sunday morning, but those that were didn't survive. Over the days that followed some of the injured died and some folks just walked away. I'm assuming they didn't make it, only because they didn't seem to want to make it. By that time there were only a couple dozen people besides me left. Then eight days ago a caravan of big, black SUVs came through. The woman leading them said that her town was a sanctuary. Most of the women and the couple of men who were still alive went with her."

"Why didn't you go?" Stella asked.

"I didn't like her eyes, and didn't like the way she talked to the men who were with her," Marcus said.

"Was she, perhaps, a redhead named Amber?" Mercury asked.

Marcus nodded slowly. "She was."

"Good instincts not to go with her," Stella said. "She's a fucking monster. Madras isn't a sanctuary. It's a gilded cage."

"Damn," the big man sighed. "I hate that for the folks who went with them." He looked from Stella to Mercury. "How do you know about her?"

"We've been to Madras. We almost didn't get out," said Mercury. She turned to Stella. "Eight days ago was the morning we escaped. Do you think that bitch was looking for us?"

"Probably, though I'm not surprised that they're also sweeping the area for women," said Stella. She looked at Marcus. "You said there were bad guys on motorcycles that came through here the day you broke your leg."

"Yeah, that was a week ago. I was foraging in the ruins when I heard them come into town." He paused and his jaw clenched and unclenched. "I'd just started out to see what was going on when the beam came down on my leg. I got it off and dragged myself out of that mess." His gaze shifted to stare out the glassless window again, and his words were clipped as he finished. "If there'd only been one or two of 'em I'd a set Badger on 'em, but there were half a dozen or so, and they were all armed. Not a damn thing I could do but watch and clean up afterwards. From then on it's been Badger and me."

Mercury and Stella shared a look before Mercury asked, "Did you get a good look at the guys on the bikes?"

"I did."

"Did they have a leader?" Stella asked.

"They did. I heard his men calling him Boss Man. Tall, blond guy. Bloody nose. Mean and dangerous," said Marcus.

"He's none of those things anymore." Mercury's voice was hard and as clipped as Marcus's. "He's dead. I killed him."

Marcus met her gaze. "Good."

8

"OKAY, THE BED of the truck is packed full of books, but there's still enough room back there for Marcus and Badger," said Mercury.

"And I just got Marcus's stuff and Badger's"—Gemma paused to grin at the big shepherd—"loaded in the back seat of his Jeep."

Marcus had remained in the chair as the women quickly found the rest of the books they needed and then packed them in the truck. He'd told them his Jeep, which had been off at the time of the EMP from the bombs, was parked behind the library—where it'd been since he'd broken his leg. Stella had brought the Jeep around front, where it idled near the truck.

"You guys, really. I can drive the Jeep. Remember I said I'm good with a stick shift?" Gemma said.

"I don't doubt your driving skills," said Mercury. "But I do doubt my doctoring skills. So I'll drive the Jeep and you keep your doctor eye on Marcus." Her gaze shifted to the big man. "How groggy are you feeling?"

Gemma had found a *Physician's Desk Reference* and used it to figure the maximum codeine dose for Marcus—and then dosed him while they loaded the vehicles. She'd also found several other medical books, and squealed in delight as she packed them with their other reference books.

The big man's eyes barely focused on Mercury and his grin was drunk. "You're bossy."

Stella made no attempt to hide her amusement. "He's groggy, but he's not wrong about that."

"Well, good. He needs to be groggy. Those gravel roads are going to jar the crap out of his leg and hurt like hell," said Mercury.

"I'll see if I can help with that after we get him in the truck." Gemma spoke softly.

"Alright, our time is more than up here. We should've left a good thirty minutes ago. My skin's been crawling ever since," said Stella.

Mercury stepped closer to her best friend. "Are we in trouble?"

Stella shook her head and then shrugged. "It doesn't feel like that. It feels weird—like we're late. Remember how I felt compelled to get us off the mountain ahead of that snow?"

Mercury nodded.

"In retrospect, I think my compulsion was more about getting to Georgie, Cayden, and Hayden—and Ford—in time than it was to actually be off the mountain. I've been feeling a little like that. Like we need to be away, and that we've missed a deadline. I can't tell if it's because we needed to be somewhere, or needed to *not* be somewhere." In frustration she blew out a long breath before she continued. "I really hate it when my intuition is so fucking vague."

"Either way let's get out of here and keep our eyes open as we drive home as fast as possible," said Mercury.

"Home." Stella smiled. "I like how that sounds."

"Where *are* we goin'?" Marcus asked as he slurred his words.

"To our campsite. You'll like it," said Gemma. "We even have a real latrine, and a lot of wine. Even though most of it's red, but I'm getting used to that."

Marcus's bleary eyes found Stella and Mercury and he squinted accusingly at them. "You let baby girl drink?"

"She's only a baby on the outside. You'll see," said Stella as she and Mercury walked over to Marcus's chair. "Okay, big guy, lean as much as you want on Mercury. Like Gemma, she's a lot more than she seems. We have a bed all made up for you and Badger under the camper shell of our truck. The trip will not be a fun one for you, but at about the halfway point we'll stop and drug you up again."

"If you're lucky you may pass out," said Mercury. He held out one huge hand to her and she took it, easily pulling him to his feet, where he stood, swaying, as he blinked down at her in surprise. "Told you I'm stronger than I look."

Together, the three of them, flanked by two dogs, managed to maneuver Marcus through the low, empty window and out to the waiting truck. The tailgate was down and the camper shell was open. Marcus sat on the tailgate and Mercury scrambled around him into the truck bed, wrapped her arms around his chest, and then she pulled him backwards until they could close the truck without hitting his feet.

"Damn, you're sssstrong," he slurred as Mercury scooted past him.

Gemma took her place. She put bottled water and a pbj sandwich within his reach. Then she patted his shoulder. "It's going to be okay. Stella's used to having hurt people back here. She'll be careful."

"You're nice, baby girl." Marcus patted her shoulder, almost knocking her over.

"You're nice, too. Now I'm gonna move so Badger can get in here. Then I'll check on your leg once more and we'll be off."

Gemma left the truck bed and Marcus called, "Badge, hup!"

The big shepherd immediately jumped into the bed and lay beside Marcus. Then Gemma put her hand on his injured leg. She closed her eyes and concentrated. In the shadowy interior of the cab, green luminescence glowed beneath her hand. It made the rich earth color of Marcus's skin appear to take on a deep jade tint.

Mercury watched Gemma closely, and when sweat began to bead her hand and drip from her arm she stepped forward and touched the girl's shoulder. "Gemma, that's enough for now."

Gemma staggered back, breaking contact with Marcus's leg. She gulped air as if she'd been holding her breath. Her hands trembled as she wiped them on her jeans and used her sweatshirt to mop more sweat from her face.

"Drink this." Stella handed her a bottle of water, which Gemma drained.

Mercury peered into the cab. The shepherd's eyes were watching her with what seemed like human sharpness, but Marcus's face had relaxed. His eyes were closed and he snored softly. Mercury closed the tailgate and clicked the camper shell shut before she turned to Gemma. "Are you okay? I want you to eat a sandwich right away."

"I'm tired. And hungry. And my leg hurts, but that'll go away," Gemma said.

"There're some apples in that bag of sandwiches too," said Stella. "Eat at least one of those along with a sandwich."

"You two don't need to worry. I'll feel lots better after I eat and then sleep. It'll be fine," said Gemma, who patted Khaleesi on the head and then limped to the cab of the truck.

"She's limping on her right leg. The same as his broken one," said Mercury.

"Acorn, you don't remember because you were passed out and almost dead, but after Gemma healed your bullet wound her shoulder and back looked terrible. She had deep, awful bruises and horrible welts exactly where your bullet wounds were." Her gaze followed Gemma as she gingerly got into the truck. "She's gifted, but that gift doesn't come without a price. She pays that price in pain."

"I wonder what price we'll pay for our gifts?" Mercury murmured.

Stella's blue eyes found hers. "I could spout some platitudes like *nothing good comes without a price* or *we need pain to balance joy*, but I think that's bullshit. I mean, I can definitely embrace some joy and goodness without one fucking bit of pain. But I will say that you and I have already paid a price for our *gifts*."

Impulsively, Mercury hugged her best friend. "I'm glad we're in this apocalypse together."

"Me too, Acorn. Now let's go home. Stay close behind me, but not so close that you'll run into me if I have to stop suddenly."

"Got it." Mercury glanced down at Khaleesi, who was sitting beside her, but gazing longingly at the camper shell. "I get it. Badger is a handsome boy." Then she lifted her gaze to Stella's again. "I wonder if Khaleesi's been spayed."

Stella grinned. "Well, I saw Badger's big, swinging balls—fully intact—so we're definitely going to find out."

"Hum . . . puppies would be nice." As Stella turned to head to the cab, Mercury called, "Hey, I just have to ask it out loud. Marcus is one of the good guys, right?"

"Right. You can relax. You know I would've said we're leaving his ass here if I wasn't one hundred percent sure that he's one of the very good guys." Stella's white teeth flashed in a smile before she slid behind the wheel of the Chevy.

"I think the apocalypse is making me grumpy," Mercury told Khaleesi. "Come on, let's go home."

With Khaleesi in the passenger's seat, nose stuck out the half-open window, Mercury put Marcus's Jeep into gear and followed the Chevy. Stella made a quick turn in the middle of Main Street, which Mercury copied, then they snaked their way around a few stalled vehicles and a lot of rubble and broken asphalt as they left Condon in their rearview mirrors.

Mercury was surprised at how relaxed she felt. They were headed home, and all in one piece. Khaleesi was good company and at least the road between Condon and Mayville was free of green mist and vehicles.

"That's good," she told the pit bull. "Have I mentioned lately how much I dislike dead things?"

Khaleesi's tail swept the seat in response, but the pitty kept her nose pointed out the window, sniffing the cool midday air. It was still bright and the wind blew strongly from the north, but the day had definitely heated up and the breeze felt good.

"As long as there's nothing green out there we can leave the window open, but if I see any of that mossy colored stuff I'm closing everything up. So enjoy it while you can because you remember how awful it was in Fossil, right? I doubt that's changed much."

Ahead of her, Stella slowed the Chevy, making Mercury sit up straight and look around the truck to see what kind of obstacle was ahead.

"I don't remember any wrecks at all just outside Condon," muttered Mercury.

Then Khaleesi started to whine, and as the Chevy's brake lights blazed, the pitty's whine turned into rough barks punctuated by growls as the dog's scruff stood up and her stance became rigid.

"What the—" Mercury put the Jeep in neutral. Something to the right of the highway caught her gaze. She couldn't tell what was moving at first, and then everything came into focus. A man was staggering toward the highway, waving one hand and shouting. "Shit. Stay here, Khaleesi." Mercury engaged the parking brake and got quickly out of the Jeep.

Stella and Gemma had already exited the truck and were staring out at the man staggering toward them. As they watched, he fell to his knees, struggled back to his feet, waved one arm over his head at them again and shouted, "Help! Help me!" Then he stumbled back to his knees.

"He's hurt. He's clutching his right arm against his body. I can see blood from here," said Gemma. She hurried around to the back of the truck, put down the tailgate, and opened the camper shell.

"What'ssss happing," said Marcus sleepily.

Gemma crawled into the bed quickly, grabbing the bag of medical supplies she'd brought with them, including one of the bottles of pain-killers Marcus had contributed. "Someone needs my help."

"Who?" Marcus struggled to lift himself on his elbows and look out the camper shell window.

"We don't know," said Mercury from outside the truck. "Some guy out in the desert."

Marcus grunted and blinked several times. When he spoke next his voice sounded less groggy. "Baby girl, take Badge with you. I'm going to give him a command and he'll be sure no stranger will hurt you, but if you want to help this guy you'll need to tell Badge 'It's okay, platz' and he'll lie down by you."

"What if she doesn't do that?" Mercury asked as she peered into the bed of the truck at Marcus.

"Think of Badge like you would a cocked and loaded firearm with no safety. He'll go off."

"You got that?" Mercury asked Gemma.

"Totally, and thanks, Marcus," said Gemma, but she wasn't looking at Marcus or Badger. She was staring out at the man, who had fallen again and was lying silently on the ground about fifty yards from them.

"Badge, guard her!" Marcus commanded, pointing to Gemma.

The big shepherd jumped from the truck and went to Gemma's side. She immediately started jogging from the highway, through a little ditch, heading to the fallen man. The shepherd kept pace with her.

Mercury jogged on one side of her—Badger on the other. Stella was close behind them. Mercury kept her hand on the .38 holstered in her waistband.

When they reached the man, he was lying on his side. Gemma told the shepherd, "Badge, it's okay. Platz." Badger lay down close to her, alert amber eyes never leaving the stranger. Then Gemma went to her knees beside the man and his eyes blinked open.

"Help me." His voice was hoarse and his lips were cracked.

"I'm Gemma. I can help you. Where are you hurt?"

With a moan he shifted his body so that his right hand, the one he held tightly against his chest, was visible. There were puncture wounds on his wrist and the meaty pad beneath his thumb. The hand and wrist were already grotesquely swollen and a terrible purple-red color. The wounds wept blood-tinged pus.

"Rattlesnake." He said. "I tripped a while ago. Fell, and my hand landed on top of the rattler. Bit me three times. Help me!"

Mercury and Stella exchanged a glance that said as Okies they knew how deadly venomous snakes were—even when antivenin was available.

This is bad, Mercury mouthed to Stella.

Stella nodded in solemn agreement.

Gemma's focus never left the man, who Mercury realized after closer inspection was more boy than adult. Even though he was sunburned and looked terrible, he couldn't have been much older than twenty-one.

Gemma took his arm and rested it gently across her lap as she poured water from a bottle she'd taken from the medical supplies bag over his wounds. The moment she touched him, the guy's face lost its grimace and his blue eyes widened, fixing on Gemma.

"Feels good," he said softly.

Gemma smiled. "It's going to be okay." Then she shifted her attention to Stella and Mercury. "I have to heal him. If I don't he's going to die."

"What? Die? No! Help me! Please!" The guy started to try to sit up, which had Badger growling deep in his throat.

"Sssh," Gemma soothed as she pressed his shoulders back so that he lay prone on the ground. "I'm not going to let you die."

"Kid, come over here for a sec," said Stella.

"He'll feel better if I touch him," said Gemma.

"It's important," Stella insisted.

Gemma sighed and told the young man. "I have to talk with my friends about how best to help you. Here, take a nice drink of this water." She helped the guy slurp water from the bottle, then guided him to lie back down. "I'll be right back."

The young man grabbed her hand with his good one. "Don't leave me!"

Gemma patted his hand as Badger growled. "I won't, but be still so you don't piss off Badger." She gestured at the shepherd who watched from just a few feet away.

The guy let go of her hand, swallowed audibly, nodded, and then lay still.

Gemma moved a few feet away with Stella and Mercury. "You guys, I need to heal him fast. Snakebites are super bad news. Even with me helping him, he'll probably be sick for a good long while."

"Kid, you know I'm not one to sugarcoat shit to try and make it sweet, right?" Stella said.

"Riiight," Gemma said reluctantly.

Stella spoke quickly and softly. "I have a bad feeling about this guy."

"How bad?" Mercury asked.

Stella shook her head. "I can't tell if it's bad because of the extent of his injuries or if it's bad because he's a douchebag. I just know it's bad." She cleared her throat and met Gemma's gaze. "I think we should give him a bottle of pain pills and some water, maybe Mercury can carry him over there under those junipers, and then we should leave him."

Mercury felt the jolt of shock that shook Gemma's body.

"No." Gemma said firmly. "I'm not leaving someone I can help out here to die alone. He doesn't have to die at all. I know I can heal him."

"At what cost?" Mercury asked.

"Would you ask Doc Hilary that?" Gemma shot back. "No, you wouldn't, and why? Because she's an adult. Because she's a 'real doctor,'" Gemma air quoted. "I saved your life." She glared from Mercury to Stella. "And when I did, you told me that I have more inside me than any surgeon or hospital or adult. That makes me *more* than a real doctor, and real doctors take an oath to save lives. I have that oath pounding in my blood. I *will not* leave him out here to die. Also, if we leave him just because you maybe don't like him, or healing him might be hard for me, then we're no different from that Al guy or those awful people in Madras. And we have to be different. Do you get that? Do you *really* get that?"

Mercury nodded slowly. "Yeah, I get that."

Stella sighed. "I do too. Kid, you're right and we're definitely wrong. Heal him enough to make him stable, but I have to tell you that I'm truly worried that my bad feeling means that this snake poison is too much for your body to handle."

Gemma opened her mouth to protest, but Mercury's raised hand stopped her.

"Stella has a good point. You can't help anyone else if that snake poison kills you, and it might if he's too far gone. You feel our wounds." Mercury's voice softened as she rested a hand on the teenager's shoulder. "We know you do. It's obvious. So try to get him stable, but if I have to, I'll pull you away from him and drag you kicking and screaming back to the truck."

"Remember Marcus," Stella added when Gemma glared at Mercury and opened her mouth to complain. "This snakebite guy is not the only one who needs you, and we know Marcus is one of the good guys. We don't know anything about him." Stella jerked her chin in the direction of the wounded young man.

"Yes, we do," said Gemma. "We know he'll die without my help, and that's enough knowing for me." The teenager spun around and went back to the prone man.

"I don't like this," said Mercury. "He's conscious enough to realize Gemma has healing powers."

"I don't like it either. But the kid has a point. She's a healer and I think it would break something inside her if we dragged her away from here. She wouldn't forgive us," said Stella.

"Gemma also had a point about us being no different than Rutland or Eva Cruz if we leave him out here to die." Mercury ran a hand through her hair and fought the urge to scream her frustration. "So we make sure she doesn't poison herself and then load this guy up and take him with us, but we'll drug him and hope he's out of it enough that he doesn't realize where we are when we get home. Then when he's better, *if* he gets better, we'll decide what the hell to do with him."

"Agreed." Stella stepped closer to her friend and whispered. "I'm worried that this is why I knew we needed to leave Condon half an hour ago. If we had been on time we would've missed him completely. Gemma would've never seen him."

"Next time you say go I don't give a shit whether we're ready or not—we go," said Mercury.

"What's your name?" Gemma was asking the guy as Mercury and Stella rejoined them.

He cleared his throat and said, "Chad. Chad Condon."

Gemma grinned. "Condon? Like the town?"

He nodded and then grimaced. "I think my hand is bad. Real bad. Am I gonna die?" His blue eyes were shiny with fever and sweat covered his face. His skin was a sickly, sallow color and his breathing was rapid.

"No. I won't let you die." Gemma sat cross-legged beside Chad. She took his injured arm and rested it across her lap.

Chad relaxed visibly as soon as Gemma touched him, but his fever gaze narrowed on her. "Why are you just sitting there? Aren't you going to give me a shot of antivenin or something like that?"

Mercury stepped forward. "Shut it, kid. Gemma is better than antivenin. Just lie back and relax and be thankful we stopped for you."

Chad's blue eyes lit on Mercury. "Who're you?"

"Someone who protects Gemma," said Mercury. "Think of me like that dog over there, only I don't give warning growls."

"Okay, stop it. I need to concentrate and you're not helping," said Gemma.

Mercury closed her mouth, though she continued to lock eyes with Chad. He was the first to look away.

Gemma closed her eyes again and placed both of her palms against Chad's skin. One palm rested on his wrist. The other cupped his swollen, discolored hand. She took several deep breaths and then a moss-colored light began to glow from where her hands touched his.

Chad gasped and his gaze went from Gemma's face—brow furrowed in concentration, eyes tightly closed—to her hands. His mouth went slack with shock. And then Mercury stopped looking at Chad and focused on Gemma.

"Do you know how to tell when she's had enough?" Mercury asked Stella.

"I think so. Watch her hands. His are discolored. When hers start changing color the poison will be draining out of him. That's when we need to make her stop."

"Wait, what?" Chad was looking from Stella to Mercury. "She's pulling the poison from me?"

Both women ignored him and kept their focus on Gemma. The teenager's face had paled to curdled milk. Then her skin slicked with sweat. As she started to tremble, her hands began to change color—taking on an unhealthy purple-red tint.

"That's it," said Stella.

"Got it." Mercury moved to Gemma and crouched beside her. "That's enough, Gemma. You need to stop now."

Eyes still tightly closed, Gemma spoke through gritted teeth. "Just a little more."

Mercury glanced down at Gemma's hands. They were beginning to change shape—to swell. "Nope. Now." Gently but firmly, Mercury took the teenager's hands by the wrists and pulled them from Chad's skin.

Gemma's eyes opened and she frowned. Her voice was weak when she said, "I could've kept—" Then her eyes rolled to show their whites and Gemma fainted.

Mercury moved fast and caught her before she slumped to the ground. She lifted the teenager in her arms. Chad cried out as his hand thumped against the hard-packed earth. "Can you walk?" Mercury asked him.

He cradled his hand against his chest as he stared at Gemma. "Maybe. With help."

"I'll help him," Stella said. "You get Gemma back to the truck. She'll wake soon and will need water and food."

Mercury nodded and called to the shepherd. "Badger, with me!"

With the dog padding beside her, she carried Gemma back to the truck. Behind her she could hear Chad crying out in pain as Stella helped him stand and then supported him as they followed at a much slower pace.

9

✤

"SERIOUSLY, I'M FINE," Gemma repeated.

"Hey, can I get some more water? Please?" Chad called from the back seat of the Jeep where Mercury and Stella had put him after they'd distributed Marcus's belongings between the bed and cab of the truck. Currently, Mercury, Stella, and Gemma were standing in the road closer to the truck than the Jeep. Badger had returned to Marcus's side in the bed of the truck, and Khaleesi was sniffing around them, looking for a place to pee.

"In a minute," Mercury called to the Jeep without looking at Chad.

"If you don't give him some water I will," said Gemma stubbornly.

Stella sighed, reached through the open camper shell, and grabbed a bottle of water from the bag of foodstuff they'd packed early that morning. "I'll take it to him, but I'm also taking him a heavy dose of those painkillers." She lowered her voice and made the teenager look at her before she continued. "That boy already knows too much about us, you in particular. He doesn't also need to know how to get to our campsite, so I want you to be sure he stays drugged and, hopefully, as out of it as possible for the trip home."

Gemma frowned, though she kept her voice low. "You weren't worried about Marcus coming to our campsite."

Stella's response was immediate. "Like when we met Ford, I knew right away Marcus could be trusted. I can't say the same for the new kid."

Before Gemma could continue to argue, Stella said, "Hey, you know me. You know *us*." Her gesture took in Mercury. "So stop and think. We're not being mean or unfair or draconian. We're being careful and listening to our guts, because that has kept us alive so far."

"And we want all of us to continue to stay alive," said Mercury.

Gemma's shoulders drooped and she looked down at her feet. "I know. Sorry. I just . . ." her voice trailed off.

Stella put a hand on her shoulder. "I get it, kid. He's young and cute and you're young and cute. Just remember—this is the apocalypse and not prom."

Gemma looked up at her as she tried unsuccessfully to hide a smile. "Prom? Really?"

"I think you get my meaning," Stella said. "How many hydrocodones can I give him without killing him?"

"I'm pretty sure he can have three of the kind we gave Marcus," said Gemma.

Stella took the water and the pills and headed to the Jeep.

"Gave me more than that." Marcus's groggy voice came from the open camper shell.

Mercury peered in at him and grinned. "That's because you're mountain-sized and that boy is definitely not."

Marcus's rumbling chuckle was her only answer.

She turned her attention back to the teenager. "Let me see your hand." Mercury held hers out, palm up, and gestured at Gemma.

Reluctantly, the teenager put her hand in Mercury's. It was still discolored, but it had stopped swelling and the red striations that had begun to spread up her wrist had faded.

"How's your headache?" Mercury asked her.

Gemma shrugged. "Getting better, and definitely good enough for us to start driving again. I'll probably just go to sleep, and when I wake up I'll be good as new."

"I'm going to agree with that. We need to get going." As Stella rejoined them she pointed back to the north where the wind was blowing a line of emerald in their direction.

"I want to ride in the Jeep to keep an eye on Chad's hand," said Gemma. Then at Mercury's narrow-eyed look she hastily added, "There's no room for me in the cab of the truck what with Marcus's stuff in there anyway."

"Okay, but you're not riding in the back seat with him." Mercury held up her hand, cutting off Gemma's complaint before she'd even spoken it. "Nope. No argument. He needs to stretch out and sleep, which means he'd have to put his legs across your lap, and I know damn well you'll be sending little zaps of healing mojo into him. Your body can't take that on top of all the rest of the healing you've done today."

"She's right," said Stella.

Gemma sighed. "I know. And I know I have to rest. I'll sit up front, 'kay?"

"Okay," said Mercury. She glanced at the pitty, who was chasing a puff of sagebrush across the road. "Is there room for Khaleesi in the cab of the truck?"

"Got room for her back here." Marcus said.

The three of them turned to look into the bed at Marcus and Badger, who had scooted more toward the cab to make room for Khaleesi.

"How's your leg feeing?" Gemma asked him.

"Not bad enough for you to hurt yo'sssself to try and fix," said Marcus, his keen observation in contradiction to his slurring words.

"You don't miss much, do you?" Stella asked.

Marcus just blinked at them and moved one massive shoulder up and then down in a half-shrug.

"Well, *you* said we could trust him," quipped Gemma before she headed to the passenger's side of the Jeep.

Marcus's white teeth flashed in the darkness of the truck bed.

"I'm smoking an entire damn joint tonight. By myself," Mercury muttered. "Come on, Khaleesi! You're gonna ride with Badge and Marcus." Like a perfect lady, the pitty jumped delicately up onto the open tailgate and then went to Badger. The two touched noses and, before she curled up in front of the shepherd, she licked Marcus's cheek. Mercury closed the tailgate and the camper shell on the big man's deep chuckle.

"Hey," Stella called to her just before she got in the cab of the truck. "Give this to Gemma. She can use it as a pillow." She tossed Mercury Gemma's hoody. "And I promise to open one of the really good bottles of wine tonight."

"Something that pairs well with weed?" Mercury asked.

"Hell, *all* wine pairs well with weed." Stella laughed and got into the cab.

Mercury slid back behind the wheel and handed Gemma her hoody. "Try to get some sleep."

Gemma yawned, nodded, and then glanced in the back seat. "How you doing, Chad?"

"Better. Be glad when these pain pills start working, though," he said. "Hey, what happened back there? What was that green glowing stuff that came from your hands? Do you have special powers or something?"

Mercury met Chad's gaze in her rearview mirror. "Go to sleep."

"No, but seriously. My hand is way better and I saw the green glowing stuff and then I saw that her hand had started to look kinda like mine," said Chad.

Gemma and Mercury shared a glance and Mercury quickly shook her head.

"Like I said, go to sleep." Mercury told him. "If you don't rest you won't heal."

Chad quit asking questions then, but in the rearview mirror Mercury could see that he continued to stare at Gemma until the hydrocodone had his eyes unfocusing and he finally slept. Gemma slept, too, leaving Mercury alone with her thoughts. She kept glancing in the rearview mirror at Chad Condon's face, wondering how worried she needed to be about this new addition to their group.

Stella stopped the truck just outside Fossil and waved Mercury to pull the Jeep up beside her. The mist hadn't left the town in the hours since they'd passed through. Fossil still appeared to be veiled in a low-hanging, moss-colored shroud. Green pockets were tucked close to ditches and sidewalks, lifting only briefly with the cool breeze before it settled against the skin of the streets again. Gemma barely stirred when Mercury opened her window so she and Stella could talk.

"You remember how on our way through the truck made it look like that green stuff was a sea it parted?" Stella began without any preamble.

"Yep," Mercury said. "I remember."

"I want you to stay close to me, like you're a boat riding in my wake. I'm pretty sure Marcus is okay back there, but that Jeep doesn't even have a real rear window—just zippable plastic. You and Gemma would probably be fine, especially as we're going to get through this damn town as fast as possible. But the boy . . ." Stella cut her eyes to sleeping Chad and shrugged.

"Got ya. I'll stay close."

Stella nodded. "Both vehicles are all gassed up, so we won't stop again until we take the second gravel road."

Mercury nodded. "The one with the not-so-friendly gun people."

"Yeah, by that time the guys will need more pain meds and Gemma should be awake enough to tell us when we have to leave the road to avoid any unpleasantness with the gun people," said Stella.

"I'll be awake." The hoodie pillow muffled Gemma's voice. She yawned and appeared to go right back to sleep.

Mercury's gaze went to the western horizon, which the sun was working its way down to. "You think we'll be home before dark?"

"I'm planning on it. I know it's going to jar the hell out of both those men, but I do not want to be out on the road after dark."

"I'm totally with you."

They made sure all the windows were up and the external vents in the vehicles were closed, and then Stella began to lead them through the emerald city.

Mercury hated every moment of it. Her stomach clenched and her palms were sweaty, even though her hands were cold. Stella kept up a speed that made adrenaline course through Mercury's body. She gulped air as if she was running alongside the Jeep as she wrenched the steering wheel to the left and right, tailing the Chevy as closely as possible. The Jeep's fat tires squished over the putrid remains of people as she dodged around stalled vehicles.

Mercury couldn't help thinking about the dead people—especially the dead women. How much green mist was too much? One sniff of it killed men, but she and the other women survivors had definitely breathed it in deeply. She and Gemma had even had a second dose of it, and they seemed fine.

Well, fine but changed. She was stronger and faster. Gemma had remarkable healing abilities. But when did those changes shift into the danger zone? When did too much exposure kill them?

As thoughts of the green mist buzzed through her mind they came to the heart of Fossil's Main Street and Stella had to slow the truck to weave around a group of more than a half dozen motorcycles that had been abandoned in the middle of the road. Beside the bikes were what remained of their riders—mostly just leather and boots, teeth and hair. Mercury's gaze shifted from the globs of male leftovers to a nearby brick building that was still standing. Painted in the front picture window that was intact, but spider webbed with cracks, were the words FOS-SIL MUSEUM. Outside the museum, where someone had attempted to landscape some bushes in the hard dirt, her attention was drawn by the body of a woman slumped against the side of the building. There was something off about the corpse. Stella slowed again to avoid a truck that had collided with one of the bikes, giving Mercury a chance at studying the dead woman.

Shock skittered down her body and pooled in her belly. Growing from the dead woman's abdomen, like something from the old Sigourney Weaver *Alien* movies, was a riot of thick roots. They arched out of her torso, their ends connecting to the earth where they burrowed so deeply the nearby sidewalk buckled and cracked.

Then Stella sped up and they shot out of the dead heart of Fossil. Even after the town was only a green stain in her rearview mirror, it was several miles before Mercury was able to relax her grip on the steering wheel and roll her shoulders.

The only thing remarkable about the rest of the trip happened just before they turned from the second gravel road, which Gemma had named Gun People Lane, onto Bridge Creek Road. Gemma had been wide awake and chattering softly but nonstop at Mercury since their break to pee and administer more painkillers to the wounded men, when she suddenly pointed off to the right of the Jeep.

"Goats! And there're babies with them! Can we stop? Can we try to catch them?" The teenager almost wriggled with excitement.

Mercury glanced at the little herd of goats and kids. "Even if we could catch them we don't have anywhere to put them. The bed of the truck's full and we don't have a pen made for them."

Gemma's kind brown eyes beseeched her. "Pleeeeease, can we come back when the truck's empty with some rope and try to catch them? At the library I heard Stella say she found a book about cheese making—Stella can practically make anything. Fresh goat cheese would be really yummy."

"You're not wrong about either of those things." Mercury grinned at the girl, glad Gemma wasn't the kind of teenager who sulked and turned every no or even disagreement into a grudge. "I have been thinking about goats, and horses—" She paused, her grin widening at the excitement that flashed across Gemma's pretty face at the word *horses*. "Ford said we should gather some farm animals. Gas is going to run out sooner rather than later. We can't grow more of it, but we can . . ." Mercury let the sentence fade as she glanced in the rearview mirror where their passenger appeared to have been drugged into a deep sleep—but appearances could be deceiving.

Gemma seemed too excited to notice her hesitance. "Oooh! I'll bet we can take some of the pellets we've been feeding the bunnies and put it out there for the goats, a little at a time. That has to be way better than whatever they've been eating. They'll probably come right up to us if we start feeding them. And when they do, we'll catch them, put them in the back of the truck—with the camper on 'cause I know goats can jump like crazy—and bring them home!"

Mercury nodded. "That's a good plan." The thought flashed through her mind that they really should return to Mitchell and pillage the rest of the feed from the store there, but she pushed it aside for later. "I had a goat when I was a little girl. I called her Doty Goaty. I remember my dad said that I hung out with her so much that I was starting to look like her."

"Seriously? That was mean!" Gemma said.

Mercury laughed. "Nah, Doty Goaty was adorably cute!"

"Bridge Creek Road!" Gemma said happily as Stella turned the truck from the gravel one-lane. "We're almost home!"

Mercury looked at the darkening horizon. The fuchsia, orange, and sapphire that stained the huge sky said sunset was close and she felt a wave of relief when Stella finally left Bridge Creek Road and drove several yards until the truck and Jeep could be tucked behind a copse of junipers. The women made quick work of covering their tracks before returning to the vehicles to bump along the rough ground, winding around scrub and rocks while they followed Bridge Creek, which would eventually lead them to their campsite—their home.

Chad groaned after the Jeep bounced out of a rut. Holding his injured hand against his body, he sat, yawned, and looked around them. Mercury watched him in the rearview mirror, relieved that dusk had darkened the area so much that both vehicles had turned on their lights. They were well away from any road, but she couldn't help but be glad the boy hadn't crawled out of his painkiller fog until then.

He cleared his throat and Gemma immediately took a water bottle from the medicine bag by her feet and gave it to him. "Try to drink all of that. You need to stay hydrated."

Chad nodded and then took several gulps before asking, "Where are we?"

Gemma's smile was brilliant. "Almost home!"

"Home?" He frowned out at the darkening land that stretched uninhabited and silent around them. "There're houses out here?"

"No." Gemma's smile didn't dim. "Better. Our camp is awesome. You'll see."

"You're camping out here?" Chad's voice was incredulous and Mercury saw him give the land a disgusted look.

"Not camping," Mercury said. "Living."

Chad smirked and Mercury was sure he was going to say something asinine, but he caught her gaze in the mirror, changed his mind, and closed his mouth.

They followed the bottom of one sheer-topped hill, and the sight of flickering flames dancing within the opening of their cave-like camp washed away the irritation Chad made her feel, replacing it with a rush of warmth that said *home* more thoroughly than words ever could.

And then the rest of their little group—Imani, Karen, Georgie, Cayden, and Hayden—rushed out to greet them, carrying precious flashlights to illuminate their way.

10

THERE HAD BEEN quite a bit of excitement about the new additions to their group, though most of it had been for Badger, who clearly loved children. The kids had been leery of Marcus at first, but his kind smile, gentle manner—and the fact that Badger belonged to him—had them warming to the big man quickly.

The group had been productive while the three of them had been gone. Along with another large salmon, they'd caught three steelhead trout, which they'd cooked intending to feed Mercury, Imani, and Gemma—and then use the rest in a wild-foraged veggie stew. Instead, there was plenty to feed the two men.

Exhausted from their busy fishing day, the children went to bed not long after dark, leaving the adults to cluster around the campfire, looking through the stacks of library books they'd brought home as the women sipped wine and passed a joint around. Gemma had forbidden alcohol for the men, reminding them how dangerous opioids were when mixed with booze, but they were allowed to share a joint.

Marcus settled in with them almost immediately. The big man was affable, even though his leg had to be painful. Though he'd been smoking weed since dinner and was, as Stella said, *drugged to the gills*, his gaze was sharp and inquisitive.

"This campsite is smart," said Marcus. He was reclining on the hard ground of the cave, his broad back resting against one of the logs they used as chairs. Gemma had carefully propped his leg up under a rolled sleeping bag. Badger rested beside him, and Khaleesi lay next to the shepherd. Marcus sipped water from a bottle and nodded as he looked around. "Bridge Creek is full of fish, and the little waterfall stream at the rear exit of the cave is really handy."

"Wait till you see the area in the daylight," said Imani. "This campsite isn't where we're planning on settling permanently."

"Yeah," Gemma grinned as she looked up from a medical book she'd been reading in the flickering light of the campfire. "Imani is going to build us homes in the clouds."

"What doesss that mean?" Chad's words were slurred from weed and pain meds, but now that he wasn't begging them to save his life, his tone—when he bothered to speak at all—had an arrogant edge to it. Since they'd arrived, Chad had been a lot quieter than Marcus, which had Mercury's nerves prickling. She'd watched him study the cave, the campfire, the sleeping areas—everything. Marcus had studied the area too. The difference was Marcus had engaged them in conversation about it and the boy had just stared, as if he was cataloging everything.

The truth was Chad Condon reminded Mercury far too much of the wealthy, entitled kids who formed exclusive, mean little cliques in the Tulsa schools, though she wondered if she judged him too harshly. He was really just a kid—and an injured kid at that.

Gemma didn't seem to notice Chad's arrogance. Her grin widened as she answered him. "It means Imani, who is a super smart engineer, is going to figure out how to make us adobe homes in the cliffs above here, just like the ancient Pueblo Indians in . . ." Her voice trailed off as she looked to Imani for help.

"In Mesa Verde. And the ancient name for them was the Ancestral Puebloans." She held up one of the thick reference books they'd brought back from the library. "There's a great article and illustration in this adobe brickmaking book about them."

"Yeah, that's it," said Gemma. "It's going to be cool *and* beautiful *and* safe. Like Themyscira."

"What'sss that?" Chad slurred.

"The name of the Amazons' island," said Marcus. His gaze shifted to Imani. "An engineer, huh? Well done, queen." He bowed his head in acknowledgment of her black girl magic.

Imani's lips lifted. "Thank you, but engineering was just my minor. Though I'm confident now that I have some reference books that I can create our cliff homes." Her warm gaze swept the room. "With help, of course."

"Why not just find a town and move in?" Chad asked, suddenly sounding more sober. "It's a lot less work."

"And a lot less safe," said Stella.

Karen had just returned from a trip to the latrine. "What's less safe? And may I have a glass of that lovely red wine too?"

"Absolutely," said Stella, who poured her a glass. "We were just explaining to Chad that we're going to build our homes in the cliff and he asked why there instead of living in an abandoned town."

"Thank you," Karen said as she took the offered glass from Stella and then sat on the empty log near Gemma. She smiled across the fire at Chad and said, "Because it's a lot safer than down here or any town."

"Safe? Like from the mist?" Chad asked.

"Yes," Imani said. "It tends to pool in low areas. But also living in the cliffs allows us protection from marauders."

"Marauders?" Chad barked a sarcastic laugh. "For real?"

Before anyone could answer, Marcus asked Chad a question of his own. "You said your name is Condon? Are you Gertrude Condon's grandson?"

Chad's gaze went to him. "Yeah. That's me. Why?"

"Thought you were away at college. What were you doing out there in the desert?" Marcus's tone was casual, but Mercury could sense something under it, like a wolf waiting to spring on a rabbit.

"I was, but I was staying with Grandma for spring break." Chad's words were short, clipped, and he wasn't slurring anymore.

Marcus nodded. "Yeah, I remember now. That's what your grandma said. That you were spending some time with her instead of joining your folks in Seattle. Doesn't explain what you were doing out in the desert."

Mercury could almost see the wheels inside Chad's brain turning as he spun a story. "When the shit hit the fan I took off for our cabin over by Snyder Ranch. I, uh, was scouting it out to see if it was still standing after those quakes, and making sure that green crap wasn't there."

"Oh, honey," Karen said. "You were trying to get there on foot?"

"No." Chad answered quickly. "I took my motorcycle."

There was a tense silence as they watched Chad expectantly, waiting for him to say more. When he didn't, Stella prompted, "What happened to the motorcycle?"

Chad looked off to his left. "Ran outta gas when I was on my way back."

"Oh, no! Your grandma isn't out there stranded alone in a cabin, is she?" Karen asked as she touched the crucifix that always dangled from a gold chain around her neck. "You should have said something earlier!"

Chad shifted on his log chair. "Nah, Grandma wasn't with me."

Anger pooled in Mercury's stomach. "You left her in Condon when you went to the cabin."

She hadn't phrased it like a question, but Chad's blue eyes narrowed at her as he answered. "I had to. Wasn't safe for her to go with me. I had to make sure it was okay first. It mighta been a heap of logs or nothing but ashes. I was . . . I was coming back for her when I, uh, ran out of gas. That's why I was walking back to town when the snake bit me." He finished in a rush. Then, as if he just realized that Marcus was also from Condon, Chad turned to the big man and asked, "Hey, you know my grandma, right? Why didn't you bring her with you?"

"Because she was killed a week ago when those marauders you were just laughing about came through Condon," said Marcus.

Chad's face flushed a deep red. "What? Grandma's dead?"

"Yes, she is." Marcus pressed his lips into a line and looked away from Chad into the fire, but not before Mercury saw the disgust that flashed across the big man's face.

"Well, that is very sad," said Karen softly. "I shall say a prayer for Gertrude Condon."

"Thanks," Chad said and then added, "ma'am."

"I'm going to take my walk now." Imani stood. Her face had a far-away look that Mercury had come to recognize. She knew Imani was going to perform her nightly ritual of standing on a rise near Bridge Creek where she faced the southwest and thought of her two babies and her husband—all three had perished in the bombs.

Imani paused at the mouth of the cave. "Do you need my help to get Marcus or Chad situated?"

"No," Mercury said. "We can handle it."

Imani nodded and walked silently into the night.

"She's going for a walk in the dark?" Chad asked as he stared after her.

"Yeah," Gemma said. "Imani lost her—"

"Why don't we help Marcus and Chad to their sleeping pallets," Mercury interrupted.

"It'd be nice to turn in," said Marcus. "I truly appreciate all you ladies have done for me."

"Well, get a good sleep," said Gemma as she put the medical book aside and stood, brushing dirt from her butt. "I've just read in the ortho-pedic section that I'm going to need to reset that broken bone. And that will not be pleasant for either of us."

"Baby girl, I will willingly put my leg in your hands, though I will also be glad that I can take some pain pills first and smoke more of this excellent weed." He grinned sleepily at the women. "I'm already better."

Stella snorted. "You're just medicated. That's doesn't make your leg better."

"It does make it more bearable, though." Marcus winked at Stella.

Mercury watched Stella blush an attractive shade of light pink, which had Mercury smiling. "Are you feeling better enough to stand so we can help you hobble back there to the sleeping area we fixed up for Chad and you?"

"I surely am," said Marcus, returning her smile.

Mercury approached Marcus and glanced at Chad. "If you have to use the latrine, now is the time."

"I can show you where it is," said Gemma.

"Oh, yeah. Okay," said Chad. "But I was going to finish this joint before I went to bed."

Mercury met his gaze. "Finish it while you're peeing. You need to rest. Now."

"Come on." Gemma took one of precious flashlights from a ledge-like area near the entrance to the cave. "I'll even use one of these to show you the way."

Chad got slowly to his feet and shuffled after Gemma. His voice car-ried back through the cave. "You mean you go out here at night without a light?"

"Oh, sure! It's not hard once you know your way . . ." Gemma's enthusiastic response faded.

"I'll turn down the bedrolls for our two guests," Karen said as she put her empty wineglass aside and stood. Then she paused to cover a huge yawn. "I feel as tired as the children. I do believe I will show myself to bed, too. Good night, everyone. You did well today at the library."

"Thanks, Karen." Mercury nodded at Karen, and then she took Marcus's large hand in hers and easily helped guide him to his feet. Stella stood close beside him while he balanced on one leg.

He looked down at Mercury. "You're strong."

"I am," she said, returning his gaze steadily.

"Unless I am vastly mistaken, which I usually am not, I'd say your strength is a lot like Gemma's doctoring skills."

Mercury met Stella's gaze, and her friend responded for her. "You are not mistaken—vastly or not."

Marcus grunted. "Thought so." He looked from Mercury to Stella and lowered his voice. "Your blood can grow things, can't it?"

Mercury felt a jolt of surprise, but her best friend didn't seem rattled at all. "Yes, it can," she said.

"Thought so."

"How did you know?" Mercury asked as she took most of Marcus's weight across her shoulders. Stella was on his other side, her arm around his waist. The two dogs followed them as they walked slowly to a rear section of the cave, separated by a curving wall from the rest of the group, that they'd prepared as sleeping quarters for the two men.

"Gertrude Condon was a friend. A good friend," Marcus said. "After the bombs and the mist she could grow things too. She showed me. She also knew things."

"Like what?" Stella asked when he volunteered nothing more.

"She always knew when the mist was going to blow into town. The others didn't pay any attention to her. They just thought she was a crazy, rich old lady. She and I have been friends since I came to town and bought the café two years ago. She trusted me, so she showed me what her blood could do. She also told me when the mist was coming."

"None of the other women in town had any special powers?" Stella asked.

Marcus shrugged his wide shoulders. "If they did, they didn't say anything about it to me. I was just the cook, ya know?"

"Does Chad know about the changes in his grandma?" Mercury asked as she helped Marcus down to his sleeping bag.

Marcus grunted in pain and then relaxed with a sigh when he was finally prone. Badger immediately curled up beside him. "Don't see how that boy could know anything about it. He lit out the first day—right after the mist cleared. Gertrude didn't discover her powers until day three."

"Guys, Marcus needs to keep that leg elevated." Gemma hurried into the sleeping area, the rolled-up sleeping bag she'd used to prop up Marcus's leg by the fire under her arm. Chad trailed slowly behind as he sucked on the end of his joint.

As Gemma fussed over Marcus's leg, Chad kicked off his shoes and started to undo his jeans.

"You can wait until the ladies leave to take those off," Marcus said sharply.

Chad shrugged and flipped the joint on the floor.

"And you can pick that up and field dress it," Marcus added.

"What does that mean?" Chad asked.

"That means you pick it up and shred it with your fingers until there's no mess left behind," said Marcus.

Chad sighed deeply, but bent, and with his good hand did as Marcus directed. "That good enough?" He asked the older man sarcastically.

"For now," Marcus said. Then his tone lightened. "Thank you, ladies. Truly."

"We're glad we can help," said Stella.

Marcus's smile flashed in the dim light. "Tonight will be the first full night's sleep I've had since the bombs."

"We know how that feels," said Gemma. "But you're safe here, so you can get some really good rest. Right, Stella?"

Stella nodded. "Absolutely. Good night."

"'Night," Mercury and Gemma said.

"Hey, what if my hand starts hurting during the night?" Chad asked as they turned to go.

"Oh, here you go." Gemma went to Chad and shook out a couple pills from the bottle she'd tucked into her jeans pocket. There was already a bottle of water near the head of each of their sleeping bags. "If you wake up in pain, just take these two, but go to sleep first. You've had enough painkillers and weed that you should be able to rest well." Then the girl went to Marcus and shook out two more pills for him. "And for you too." She glanced at his leg and started to press her hand to it as she asked. "How's it feeling? I know that trip was hard on you today."

Gently, Marcus intercepted her hand, patted it and smiled up at her. "It's just fine, baby girl. Save that for yourself."

Gemma's brows went up, but she nodded and said, "'Night."

The women returned to the main room of their camp, with Khaleesi padding beside Mercury. Imani still hadn't returned and Karen's soft snores echoed from the communal sleeping area.

"Hey, I'm going to bed. I'm super tired," said Gemma.

"You did great today, kid," said Stella as she hugged her.

"Yeah, you're one hell of a healer," said Mercury.

"Thanks!" Gemma shot them a proud smile before she disappeared into the darkness of the cave.

"Want another glass of wine?" Stella asked.

"Definitely." Mercury sat on a log beside her friend, who refilled their glasses. The two women sipped silently until Mercury said, "What do you think is going on with those two men?"

Stella didn't hesitate. "What Marcus tells us is the truth, but he's not telling us everything. For instance, he's ex-military."

Mercury blinked in surprise. "How do you know that?"

"Because I dated a fighter pilot. He used to 'field dress'"—she air quoted—"his cigarettes. And Chad is straight-up lying—I think almost everything he says is a fucking lie."

"So you still have a bad feeling about Chad?"

"Yep." Stella sipped her wine silently for several minutes, and then she continued in a voice so low Mercury had to lean toward her to hear. "Gemma's ethics are commendable, but sometimes doing what's best isn't the same thing as doing what's right."

"We should have left Chad out there."

Stella swirled the red wine, watching the scarlet legs run in rivulets down the inside of the glass. "We absolutely should have left Chad out there."

Imani returned to the cave. Mercury glanced up at her and saw an emerald glow fade from her dark brown eyes.

"We need to get our cliff homes started immediately," said Imani.

"What's happened?" Stella asked.

"Something is stirring. Something that's angry and restless and questing."

Mercury felt a chill finger down her spine. "Questing for what?"

"Power and control, I think," Imani replied. "Mixed with revenge."

Stella brushed back her hair with a hand that trembled. "Do you know what this thing is?"

"I can't see it. I can only feel it, and it's not like anything I have ever known before." Her smooth, fawn-colored brow furrowed. "I don't think anyone has known anything like it—not for many, many lifetimes."

"Is it what you felt a few days ago? The man you called the Destroyer?" Mercury asked.

Imani nodded. "Yes. He's somehow attached to the earth. That's how I feel him. Because I can feel things through the earth."

"Like your kids and your husband?" Mercury asked softly.

"Yes, like them. I can feel an echo of them, and it comforts me. And also other things—things that are more difficult to understand, like the Destroyer. My babies and Curtis are gone. He's not. He's something, some*one* new. Alive, but calling him a man isn't entirely correct and I don't know why. I wish I understood more of what that green mist did to me—more of how I can use the senses it's given me."

"I'm with you on that," said Stella. "I try to understand too, but mostly feel like I'm just guessing."

Then Imani shook herself as if she'd just come in from the rain, and her gaze focused on Mercury. "We need to get busy. Now. What I've read in the reference books reinforces what I thought. We can get away with not having to fire the adobe bricks, which will save us a lot of time."

"Then how do we dry them?" Stella asked.

"The sun dries them," explained Imani. "We'll need a good clay to sand mixture—about thirty percent clay and seventy percent sand."

"Where are we supposed to get sand?" Mercury asked.

"All along Bridge Creek. As we mix the bricks we can add grasses and such to help strengthen them." She sighed. "I wish we had wooden molds for the bricks so they'd be more uniform, but they can be shaped by hand. We'll lay out those big paint tarps from the Chevy and let the bricks dry on them. Then we can build the walls with the dried bricks, adding more of the wet clay mixture as mortar. What with the shovels and other supplies that you got from Mitchell, we have everything we need to begin making them, but I also have to figure out several lift and pulley systems to haul a whole bunch of adobe bricks up to the cliffside."

Stella cleared her throat. "I'm not a science person, so this might not work, but what if we make the bricks up there, either on top the cliff or around the areas you've decided to build our homes."

Imani's dark brows lifted. "This whole damn time I've been trying to figure out how to create pulley systems to haul bricks up there and the answer was a lot simpler." She sighed and sat heavily on a log as she rubbed a hand across her face and then asked, "Can I have some wine?"

Stella got her a glass and filled it with red wine.

"So, it's a good idea?" Stella asked.

"It's a great idea. The top of the cliff is pretty flat. There are boulders and such up there, but a good wide area before the sides sheer off, and even then they do so in layers, like a giant wedding cake." Imani's voice had gone from worried and tense to excited.

"Yeah, I haven't been up there, but even from down here I can see the tiers. Some of them look cave-like already," said Mercury.

Imani nodded enthusiastically. "They are! It'll actually be fairly simple to finish those out with walls, especially if I don't have to worry about hauling adobe bricks up there."

"We'll need to get water up there, though," said Mercury. "Not just for the brickmaking, but for living when we move there."

Imani and Stella grinned at her and Stella said, "Forgot to tell you that while you were depression sleeping, Imani and I climbed to the top of the cliff. You know the little stream that runs along the back of our cave and flows into Bridge Creek?"

"Yeah, of course," said Mercury.

"It originates up there." Imani finished for Stella, pointing upwards.

"Seriously?"

Stella and Imani nodded.

"But how is that even possible? It's the high desert," said Mercury.

"The pool is filled by runoff from the top of the higher cliff behind ours." As Imani described the area her voice held a focus and an intensity that was almost tangible. "It's great and I'm glad it's there, but it would be even more helpful if it was bigger, deeper, and elevated, or at least had a higher bank. Then it'd be easy to cut into the bank, or even fashion a hose system to irrigate the crops we need to get planted up there."

"Wait, we can plant crops up there?" Mercury felt as if her head was spinning. She'd slept for a few days and everything seemed to have changed.

"We can. The soil has a high clay content. Some crops like that and some don't. I'm hoping our blood will be enough to help out the ones who *don't* like clay," said Imani.

"If we can grow crops up there and have shelter and a reliable water source, it really will be a fortress," said Mercury.

"I like to think of it as more sanctuary than fortress," said Imani as she poured herself some more wine.

Stella sipped her wine and added, "It'll be nice to have Jenny here. Her botany major is going to come in handy."

"Yeah, Jenny's plant knowledge is going to be a big help. And that pond up there will work for part of the year, but if it's just a runoff, it'll dry up in the summer." Mercury sighed. "At least that's something we don't have to worry about for a month or so."

Stella's smile was knowing. "I have a *feeling* we're never going to have to worry about that."

"How so?" Mercury asked. "It'd be great, but if the snow's gone that means the water will be gone."

Stella replied with a question of her own. "How does our blood make plants grow?"

Imani took up the thread of the conversation. "Exactly. How can you be so strong and Gemma heal and Karen see spirits and Stella *know* things?" Then she laughed softly. "And me—well, I'm not sure what all is going on with me, but I'm starting to accept that I have a connection to the earth that's more than just liking to hike. So how can all that be possible?"

"Magick." Mercury said the word like a prayer.

"It's how I knew we had to settle here," said Stella. "Everything we need is either already here, or we can create it here."

Imani's gaze was unfocused as she looked out at the dark, silent land beyond the entrance to their shelter and echoed Stella. "Everything we need is here, or we can create it."

"It's incredible," said Mercury.

Stella leaned forward, her eyes bright with more than the firelight. "It's a new world, a new era, a whole new way of living."

Imani pulled her distant gaze back to them. "Yeah, but we're going to have to fight to make it happen," she said. "And that means we need to get ourselves up there where it's safer, easier to defend, a.s.a.p."

"What do you need from us?" asked Mercury.

"I've already read through the sections of the reference books that deal with adobe brickmaking. Like I said, we have all the clay and sand and water we need. We can add grasses and twigs to help strengthen them and I can teach everyone how to fashion the individual bricks," Imani continued. "It would still be a very big help if I could create a pulley system to lower the bricks from the top of the cliff down to our home sites. I can make some simple pulleys to lift and lower bricks on pieces of plywood, or even two by fours side-by-side, if I had some lumber." She paused and added. "And if I had lumber, I could make molds for the bricks, which would be faster than forming them by hand. Also, I need a lot of rope and something like big hooks or, better yet, carabineers for those simple pulleys."

"Didn't we bring a bunch of ropes back from Mitchell?" Mercury asked.

Stella nodded. "Yeah, and we've used most of it to make climbing up to the top of our cliff possible."

"Huh?" Mercury's brow furrowed. "We're climbing ropes to get up there?"

"No." Imani smiled at her. "There's a rough deer trail that leads up to the top, but it's really steep in some places."

"Yeah, and the dirt on the path is rocky and loose," added Stella.

"So, until we can build some kind of steps, we've made a basic guiderail to hold on to so it's not as dangerous," added Imani. "And that used almost all of our rope."

"Hmm, that makes sense," said Mercury. "Stella and I didn't go into that feed and grain store in Mitchell, but it basically looked like a Southern Ag, and they carry a lot of farm and ranch stuff," said Mercury. "They'll for sure have rope, or at the very least a bunch of horse lead lines and dog leashes. I'll bet you can make those work for your pulleys."

"And if we have to, we can pillage lumber from one of the abandoned homes in Mitchell." Stella grimaced. "It won't be pleasant."

"It'll be less pleasant to be caught down here by something malevolent," said Imani.

"Agreed. We'll scavenge," said Mercury.

"Okay, let's make detailed dream lists so we know exactly what we're looking for." Mercury stood and started toward the pile of dried branches and logs they collected every day for the fire. "I'll build up the fire so we can see better."

Stella headed to the area of the cave where they stored the books and their precious pads of paper, pencils, and pens. "And I'll be our secretary and write the lists."

"It'll be a sad day when we run out of paper and pencils," said Mercury wistfully.

"No it won't," Stella called from over her shoulder. "I'm an art teacher, remember? I can make pencils from charcoal and I'm excellent at pulping paper."

"We have a kickass team," said Mercury as she fed the fire.

"We definitely do. And I think the addition of Marcus will only strengthen our team," said Imani.

"Agreed." Stella returned with paper and a pencil and took her seat on the log. "Chad is a problem, though."

"He's a sullen, entitled kid who thinks he's a man," said Imani. "But let's get one problem handled at a time. Hey, tomorrow the children can collect twigs and grasses and such for the bricks. I'll show them what's best to use and give everyone a demo on brickmaking. Then we can get those tarps and supplies up to the top of the cliff. There's no reason we can't start making the adobes right away."

"Good idea. I'm putting that at the top of the list," said Stella.

"We should take one of those horse troughs Ford scavenged from the feed store up to the top of the cliff," said Imani. "It'll be perfect to mix the mud in. Hey, this might sound frivolous, but it would be really nice if we gathered some of that brightly colored clay from the Painted Hills to add to our mixture for the bricks." Imani's lips tilted up. "Think about how beautiful it would make our new homes."

"I don't think it's frivolous," said Mercury.

"That's because frivolous isn't the right word," said Stella. "It's artistic. It's pleasing to the senses. It's beauty and civilization in a world that feels lacking of both right now."

In complete agreement, the three teachers got to work.

11

MERCURY FELL INTO her sleeping bag about the time the sky was beginning to blush with dawn.

They'd finished their lists and ordered what they needed to get done: (1) Teach the kids, Karen, and Gemma what to gather for the bricks. (2) Lay out the tarps on top of the cliff and near the most accessible home sites. (3) Show everyone how to mix and mold the bricks, as well as how to place them out in the sun for drying. (4) Get a full night's sleep and then go to Mitchell to get as much of their supply list as possible. (5) If they are able to scavenge enough supplies in Mitchell, make the pulleys—if not, go on a quest to see what they can find in abandoned houses. (6) Under Imani's direction, begin building their new adobe homes.

The six things on their to-do list swirled around and around in Mercury's sleepy brain, which was a lot like counting sheep. She hadn't even gone through the list twice when her eyes closed and exhaustion claimed her.

Ford came to her again. Since that first night—when she'd awakened to find a wildflower on her pillow—his presence hadn't been as strong in her dreams. She could feel him, and always woke with him on her mind. Mercury often even dreamed he called her name, especially his nickname for her, *Bellota*. But he'd been distant, fading from her subconscious, which made her sad, though she supposed it was the way of things. For the living to move on, the dead must fade.

Not that night. Not in that dream.

Mercury could feel Ford's presence, strong and near. In the dream she was curled on her side and his body was warm and solid as it spooned against her. One arm was under her head, and she used it for a pillow. The other wrapped around her, holding her against him. His lips were near her neck and he'd brushed aside her hair so that when he spoke his breath tickled her skin.

"This is nice, Bellota. I like holding you like this." Ford's warm breath made her shiver.

"I miss you," she whispered.

"I'm right here," he replied and kissed the skin of her neck.

She shivered again and remembered she only had on a T-shirt and panties when she felt his erection. "This is a delicious dream, but next time I think I'll remember to dream that I sleep naked."

His teeth found her earlobe and he tugged teasingly on it. "Bellota, you'd need to go to sleep naked for that to work."

His words sent a little shock through her. "Why? I can dream things that aren't true. Why not just dream I'm naked? I dreamed you here, alive, holding me and wanting me."

Ford kissed her again and his tongue tasted her skin before he replied. "But did you, Bellota? Did you dream me, or am I truly here?"

"You're dead," Mercury said softly, and the pain those two words caused spread grief throughout her body with her heartbeat. In response, she began to lift from her dream.

"I was," Ford said.

"Was?" Mercury's heartbeat increased and her sadness began pulling her from the dream, and as she came closer to waking, Ford started to fade. His touch wasn't as warm. His breath didn't tickle her skin. She wrapped her arms around his, willing him to be real. "Don't go. Not yet."

He hesitated, allowing her to hold tightly to him. "You are not ready for me to come to you."

She hugged his arm closer and snuggled back against him. "I feel ready."

His laugh was low and intimate. "I wish it was that simple—just our desire—you and me together. But it is not. Others are involved. A *world* is involved." He kissed her neck again. "And I am different—changed. You may not like it. May not accept the new me."

Mercury suddenly felt cold. "But is it still *you*?"

Ford paused and finally, very softly, said, "Yes and no."

She loosened his arm and reached back to touch him. He was still on his side, pressed to her. Her hand was on his strong thigh. And that thigh was covered with fur. Not a man's leg hair. *Fur*.

Mercury came completely awake. She sat and blinked sleep from her eyes as she stared around the cave. It was still predawn and the only illumination in the cave came from the front area where the entrance showed a sky that hinted at sunrise with a splash of pastels. No one stirred, so only a little time had to have passed since she'd fallen asleep.

At her feet, Khaleesi's tail thumped. Mercury petted her. "Am I going nuts, pretty girl? That dream. It was so, so real!" Mercury shook her head, fluffed the pillow of her sleeping bag, and lay down, but before she closed her eyes a strange mark on the cave floor beside her pallet drew her gaze. She lifted herself on one elbow and leaned closer to study it, and as she did Mercury realized that the mark was a vague outline of a large cloven hoofprint. Her fingers traced it before it faded into the hard-packed soil.

Mercury lay down again, curled on her side, and as she closed her eyes she wished, *Come to me again.*

CHAPTER

12

H E COULD SMELL her before he saw her. It was strange and wonderful that his reborn body came with more bells and whistles than a new Range Rover. He could now admit to himself something he would have never allowed himself to think, let alone embrace, *before*. He'd always been a predator. But in the *before* he hadn't had the senses or the powers or the freedom to act.

He did now. Now he was an *apex* predator.

He strode through Oregon's high desert. This section, just south of the place he'd been mortally wounded, was desolate, but not completely deserted. There were pockets of sweetness here still. He could smell them. He could smell *her*.

As he came within sight of the little group he paused, cloaking himself in the shadows at the base of a canyon. Manipulating shadows was just one more bell and whistle he'd attained since his death and resurrection.

Resurrection. He almost laughed. It sounded a lot more religious than the experience had actually been.

One of the things under his shirt wriggled against his skin and he scratched at it gently. "Be still, my friend. You can come out soon." He whispered to it and then his attention returned to the group.

They had three black Ford Expeditions and quite a few guns, which three men toted. There was a skinny redhead who talked a lot, mostly to the men, and mostly with a hard, sarcastic edge to her voice. But he wasn't watching her or the men. They were irrelevant. He watched *her*. She was obviously in charge. She was also blonde and beautiful—sexy as hell. He was surprised to feel his cock stir. He hadn't thought about sex since the *before*, but now he remembered how much he'd liked it—how good it had felt. His smile was feral as he thought about taking her, tasting her, claiming her. She was attractive, but that's not all she was. She was like him—a predator who had been set free by the bombs.

He scented the air and knew the mist had changed her, but not enough. She hadn't evolved enough. Yet. He'd show her how and then watch her embrace her nature more fully.

Maybe, if she was real good, he'd let her rule beside him, or at least let her believe she ruled.

It was midday and they must have stopped for lunch. They'd built a fire and had heated a pot of coffee over it. The scent of the dark drink mixed with that of the woman. Both made his mouth water. The three gun-carrying men were wiping their mouths with their sleeves as they finished eating. The little redhead picked the last of the meat off a drumstick. The blonde, *his* blonde, finished a red apple with hard bites of her straight, white teeth. Without looking at anyone she said, "Amber, I need napkins."

Amber licked chicken fat from her lips before she glanced at one of the men. "You heard her, Wes. Get the mayor some napkins."

Mayor. His lips lifted in a feral smile.

"I'm on it."

Wes hurried to one of the SUVs and then returned with a handful of napkins, which the mayor took without thanking him. She wiped her hands delicately and then dabbed her mouth before reaching into a little purse that rested on a log beside her. She took out a tube of lipstick and applied it to her bow-shaped lips, turning them the red that warned sailors of a morning. Then she stood.

"Amber, I'm going to use the primitive facilities. Get the fire banked. I don't think we're going to find shit out here. These people were too damn poor to have anything we want, and there are none of them left alive." She snickered. "Let me rephrase that. There are none of them left alive who are sane."

"That's for sure, Eva," muttered Amber.

Eva . . . Her name shivered through him.

The men didn't speak.

"Let's head back to 26. Bend's a mess, but we can bypass it. We haven't checked south of it much and I know damn well there are some bougie mansions masquerading as cabins there, especially near Sunriver." Without waiting for a response, Eva picked her way around rocks and scrub carefully as she headed toward the edge of the canyon and the shadows that hid him.

He breathed deeply as she approached, oblivious to his presence. She walked past him, too intent on not tripping in the ridiculous stiletto boots she wore to notice that he watched from within the shadows. She had on jeans that hugged her curves and a long-sleeved sweater that accentuated her large, high breasts. He clenched and unclenched his fists, thinking of how those breasts would feel in his hands.

When she ducked around the curve of the canyon to be out of sight of the others by the SUVs, he followed and watched as she undid her jeans and pulled them and black lace panties down, squatted, and relieved herself, using the napkins to dab dry and then leaving them to flutter damply in the wind, like dying birds. She stood and fixed her clothes.

That is when he stepped from the shadows.

"Hello." He knew what his smile had done to women in the *before*, and he used it then. He watched her eyes narrow and was pleased to see irritation rather than fear flash through their cool blue depths.

"I don't like to be snuck up on," she said.

"I'll remember that in the future," he said. "My intention wasn't to startle you."

She gazed steadily at him. "I wasn't startled. I was annoyed. Who are you?"

"I'm many things, Eva, but I'd like it if you called me Al," he said.

"How do you know my name?" she asked.

"I heard the redhead call you Eva, and mayor. Congratulations," he said with another charming smile. She appeared unmoved by his smile, but Al could smell her arousal as well as her curiosity.

She tossed back her thick blonde hair. "Are you alone?"

"There are no people with me," he said.

She raised one perfect brow. "You've been out here, alone, for two weeks and you look like that?" She jerked her chin at him.

Al glanced down at himself. It'd taken days to find a home that had decent clothes of his size. The jeans were clean and fit him well. The button-down dress shirt that fit over a white T-shirt wouldn't have been his first choice, but he liked how it showed off the width of his chest. He also liked what it hid. He was bathed, clean-shaven, and handsome. He looked up and trapped her gaze with his. "That's right, but now I'm going to join you."

Eva's laugh was musical and dangerous, like sleet against a tin roof. "I haven't asked you to join me."

"You will," he said.

Eva smirked. "And why should I do that?"

"Protection. Information. Power." He spoke the three words clearly, making them sentences of their own.

"Those men have guns that protect me." She jerked her chin in the direction of the waiting SUVs. "I've been gathering information since those bombs dropped, and I'm the mayor of what is probably the only city functioning in this part of the country."

"You misunderstand. What I offer is unique," said Al.

Eva's red lips twisted into a sneer. "Men always believe they're unique, and they so rarely are."

"You make a good point. Let me give you a small demonstration so you can see that I'm not one of those men." Al grew very still. He felt the shadows that hugged the canyon and the darkness beneath the trees and scrub. Within that darkness and shadow, he quested and found it. The small one sleeping in its burrow. "Come to me." Al spoke the words with a whisper, but the sound reverberated within every dark nook and cranny around them, rousing the small one and calling it forth.

A surprised little *oh* slipped from Eva's scarlet lips as the rabbit hopped to Al. It stopped just a few inches from him. The creature's breath came in gasps. Its eyes were wide and glassy with fear.

"Prey recognize a predator," Al explained as Eva looked from him to the rabbit. "Instinctively it knows how helpless it is. To prey, death is a relief because it is an end to fear." Slowly, Al undid the top two buttons of his dress shirt so that his hand could slip down inside his T-shirt and scoop them off his chest. When his hand emerged it held a writhing nest of leeches, as black as the deepest shadow on a moonless night. Without a word he flung the leeches on the rabbit. They dropped onto the little creature—covering it, draining it, killing it.

Al looked from the corpse to Eva as the leeches slithered along the ground back to him.

Eva didn't appear horrified or frightened. She studied him, only occasionally allowing her gaze to drop to the leeches. "They belong to you and are commanded by you?"

"They do. They are," he said.

"How?" She snapped the single word question at him.

"The green mist. It changes things. It changed me."

She raised one perfect brow again. "But the green mist kills men."

"Yes," he said. "It also resurrects and grants a multitude of powers."

She shook her head. "No. I've tried that. It has granted me nothing."

He shifted a little so that the leeches could slither from his shoes and move up under his pants to return to his body. Al asked her, "Does your blood grow plants?"

Her beautiful face twisted. "No! Whatever my blood touches blackens and dies."

Al smiled. "That is excellent news. You gave up too soon. The mist isn't done evolving you." He held out his hand, beckoning. "Would you like to learn more?"

Eva didn't hesitate. She took his hand and allowed him to thread her arm through his, as if they were going for a walk in a park. "If it means power—yes, I would like to learn more."

"Then I will teach you."

13

MERCURY DREAMED NO more and woke not long after the sun had completely risen, still groggy but restless. She didn't get up immediately. Instead, she thought about the oddness of her dream as she stroked Khaleesi's soft head. Imani and Stella were still sleeping soundly on their pallets not far from Mercury's.

Laughter pulled her attention to the front room of the cave, and her gaze went there. She could see Marcus's large body outlined against the fire. He sat where he had the night before, his broad back leaning against a log with his leg propped in front of him. Loyal Badger was lying beside him. He sipped from a mug, which Mercury knew by its enticing scent was filled with coffee. There was also another familiar smell drifting around the cave, and as Marcus lifted a joint to his lips and took a deep draw from it, Mercury found its source.

Another burst of laughter had her gaze moving from Marcus to the two figures who sat close to the mouth of the cave. Gemma's head was tilted toward Chad's, and when she laughed again she leaned against him. Mercury sighed. *That flirtation is going to be a problem.*

Quietly, so as not to disturb Stella and Imani, Mercury pulled on her jeans and her boots, grabbed her toothbrush, toothpaste, and a bottle of water, and left the sleeping area.

Marcus looked up and smiled at her as Khaleesi and Badger greeted each other. "Morning. Got coffee there."

"Good morning. I'm counting on that coffee. I'll be right back for it."

At the sound of her voice Gemma straightened and turned quickly around. "Oh, hi, Mercury."

"Hi." Mercury smiled at the teenager and then nodded at Chad. "How are your patients this morning?"

Gemma's grin made her look so young it wrenched Mercury's heart. "They're doing really well. Chad's hand is so, so much better. Marcus feels better, but I'm glad you're up 'cause I need you to help me fix him."

"How am I supposed to do that?" Mercury asked.

"It's what I was talking about last night when I said Marcus needed to get a good night's sleep." She looked over her shoulder and let her grin include him. "The broken bone in his leg is pressing against his skin and needs to be put back into place so it can heal properly."

Mercury sent an apologetic look to Marcus. "That sounds painful."

"So Gemma has told me," said Marcus, who lifted the joint. "Which is why I'm smoking this and my young doc has given me several pain pills this fine morning."

"I'd like to have some of those pain pills," muttered Chad.

Gemma butted him with her shoulder. "Your hand doesn't need them, silly. You're way better today." Then she turned her attention back to Mercury, not noticing the way Chad lifted his lip in a sneer at her. "Anyway, I need you to pull Marcus's leg straight. Then I'll help it finish healing and set it again."

Mercury cleared her throat and told her stomach to settle down. "Okay, I can do that. Just give me a sec—and a cup of coffee." She didn't allow herself to take much time with her toilette. If she thought too long about what she was going to have to do, Mercury was afraid her hands would shake so hard she'd thoroughly screw up the resetting of Marcus's leg.

As she hurried back to the cave, the rhythmic sound of drums and the high, sweet trilling of a flute mixed with the laughter of children drifted on the warm morning breeze. Mercury shielded her eyes as she gazed at Bridge Creek. Karen sat on the bank with the three children. She was alert and scanned the creek for mist. Georgie and the twins were sitting not far from her. Each had one of the big drums she and Imani had found in the RV between their knees, and their sister held the flute to her lips. Together they were creating a compelling melody that had Mercury tapping her foot with the beat. The instruments had intrigued the children from the moment they'd seen them, and Mercury loved that they were making such beautiful music together. Georgie shrieked happily and handed Karen the flute before she raced a few feet down the bank, grabbed a pole that had been propped there, and reeled in a large fish that flopped on the bank. One of the twins jumped up from where he sat to take it off the hook for his sister. Karen waved, which Mercury returned before she reentered the cave to find Stella and Imani yawning sleepily and pouring steaming cups of coffee.

"I just saw Georgie catch a fish," said Mercury, happily accepting the mug of coffee. "And the kids are doing really well with the drums and flute."

"Georgie is becoming an excellent fisherwoman," said Imani. Then she added with a grin. "Even though she doesn't like to take them off the hook."

"I noticed that too," said Mercury. "Can't really blame her."

"The kids are definitely musically talented. I'm glad you two found those instruments," said Stella. "And Georgie's fish catching ability is definitely good news." From where she sat beside Marcus, Stella reached out and petted Badger and then Khaleesi.

"I'll be glad when this leg allows me to join Georgie. I do like fishing," said Marcus.

"I'll be glad when our chickies get big enough to give us eggs so you can cook us up some of your famous breakfasts." Gemma spoke as she and Chad joined them around the campfire.

"You're good at making breakfasts?" Imani asked Marcus.

Gemma answered for him. "He's the best! He's the owner of that café I told you about in Condon. The one with the awesome breakfasts."

"Thought you were just the cook," said Chad, sending Marcus an appraising look.

"I'm not surprised that's what you thought," Marcus said as he blew out a cloud of fragrant smoke.

Chad narrowed his eyes. "What's that supposed to mean?"

Imani skewered the boy with her dark gaze. "It means you saw a black man and automatically made assumptions about him. Try not to do that in this new world."

Gemma spoke up quickly. "Okay, so, how medicated are you feeling, Marcus?"

The big man smiled. "I am feeling no pain."

Gemma nodded and shifted her gaze to Mercury. "Let's do this quickly then."

"Do what?" asked Stella.

"Mercury is going to help me reset Marcus's leg. I need you and Imani to hold him." Gemma went to Marcus and crouched beside him. "This is going to be awful, but Mercury's real strong and she'll be quick. And I'm going to try to help your pain while she's doing it."

As Gemma reached out to touch the big man, he took her hand gently in his and looked down, studying it. "Baby girl, I still see some redness and bruising in this hand. I know you pay a price for what you do, and I think you've already done some healing this morning." His eyes flicked to Chad and back to Gemma. "So how 'bout I just deal with the pain and then you can work your magic on me after so as you don't extend yourself too much."

Stella went to Chad. "Let me see your hand."

He lifted it, and they saw that almost all of the swelling was gone and the discoloration was no worse than if he'd had a minor injury with a little bruising.

Stella blew out a long breath before she said to Chad, "Gemma won't be doing more healing to your hand. And you don't need those pain pills anymore, either." Then her gaze went to Gemma. "Kid, you need to think about triaging. You're our only healer—our only doc. Your heart is sweet and compassionate, but you also have to be wise. Do you understand me?"

Gemma nodded. "I do. It didn't take much to give Chad a little boost this morning."

"Honey, it also wouldn't have taken much for Chad's hand to continue to heal on its own," said Imani.

"Hey, so, she can really heal people, right?" Chad said.

Mercury looked at the boy. There was no reason to continue to evade his questions and it'd do no good to lie. "Right."

"Wow, that's crazy."

Gemma grinned at Chad, but the rest of the group ignored him as Imani went to one side of the big man and Stella moved to his other side, and then paused. "Maybe Badger and Khaleesi should go out with the kids. Your dog may not like the kind of pain you're going to be in," said Stella.

"You got a point there," agreed Marcus. "Badge, go to the kids." He pointed out the front of the cave toward the creek. The shepherd got up and padded to the entrance, where he paused and looked back at Marcus. "Go on. It's okay."

"Khaleesi, go with him." Mercury shooed the pitty to the entrance, and both dogs padded down to the creek.

"He listens to you really well," said Gemma. "Did you train him yourself?"

"No, he came to me trained, but we've been together for many years and have gotten through some tight situations. Sometimes I think he knows my mind better than I do."

"I think Badger's really cool, and so big and beautiful." Gemma chattered about the dog as she rolled up the cut leg of Marcus's jeans to expose his break and began unwrapping the splint she'd made for him the day before.

When his leg was bare from the knee down, the break was obvious. Mercury's stomach tightened as she saw the swollen, distended flesh of his shin, pushed in an awkward manner by the out of place bone. She wiped her wet palms on her jeans. "What do I need to do?"

"Hold his foot like this." Gemma demonstrated as she cupped Marcus's heel with her right hand. Her left hand rested across the top of his foot. "The diagram in the book on orthopedics said to draw his heel forward as you pull the foot back—hard. The bone should slide into place then." She looked up at Mercury, who stood behind her staring down at Marcus's injured leg. "When I say hard, I mean really hard. They'd usually do this with the patient under anesthesia." Her gaze shifted to Marcus. "I'm really sorry, but the book said if this isn't done your leg's not going to heal right."

"I get it, baby girl. Do what you need to do. I would appreciate a stick or some wood to bite on, though, so's I don't slice my tongue in half," said Marcus.

Imani disappeared outside the cave and returned shortly, brushing off a stick before handing it to Marcus. He nodded, took it from her, and bit down on it. "Just do it."

Mercury took Gemma's place on her knees in front of Marcus. She placed her hands in the position Gemma had demonstrated, then she glanced at the big man. "On three?"

He nodded.

"One . . . two—" Purposefully, Mercury didn't wait to count three. Instead, at two she focused all of her strength into her arms and hands and with one swift, strong motion she snapped his bone back into place.

Marcus made a choking sound and then his eyes rolled to show their whites and he passed out. The stick, snapped in half by his teeth, tumbled from his mouth.

"Okay, see that pile of bandages and branches over there?" Gemma spoke quickly as she pointed. "Get those for me. I'm gonna do some healing and then, hopefully while he's still out, splint his leg again."

While Stella supported Marcus's weight so he didn't slump forward, Imani hurried to get the splinting supplies Gemma had gathered earlier.

Mercury moved out of Gemma's way and the teenager sat crosslegged beside Marcus's leg. She drew a deep breath, placed her hands over the break, and closed her eyes. Mercury remained close to Gemma. She watched the girl, and when sweat beaded and then fell from her skin and her breath came in pants as her body trembled, Mercury crouched and touched her shoulder. "That's enough, Gemma."

Like she was waking from a dark dream, the teenager's eyes fluttered open. They were filled with pain, and Mercury saw that the sweat on her face was mixed with tears and snot.

"Maybe just a little more?" Gemma's voice was weak, barely above a whisper.

Imani was there, placing the new bandages beside Marcus. She put her arm around Gemma and gently pulled her hands from his leg. "No, honey. You've done enough for now."

Mercury went quickly to where they kept their supply of boiled and bottled water and brought two full bottles back to Gemma. "Drink one and sit over here beside Marcus."

"But I need to rewrap his leg," she said.

"Just tell me how and I'll do it," said Imani.

"Listen to us, kid," Stella said, still holding Marcus in place. "Remember what we said about you being our only doc."

"I'll be glad when Doc Hilary gets here," Gemma said wryly, but she scooted painfully around so that she, too, leaned against the log. Slowly, wincing, she straightened her legs.

Mercury didn't need to pull up the teenager's jeans leg. She knew what she'd find—an injury like Marcus's on her shin.

"Man, that's really something," said Chad. "How come she can do that?"

Mercury looked at the young man. His eyes were bright with excitement as he stared at Gemma. The part of herself that was a teacher wanted to give Chad a chance. He was entitled and selfish, that was clear, but lots of young people were—and many of them grew up and grew out of it. But the other part of her, the warrior she was becoming, wanted to pick him up by the scruff of his shirt and toss him out of the cave and tell him to go the hell away. She shook herself mentally and chose a path somewhere in the middle of the two parts of herself. "The green mist," Mercury said bluntly. "It kills men, but it changes us. It changed Gemma."

His eyes shot to her. "Did it change *all* of you?"

"Yes, it did." She held his gaze until he looked away without asking her any more questions.

14

M ARCUS RECOVERED QUICKLY from the resetting of his leg, which said a lot about Gemma's evolving skills as a healer. Gemma did not recover as quickly, which also said a lot about her evolving skills as a healer—Mercury believed it was more proof that they needed to be careful with the teenager. One day she might *not* recover from healing someone, and that possibility was terrible.

They helped Marcus to hobble out by Bridge Creek, where Imani had set up an adobe brickmaking area. There the big man relaxed with his leg elevated and Badger by his side. The entire group, minus Gemma, who was sleeping, clustered around Imani.

"Okay, I'm going to give you some basic instructions down here, but we'll make the bulk of our bricks up there." She pointed up at the jagged cliff. "First, because that's where we're making our homes and second because up on top of that cliff is an excellent place for the bricks to bake in the sun and dry."

Georgie's hand shot up.

Imani smiled. "Yes, Georgie?"

"What if it rains on the bricks?"

"That's a good question," said Imani. "After they're dry that won't be a big deal. They'll be fairly watertight, especially as the cliff dwellings will have a natural roof up there. But if it does rain before they're dry and in place, we'll need to stretch a tarp over them. Here's hoping it just continues to be hot and sunny. That'll dry the bricks quickly and we can start building our adobe walls." She glanced at Stella. "We need to add more tarps, or at least plastic covers of some kind, to our list."

Stella nodded. "I'll write it down as soon as we're done here."

"So I'm going to show you a miniature version of what we're going to do clifftop," continued Imani. "But the ratios are the same. We're going to take thirty percent clay."

Imani picked up the bucket that had some of the rust-colored clay Mercury had gathered from the Painted Hills and poured a little of it into one of the two big aluminum water troughs Ford had found in Mitchell. Mercury felt a moment of sadness at losing the trough as a bathtub. Stella bumped her with her shoulder and whispered, "There's gotta be another trough back there in Mitchell. Don't worry, Acorn, I'll add bathtub trough to our list."

"Stop reading my mind," Mercury whispered back.

"Never." Stella teased.

"So then you add to the clay this sandy dirt that's by the creek. Up there on top of the cliff there's also plenty of this same sandy dirt surrounding the pond-like area that feeds our little waterfall, so we shouldn't have to haul dirt up there. The ratio is thirty percent clay to seventy percent sandy dirt." She demonstrated as she continued to instruct. "See these dry grasses and twigs?" Imani held up a handful of brown stuff. "Technically, we can make adobe bricks without these, but I want to give our bricks a little extra strength. So in they go. Then we mix in the water—enough to make it pourable. Like this." Imani poured creek water from a bucket she'd already filled. With her hands she stirred the mud until she was satisfied. Then she filled a big cup with the goop. "See how this pours?" She emptied the cup slowly back into the mixture. "That's the consistency we need. Now all we do is form the bricks. They should be nice and big, and try to make them about the same size." She glanced at Stella again. "Let's really try to find some two-by-fours. I could build simple molds that would make this process a lot quicker and more uniform." Her attention returned to the rest of her audience. "But we don't have to have molds. Without them we just form bricks by hand." She used the bucket to scoop out the mud mixture and then poured it out on part of one of the tarps she'd laid nearby. "It's a little like working with sloppy play dough," she said as she formed a brick that looked about two feet long, one foot across and four inches deep.

She stood and flicked mud from her hands as she smiled at the little group. "That's all there is to it. We wait for the bricks to dry enough to sit up on their sides, where they'll continue to dry. When they're hard enough we'll start forming walls up there, using more mud for mortar. I'll also add some rock between the adobes and mortar for added strength. Questions?"

Karen asked, "About how long will the adobe take to dry?"

Imani shrugged. "That depends on the weather. The hotter it is, the faster they'll dry. In the summer it'd probably only take a day or two. Right now we'll need to double that, which is why we have to get busy. Today." Her gaze went to Mercury. "Do you think you can carry that trough up the cliff?"

Chad, who had been silent during the demonstration, made a scoffing sound, which he tried to cover with a cough. Mercury ignored him. "Yeah, of course. It's going to be an awkward carry, though, and if it's as steep as I think it's going to be I'll probably drag it a good part of the way. But you can fill it with buckets and the tarps and even the shovels."

"You think you can carry that trough filled with stuff all the way up there?" Chad looked her up and down and added, "I mean, you're in okay shape, but I don't even think the big guy could carry that up there." He jerked his chin at Marcus, who was watching him with his brows raised in amusement.

"I don't *think* I can carry that up there. I *know* I can." Mercury turned her back to the boy. "Get the stuff you need in the trough and while you're doing that, Stella can show me the path up there. It'd be smart for me to walk it first so I know where the really steep parts are."

"Sounds good," Imani said. "I'll gather the tools right now." She hurried off in the direction of the cave.

"I wish I could help you ladies with this part, but I won't be able to climb up there until my leg has healed more," said Marcus. "So how 'bout I make myself a spot over there on the bank and do some fishing instead?"

"That sounds good," said Stella. "You'll need some help, though, and we're going to put Georgie and the twins to work making bricks."

Her gaze went to Chad. "I'll bet Gemma would say that you need to keep that hand out of the mud for a few more days until those bites scab completely over, so you can stay down here and help Marcus."

"I'm feeling kinda tired. I thought I might go back to the cave and take a nap," said Chad.

"Help Marcus instead," said Mercury. "Go to bed early tonight so you're not tired tomorrow."

"Mercury?"

The soft sound of her name surprised her, and then she felt a rush of joy as she looked down to see Cayden smiling up at her. *He'd spoken!* She heard Karen's gasp of surprise and Stella's sharp intake of breath, and then everyone went completely still. Mercury wanted to cheer, but she also didn't want to make a huge deal out of the first words he'd uttered since his parents had died in case that caused him to stop speaking again. So she crouched in front of the little boy, whose twin brother, Hayden, stood behind him watching her with big, expressive eyes. "Yes, Cayden. Did you want to ask me something?"

He nodded vigorously. "When we make our houses up there, will that keep the bad men from getting us?"

Mercury smoothed his hair back from his forehead. "Yes. We'll be safe up there. But I want you and Hayden to know that I won't let the bad men get you. Not now and not after we're living up there."

"We know." The little boy reached out and took her hand. "You're our warrior."

Hayden moved up to stand beside his twin and took her other hand. In a voice softer than his brother's he repeated. "You're our warrior."

"I absolutely am." Mercury felt as if her heart would burst from her chest as she hugged the little boys close to her and kissed both of their foreheads. "And I really like hearing your voices. Now, want to race me to the top of the cliff? We have bricks to start making!"

"Yeah!" the boys said together as they sprinted away toward the cliff.

"Hey, wait!" Georgie shouted. "I'm gonna make bricks too." Then she raced after her brothers with Khaleesi at her heels.

Beside Marcus, Badger whined softly and the big man smiled. "Oh, go on." The shepherd shot after the kids and the pit bull.

Karen was dabbing at her eyes as they watched the boys. "I'm so glad they finally spoke."

"What's wrong with them?" Chad asked.

Stella turned to him. "They watched their parents burn to death."

"Oh. Sucks for them," muttered Chad.

Karen's thin lips pressed together as she studied the boy. "Chad, I'll show you where we keep the fishing gear so that you and Marcus can get busy catching our dinner," she said. Then she turned to Mercury and Stella. "I'll get them settled and check on Gemma before I join you clifftop."

"You can stay down here if you'd like," said Stella. "That climb is rough."

Karen nodded. "It is, and that is exactly why I need to make myself do it at least once a day. Someday I may need to get up there—fast, and I want to be able to do so." She patted Chad's shoulder as she passed him. "Come on, young man. No sense in dillydallying."

Chad sighed and shuffled after her.

"That boy needs an attitude adjustment," said Marcus.

"I'm afraid if an apocalypse didn't adjust his attitude nothing will," said Mercury.

Marcus nodded. "Good point, but maybe he just needs some guidance. I'll see what I can do."

Stella's snort echoed Mercury's thoughts, though she told herself *Marcus could be right. The boy might just need some guidance to become a decent man.*

"Fat chance, Acorn," Stella said softly as they followed the children and dogs more slowly.

The climb to the top of the cliff was steep and parts of it were difficult, but it wound like a snake, coiling up the canyon-like hill, which made the climb manageable. The ropes were helpful, though the kids scampered ahead of them like mountain goats and didn't use them at all.

Mercury wiped sweat from her forehead and drew in several deep breaths to steady her heartbeat as she finally reached the clifftop. The kids and dogs were already up there. They were throwing sticks for the dogs and giggling as Khaleesi and Badger raced each other to see who could retrieve them fastest.

"Remember when you used to have that kind of energy?" Mercury turned to ask Stella, who was just emerging from the little trail.

"Holy fucking shit!" Stella said.

"Well, that's a weird response. You're not *that* damn old."

"Not that." Stella pointed to a place behind Mercury. "*That.*"

Mercury turned to look across the rugged top of the cliff. Though the edges were jagged and rough—some were even pointed—the land that stretched the length and width of the cliff was flat and dotted with rocks and spindly evergreens. Not far from where their little trail tucked against the rounded mound of the hill that adjoined their cliff, was the pool Stella and Imani had told her about the night before. Like rays of the sun stretching from it were the furrows of the garden they'd already begun digging.

Mercury was amazed at the beauty of the area. "Y'all didn't tell me there's an oasis up here. This is incredible." Mercury walked toward the pool. A waterfall that fell, veil-like, from the much taller hill that butted up to their clifftop, fed it. It flowed into a round, clear pool that was elevated on a high bank, making it look like it was a giant's soup bowl that was chipped. From that chip leaked the much smaller waterfall that ran down the rear of their campsite. The high bank of the bowl-like pond was lush with green grasses and dotted with brilliant golden poppies, shimmering like miniature suns.

"It's so pretty, isn't it, Mercury?" Georgie ran past her, giggling as she let her hands caress the golden flowers, causing them to dance in her wake.

"It sure is," said Mercury as she climbed the steep bank and dipped her hand in the pool. It was clean and clear and cold. She looked down at Stella, who was still staring at the pond. "Isn't this steep and deep enough to be used for irrigation?"

At a jog, Imani suddenly topped the path. Her gaze went to the pool, and she stumbled to a halt and her sweat-streaked face went blank with shock. "Oh, shit! It actually worked!"

Mercury half slid, half climbed down the bank. "Will you two please tell me what the hell is going on?"

Stella pointed at Imani. "This is all her."

Imani walked slowly to the raised bank of the pool. Reverently, she bent to caress the grasses. Her fingers gently stroked a striking yellow poppy before she turned to look at them. "Thank you." Her words drifted to Mercury with the soft breeze. When she faced them her brown eyes were bright with unshed tears and her smile was radiant. "This is exactly what I pictured last night when we talked about it—when I said that the pool up here was great, but that I wished it was deeper and raised." She wiped sweat from her face with a trembling hand. "My heart told me that my connection to the earth was special—that there was more to it than I realized. So I pictured this, all of this, even the California poppies."

"This wasn't here before?" Mercury asked, still struggling to comprehend what her eyes and her friends were telling her.

"No," said Stella. "Just a couple days ago it was a shallow, round basin with almost no bank."

"There were very few grasses," Imani added. "And no poppies."

"Imani, you created this." Mercury felt flushed as a rush of joy and excitement coursed through her.

Imani shook her head. "I'm not a creator. I didn't do this. The earth did, but she did it because she can hear me, and I believe she, the earth, wants to help us."

"This is some serious black girl magick," said Stella.

"Truly," said Mercury.

"We are going to be very happy living up here," said Imani firmly. "And we need to start moving our things up here right away. Not everything, of course. Not until we move up here permanently. But our extra supplies should be stored here where it's safe."

Mercury nodded. "Sounds good to me."

"My gut says ditto," Stella agreed.

"And now that our water supply has been altered, we can begin planting those seeds you brought back from Mitchell." Imani gestured at the area adjoining the pool that was already furrowed. "All of this can be our garden. Stella, add hoses to your list—the more the better, the longer the better. With the new height of the bank and the pool I can easily rig hoses to irrigate."

"I'll add it to the list. I'll bet there are hoses in that ag store," said Stella.

Mercury gazed across the top of the cliff, awed by the stark beauty of the area. It was like they had been lifted into the sky. The flat area atop the cliff was about the size of a football field. The far end of it curved and narrowed, with rocky spires that jutted up. She gestured to that part of the cliff. "Hey, that looks a little cave-like over there."

Imani nodded. She sounded more like herself, though her gaze periodically was drawn back to the pool, as if she needed to check that it was still there. "It could be a temporary shelter, but it's pretty rough and there's not enough space within those rock formations for more than just a few people to live comfortably."

"I think we need to seriously consider moving our campsite up here, and not just our extra supplies, as soon as Marcus's leg can tolerate the climb," said Stella. Imani and Mercury turned to her and she nodded. "And yes, that's definitely a gut *feeling* I just got."

"Well, right now with the use of tents and tarps we can create a shelter against those spires for the number of people we have," said Imani as they began to walk from the pool across the flat expanse of the clifftop. "But when Jenny and the Timberline group get here, there will absolutely not be room for them. It gets cold up here at night, and soon it'll be very hot during the day, which is why we're going to build our homes into the side of this cliff instead of on top of it."

"Should we have told them not to come?" Mercury spoke the thought aloud that had been niggling at the edge of her mind since she'd spoken to Jenny.

"No," said Stella firmly. "If Timberline was still a viable shelter they wouldn't leave."

Imani nodded. "Yeah, especially because there's still a lot of snow at that elevation. We can't turn away thirty people. Also, with more people we can make bricks faster," added Imani. "They won't be down there long." She stopped near the edge of the cliff where there was a gap in the rocky side. Another rope was there, secured around the tip of a rock. "Follow me." Imani grabbed the rope and confidently half climbed, half rappelled down the cliff.

"Do I have to?" Mercury said, only partially kidding.

"It's not as bad as it looks. It goes straight down to a pretty wide ledge. You can do it, Acorn." And with that Stella stepped in front of her, grabbed the rope, and went down over the side.

Mercury sighed, drew in a deep, shaky breath, and followed.

Stella had been right. She only had to scramble down about six feet and then she was standing on a ledge that was several yards wide. Like broken teeth, rocks jutted up at the edge of the ledge, forming a comforting barrier that had Mercury's stomach righting itself.

"I'll make us a ladder as soon as we get some lumber. This way," Imani called, and Mercury followed her and Stella to the right where the ledge cut back into the cliff, where a rocky outcropping formed a dome-like roof. It was expansive and Mercury could easily envision snug adobe homes, like a honeycomb, resting safely, side by side, far above the vulnerable land below them.

"Was this here when you first looked up here, or did you change it too?" Mercury asked as she gazed around, awed by the perfection of the site.

Imani grinned. "It was already here, and I didn't change the pool. The earth did. All I did was ask her."

Mercury turned and stared out at the world around them. In the distance she could just glimpse the colors of the rolling Painted Hills, and that was where she focused her eyes—instead of the plumes of smoke that feathered all across the horizon or the stains of green that spotted the land. The endlessness and strangeness of it made her feel small and frightened and very mortal—and then she thought of the remarkable pool, Gemma's healing touch, Stella's intuition, Karen's connection to spirit, and her own strength and resiliency. Mercury held tightly to the comfort and the magick they'd found and promised herself that she would do anything to keep her people safe and thriving.

"All right, let's build a city in the sky," said Mercury.

"We're ready," said Imani.

"Fuckin' A right we are!" added Stella.

15

❧

THE SKY WAS just beginning to lighten with dawn when Eva felt someone touch her shoulder. She woke instantly, grasped the 9 mm under
her pillow, and rolled onto her back as she raised the gun in a two-handed
grip.

Al lifted his hands. His white teeth caught the wan light from the
window as he smiled charmingly. "I come in peace."

Eva didn't immediately lower the gun. "How did you get in here?"

He crossed his arms over his chest and leaned against the bedroom
wall. "What can I say? The shadows like me."

Eva made a mental note to chastise Wes, whose turn it was that
night to guard her and prevent any unfortunate surprises—like someone
sneaking into her bedroom.

"What do you want?" Eva asked. She couldn't say she actually liked
Al. She couldn't say she actually liked many people. But Al Rutland
intrigued her, so much so that she'd allowed him to join her in Madras.
She even found him attractive, though she wasn't sure she wanted to
discover exactly what was hidden under his clothes.

"Fulfilling your request. You said you want to learn how to gain
power from the green mist. I'm here to teach you."

Eva lowered the gun. She despised the kind of man who believed
every fucking thing they had to say was a golden kernel of wisdom, especially when imparted to a woman, but Al had powers. She'd witnessed

his control over the leech-like creatures he somehow carried with him. And now he'd managed to slip into her bedroom using shadow to cloak himself.

Eva wanted power. She *needed* power to remain in control of Madras. She sat and shook back her hair. "And how do you plan to teach me?"

"Come with me. It's better to show and not tell." He glanced down her body. The bed linens were pooled around her waist, exposing the thin silk chemise she slept in. The corners of his lips lifted in an appreciative smile. "I'll turn my back while you get up and get dressed."

With no hesitation Eva threw off the linens and stood. She paused to meet his gaze steadily. "No need." Unhurriedly, she walked past him, stopping at her closet long enough to gather a pair of skinny jeans and a form-hugging shirt before going to her dresser and taking her time picking out a lacy bra and panties set. Then, without looking at him, she said, "I'll only be a moment," and disappeared into her bathroom. She got ready quickly, choosing to only apply mascara and her signature red lipstick. Eva studied herself in the mirror. *I'm perfection.*

As she emerged and went to the shoe section of her closet, Al said, "As much as I appreciate those stilettos, you'll probably be happier if you wear something flat for this lesson."

Eva's hand paused on her favorite black knee-high boots. She glanced over her shoulder at him. "I'm not into hiking."

His charming smile widened. "Noted. We won't hike."

Eva hesitated only a moment, and then pulled a pair of vintage turquoise cowboy boots from the corner of her closet. As she slipped her feet into them, Al spoke again.

"Does owning a pair of cowboy boots make you a successful rural Oregon politician?"

"No," she snapped as she walked past him to the door. "Exploiting ignorance and racism *made* me a successful rural Oregon politician. Power and control will be what assures I remain successful in this *brave new world.*" She laced the end of the sentence with sarcasm.

Al chuckled as he followed her out the door and down the long, dark hallway.

This wasn't Eva's home. That had been a 6,500-square-foot chalet on a sizable ranch, the boundary of which began at the edge of Madras. Her home hadn't made it through the quakes and was currently a pile of expensive rubble. Sadly, Eva now called the only suite in the Madras Inn, along with several adjoining rooms, her home. It was only adequate because it was temporary.

At the end of the hallway by the closed door to the stairwell, Wes stood abruptly as she and Al approached him. Eva looked the pathetic man in the eye.

"Can you tell me how Al managed to enter my room and wake me?"

Wes's gaze darted from Eva to Al, and then back to rest on Eva. "N—no, ma'am. I swear I haven't moved from here."

Eva reached out and took the AR-15 from Wes and held it against the curve of her hip as she pointed it at him. "If anyone *ever* gets past you again I will shoot you. Do you understand?"

"Yes, ma'am."

She tossed the weapon at him, and as he scrambled to catch it, Al slipped past him and opened the door for Eva. "After you, Madam Mayor."

Eva strode into the stairwell. Her suite was on the third floor of the inn, which was the top floor, and her boots made a sharp *tat-tat-tat-tat* as she went down the cement stairs.

"The apocalypse has made good help damn difficult to find," said Al at her side.

"Yes, I'm aware."

He smiled at her. "Perhaps you shouldn't sleep alone."

"Perhaps you should mind your own business." She returned his smile with one of her own, laced with poisonous sweetness.

"Noted."

They emerged from the stairway and made their way through the silent lobby. The front windows of the inn and the cheap, automatic glass doors had been shattered and boarded up, but workers had managed to rig a wooden door in place of the electric ones and Eva paused before it.

Though she didn't so much as glance at Al, he stepped around her and held the door open for her.

"Thank you," she said.

"It is my pleasure," he said.

Eva stopped and squinted up at the lightening sky, brushing back her hair as the wind whipped it across her face. The rising sun was painting brilliant splashes of fuchsia and saffron against the horizon.

Eva had to stop herself from grimacing. It was going to be another clear, warm day—and from here on out it would just keep getting warmer until October. Eva hated hot weather. *I'm going to get one of those damn generators for my suite and keep it so fucking cold in there I won't have to put my wine in the fridge.* She sighed and turned to Al. "Now what? Do we need to take one of the SUVs?" She nodded in the direction of several sleek Ford Expeditions parked silently side by side in the most undamaged part of the circle drive to the inn.

Al barked a laugh.

"What?" She frowned at him. "Is there something wrong with the SUVs?"

"You mean besides the fact that they guzzle gas and that's a very limited commodity?" He laughed again. "I prefer a bike."

"A bicycle? I didn't picture you as one of those metrosexuals who bike to work."

"A motorcycle. They require a lot less gas and provide a lot more freedom," he said.

"Yeah, I've already thought of that. I've collected some of those. If we need one right now I can show you where they are. If not, I'll let Wes know you can have your pick of them."

"That's generous, and I'll take you up on it, though we don't need one for where we're going at the moment. It's an easy walk." He glanced down at her cowboy boots and his lips tilted up in a wry smile. "At least it's easy in boots that don't have three-inch heels."

She raised a blonde brow. "Four-inch, not three."

He grinned. "My mistake. This way, Madam Mayor."

Al led her around the back of the inn and helped her scramble up a half-crumbled stone retaining wall. They crossed a street and then climbed a hill that looked like a scoop of brown ice cream situated directly behind the inn.

"I told you I don't like to hike," Eva said as she trudged up the hill beside him.

"Think of this more as a field trip than a hike," he said. "And it's a pretty small hill."

She said nothing, but was relieved when they got to the top, which was rocky and dotted with a grove of junipers. Eva turned to Al. "How is this hill teaching me about the power of the green mist?"

"This hill won't. *That* will." Al pointed past the junipers where, about halfway down the far side of the hill, there was a dip in a rocky area. In the pale morning light the green mist that filled it was the color of moss. It seemed to play in the wind, lifting lazily with each gust and spilling over the dip like a cocktail made with dry ice.

Eva stared down at the pool of mist. "Is it supposed to show me something?"

"Not from here it won't. You need to go down there. Walk into it. *That* is your lesson."

Eva's gaze went from the mist to Al. She frowned. "I told you, I've already been exposed to the damn mist. It did nothing for me except make my blood toxic to plants, which is the opposite of useful."

"And as I said, you haven't evolved enough yet. You need more exposure to it. So go down there. Circle around where it's puddled so that you're heading into the wind when you reach it. You'll pass out, but won't get overexposed because it'll blow past you. And when you wake I'll be there," he finished with a little flourish and a bow, like he imparted his wisdom with Barnum and Bailey–level showmanship.

Eva put her hand on her hip and cocked her head to study Al. "If the mist is so great, why don't you come with me and get another dose yourself?"

"That's not how it works for men. I've had one dose. That's all I can have."

Eva's brows lifted. "Is walking into the mist how you gained your powers?"

The open, friendly expression on Al's handsome face shifted. He turned his gaze from hers. His eyes went flat with anger and the side of one lip curled up as he clenched his fists. He spoke sharply. "Not exactly." Then, under his breath, he said, "Fucking teachers."

"Did you say teachers?"

Al blinked, and when his gaze returned to her most, but not all, of the anger had drained from his face. "Yeah, women, two in particular, and a man. They caused me"—he paused and then enunciated the word carefully—"*difficulty.*"

Eva brushed her windblown hair out of her face again. "I think I know who you mean. Was the man a Mexican?"

"Yes."

"That's them. They were also *difficult* here in Madras. They managed to slip away from Amber. Not her finest hour. I would love to happen across them," Eva said as she wondered what they'd done to piss Al off.

"As would I. But you should know the mist changed them. Made them *more*." His blue eyes took on a malevolent glint. "Well, the women. The man is no longer a player."

"They can do more than grow plants?" she asked, annoyed and intrigued at the thought.

"Yes, I do believe so," he said.

"Then I'd better even the playing field." Eva started down the side of the hill. She hated hiking and all things out-of-doors, but Eva was obsessed with working out, and her fit body moved quickly and gracefully as she kicked into a jog, skirting the pooling mist. She continued to jog several yards down the hill from it before she turned to face it. The wind blew into her face, cooling her skin. She could feel Al watching her, but she didn't look at him. This wasn't about him. This was about her and power. She gathered herself and then launched forward, sprinting into the mist.

The green stuff that had already been blown from the dip in the land swirled around her legs, lapping against her more like water than fog, and then the ground sloped down and the wind lifted the mist from her legs to her chest, and finally it engulfed her.

For a moment Eva held her breath. *No. I have to breathe it in. If those idiot teachers can do it, I can do it better.* Eva halted and drew in a long breath—so long that her chest rose, her breasts straining against her snug shirt. Even then she forced another sip of air into her lungs, and held it. The mist exploded within her—stinging—stinging—stinging. The scent was as it had been the day of the bombs; it was like she stood in a swamp breathing in stagnant water, mud, and overripe fruit. Then her breath released in a rush. She drank in another deep breath and the stinging was worse. The pain was terrible. It felt as if the mist had become sentient within her and, trapped, it was trying to claw its way out—through her lungs, her chest, her abdomen. *No! I'll hold it in. I won't let it go!* She held her breath as she tried to see through the thick green shroud and stumbled forward, attempting to get out of the low spot—to get to clean air—but her legs jellied and she fell to her knees as she released her breath in a shriek of agony. Then everything went black.

Before Eva opened her eyes she was aware of *them*. She could feel their presence. They filled her, much as the stinging mist had, only the feeling wasn't painful. It was a comfort. Eva had always been a leader, even when she was a child. Her father had made sure of that. Her mother had not given him the son he craved, so he'd created his firstborn into an image of himself—clever, tough, and focused on one simple truth, that the end justified the means. Eva regretted nothing about her childhood or her life, but except for occasional lovers she had been alone. Now she was not.

With the knowledge that she was not alone came something else—a tidal wave of scent. *Eva could smell everything.* She knew Al sat beside her. She could smell him. His breath, his skin, his blood. There were creatures all around her—squirrels, chipmunks, birds, and even a snake that stirred from the base of a tree not far from her. She could smell all of them, especially their breath, and she knew if she got closer she would be able to scent their skin, their sweat, their blood.

Her eyes opened. She lay on her back. She gazed up at the sky, which was almost painfully blue. She took in the scraggly branches of the junipers that surrounded her. Her eyesight was so clear—preternaturally so. She sat.

"Slow down. You might still be dizzy." Al put his hand under her elbow as if to support her.

Eva shook him off. "I'm fine." Even her words were sharper, clearer. She turned to look at him. "Say something."

His brows lifted, but he complied. "How are you feeling?"

Eva thought for an instant that she could see his words, but she quickly realized that wasn't correct. It wasn't his words she could see; it was the breath he exhaled. It curled between them, delicate, gossamer, and beautiful, like a spider's web.

Al smiled. "You've evolved."

"I have." Eva stood and Al got to his feet as he watched her closely.

"What gifts have you been given, do you know yet?" he asked.

She was only slightly annoyed by the eagerness in his voice. This was private. This was *hers*. She started to tell him to back off, but there was suddenly a terrible tickle in her throat. Eva gagged and then covered her mouth as she coughed violently. She was going to wipe her hand on her jeans when something in her palm caught her gaze. She'd coughed up dark speckles, almost like pea-sized coffee grounds, which didn't surprise her. The smell of the mist was rancid. Who the hell knew what crap it was made of? But as she looked closer she saw that the dark speckles *moved*. Intrigued, Eva lifted her hand, palm up, as the insects opened their translucent wings. They each had six delicate legs, and as she marveled at their beauty, they turned to face her.

Eva could feel them, this incredible swarm. They knew her and she knew them. They were part of her. They filled her, *and they obeyed her*. "You are exceptional," she told them in an echo of her father's voice. She glanced at Al, who was staring at her with a half smile curving his lips. "Bite him," she commanded.

Instantly the six large, beautiful mosquitoes obeyed. They lifted from her palm and, like a flight of miniature F-16s, attacked Al.

"Shit!" He swatted at the air, knocking several aside. "Call off the little bastards or I'll fucking squish them."

"Leave him," Eva said. The insects returned to her. They went to her shoulders and perched there like tiny, well-trained birds. She frowned at Al. "Do not hurt them."

"Then keep them away from me." His voice lost its charming edge. "Remember that I, too, have *companions*." Gently, he scratched a spot just above the waist of his jeans where there was a soft, wriggling bulge.

Eva nodded shortly. It would be a mistake to make him an enemy. "You are correct. I will keep them away from you." Just above her in a cavity of the juniper was a squirrel nest. She could smell the rich scent of multiple babies, still so young their breath was milky and warm. Eva concentrated. There were three of them, and they were alone. The mother must be out feeding. Eva smiled and concentrated on the babies. She cleared her throat twice and then she inhaled deeply until her breasts once more strained against the soft fabric of her shirt. Again, she sipped in just a little more air, held it, and before she exhaled she thought *Bite them, cover them, drink them dry*. Eva tilted up her chin and blew out a long breath through her pursed, scarlet lips.

Mosquitoes swarmed from her mouth. Their wings made a deliciously dangerous buzzing sound that filled the area around her, but her insects didn't pause to greet her or hover about her. They flew, arrow-like, up to the nest in the tree. In a dark, living cloud they entered it.

Eva entered with them. Not literally. She couldn't see through the eyes of the swarm, but she was joined with them, so she felt their need for blood and their fierceness as they attacked.

As the baby squirrels shrieked and died, Eva Cruz laughed.

"You'll have to be careful now," said Al.

"Now?" Eva laughed again. "No, *now* I'm more powerful, which means I can be less careful."

"You misunderstand. What I meant is you'll have to be careful with the green bloods. They could have extra powers of their own," he explained.

Eva scoffed. "Those women? No. They have given up their power. I know their type all too well. They're the women who willingly subjugate themselves, whether to a man or a religion, because they're either too stupid or weak or broken to stand up. Those women are no threat to me, and the very few who might be, I'll do away with."

"You are spectacular."

Still laughing, Eva turned to face Al. His gaze swept hungrily down her body. She was filled with such power, such energy, that sex would give her a glorious release. And Al was handsome—tall, blond, square-jawed, and muscular. He was definitely the type she liked to play with and then discard. Her smile was slow and seductive. Her hand traced the swell of her breast as he watched.

Eva closed the space between them. She draped her arms around his broad shoulders and pressed her body close to him, but as she tilted her face up, lips parted for his kiss, he made the mistake of speaking.

"I'm all for this, but let's *not* kiss until you've spent a little more time controlling your new companions."

Eva froze. She undraped her arms from his shoulders and briefly patted his cheek. "Pity, but I do have a staff meeting this morning and I loathe being late." Eva began walking back up the hill with Al at her side. She glanced at him. "You're welcome to join me in the staff meeting. I'll be talking about my security—or lack thereof. Though I feel considerably safer now." She coughed delicately and caught the mosquito on her finger, smiling as it lifted to buzz affectionately around her head.

"I appreciate the invite, but I've had enough staff meetings to last a lifetime. Instead, I'd like to take you up on that offer of a bike."

Eva shrugged. "You do you. Wes will be in the meeting. I'll tell him to show you to the motorcycles. He's crap at security anyway." When they reached the road Eva turned to him. "Should I expose myself to the mist again?"

Al ran his hand through his thick, blond hair. "Probably not. You've evolved. You've been changed and given gifts, but there is a line, and if you cross it there is no returning to humanity."

His vagueness irritated Eva. "What does that mean?"

"It means that we can only change so much until we are unrecognizable."

She grimaced. "You mean I'd become monstrous and unattractive?"

He smiled. "Quite possibly, but perhaps only on the inside. I've seen things out there." His gesture was sweeping. "And I do not believe you would like to become some of those things."

She narrowed her eyes. "Can you not be more specific?"

"No. There is no rule book. I'm just speaking from my gut and my experience."

She sighed. "Fine. This will do . . . for now."

Al reveled in the feeling of the wind against his skin as he roared down the empty road on the Harley XR750 he'd been pleasantly surprised to find in the group of bikes Eva had collected in Madras.

Eva . . . she would be a challenge. He'd need to control her without her realizing he was pulling her strings. Normally, he'd charm her into falling in love with him and then begin to slowly isolate her from others and subtly work on eroding her self-esteem until she questioned every decision she made and had to look to him as her savior.

That wouldn't work on a woman like Eva. She didn't count on friends or family to support her. She counted on herself—on power and control. Her self-esteem wasn't set by the opinions of others. She was far too strong and self-assured for that nonsense. And now she had a very real amount of power in those insects that incubated inside her.

Fascinating. No, a woman like Eva Cruz couldn't be bullied or intimidated. He had to be of value to her. He also had to be dangerous. Not enough that she tried to dispense with him—just enough that she was forced to respect him.

That was fine. Al knew things about this new world. Not everything. Not even as much as he wished he knew, but he'd proven today that he knew more than Eva. He would keep proving it. He would also fuck her. His laughter was caught and blown away by the wind. Though he wouldn't kiss the bitch. The swarm under her control might fascinate him, but he was not going to allow her to breathe them into his body.

The town of Prineville came into view and he stopped the bike. Patches of green mist rolled with the steady morning breeze and he decided to skirt the town—it was a shithole anyway, and as he was on a bike he really couldn't scavenge much. The bike handled well off road, though he had to slow and was glad when the town was behind him and he could get back on highway 26. Originally, he'd headed south, thinking that he'd reconnoiter in Sunriver and check out the multimillion-dollar homes there. If any were still standing, they would interest Eva, and the more he could pique her interest the better for him. Not that he needed Eva's approval. It wasn't that. He could kill her today and take her place, but that would be a lot less entertaining than manipulating her into believing she needed him so much that she handed him the keys to her city—literally and figuratively. He would build an empire to control in this new world, and the simplest way to go about that was to begin in Madras, where Eva Cruz had already attained control over the sheep she'd gathered.

Also, it would be enjoyable to conquer Eva. She was conquest worthy—a female version of himself. He looked forward to bending her to his stronger will.

So he would take the bike down to Sunriver and see what of interest he could find there. But first he needed to return to the place it had ended and begun. Eva was busy keeping an iron grip on her people, and it would be good for her to wonder where he'd gone, what he was doing. And because he'd awakened her so early, it was barely midmorning. Al had all the time he needed.

Al's bike flew up the highway, easily dodging around wrecks and sinkholes. He saw a few people, mostly dead, though a couple times he noticed someone stirring around the crappy properties that had been built off the highway. He made mental notes of where they were, but felt no compulsion to stop. He felt only one compulsion.

It didn't take long to get to Mitchell. The bike was fast and it wasn't like he had to deal with rush hour. The wind had remained brisk, which meant it was blowing mist in and around the town, so he'd be quick.

He guided the bike to the spot he'd been killed and halted there briefly. The road was still stained with his blood as well as the Mexican's. It was a dark, rust-like blemish that marked his end and his beginning. He'd returned here often, hoping that those women would also be compelled to return. He ached to find them—to show them that they hadn't conquered him—they had only helped to make him better, stronger, more dangerous. And then he would show them what else he was, and their endings wouldn't be as poetic as his.

On the bike Al continued to the heart of the little nothing town. The stench of death was thick and he was glad of the reprieve the breeze brought. He stopped again in front of the Feed'n'Farm and got off the bike. Across the street was a general store. If the women returned, they would come here, so here was where he would leave his gift for them.

Al walked around the side of the Feed'n'Farm to the rear where brown grass attempted unsuccessfully to choke out weeds. He kept walking through knee-high grasses and weeds until he came to the bank of a little stream that wound its way through the town. It wasn't much—a dried-up ditch most of the year, but it was still early enough that some water dribbled over the rocks.

That's where he left his little friends—in the stream. Al whispered to them first, sharing his will with them. His leeches understood. They didn't speak, of course. That would be insane. But they were part of him, which meant they understood him completely. They didn't need to speak for him to be sure that they would wait and do as he willed. And he would know if they were successful. He would know . . .

16

"MERCURY, SERIOUSLY, I wish you guys would stop treating me like a child! It makes sense that Chad and I take Marcus's Jeep to get the colorful clay while Karen and the kids keep making bricks and you guys go to Mitchell for more supplies. I mean, the kids are going to run out of the Painted Hills clay soon and there's no reason we should stop making bricks until whenever you guys get around to bringing us more clay. Chad and I can get it right now." She paused and then added. "Or we can just make a bunch of boring dirt-colored bricks."

Stella snorted and Mercury hid her smile.

"We're not treating you like a child," said Imani. "We're being smart. Sending you and Chad out alone isn't a good idea."

"Gemma, I don't have to remind you how dangerous it is out there, do I?" Mercury asked as she dunked a bucket in the creek and then splashed water from it onto her face, washing off the sweat and dirt that had caked her skin. She stepped aside and Imani took her place, sighing in pleasure as the cool water cascaded over her face. The day before, Mercury had carried a trough filled with their brickmaking tools clifftop, and since just after dawn that morning she and Stella and Imani had been schlepping their extra food and supplies up there. She'd climbed that damn steep path six times—twice the number of times her friends had gone up and back— between dawn and midmorning, and even with her super strength it had been sweaty and difficult. She was in no mood to deal with Gemma's whiny insistence that she needed to do something more than fish to help, even though she was still favoring her leg and the dark circles under her eyes looked like bruises.

Stella washed her face and then turned to Gemma. "Kid, you know how much we care about you and respect your gifts. We're not trying to be assholes. We're just trying to keep us all alive and safe."

"Hey, I'll keep her safe. I can handle myself," said Chad. He winked at Gemma, who smiled back at him.

Mercury wiped her face with her shirt. "Yeah, we saw how well you could handle yourself when we found you."

"Anyone can get snake bit," muttered Chad.

Stella snorted and splashed more water on her face.

"What if I go with them?" Marcus spoke up from where he was sitting near the bank of the creek gutting and scaling the fish he, Gemma, and Chad had caught that morning. "My leg is hardly causing me any pain and I won't be walking on it anyway." He turned his dark eyes on Chad. "I'll be chaperoning. And I'm good with weapons. I won't let anything happen to the kids, and baby girl is right. It's a waste of time to sit around here not making bricks, or making *boring bricks*, as Cayden and Hayden call them, without the colorful clay."

"You sure your leg is up to it?" Mercury asked him.

He looked at Gemma. "What do you think, Doc?"

"I think the short ride to the Painted Hills will be a little uncomfortable, but I won't let you do any walking, so you should be fine," she said.

"There," said Marcus. "We all know she wouldn't let me do something that would mess up her handiwork." He patted his injured leg.

Mercury looked at Stella. "What do you think?"

"I think Marcus is an excellent chaperone."

"Then we can go?" Gemma asked, bouncing a little on the balls of her feet.

"Which do you prefer—a .38, a Glock, or a rifle?" Mercury asked Marcus.

"The Glock," said the big man.

"I'll get it for you. Karen and the kids are clifftop making bricks and finishing readying the garden rows for planting," said Mercury. "If you hurry, you'll be back from the Painted Hills before any of them even know you're gone. Gemma, I'll put the buckets and a bunch of those shopping bags we got in Mitchell in the Jeep, but I don't want you to carry any of them up the cliff after they're full. Your leg still isn't a hundred percent." She turned her gaze to Chad. "That means you'll be hauling the clay up the cliff when you get back. Karen and the kids will want to help you. Let the kids, but it's a lot for Karen just to get up the cliff. Don't let her do too much."

"Well, okay, I'll try. But you know my hand—"

Mercury cut him off. "How's his hand healing, Gemma?"

Gemma answered quickly and honestly. "Doing really well. I still want him to keep it out of the mud for another day or two, but it's good."

"Then you're cleared to carry clay," said Mercury. "And you're a lot younger than Karen."

"He'll do the carrying," said Marcus. "Because it's the right thing to do. Isn't it, Chad?"

"Yeah." Under Marcus's steady gaze the boy's response was quick.

"Good, then it's decided. I'll wash off these fish guts, then Chad can help me stash the fillets in the fish cooler and I'll be ready to go," said Marcus. He grinned at the big shepherd who was lapping the creek water with Khaleesi and added. "I'll take Badger. He's also a good chaperone, and he moves a lot faster than I do."

"Excellent idea," said Mercury. "Take Khaleesi, too." She watched Chad's gaze go from the big man to the well-trained shepherd, and she didn't like the frown that pulled the corners of his lips down.

※※※

In the Jeep, Gemma followed close behind the truck so that when the two vehicles came out on Bear Creek Road they only had one set of tracks to obscure. Then Gemma turned to the right to head to the Painted Hills, and Stella went left where Bridge Creek Road would take them to highway 26, which went directly through Mitchell.

Gemma stuck her arm out the window and waved happily. Mercury craned her neck, watching the Jeep until it disappeared around a curve in the two-lane road.

"They'll be okay," said Stella. "The dogs are massive deterrents, and even with that messed-up leg, Marcus is formidable."

"Yeah, unlike Chad he can *actually* handle himself," added Imani.

"I'm really trying to like that boy," said Mercury.

Beside her, Imani nodded. "Ditto, sis."

Stella said nothing. She kept two hands on the wheel with her focus on the road.

"It's just that I get a really bad vibe from him," said Mercury.

"He has a serious case of *look at how cool I think I am*, which is annoying as hell," said Imani.

"What's really annoying is that Gemma is falling for it," said Mercury.

Imani shrugged. "She's sixteen. He's, what, eighteen, maybe twenty? To Gemma he's an older *man* with a charming smile who's paying a lot of attention to her. I'm not surprised she's falling for it."

"I just wish I knew if we dislike him because he's irritating, entitled, and lazy—or if we dislike him because he's a danger to us." When Stella remained silent, Mercury bumped her with her shoulder. "Woman! Have you nothing to say about this?"

Stella guided the truck around a sinkhole before she answered. "I've already said I don't like him and I don't think it was in our best interest to pick him up. But I'm also not infallible. Hello! Ford's death proved that." She paused and then blew out a long breath and continued. "I don't know what else to say. Plus, what if I did *know* he was going to do something that put us in danger? What can we do about it? He knows where our settlement is and that we have powers. Gemma has a crush on him. Short of snatching him in the middle of the night, taking him outside of camp somewhere, and killing him there's not a damn thing we can do."

"I would not be for taking him out and killing him," said Imani.

When she felt her friends' eyes on her Mercury spoke up quickly. "I wouldn't be for that either. I guess I just needed to vent about him."

"Hey, I didn't mean to sound bitchy," said Stella. She wiped her palms on her jeans. "It's returning to Mitchell—it has me tied up inside."

Mercury nodded. "I get that."

"It's a lot for you two," said Imani. "Which is why it's good we have our list." She held up the piece of paper filled with Stella's distinctive scrawling cursive. "Let's get in, check off the items we need, and get the hell out."

"And worry about Chad later," said Mercury.

Stella and Imani nodded and the cab fell silent. Mercury stared out at the desolate landscape. It was a little over two weeks since the bombs had dropped, and she'd imagined that people would be making themselves known again. They were not. Or at least they were not anywhere within sight. No one stirred. The skeletal ruins of homes were commonplace, though in fairness the land between their campsite and Mitchell had only been sparsely populated before the bombs. Mercury made a mental note of homes that were still standing and had outbuildings, especially barns. She liked Gemma's idea of luring goats to them, and once they'd caught their own flock they'd need hay and such until they'd grown their own feed. Maybe they'd even manage to find a few horses.

Thinking of horses reminded her of Ford, and her last dream of him came back with a tidal wave of conflicting emotions. Had she really seen a hoofprint on the floor of the cave beside her that morning? She hadn't told anyone—not even Stella—about the incredibly realistic dreams she'd been having about him. How could she? She'd felt horns on his head and his leg had been covered with fur. Then she'd seen a hoofprint. *A hoofprint*, which disappeared.

Mercury's mind went round and round, replaying the dreams until she convinced herself that of course she was having super vivid dreams, she'd lived through a fucking trauma! It was normal for her subconscious to process it via dreams. If she did tell Stella, her best friend would just say she should relax about it. As long as she wasn't waking covered with sweat and screaming from night terrors, all would be well.

It didn't seem as if they'd been traveling long when Stella braked the truck on the incline that looked down on Mitchell.

"Well, it's not totally covered in green fog," said Stella. "But it's definitely floating around down there."

"It's too windy today for that stuff to stay still," said Mercury.

"That means we're going to be on high alert. No one needs another exposure to the green." Stella spoke firmly.

Mercury, remembering what she had seen in Fossil, nodded. "Yeah, let's avoid that." She looked at Imani. "It's gross down there, so prepare yourself."

Imani nodded shakily. "I remember you said there were dead bodies everywhere."

"There still are," Stella said grimly. "I'm going to turn around and park the truck where we did before, in the middle of Main Street between the grocery and the feed store. I've been checking in with my intuition and I don't feel like I did last time when I said we needed to be quiet, but my gut is uneasy. As per usual, I can't tell for sure it that's because of what happened when we were here before, or because there's danger lurking, or just because we're heading into a town full of bloated, rotting corpses with green mist swirling around."

"So we stay within view of each other," Mercury said.

"I have zero desire to wander around by myself," said Imani.

"Okay, here we go." Stella drove the truck down the highway that fed through Mitchell's Main Street, frowning as she focused on steering around stalled vehicles.

But before they got to the heart of the little town Imani shouted. "Hey, stop!"

Stella braked hard and Mercury put her hand on the revolver she'd tucked into the waist of her jeans.

"That falling down sign on the store over there says Redwood Bench and Table Company, and the building is still standing." Imani pointed to their right.

"Holy fucking shit," said Stella. "We didn't even notice it last time we were here."

"We were too focused on the groceries and the feed store," said Mercury, feeling a little trickle of excitement. "Ohmygoddess, look! The sign on the door says unfinished furniture."

Imani's voice echoed her excitement. "They should have at least enough lumber in there for me to make brick molds."

"I don't feel like there are any booger monsters close, but I'm leaving the truck running." Stella put the Chevy into neutral and set the parking brake. They exited the cab, each grabbing one of the flashlights they'd brought.

"Oh, thank the Goddess," Mercury murmured as she saw the CLOSED SUNDAYS sign on the glass front door. "Means we won't find a bunch of bodies inside."

"But it's locked," said Imani.

"Not a problem." Mercury looked around the front of the building, found a bread loaf–sized rock, and told her friends, "Move away from the door and turn your backs." Then she closed her eyes and threw the rock at the glass door, which shattered with a sound so loud Mercury cringed.

"It's okay," Stella touched her shoulder. "I do not feel any people near. I'm sure of it."

"Careful with the glass," Mercury told Imani as she picked her way through the shards, slipped her hand within the newly made opening in the door, flipped the lock, and went inside, flicking on one of their precious flashlights.

"Okay, I see a lot of raw wood shelving, which I can use after I take it apart, but it'd be easier if I could just find some two-by-fours."

They followed Imani through the store to a door in the rear that was marked STAFF ONLY. It was unlocked and opened to a workshop that had Imani squealing with joy. "This is perfect! Look at this raw wood! Oooh! And there are tools! Lots of tools! And nails! I can make a railing for the path up to the cliff *and* a sturdy ladder so we don't have to rappel over the side to get to our home. Karen has been seriously worried about that. Not that I blame her."

Mercury smiled at her. "I'm gonna dump out those garbage cans that are catching the wood shavings. You can put all the tools and nails you need in the cans. Then just tell me which lumber you want and I'll load the truck."

"Hey, let's pour out the wood shavings in a big pile," said Stella. "We can come back and fill the bed of the truck with them. They make great bedding for the rabbits and the chickens, as well as excellent fire starters."

They worked quickly. Imani was efficient. She knew exactly what she needed and filled three garbage bins and then stacked a large pile of wood. "That's it. I've marked a bunch of my items off our list."

They made their way back through the store, and Mercury stopped by a line of wooden rockers. "Is it ridiculous of me to wish we could take these back with us? I mean, imagine the view—rocking while we watch the sunset from the top of our cliff."

"It's not ridiculous at all," said Imani.

"If we don't have room this trip we'll for sure come back and get them and the wood chips. I can't wait to sip wine, rock, and watch the sunset," said Stella.

"That's my kind of civilized." Imani sighed happily.

Mercury said, "Ditto."

Smiling, the three women got back in the cab—and then their smiles faltered as they reached the center of Main Street. As before, bodies littered the street. And as before, carrion birds lifted from their meals and then resettled in their wake. Stella couldn't steer around all of the corpses, and every time the truck rolled over one the three women cringed and gagged.

"It smells worse than before," said Mercury, covering her nose with her hand.

"Yeah, it's fucking awful, but it'll just remind us to hurry," said Stella as she drove past the feed store and grocery, preparing to turn the truck around so that when she parked it they'd face the way they'd arrived.

Like a moth to light, Mercury's gaze went to the spot where she'd killed *him*, that monster Al Rutland, just after he shot Ford. And a little zap of electric surprise sizzled through her body. "Stella, he's gone."

Stella braked the truck and looked at her. "Rutland?"

Mercury nodded and pointed at the spot in the road that was stained dark rust, but that was all that was there—the stain—no body.

"Coyotes must have dragged him away," said Imani softly. "Things have been eating the rest of the bodies. Some of them were probably dragged away too."

Mercury shuddered with a terrible *someone just walked over my grave* feeling, but said, "Yeah, that makes sense."

Stella said, "He's dead. We know that, and that's all that counts. I don't give one single shit about what happened to his maggot-ridden corpse." She made a U-turn and then parked between the grocery and feed stores. "Okay, we wait for the wind to blow that splotch of green away." She nodded at the emerald mist that whipped past the truck in the brisk wind. "I'm going to leave the truck running again. So let's not waste time or fuel. What do you think, Acorn, grocer or feed store first?"

"Grocer," said Mercury. "We cleaned it out pretty well our first time here, except we left some clothes and fishing equipment in case someone else came by and needed them. But now we're expecting thirty more people soon."

"So we'll grab the rest of the stuff," said Stella.

"Right. Then we go into the feed store." Mercury and Stella shared a look, and then Mercury turned to Imani and continued. "Ford was the only one who went inside the feed store before. He said there were dead animals in cages—so prepare yourself."

"Nasty," said Imani with a grimace.

"And there are bodies inside the grocery," said Stella. "But I covered them." She grinned. "Pretty much the only use I have for a Confederate flag." Imani grinned back at her.

"Okay, the mist has cleared. Let's go," said Mercury, and they piled out of the cab.

The bodies inside the store had bloated under their shrouds and the disgusting sound of busy flies filled the heavy, rancid air. "Oh shit, this is gross," said Mercury. "I'm going to prop the front door open."

Imani gagged and then said, "And I'll look in the rear of the store. Maybe there will be a back entrance and we can get a cross breeze."

"Just keep an eye out for any green mist that might blow in here," said Mercury.

"While y'all do that, I'll grab anything I think we need." Stella hurried to the dry goods aisles, which they'd picked clean. "Though I don't see much left."

"Hey, guys, look at this!" Imani called from the rear of the store.

Stella and Mercury joined her. She was standing in an open doorway, which didn't lead to the outside, but instead to a large storage room.

"Holy shit," said Mercury. "I don't even remember seeing this door."

"We were too busy grabbing stuff from the shelves to notice it, but this is fucking fantastic." Stella stepped into the room. "It's like a dream!" She went to the stacked metal shelves and ran her hands over bags and cases that proclaimed RICE, SALT, FLOUR, and OLIVE OIL in big, bold letters and sealed boxes labeled SOUP and BEANS and a lot more. "I was worried about how we were going to feed the Timberline people until we can get our gardens planted and veggies grown." Her white smile flashed. "*This* is how we'll feed them. Acorn, get your super strong ass in gear and let's load all of this into the truck."

"Check this out. These boxes have inflatable rafts in them," Imani said from the side of the storage room. "I'll bet these will help with the fishing."

Mercury remembered what Gemma had said about their creek being a good escape route and nodded grimly. "Yeah, among other things. How many of them are there?"

"Three, brand new still in the box. And it says they come with a hand pump to inflate them. There's a pile of plastic-wrapped life jackets, too," said Imani.

Stella joined them. "These are great, but I'm not sure if we'll have room this trip, and food is more important. Do y'all agree?"

Imani and Mercury nodded, and then Mercury added, "But we need to come back soon. Gemma was talking about our creek and how it would be a good escape route because it flows to the John Day River."

"The kid's smart," said Stella.

"Yeah, let's load up all the food. Then see if the feed store has the rest of the supplies on our list. If there's room we take the rafts. If not, we'll come back. Soon," said Imani.

"Perfect. Start pulling the food off the shelves and I'll get it loaded," said Mercury.

It didn't take them long to pack the truck. They had to wait on the porch of the grocery for more green mist to be blown out of their way before they headed into the feed store. The three of them paused in front of the partly open door for just a moment and then they entered.

It did smell bad inside, but not as horrible as the grocery had smelled. Mercury saw the area that held cages. Her eyes flicked past the dark, unmoving blobs within. "Hey, y'all, don't go down that row. That's where the, um, dead things are."

Her friends nodded and Imani began reading off the items left on her list. "Rope. I really need as much of that as possible, and hoses—lots of hoses."

"Found rope over here!" Stella called from one of the aisles. "And there are also a bunch of lead ropes for horses."

"Grab all of them," said Imani.

"I found the hoses. They're in a big pile," said Mercury, filling her arms with the snake-like coils of hoses.

They worked quickly in the feed store, too, filling the bed of the truck to the brim with rope and hose, as well as a box of rope and tackle pulleys that had Imani squealing with delight. Then they piled in bags of dog food, rabbit and chicken feed, and even some bags of something called Purina goat chow, which made them laugh. Finally, they cleaned out the rest of the vegetable seeds, as well as a big box of potato starts, which made Stella do a little impromptu happy dance.

Mercury wiped her hands on her jeans and surveyed the bulging bed of the truck. "Okay, that's all we can carry. We'll have to come back for the rafts."

"And the rocking chairs," Imani added, smiling.

"Definitely," Mercury said. She looked up at the sky and the brilliant yellow sun that glowed above them. "It's noon, which means if we tie all this down and head home, we'll still have time to get most of this stuff clifftop before it's too dark to use the path." She rolled her shoulders, anticipating how stiff and sore she'd be the next day. They used some of the rope to secure the load and then the three women grinned at each other.

"We did good," said Imani.

"Real good," said Mercury.

"I'm going to pee before we leave," said Imani as she headed around the side of the feed store.

"Don't go far," called Mercury.

"Oh, please," Imani said over her shoulder as she hurried away. "Between the dead bodies, green mist, and the snakes I'm sure are lurking everywhere I'm not going anywhere."

Stella and Mercury leaned against the side of the truck, sharing a bottle of water from one of the cases they'd taken from the grocery storage room.

"Is our wine supply low enough yet for us to go back inside that pub where we found Khaleesi and grab those bottles?" Mercury asked.

Stella's expression looked as if she'd just sucked a lemon. "No. Not yet. Give me another couple weeks or so and perhaps. That place was full of bodies, dog shit and piss before—it's marinated for more than a week. It's gotta be shitty death soup in there now."

"That is so disgusting that I—"

Stella's lifted hand cut her off. "Did you hear that?"

They froze and listened. The sound came again. It was like the distant cry of a baby, and it drifted on the wind from the rear of the feed store—the direction Imani had gone.

"Oh shit!" Stella said.

"Imani!" Mercury called as the women hurried around the side of the feed store.

Imani wasn't there.

17

THE SOUND CAME again, drawing their gazes across a brown stretch of sage grass that met the green of a stream bank, which Imani was jogging toward. The sound was coming from the stream.

"Fucking hell, there's green mist there, coming our way fast." Stella pointed upstream, to the right of where Imani stood on the bank, where a tide of green was being blown toward her.

"Imani! Wait!" Mercury called. "There's green mist coming!"

Imani turned her head as she reached the bank. "It's okay!" She called back to them. "I see it! But there's a kitten down there by the stream. It's hurt. I'll get it and be right back." Without any hesitation Imani started down the bank.

The green mist blew closer.

"Fuck! I'll get her." Mercury sprinted forward. She kept glancing to her right, at the waist-high wall of green that drifted lazily closer and closer.

Mercury was fast, and she reached the bank quickly, barreling over the edge of it and half staggered, half ran to Imani, who was on her knees at the edge of a little stream.

She looked up at Mercury. "Good, you're here. Take this baby and run it back to Stella. She needs to break out the salt that we packed and get these awful things off this kitten."

Imani shifted so Mercury could see a little white fluff of a kitten, not much bigger than her hand. It was lying half in and half out of the water. At least half a dozen fat, disgusting black things were attached to the little thing's belly. It looked up at her and belted out a meow scream that should have come from a cat a lot bigger. "Leeches. Disgusting," said Mercury.

"Yeah, get her to Stella." She scooped up the kitten and handed her to Mercury. "I'll be right behind you."

Mercury grimaced. The kitten's body weighed almost nothing. The swollen leeches were firmly attached to its belly. The poor little thing looked skeletal, more dead than alive.

"Well, hurry! You said there's green mist coming." Imani shooed her toward the bank.

"Yeah, right. There is. So hurry the hell up and get outta here." Then Mercury sprinted up the bank and, holding the kitten close to her, raced back to Stella.

"What in the holy fucking shit is that?" Stella took a couple steps back, stopped, and then moved closer to Mercury.

"A kitten covered in leeches. Get the salt out that we packed. It's the fastest, easiest way to make them release," said Mercury.

"Jesus Christ that's gross. Poor kitten." Stella hurried to the truck and opened the tailgate, pulling tightly packed foodstuffs out of the way. "Got it!" As Stella pulled one of the bags of salt from the truck she glanced behind Mercury. "Where's Imani?"

"Shit! She was supposed to be right behind me. Take the kitten. Pour salt on the leeches. I'll be right back." Mercury quickly retraced her path to see Imani standing just a few feet from the bank. She faced Mercury, and there was a river of green between them.

"Stay there," Mercury called. "The wind will blow it away."

"Where's the kitten?" Imani asked.

"Stella's got her and the salt." As Mercury watched, the edges of the green river lifted and lapped at Imani's feet.

"I don't like this," Imani said. "Maybe I should just run to you. It doesn't look like it'd be much above my waist. I should be fine."

"I don't know . . ." Mercury chewed her lip. She didn't like how the green stuff was rising and falling, like waves washing against a rocky shore. "I don't like how—" she began, but Imani cut her off.

"I can't just stand here. I'm coming!" Imani jogged into the river of green.

"Slow down!" Mercury said. "The ground isn't level and you do not want to trip."

"Okay, yeah, got it." Imani nodded jerkily. She kept glancing down at the tide of mist that had lifted to the middle of her thighs.

"It's going to be okay. Just look at me and keep walking," said Mercury.

"What the fuck?" Stella joined her. She was holding the kitten—now leech-free—cradled against her.

"Is the kitten okay?" Imani asked.

"Yes. It's fine. You just focus on you," said Stella.

Imani was a little over halfway to them when a thick tendril of green, like a giant tongue, lifted. It stroked against the side of Imani's body and then the warm wind gusted and it surged, completely covering her.

"Mercury, Stella, stay there! I'll be—" Imani screamed, gagged, staggered forward a couple more feet, and then she fell and was swallowed by the mist.

"No!" Mercury lunged forward, but Stella grabbed her arm and jerked her back.

"You've had two exposures. You *cannot* have another! Imani knows that. It's why she said to stay here."

"But we have to get her!"

"We will. Look, there's the edge of the mist. The wind is pushing it away." Stella pulled on Mercury's arm hard enough that she had to turn to face her friend. "If either of us go out there now we won't be helping her. We'll pass out, just like Imani. Listen to me, Mercury Elizabeth Rhodes. If I ever get covered by the mist again you keep your ass out of it and let it pass over me. I'll be fine, just like Imani will be fine. You and Gemma taught us that we can take two exposures. We do *not* know if we can take three."

The wind gusted again, causing the green river to wash over and past Imani's still form. Mercury loosened Stella's grip on her arm and she sprinted to their friend. Gently, she rolled Imani onto her back. Stella was there in a moment, handing Mercury a bottle of water, which she opened and then sprinkled on Imani's face.

Her eyelids fluttered and opened. For a moment Imani's dark eyes glowed green, a perfect match for the river that had just engulfed her, and then she blinked and focused. "Water," she said.

Mercury helped her sit and handed her the water, which Imani gulped. She wiped her mouth with the back of her hand and shook her head. "That is so damn unpleasant. It smells good, like a giant Christmas tree grove, but why does it have to feel like it's prickling from the inside out?"

"I don't know, but it was the same for me. Are you okay?" Mercury asked.

Imani nodded and got to her feet, where she swayed once and Mercury steadied her with a hand under her elbow. Imani's gaze went to the little white ball of fluff Stella was holding.

"You got them off her?"

Stella shuddered. "Yes. And they were fucking gross. I've never seen anything like that. I didn't even know they attached to pets. Is she going to be okay?"

Imani took the kitten from Stella. Its sunken belly was dotted with bloody spots that were still weeping red. "She should be. I know a little about leeches from my grandma, who was seriously into old homeopathic remedies."

"Did your grandma put leeches on you?" Mercury's skin shivered at the thought.

Imani smiled. "No, but she would have if my mom had let her. My grandma told me leeches inject an anticoagulant where they attach, which is why the kitten is still bleeding, but that'll go away and she'll heal. I didn't think they could do any real damage. They usually drop off of whatever they're feeding from when they're full, but there were two other kittens down there." Imani paused and shook her head. "They were covered with the things and dead."

"That is revolting," said Stella.

"Uh, y'all, more green is coming." Mercury pointed. Another emerald river rolled toward them, pushed quickly by the warm, gusting wind.

"That's it. We're outta here," said Stella.

"I couldn't agree more, except I'm going to take a slight detour inside the feed store," said Imani. "I know this little one can eat fish, but I'm worried about how tiny and thin she is, so I'm going to grab some cans of cat food."

"I'll do that." Mercury was already moving toward the door to the feed store. "You should drink another bottle of water and see if you can get the kitten to drink some too. I'll be out in a sec."

Mercury jogged into the store. The much smaller cat section was beside the dog food area, which they'd cleaned out. She easily lifted a couple cases of wet cat food and some kitten kibble, and hurried back to the truck, where she kept one can with her and somehow shoved the rest of them into the bed. As she slammed the tailgate closed something on the ground caught her eye and she glanced down to see three fat leeches crawling toward the grass that led back to the stream like inchworms.

Even though several had already disappeared into the grass, Mercury stomped on the stragglers, shuddering at the squish they made and the blood that squirted from them. Then she wiped her boots in the dirt and got back in the cab.

"When we return for the rafts and the rockers, let's make a pact not to go down to that stream," said Mercury.

"Agreed," said Stella.

"Absolutely," said Imani, who held the purring kitten as she ate ravenously from the can of cat food Mercury had opened. "But I gotta say that rescuing this one was worth it."

"Well, we did get our cat," said Stella.

"I hope the dogs are cool with her," said Mercury.

Stella cocked her head as if listening within. "They will be, and that's a definite *feeling.*"

"Hey, stop a sec," Imani said when they were on the outskirts of Mitchell.

Stella stopped the truck. "What now?"

Imani jerked her chin to the right of the road. "Do you see that?"

Mercury said, "You mean that messed-up looking building?" There was a little shack-looking storefront that drunkenly leaned to the side. The tin roof over the porch was slanted and a faded sign that said JUDY'S PLACE hung lopsided above it.

"Well, yeah, but more specifically, look in that busted-out window," said Imani.

"What is that?" asked Stella, squinting at the store.

"It's a big tulle skirt, like something a ballerina would wear." She handed the kitten to Mercury. "Here, hold her. I'm gonna go get it."

"You're what?" Stella asked.

But Mercury grinned. "For Karen. She's getting it for Karen."

Stella's expression lightened. "That's an awesome idea."

Imani hurried from the truck, picked her way through the debris, and then reached through the broken window and lifted the mannequin out. Quickly, she pulled the ballerina pink tulle skirt off, as well as a pretty if a little moth-eaten wraparound matching pink sweater. Then she jogged back to the truck, folded the clothes carefully, and put them behind the seat.

"For our ballerina," said Imani.

"For our ballerina," Stella and Mercury echoed, and their smiles lasted all the way home.

The sun was high overhead when pain radiated through Al's body and he had to slide the bike to a quick stop in the middle of the road. He wrapped his arms around himself, feeling as if his insides were being squished like a tube of toothpaste. The horrible sensation faded as quickly as it had begun, and he drew a deep, shaky breath.

"What the fuck was that?" Al muttered. Then his leeches writhed and squirmed against him, more agitated than he'd ever known them to be. He passed a hand caressingly down his torso, gently soothing those that were attached to his chest feeding, or simply curled against him. "What is it? What has happened?"

As soon as he verbalized the questions a wave of images cascaded over him. Strange, blurry, black and white pictures flooded his mind, along with sharp, specific scents. He couldn't make sense of the images, but he easily identified the different smells.

Felines—several of them. His leeches fed and fed from them. "Good," Al said. "Cats are useless anyway. Hell, I hear they taste a lot like rabbit." His bark of laughter was interrupted as a hulking image came to him. He breathed deeply. It was a woman. Then there was a second indistinct image and he smelled another woman. Al's jaws ached as he ground his teeth at her scent.

It was one of the teachers. The younger one. His sense of smell hadn't been preternatural the two times he'd been near her, but his brain had logged her scent. It was her—Mercury. He was sure of it.

The old hen, Stella, was there too.

Then Al felt the remembrance of the burning of the salt through their sensitive skins as they were forced to stop feeding from the feline. They tried to get to safety, but Al felt the death of several of them, murdered under Mercury's boot.

Once again, his hand caressed the creatures hidden beneath his shirt. "Be still. All is well, my friends." As they settled, his own calm was restored and his jaw relaxed so that he could bare his teeth in a predatory smile.

The bitches had been there twice. They'd return.

And so would Al.

18

❧

"THAT'S ENOUGH, ACORN. Seriously. How many times have you been up and down the side of that cliff today?" Stella blocked Mercury's way as she headed, again, for the path, cases of beans piled in her arms.

Mercury shook her head, sending sweat flying around her. "I lost count, but my sore shoulders say a lot. You and Imani have also been up and down a bunch of times today, and I don't see you stopping."

"Oh, we're going to." Imani joined them. "Give it here, sis. I'll take one case and Stella will take the other." She held out her arms. "We can manage these, then we'll call it a night—and I do mean night because sunset isn't far off. Marcus lit the grills and is getting the coals ready to fry all that fish they caught this morning, and with these extra supplies we're going to feast. While we're finishing, you can wash up. We're all sweaty messes, but you are a whole other level of funk."

Mercury frowned as Stella and Imani took the cases from her. "It's because of my super strength. I also have super sweat."

Stella snorted. "You're super stanky, that's for sure. Wash. Change out of those drenched clothes. Relax for a damn minute. When Imani and I get down from carrying this last load, we'll bring Karen and the kids down with us and it'll be time to eat."

"And rest," said Imani.

"And drink?" Mercury asked hopefully.

"Definitely," said Stella. Then she sighed. "I'll add going back inside that awful pub and liberating their wine to our short list of return items to grab from Mitchell."

"Liberating?" Imani asked.

Stella nodded. "We're definitely going to set it free when we open it and drain those bottles."

Mercury laughed and wiped the sweat from her forehead with her shirt; then she grimaced as she looked down at herself. "You're right. I'm a mess. I'm gonna grab some clean clothes and then dunk myself in the creek."

"It's cold," said Stella.

"Good. Maybe it'll help me stop sweating." She grinned at her friends as she headed away from them and toward the opening of the cave-like campsite. Marcus was sitting on a log he'd asked Mercury to place close to their Weber grills. Currently flames were licking golden tongues above the coals as Marcus hummed a tune under his breath. Badger and Khaleesi lay near him, and tucked against Khaleesi's belly was the little white kitten who the kids had quickly dubbed Dandelion because she was so fluffy and white—though they'd already shortened it to Dandy. Mercury smiled at the dogs. "I'm really glad they like the kitten."

Marcus laughed. "Had I been with you when you found her I woulda told you that my Badger likes all animals, especially little animals—it's only some humans he has a problem with."

"Good thing I finally passed his test," she said.

"He was fine with you once he understood you weren't going to shoot me."

"He's a smart boy." Mercury petted his wide, intelligent head and he gave her a sleepy, doggy smile. Khaleesi's tail swept against the ground, but she didn't move. Mercury grinned and ruffled her ears. "You're being a really good surrogate mom." She turned her grin to Marcus. "I'm grabbing some clothes and then I'll go to the creek and wash up. Imani and Stella say they're bringing everyone down when they come."

"Good, the coals will be ready by then and fish cooks fast. Already got rice and beans and a mess of greens bubbling over the fire inside."

Mercury hurried to her sleeping area and gathered a new pair of sweatpants she'd *liberated* from the Mitchell General Store, as well as a new T-shirt that said *Mitchell—Gateway to the Painted Hills* in rainbow colors. She also grabbed two precious bottles, one of shampoo and the other of conditioner. She scratched at her dusty, sweaty hair and headed back through the cave.

She hesitated beside Marcus; taking advantage of the fact that no one could overhear them, she asked, "So how was it with Chad and Gemma today at the Painted Hills?"

"Mostly like it was here with them for the rest of the day. Baby girl sticks pretty close to the boy, except when it was just us at the Painted Hills they held hands whenever they thought I wasn't looking. I'm also pretty damn sure there was some kissing going on."

"Ugh," Mercury said. "Gemma has a major crush."

"That's for sure, but I can't tell how interested he is in her. He likes that she pays him so much attention. He's young, though." Marcus shook his head and stared at the flickering flames.

"He's older than Gemma. She's only sixteen," said Mercury.

"Yeah, well, she's a lot more mature than he is, but that's typical for boys his age. What I meant by him being young is that I don't think he's capable of looking for a real connection," said Marcus.

"He's going to break her heart." Mercury felt a tickle of relief. A first crush heartbreak was tough, but almost everyone went through it and recovered just fine. If that was all Stella's bad *feeling* was about, it would be sad for Gemma, but not life threatening for her or any of them. Mercury sighed. "We'll be here to pick up the pieces, though."

"And after he messes up with baby girl, maybe the boy will grow up and not be such an entitled little shit," said Marcus.

"Here's hoping. See you in a little while."

Mercury headed to the creek. She went downstream from where the kids and Marcus liked to fish from the bank to a place where there was a bend in the creek so that it pooled deep and the current wasn't as fast. She draped the clean clothes over a big rock and then peeled out of her dirty, sweaty things. Carrying the shampoo and conditioner, she picked her way carefully over to the creek's edge, enjoying how the wet sand squished between her toes.

The creek was cold, but it felt wonderful against her flushed, sweaty skin. She waded in only far enough so that when she sat the water covered her shoulders. Then she got to work on her hair, washing and dunking it three times before she piled it on the top of her head and let the conditioner sit as she used a little more of the shampoo to lather up and scrub her body. Mercury wondered vaguely what they'd do when it was all gone, and then made a mental note to go through some of the wilderness survival books they'd found to see if there were any recipes for things like *how to make shampoo and conditioner out of plants.*

When she felt clean again, she dunked down to rinse out the conditioner, wrung out her hair, and headed back to the place she'd left her clothes.

"Well, shit," she muttered to herself. "What the hell am I going to use to dry?" Mercury opted to dab herself with her dirty tee after she turned it inside out. Then she dressed in the clean clothes. She'd turned to head back to the cave, but she didn't hear the voices of the children yet, and the solitude by the creek was seductive. Mercury folded the dirty clothes and put them in front of the rock and then, with a sigh, she sat on them and used the rock for a backrest as she stared out at the creek.

Birdsong serenaded her from the cedars that grew near the creek. A shadow flitted past and she looked up in time to see a huge golden eagle circling above her. She smiled at the majestic beauty of the big raptor, and then her gaze drifted down lazily to the creek. She felt deeply relaxed, and when a splotch of yellow caught her eye Mercury sat up straighter as she realized what she was looking at.

"Ford's grave." She spoke the words softly, reverently. They'd buried him farther downstream where the creek was deeper and the cedars had made a lovely little grove. She hadn't visited since the night she'd danced there and her blood had coaxed beautiful yellow wildflowers to cover the mound of raw dirt. Sighing, Mercury forced her eyes from the yellow, suddenly feeling the soreness in her muscles and the weariness in her soul pressing down on her with almost unbearable weight.

"I miss you," Mercury murmured. She stared at the creek, letting the music of the water and the birdsong soothe her. Her eyelids felt as heavy as her soul—so heavy that she thought she'd just close them for a moment and rest . . .

"Acorn." His breath tickled her ear. "I wish I'd gotten here sooner. I would've liked to have done some skinny-dipping with you."

The dream was delicious. Mercury wasn't leaning against a hard rock. Instead, Ford's warm arm was around her and her head rested on his chest as she leaned against him. "I didn't skinny-dip. I was bathing."

He squeezed her shoulder. "You should have used the trough I got you and some heated water."

"Can't," she said sleepily. "It's clifftop full of mud for the adobe bricks."

"Good. It's smart to build up there," he said.

Mercury nodded and snuggled against him. "This is nice."

His hand slowly rubbed her shoulder and arm. "It is. I cannot stay long, though. I can smell the fish frying. They'll be coming to get you for dinner soon."

She burrowed closer to him. "Don't go yet."

"A little longer."

Mercury rubbed her cheek against his chest and suddenly registered the fact that she was nuzzling bare skin. "Where's your shirt?"

His chest rumbled under her ear with his chuckle. "Remember I've told you that I've changed?"

"Changed like you're a nudist?" The thought flitted through her mind that it really wasn't that weird that her subconscious had conjured a shirtless version of Ford into her dreams.

His chest rumbled again. "Something like that."

One of her arms was between them, pressed against their bodies, but her other arm was free, and she reached up, resting it on his bare chest, which was hard and muscular and so, so warm. She caressed him slowly, sensually.

He trembled.

"Being a nudist can be kinda cold," she whispered.

His voice deepened. "It's your touch that makes me tremble, not the cold."

"That's nice," she murmured as she let her hand trail down, caressingly, until it came to his waist. Mercury paused there, thought *What the hell—it's a dream*, and let her finger dip down.

They didn't touch jeans.

They didn't touch naked skin.

They touched fur. Thick, soft fur.

"Mercury! Where the hell are you?"

Stella's shout brought her abruptly out of the dream, but instead of just opening her eyes and finding herself resting against the big rock, Mercury flopped down, falling to her side. She opened her eyes to see that the grass beside her had been pressed down—as if someone had just been lying there.

Mercury quickly sat. Her eyes swept the area around her. A splash drew her attention to the right. The fading light shadowed everything around her in the muted hues of dusk, and as she peered through the cedar grove she saw a man-shaped form emerge from the creek. His back was to her, but she could distinctly see horns curling from his head. His muscular torso was bare, *and from the waist down he was covered in brown fur that met two cloven hoofs.* Then he sprinted up the far bank and disappeared into the gloaming.

"Mercury! Jesus Christ! There you are. What the hell are you doing just sitting here while I was calling and calling?" Stella stormed up to her, arms crossed, a frown creasing her forehead.

Mercury blinked and then looked up at her best friend. She almost blurted it out. *I was just with Ford and it wasn't a dream and he's not a man.* But she couldn't make her voice work.

Stella's annoyance changed to worry and she crouched beside Mercury. "You okay? Is something wrong?"

Mercury cleaned her throat and shook her head. "N—no. Sorry. I was sitting here after my bath and I guess I fell asleep."

Stella stood and held out her hand. "Well, that's no surprise. You've gotta be exhausted. Come on, let's get you fed and get some wine in you. Then I'm tucking you into bed. If you work yourself sick, Gemma is going to be pissed."

Mercury took her hand and stood. She picked up her dirty clothes and the shampoo and conditioner bottles and followed Stella, who was chattering about how awesome the prep for their clifftop garden was going and how she couldn't wait to plant tomorrow. Mercury made all the right sounds of interest and agreement as she kept glancing back over her shoulder, but all she saw was the darkening land and the silver reflection of dusk off the creek.

CHAPTER

19

⚬⚬⚬

AFTER DINNER THEIR little group gathered around the campfire. Everyone was full and content and pleased with how much work they'd accomplished that day. Mercury was glad that no one questioned her unusual silence. Stella had only to ask if she was okay, and when Mercury said, "Yep, just really tired," they all nodded with understanding.

Cayden had said softly, "Even superheroes get tired," which had made everyone smile.

Gemma went through their expanding stack of books and pulled out a paperback book titled *The Incredible Journey* by Sheila Burnford. She explained to the kids that it was the book the movie *Homeward Bound* had been based on, which she knew because the book had been one of her mom's favorites.

Mercury had been glad that the memory was a happy one, and Gemma enthusiastically launched into reading the book aloud for the kids, complete with different voices and a dramatic and comedic flair that had the adults as well as the children laughing often.

There were complaints when Imani said it was time for bed, which meant Gemma had to stop reading, but all three little ones had begun to yawn and it was clear they were struggling to remain awake. As Imani got them ready for bed, the kitten padded after her like a tiny shadow.

"That kitten is totally imprinted on Imani," said Stella wistfully.

"Jealous?" Mercury asked with a grin.

Stella nodded. "Absolutely. You know I love cats."

"I'll bet we can find you one too," said Gemma.

"How many cats do we need?" Chad asked.

Stella raised a brow at him. "There is no cat limit, especially as they'll be great at keeping vermin out of our supplies."

All Mercury could think was *Of course Chad doesn't like cats.*

Gemma yawned and stretched. "That was fun, but I'm fading like the kids." She smiled at Chad, who sat beside her. "Did you like the book?"

Chad shrugged one shoulder. "I guess. Aren't you embarrassed to do that?"

"Do what?" Gemma asked, her smooth brow wrinkling with confusion.

"Read out loud like that, you know, making up voices and stuff."

Gemma's snort sounded so much like Stella that Mercury had to bite her cheek not to laugh.

"No, I'm not embarrassed. I like reading out loud and I like making up voices and stuff."

"You're real good at it too, baby girl," said Marcus.

Gemma grinned. "Thanks! I'll read some more chapters tomorrow night." She walked over to the big man and pressed her palm to his forehead. "You didn't look feverish, but I like to check."

Marcus patted her hand before she removed it. "You're also a good doctor, and I'm feeling just fine. Actually, I think I'd like to have Mercury help me up to the clifftop tomorrow for the planting of the garden—if you give me your okay for that."

"I'll check your leg in the morning, but if Mercury helps you and you promise to lean on her and go slow, I think that would be okay. 'Night, everyone," Gemma called and then disappeared back to the dark sleeping area of the cave without so much as a look at Chad.

He stood and cleared his throat. "I, um, am going to go to bed, too. 'Night," he mumbled and headed to the separate section of the cave where he and Marcus slept.

Imani emerged in time to hear Karen say softly, "One can only hope that reality is creeping in and the crush is coming to an end."

"If you're talking about Chad and Gemma, that is very good news." Imani bent to pick up her kitten shadow. "I think the kids were asleep before their heads hit their pillows, which is a good thing because we have a really big day tomorrow."

"I am so looking forward to having fresh vegetables," said Karen as she sipped a glass of red wine.

"I'm somewhat of an expert on fried green tomatoes," said Marcus.

Karen clapped her hands happily. "I love those! I haven't had really good ones since my grandmother passed."

"Well, I will try not to disappoint," said Marcus.

"I'm going to go to bed too, but first I need to . . ." Imani's words trailed off as her eyes, already taking on a far-off look, gazed into the night.

"You still feeling okay after your green mist exposure today?" Stella asked.

"Yes, I'm fine. Don't worry about me. 'Night everyone." Imani slipped quietly outside the cave and headed to the little rise by the bank of the creek where every night, beside a big cedar tree, she looked to the southwest and thought about her lost babies and husband.

Marcus pulled their attention from their friend as he got slowly to his feet. He'd fashioned a crutch from a thick, water-whitened branch he'd found by the creek. Gemma had wrapped some cloth around the top so that it didn't chafe him to use it. Carefully, the big man made his way over to where Stella sat on a log beside Mercury. He put out his hand and said, "Stella, will you walk with me under the night sky? It won't be far or fast, but I don't believe the stars will mind."

Stella's cheeks flushed an attractive pink as she put her hand in his and stood. "I'd love to walk with you."

"With me, Badge," Marcus called and the shepherd joined him.

Mercury glanced down at Khaleesi, expecting the pitty to whine and want to follow them, but she was sound asleep, her muzzle resting on Mercury's foot.

As they went slowly out of the cave, Stella looked back over her shoulder at Mercury and Karen and winked at them, which made Mercury grin and Karen giggle girlishly.

Mercury's attention turned to Karen. The giggle wasn't all that was girlish about her. The older woman seemed to have shed a decade in the past week. She'd lost weight, but it was more than that. Karen had lost the pinched look that had caused her to appear so severe, so judgmental, so *old*. She sat not far from Mercury, the tulle ballerina skirt draped across her lap. When Imani had given it to her, Karen had gasped in delight and had to wipe happy tears from her cheeks. She'd started to thank Imani, been unable to articulate the words, and had simply thrown her arms around the younger woman. After dinner she'd brought it out and laid it across her lap, noting the beauty of the color and the lightness of the tulle. Every so often her hand would caress it gently and her lips would lift in a smile.

"That skirt is so pretty," said Mercury.

Karen's smile took another decade from her face. "It is. I haven't had anything so beautiful since I was a girl." She looked from the skirt to Mercury. "It means a lot to me that the three of you brought this to me."

"Well, we were all in agreement, but Imani is the one who saw it and told Stella to stop so she could get it for you."

Karen caressed it again. "I'm so glad she did." She caught Mercury's gaze. "And I'm glad that we have a moment alone. I'd like to ask you something that might sound rather unconventional coming from me."

Mercury lifted the wine bottle and offered Karen more, and she nodded. Then she splashed a little more in her own glass and said, "I'm intrigued. What do you want to ask me?"

"I would like you to create a special ritual for tomorrow when we plant the first part of our garden," Karen said.

Mercury's brows went way up. "A ritual? You mean a Pagan ritual?"

Karen nodded and fingered the skirt a little nervously, but continued to explain. "I've prayed about it and I believe it is right to celebrate our new world and our new selves as well as our fruitfulness by a ritual tied to the land, and thus to what you call the old gods and goddesses." She paused and then added, "I've begun to realize that honoring those old gods and goddesses doesn't dishonor Jesus." She looked up from the skirt and met Mercury's gaze. "Not long ago you chastised me about my actions and attitudes not being reflective of the Jesus in the Bible. At first I was angry and in denial about your words, but the past two weeks have changed me—opened my mind and my heart—and I have been reading and rereading the words of my Lord. You were right, Mercury. Christ is about love and acceptance and loving my neighbor as myself. So how could it *not* honor Him to be accepting of your belief that this land is ensouled?"

Mercury sat up straighter and leaned forward. "Karen, it means so much to me to hear you say that. Thank you. I would love to create a ritual to celebrate the planting and our new lives. I would also love it if you would offer a prayer along with the ritual."

"I would be most happy to," said Karen.

"And there's something else I'd like to ask you," said Mercury. This had been on her mind since Imani had taken the ballerina skirt from Mitchell. "I would like to ask you to please dance." Karen began to protest, but Mercury's raised hand stopped her. "Dance is often included in Ritual, especially in celebrations of planting and harvesting. We'll be dancing too—Stella, Imani, probably even Gemma and Georgie, and definitely me. I'd say the twins would dance, but I'm going to ask them to play the drums for our music."

"They are really very talented drummers," said Karen, nodding. "Georgie is also getting very good with that flute."

"I'll bet Marcus would dance too, if his leg let him. And, of course, if Chad wants to he'll be welcome to join us," said Mercury. "But I want you to dance with us, not just to join us, but to celebrate your new life and what I think is a new happiness that you've found."

Karen stroked the tulle, sipped her wine, and when she spoke her voice was soft and almost shy. "I haven't felt this free to be myself since I was a little girl, and even then if I didn't hear my father's admonishment to be more ladylike and more modest I felt his stern gaze on me. It made me think that anything that made me happy was wrong—that *I* was somehow wrong. And then as I got older I just accepted that it was my lot in life to follow the lead of my husband, who was also a stern man with an admonishing gaze." She paused and sipped her wine again. Mercury said nothing. She just waited, open and listening, and Karen finally continued. "When my sons were born I allowed my husband to make them in his image. I will always be sorry about that. They were such joy-filled toddlers, but as they grew up they lost that joy and became dour, disapproving mirrors of their father.

"I miss them and I mourn them, but as soon as they were old enough to follow their father's lead I lost them, much like I lost myself. And then this apocalypse happened and at first I thought I'd lost myself again, but I was wrong. I believe I have just begun to find my true self again, the little girl I'd buried so long ago. It is a wondrous thing."

Mercury had to wipe tears from her cheeks as she smiled at Karen. "That's so beautiful. Thank you for sharing it with me. I think your Jesus is happy for you."

"I think he is too. Mercury, I can see it. I can see that the earth is ensouled, and it is beautiful and amazing and everything that is the opposite of dark and evil and satanic. Is it strange that in my entire adult life I've never been happier than during this past week?"

"No, it isn't strange at all. It's wonderful. Please dance with us, Karen. Let it be the public acknowledgment of your joy," Mercury said.

Karen's gaze went to the skirt again. "Yes, I believe I will dance."

Mercury grinned. "Stella is going to love that!"

Karen waggled her graying brows at Mercury. "I think Stella is a little *distracted* right now." Both women laughed. "Not that I blame her. Marcus is a lovely man."

"He is. I'm glad we found him," said Mercury.

Karen yawned and covered her mouth. "Well, it seems my glass and a half of wine has worked its magic and I need to find my bed." She stood, holding the ballerina skirt carefully. "Good night, Mercury." As she passed Mercury, Karen bent and kissed her softly on the cheek. "It is a lovely thing to have girlfriends."

Mercury was so touched that she had to clear her throat before she called after her. "'Night Karen. Sweet dreams."

Mercury sat and sipped her wine as she gazed into the fire. She felt lighter after talking with Karen, whose new joy in life was contagious. She began to wonder if, just maybe, what was happening with Ford wasn't some kind of realistic dream. Maybe it was just another part of the magick that seemed to be awakening in and around them. Maybe she wasn't imagining it or losing her mind.

Ford might actually be alive.

Mercury startled as little Dandy padded into the cave, meowing and purring and heading to the bowl she already knew held her food. Imani followed silently behind, returning to her log and the half-empty glass of wine she'd left behind on it.

Mercury looked from the kitten to Imani in time to see that her friend's eyes still held a faint but distinctive green tint.

"Here you go. Have the rest of it." Mercury leaned over and poured the rest of the wine into Imani's glass.

"Thanks."

They sipped in silence that to Mercury felt heavy. Not uncomfortably so, but it was definitely a waiting silence. She relaxed and let her thoughts drift as she allowed her friend to decide whether she wanted to lift that weight or not.

"You got stronger after your second dose of the mist, right?" Imani said.

"I did and I also think Gemma's healing powers became more developed."

Imani nodded and then blurted. "I feel the tree."

Mercury was careful not to react with shock or a zillion questions. She could hear an edge of fear in her friend's voice and she didn't want to fuel that fear. Instead, she asked. "What tree?"

"The big cedar I stand under when I look toward my babies and my Curtis."

When Imani said nothing more, Mercury spoke nonchalantly. "There's a big elm in front of my condo. It made me stop when I was driving around midtown Tulsa looking for a place. There was something special about that tree. I swear I bought the condo because of it. I used to touch it almost every day. Ask Stella. I told her that I could feel it breathing. Is that what you mean?"

Imani moved her shoulders. "Sort of. It's hard to explain. I've felt a connection to the land since the first night I went out and looked to the southwest and thought about my family. I could *feel* them and it comforted me. I don't know if I'd still be here if it hadn't." She paused and stared into the fire when she continued. "It's gotten deeper, this connection I feel to the land—to the earth. But tonight there was even more. It wasn't just my family I could feel. I felt the land and that tree, that cedar, it was as if she wrapped me in her energy and held me. She touched me with her wisdom. I don't mean I could hear her speaking, but I felt her intelligence, her sentience. And she knows me. I'm sure of it. She knows my loss and my pain and my grief. She understands and somehow shared a little of her serenity with me." Imani looked up from the fire to Mercury. "Does that sound unbelievable?"

Mercury shook her head. "You're talking to a Pagan, remember? I believe the earth, the trees, the animals and birds, even the water and stones are filled with energy or ensouled. So it doesn't sound unbeliev-able at all."

"And it doesn't scare you?" Imani whispered the words.

"No. Why should it? I believe we share life with the elements. Air is our breath; fire is our spirit; water is our blood; and earth is our body. How can we be frightened of that from which we are made?" Mercury spoke softly, reverently too.

Imani drew in a deep, tremulous breath before answering. "It seemed the cedar wanted to tell me something, but I got scared and shut down that part of me."

"That's understandable." Mercury smiled at her friend. "But she's not going anywhere. Grandmother Cedar will be there when you're ready to listen."

Imani finally smiled. "Grandmother Cedar?"

Mercury nodded. "Well, I called my elm Grandmother Elm. I thought it fit your cedar too."

"It does indeed, and tomorrow I'll try to be less frightened," said Imani.

"Speaking of tomorrow, Karen asked me to create a ritual for our planting," said Mercury.

Imani brightened and nodded, her dark hair, which she'd begun wearing in a thick braid that began at her crown, bounced against her back. "Yeah, she mentioned that she was going to ask you. I think it's a great idea, but it's going to take a few more days to get ready for planting."

"I'm not surprised. We need a really big garden. But we'll all help." She paused and then added, "Do you mind if I use some of the clay from the Painted Hills for something special when we do our planting ritual?"

"No! What do you have in mind?"

"Let me get with our artist and I'll let you know." Mercury rolled her shoulders and grimaced. "I am sooooo sore. I think it's time for my sleepy dog and me to go to sleep. I know y'all will be waking me up way too early tomorrow."

"Thought you were going to get with our artist," Imani said.

"I think our artist is busy tonight, and like you said, we have a few days," Mercury said and they shared a smile.

"I'll stay up a little while more and finish this glass. And think." Imani's gaze caught hers again. "You for real felt that elm breathe?"

"For real. Promise. 'Night, Imani. Come on, Khaleesi, let's go to bed." The pit bull yawned and stretched magnificently and then padded after Mercury to her pallet.

Before she fell asleep Mercury wasn't sure whether she should wish that Ford would visit her again or not, so she simply sent a whispered prayer to the Goddess. "Help me walk the path that serves you best, and should that path return Ford to me, in whatever form, so mote it be."

CHAPTER

20

Al HAD TO admit that Eva Cruz was a master at manipulating her people. She kept them bound to her with ropes made of fear, lies, subtle—and not so subtle—intimidation. It worked very, *very* well. Madras appeared to be thriving, but the truth was that Eva Cruz was thriving and she towed the people of Madras along in her wake. He was eager to watch her next move. She'd explained it to him earlier that day and he'd been sure to come to the news site early to get a good seat.

He chuckled to himself. *News site.* That had been brilliance born of Eva's twisted mind. Every evening, as refreshments were made available at Sahalee Park, a spokesperson appointed by Eva would read the latest news to everyone gathered there—and a lot of people gathered for the "news."

This would be the third evening Al had joined them for the gathering. He'd quickly come to appreciate how Eva wove misinformation and fear together to form a cage that the people of Madras were all too eager to lock themselves within. She used the truth, but mixed it masterfully with insinuations and outright lies, and her choice of newscasters was spot on. She drew from a small group of people who had similar traits. They were natives of Madras, middle-aged to recently retired, and always people who believed strongly in community, were active in one of the several churches, as well as being experienced volunteers. Because of her careful choices, the audience was already predisposed to believe and trust the news because they believed and trusted the saps reading it.

The nightly newscasts made very sure the good people of Madras thought that outside their town, or even outside of the boundaries within that were marked by the big, black SUVs Eva used as barricades, *there be monsters.* The newscasters relayed horrible stories of marauding gangs that violated women and killed for no reason—of course, Eva did not have them report that many of those marauders were sent out by her to collect the women she liked to refer to privately as "green bloods." The news hinted at monsters that controlled dark forces, things that lurked in shadow, and insects that used to be pests, but were now lethal. When he'd heard that one Al had had to cover his laugh with a cough.

Al hadn't had to ask her how she kept such tight control over her city and her people. He witnessed it. Eva Cruz used the fact that the majority of the people who had survived the bombs and the mist just wanted to be safe. If that meant looking away from anything that made them uncomfortable—including provable lies their mayor fed them—they looked away, happy in not knowing.

He wondered if that would continue, or if what she had to report that night would change things. The town could easily turn on her. She was outnumbered, especially as she had no real friends. Eva Cruz had pawns, though she was good at making some of those pawns believe they were actually important to her. Amber Watson was an excellent example of that. It was clear the young woman believed she was important to Eva. Amber Watson was vastly mistaken.

Another excellent example was the group of a dozen or so specially chosen men she used as her personal guard. Those men she controlled through a clever mix of intimidation and sex. They never knew whether she'd fuck them or kill them.

The addition of the mosquitoes that incubated within her had tightened the noose hold she had on her guard. Al had been with them the day after she'd exposed herself to the mist a second time and gained control of the swarm. Eva had gone out on yet another quest to find and capture more green bloods. There were four armed men with them. They'd stopped in Sunriver at a cabin that had been built to look like a Swiss chalet. Eva had told one of the men, Michael had been his name, to do something menial for her—something so minor that Al hadn't paid any attention to it. Until Michael had balked, said that he'd do it after he finished going through the chalet with the other men.

Eva had smiled dangerously and shook her head. Then, almost playfully, she'd kissed her palm, pursed her ruby lips, and blown at him as if sending him that kiss. Instead, she sent a swarm of mosquitoes to him. They'd covered him, stinging over and over, swarming his face so that he couldn't see—entering his eyes and nose, his open screaming mouth, even his ears. Shrieking, he'd run blindly and fallen into a ravine beside which the chalet had been built.

The other men watched silently, and when she asked another to do something, *anything* for her, he had swiftly complied.

Al had enjoyed the demonstration. He'd enjoyed the aftermath even more as her personal guard suddenly was a lot less interested in coming to the mayor's bed. She hadn't seemed to hold that against them, especially as Al was ready and eager to fill that position. Though he still refused to kiss her, which Eva clearly found amusing.

"Evening, folks!"

Al's attention was drawn to the park's cement basketball court that served as dance floor for their weekly festivals and stage for the evening newscasts. That evening the newscaster was one of the town's favorites— a retired man named Frank who had been the main postman for Madras proper and was a deacon in one of the largest local churches. Frank had an incredible memory for names and looked like Santa Claus. Al thought that every damn time he saw the guy—and the man was always smiling. Al didn't trust men who smiled all the time. It meant they were either stupid or hiding something—or both. But Al wasn't like most people, and Madras loved Frank.

"Evening, Frank!" Chorused the listening group.

"We've got a real special newscast tonight," said Frank. "So I'm going to get right to it and step aside so that our special guest speaker can tell you the good news. Mayor Cruz, the stage is all yours." Frank's signature smile was even wider and brighter than usual as he stepped aside, clapping.

Al thought he looked like a fat, grinning monkey.

Eva, on the other hand, looked delicious. He loved it when she wore all white. It showed off the cream of her skin and the honey blonde of her long hair. The addition of a red, white, and blue sparkly flag lapel

pen was his particular favorite, though he was even more partial to the
red stilettos she wore. He hoped that was all she'd wear later that night.

She stepped up on the wooden stage she'd ordered constructed in the
center of the cement square. Eva's smile wasn't as warm as Frank's, but
she was undeniably beautiful.

"Good evening, Madras. As our Frank said, I have some very good
news to share with you." She paused and met the gaze of several of the
people in the crowd, so that it seemed as if she spoke to each of them
personally. "And it's past time we had good news, isn't it? The green mist
is still terrifying, though I will always have our fans set up in the heart of
town to keep you as safe as possible. Don't forget—if those whistles sound,
make your way as quickly as possible to the courthouse, behind the fans."
She paused again and smoothed back her hair, smiling gently. "But
enough of that. Let's get to the news.

"Ladies, as you know, we require everyone who lives in our wonderful town to have their blood drawn. You also know that we ask that of
you for your own good, but we haven't explained much more than that.
Tonight I will."

There were some murmurings in the crowd, and Eva waited until
they fell silent before she continued.

"Our doctors have discovered that the blood of some women who
were exposed to the mist has the power to make plants grow. Isn't that
amazing?" Eva clasped her hands together, part prayer position, part
cheerleader as the crowd's murmurings increased. She lifted a hand and
waited for silence.

"What does that mean?" Eva leaned forward on the podium, her
blue eyes bright with excitement. "It means none of us will go hungry!"

Amber started the applause, which the crowd quickly echoed.

Eva raised her hand again, and when they quieted she went on.
"Here's what we're going to do. Those of you whose blood can grow
plants will be notified tonight. You already know that many of us have
been working hard to turn Juniper Hills Park into a large, in-city garden
area. Well, at the same time my team has been readying houses that
adjoin the park for you—our saviors—the ladies whose blood will provide us with sustenance.

"Tonight you will begin moving into those snug, lovely homes so
that you can be near the gardens to help us tend them." Eva's smile

turned into bright laughter. "Oh, but do not worry! That doesn't mean you will be taken out to the gardens and bled or anything barbaric like that. We're working on a blood draw schedule for you. Think of it like donating blood to the Red Cross, which is a very apt analogy because you will be saving lives."

A woman stepped forward. She had thick, dark hair that cascaded down her back. Al thought she looked to be in her mid-thirties. Definitely pretty and the set of her spine said she also spoke her mind.

"I have a question," said the woman, whose voice carried easily across the silent crowd.

"Yes, Martina," said Eva. She was still smiling, but Al could see that her blue eyes had gone flat and hard.

"If it's going to be like a blood bank, and the women aren't going to have to go out into the garden and bleed, I don't understand why they all have to live by the park." Several women in the crowd nodded in agreement.

"That is an excellent question. I would have mentioned why earlier, but I really didn't want to taint this good news with any that might be considered bad, but I can see now that people will need an explanation. Please, try not to worry about this next part." To someone who didn't know better, Eva appeared genuinely concerned about their feelings. She drew a deep breath and said, "The doctors and I don't know what else the mist has done to these women's bodies. We need to keep a close eye on this special group and act quickly if anything . . . untoward happens. We've set up a mini-clinic in one of the houses so that the women can all receive the best of care and attention—and they should receive nothing less.

"So you see, containing the special women in one area, particularly as we have made those homes and that area pleasing—we've even added generators to the houses." At that there were happy gasps from the crowd. Generators meant lights and, more importantly, air conditioning and refrigerators.

"Can the women take their families with them?" A voice called from the crowd.

"Of course," Eva said quickly. Then she sighed. "Those family members who are left alive should never be separated. Now, if there are no more questions?" Eva paused for only a breath before her smile was back and she continued. "Excellent. Then Frank will finish the newscast, as I think we'll all agree he's much better at it than I." A few people laughed—mostly Amber and Eva's guards. "I'll wish you a good night and may God bless you, our Madras, and the United States of America."

Frank took Eva's hand and she stepped down from the podium. She smiled at the people, who parted for her, and she even stopped to speak to several women as if they were good friends. One of those women was Martina, who batted at the air in front of her after Eva passed, as if swatting at several tenacious mosquitos.

And then Eva caught Al's eye and with one curl of her finger, motioned for him to follow her.

He did. Al didn't mind that Eva thought she could command him. *Let her think she's the boss. She's doing a good job keeping everyone in order, and I'm doing a good job enjoying the show.*

They got in the back seat of one of the black SUVs Eva preferred. Wes was driving, which meant Eva could say anything she wanted to. Since Wes had watched Eva's swarm kill Michael, he had been her mute shadow and servant.

"I think that went surprisingly well," said Al as Wes drove the SUV toward the hotel Eva called home.

"What do you mean *surprisingly?*" Eva snapped at him.

Al held his hands up in mock surrender. "I'm just saying that you basically just announced that you're rounding up a group of them, telling them where they're going to live, and that they're going to be a blood bank for everyone else."

Eva lifted one slender shoulder, then dropped it dismissively. "Yes, but that's not what they wanted to hear, so it's not what they heard. They heard that we won't starve and also that the special women need to be afraid—and when women are afraid they cling to that which makes them feel safe." Her smile was vicious. "Madras and me." Her smile faded. "But that fucking Martina has got to go. She was a *housekeeper,* and she thinks she can question me?"

Al rightly assumed that was a rhetorical question, so instead of answering he asked, "Is she one of the green bloods?"

"Thankfully, yes. So when she has her 'accident'"—Eva air quoted as she spoke the word—"her blood and body will be the first to fertilize our new gardens."

"Sounds like you have them right where you want them," said Al.

Eva swiveled in her seat to face him. She crossed her long, slender legs slowly, careful to be sure Al could see that she wore no panties under her white suit skirt. "I do, and in just a few minutes I'm going to have you right where I want you too."

He smiled and thought that the only thing he would enjoy more than fucking Eva would be the day—in the not too distant future—he showed her who was *really* in control.

But all he said was, "Your wish is my happy command," as she leaned forward and stroked his thigh and then the hardening bulge in his pants. Al felt his ever-present leeches' irritation as they slithered away from her touch. *Patience, my friends*, he told them. *Patience . . .*

21

Mercury woke gently as dawn was just touching the horizon. Ford's breath still lingered on her neck, warming her, and the whispered endearment, *Bellota*, dream-like, remained with her, but only for a moment. As the sensations faded she felt the absence of both.

She stretched and grimaced. Every muscle in her body complained loudly. The past three days the camp's focus had been split between getting the garden area ready for planting and making as many adobe bricks as possible. Mercury's main job had been to carry supplies clifftop and work on increasing the temporary shelter they were creating out of the small, cave-like area up there—all physically taxing tasks. Mercury didn't complain, but just because she had super strength did *not* mean she was immune to sore muscles.

Slowly, she got dressed, waking only Khaleesi, who followed her out to the latrine and then back inside as Mercury gave her some kibble for breakfast and then stirred the glowing coals and stoked the fire. She was grateful that Marcus had brought a case of coffee with him that he'd rescued from the ruins of his restaurant. That plus the multiple cases they'd found in the storeroom of Mitchell's grocery had made all of the adults happy. Like gasoline, they knew their supply was finite, but they were determined to enjoy it while it lasted.

She brewed coffee and chose not to use a precious piece of paper for her ritual planning. Last night they'd decided the garden was ready to plant, which meant Mercury would be leading them in Ritual, and she didn't want to complicate it. She wanted to celebrate it, and thought the best way to do that was to prepare her people physically—just thinking of that made her smile—and then she'd lead them through an impromptu Gathering, following her gut. She was staring at the fire, sipping coffee and planning as Stella emerged, yawning, with her mass of blonde waves haloing her face.

"You look like Medusa," said Mercury as she poured her a mug of coffee.

"From you I know that's a compliment, so thanks." Stella took the coffee, blew across it, and then sipped. "Why the hell are you awake?"

"I'm not really sure, except that the quiet is conducive to thinking, and I'm thinking about the planting ritual I'm going to lead y'all in today," said Mercury.

"I'm looking forward to that."

"Hey, I need your artistic expertise. Do you think you could use some of the Painted Hills clay for body paint?"

Stella's brow lifted. "Hell yes. That sounds like a lot of Pagany fun. You want to make a quick run to the hills right now, before anyone is up? We can get samples of several different colors of clay."

"Absolutely. Aren't you hungry?"

"Nah, we'll be right back. Plus, I'm worried about how long it's taking the Timberline people to get here. I'd like to try and reach Jenny again, and the best place to do that is up in those hills. You can work that radio, right?" Stella looked over the coffee cup at her.

"Right."

They downed the coffee, took the pot off the fire, and then, with Khaleesi, headed to the truck. Neither said much. They'd been friends long enough that their silence wasn't at all uncomfortable. Both gazed around them at the land they'd already become so much a part of, and when they came to the road they worked together silently and efficiently to obscure their tracks. It wasn't until they were on the road that they spoke.

"So," Mercury said. "Marcus."

"Yeah. Marcus," said Stella.

"I like him."

"I do, too." Stella sighed and added, "I scarily like him."

"Oooh, that's interesting. You haven't scarily liked anyone in a long time." Mercury turned in the seat so she could study her friend. "Who was the last guy? The one with the motorcycle?"

"Yeah, and you know how that turned out." Stella's hands tightened on the wheel.

Mercury nodded, but said nothing. There wasn't anything to say. Stella's last real love had died in a motorcycle accident, and sometimes Mercury thought part of Stella's heart, the part that had the capacity to love a man, had died then too.

Stella broke the silence. "He kissed me."

"And?"

"I scarily liked it," she said softly.

"I know that feeling, but a very wise woman told me once that an apocalypse is the perfect time to take a lover." Mercury quoted Stella with a smile.

"I may have been wrong."

"Nah." Mercury waited for a few breaths and added, "I wish Ford and I had been lovers. I wish I hadn't wasted one moment with him. So kiss Marcus—a lot. Love Marcus—a lot. Regret is way worse than heartbreak." She cleared her throat, drew in a deep breath, and then on the release blurted, "Ford has been coming to me in my dreams and I think he might be real, as in he's back somehow, but he's changed and I'm not sure if I'm terrified of what he is or ridiculously grateful."

Stella's gaze snapped to hers. She slowed the truck and said, "You're gonna have to explain that."

Mercury did. She told Stella everything, starting with that very first night after she'd danced over Ford's grave and made the flowers bloom with her blood—how he'd entered her dream but somehow left a flower beside her pillow. And then how he'd been showing up in her dreams regularly since then. She told her about the hoofprint and finished with what had happened the evening when she'd fallen asleep by the creek.

Stella didn't say anything, and Mercury waited, chewing her lip nervously. When Stella still didn't say anything she asked, "You think I've lost my fucking mind, don't you?"

"If this was our old world back in Tulsa, I'd very gently guide you to therapy and major meds, but our old world is no more. In our new world, green mist kills men, gives women powers, and sometimes kills them too.

That's all we really know about it, so there's a very good chance that something magickal has happened with Ford, even if it's just that he's become some kind of tangible spirit." She glanced at her friend. "Is there anything else you're keeping from me?"

"No! I—" Then she closed her mouth, sighed, and said, "Okay. I didn't say anything about what I saw in Fossil on our way back through it. I wasn't *not* telling you. We've been busy. I just kinda forgot."

"And?"

"When we had to slow in the middle of town I saw a dead woman who looked like she must have died from the mist because she was just sitting beside a building and I couldn't see any obvious injuries. Sprouting from her body were some really big, really creepy looking roots—as in Sigourney Weaver *Alien*-level creepy. That's all."

"I'm not surprised by that. We already know the mist can kill women. We've already seen," Stella said. "All the more reason to be sure we don't keep getting exposed to it. We need to get all of us moved clifftop a.s.a.p."

"Yeah, I agree. What do you think I should do about the Ford stuff?" Mercury asked.

"He's told you that he's not sure you'll accept him, right?"

"Right."

"Then take it a step further. Next time he comes to you tell him you're ready to accept him as is." She glanced at Mercury. "If you *are* ready to accept him."

"Horns and hooves," Mercury said.

"Horns and hooves," Stella echoed.

"Could be interesting." A small laugh broke from her. "Wonder if he'd be helpful luring goats to us."

Stella snorted. "Now *that* sounds like you've lost your mind. But if you see him, ask, 'cause it would be helpful."

"Oh, hey, have you noticed that Chad seems to be annoying Gemma?"

"I have indeed, and it makes me happy. Gemma's a smart girl. I was hoping either she'd start to see through his bullshit, or he'd grow up."

"Truthfully, I'm hoping for both," said Mercury. "There's the turnoff to that parking lot place in the hills. Oh, park as close to the hills as you can get—and steer clear of that RV."

"Dead people?"

Mercury grimaced. "Yep."

Stella turned the truck around and backed it as far has she could before the clay gave under their tires like sand. They got out and as Khaleesi sniffed around, Mercury got the antenna from the glove box, extended it, and placed it on the roof of the truck.

"The beauty here doesn't seem real," said Stella as she and Mercury gazed out over the colorful, silent hills. "It's just so different than anything I've ever seen before."

"I love the layers of colors." Mercury jerked her chin off to their left and some of the lower hills. "The fog's down there."

"I see it." Stella shivered. "Let's try to reach Jenny, fill those bags with a bunch of different colored clay, and get back to camp."

Mercury pressed the talk button on the mic. "Jenny, are you there? It's Mercury." They waited and there was nothing but static. "Jenny, you there?"

"Mercury! I'm here!" Jenny's voice blared from the radio and Mercury quickly turned down the volume.

"That's loud! How close are you to the charades place?" Mercury asked.

"We're only about a day out." Jenny's voice was clear and sharp. "We'll explain when we get there why it's taken us so long."

"Hey, no problem. So you said Hilary knows the area?" Mercury asked.

"Yeah, she sure does. Want me to get her?"

"Yes," said Mercury.

"Be right back."

"What are you thinking?" Stella asked her.

"If she knows the area she'll know Bear Creek road. It's the only public road that bisects the preserve," said Mercury.

"Oh, you're going to tell her—"

The doctor's musical voice cut in. "Mercury, it's Hilary."

"Hi, Hilary. We're not exactly where we told you guys to come."

"Yes, Jenny got that much before the connection was cut off," said Hilary. "But I'm leading the group to the place you said to come to."

"Good, and you're familiar with that area, correct?" Mercury asked.

"Correct. Been there several times."

"We're neighbors to it, but off road. You know the road that has the animal in its name?"

"I do. I know it well," said Hilary.

"Perfect. Follow that road east until you come to the second word in the name of the road. And when you come to that second word, if we're not there to meet you, just stay there. We'll find you. Do you understand?"

"Yes, absolutely. We should be there tomorrow, well before dark," said Hilary. "We're really looking forward to not traveling anymore. It's been a long trip. The green mist has caused delays. Couldn't chance heading through any of it with the men."

"Well, we think it's smart to limit our exposure too," said Mercury.

"I can't say that surprises me. No one has had a second dose yet, but it's been pretty close on several—"

"Hello! Ohmygod! Hello! This is Kristi. Who are you? Where are you? My kids and I need help!"

"That's bullshit," said Mercury to Stella before she keyed the mic again and spoke quickly. "Hilary, let's get off this thing. We'll see you tomorrow."

"Got it."

"Wait! Don't go! My kids and I really need your help. You're helping those people. Would you please help us too? Or at least my kids. Just tell me where you are and I'll get them to you."

Mercury turned off the radio and took down the antenna, retracting it to stow in the glove box.

"My gut says Kristi isn't being honest. How did you know she's bullshit?" asked Stella.

"Because I recognize her voice. When Imani and I were here talking to Jenny last time, she called herself Arianna. When I told her we'd rather come to her than tell her where we are, she said she and her kids were in a town just down the highway from where Gemma kneecapped that asshole."

Stella sighed. "I'm sorry that she's mixed up with those awful men, but we can't put our people at risk on the outside chance she really does need to be rescued."

"I agree, but don't tell Gemma about her," said Mercury as she headed to the bed of the truck to gather the bags they'd brought for the clay.

"Oh, don't worry. I'm not saying shit to her or to Karen. They'd probably want to lead a rescue mission," said Stella as they approached the first of the hills made of layers of rust and buttercup.

"Karen's going to dance at the ritual," said Mercury.

Stella froze mid-scoop of the candy-colored clay. "I love that so much. And I know what I'm going to paint on her."

"What are you going to paint on me?" Mercury called over her shoulder as she headed to the side of a hill that was striped with layers of purple and moss green.

Stella's teeth flashed in the morning light. "Something fierce, Acorn."

CHAPTER

22

A S Mercury took the last few steps from the goat path over the lip of the cliffside to the top, she decided that Marcus had been even more difficult to get up there than the trough full of tools had been. Tongues lolling, Badger and Khaleesi emerged after them, and headed straight to the pool for a drink. Mercury didn't blame them. The days had been growing steadily hotter. It was almost noon and the sun was a blinding yellow giant that beat down unrelentingly. That was good for brickmaking, but less than good for intense physical activity.

Gemma was there, pacing, and when the two of them finally staggered onto level ground she rushed to her patient. Stella had already painted her face and Mercury was amazed at the transformation of the girl. With paint made from the deep purple clay, Stella had highlighted her eyes all the way up to her arched brows. From there she'd worked in the saffron in lines like sunbursts that radiated from those dark, beautiful eyes up to her hairline, and more from the center of her eyes down her cheeks to her jaw. Two bold lines were painted from her bottom lip down her chin, and the bright saffron yellow filled in the space between the lines. She was wearing boyfriend jeans that rested low on her curvy hips and her black T-shirt was tied up to expose her belly where Stella had painted more bold, brilliant lines, interchanging purple and yellow.

"Gemma, you look beautiful," Mercury told her.

Gemma flashed a grin at her before she pointed to a large, flat-topped boulder not far from the entrance to the path. "Sit right here." Gemma commanded Marcus. "Do you need a pain pill? I brought them. And I told you that you should take one before you and Mercury started up here." The teenager hovered around the big man, looking very mama bear–like.

Marcus wiped the sweat that beaded his dark brow and flashed his smile at Gemma. "Baby girl, first, I agree with Mercury. You look beautiful. Second, I told you that you need to save those pills, and your healing magick, for folks hurt bad enough to need them. All I need is some rest." His gaze went to Mercury, who was also wiping sweat from her face. "Thank you. That was a lot harder than I thought it was going to be. Glad we've moved so many supplies up here and you've been working on the shelter. I do believe I'll be spending at least tonight on the cliff before attempting a return trip."

Mercury watched Marcus's gaze shift to Stella, who was seated on another flat-topped rock not far from them. She was using her fingers to paint designs on Georgie, who had asked specifically to look like a kitty cat, as she was currently completely obsessed with little Dandy. Stella had turned Georgie cat into a witch's familiar. She had a kitty nose and whiskers, but painted on her forehead was the triple moon, full moon in the center sandwiched between two opposite-facing crescents. Feeling her gaze, Stella turned toward Mercury and she could see that her best friend had painted on herself a large crescent moon lying on its side with the curved ends pointed up to her hairline. From it she'd drawn lines across her nose and cheeks. Her white eyelet bohemian-style dress was short-sleeved, and decorating her arms were more images of the crescent moon as well as more bold lines—all in the same deep rust red. She looked like a high priestess for an ancient Celtic tribe.

"Shiiiiit," Marcus drew the word out and then whistled long and appreciatively.

At first Mercury thought he was whistling at Stella, and then she realized that Marcus's gaze was sweeping across the clifftop, and remembered this was the first time he'd been up there.

"Hell, I know *for sure* I'm not going back down there tonight. It's incredible up here, and we can see for miles and miles." He met Mercury's gaze. "This is an excellent choice for a settlement. You ladies have done a great job."

She smiled. "Thanks. It's really coming together."

"How about you sit still for a sec and I'll get you some water?" said Gemma. "Then I'll help you to the seat I made for you over in the shade where you can watch everything."

"I'll do as my doctor orders," said Marcus good-naturedly and Gemma hurried off toward the basin.

Mercury gazed across the clifftop. The basin that held the pool and runoff waterfall was to the right. It backed to the taller hill that reared from behind their cliff. Spreading out from the basin, the hard-packed soil had been worked and reworked until it looked like the pool of water was the center of a giant wheel and the furrows waiting to be planted were its spokes. It was a large area, but only a fraction of the crop space they'd eventually plow. They'd decided to get started immediately with planting what would be staples of their diet: corn, potatoes, tomatoes, beans, and several types of squashes. They'd also sectioned off a nice-sized square that would be an herb garden, and tonight they'd plant it too, with basil and rosemary, chamomile, citronella, oregano, lavender, mint, garlic, and other kitchen and medicinal herbs Stella and Marcus had insisted were necessities.

From the basin-like pool, Imani had run several hoses over the lip and secured them. They trailed down along the ground between the furrows. The part of the hoses that lay between the furrows had pinprick holes in them. Imani had explained that all she need do would be to get the siphon going on each hose and the irrigation water would flow until the ends of the hoses were lifted. She'd even driven wooden stakes into the ground near the end of each hose and fashioned a T on each stake so that the hose could be lifted to the T and tied there, waiting to be lowered for the next watering. Mercury thought, not for the first time, that Imani was brilliant.

Past the garden area and near the cliff side was the brickmaking station. Already there were row after row of colorful bricks placed on tarps to dry. Lumber and tools were mounded near the tarps, and Imani had already put together several molds, which looked a little like ladders, for the bricks.

At the other end of the clifftop, where the boulders spiked and made a small cave-like area, Mercury had been working on adding tents to expand the cave's opening, creating more covered space. There was a fire burning there in a rock pit and the cooking tripod over it held two hanging pots.

"Mercury! Stella painted us with dots for our drumbeats!" Cayden gushed as he and Hayden rushed up to her, hugging her around the waist.

She smiled down at them. Stella had, indeed, made a pattern of red and yellow and green dots that circled their faces and wove down their necks, over their shoulders to their arms and then down to the back of their hands and fingers. As the dots got closer to their hands they became larger, though none were bigger than a dime. Neither boy wore a shirt, and the pattern of dots on their narrow chests had become the phases of the moon that circled their torsos. She'd used the purple for the moons, which appeared dark and mysterious against their light skin.

"You two look fantastic!"

"Thanks." Cayden gave her one more hug before he said, "We're going to set up the drums at the front of the garden and get ready. Georgie already has her flute. Stella says as soon as you change your clothes she'll paint you and then we'll start."

The boys scampered away and Mercury's fond gaze followed them, just then noticing Chad, who lounged against the side of the basin, crushing poppies beneath him. His face wasn't painted, which wasn't a surprise. If he thought using different voices to read aloud was embarrassing, then what they were orchestrating was way too out there for him to join in. She shrugged mentally. Maybe after he saw how much fun they had he'd change his mind and take part in the next ritual.

"Oh, good, you're here." Imani appeared from around the side of the pool. She was wearing a simple white tank top that she'd tied up to expose her fawn-colored belly. She'd wrapped Stella's pashmina around her waist as a skirt. It was silver and decorated with tiny garnet-colored sugar skulls, but it wasn't the outfit that took Mercury's breath. She was a living art piece. Stella had painted her entire face a mask of light green and then, in a darker shade of emerald, she'd drawn swirls that became ivy around the circumference of her face. That same vine pattern wrapped around her curved waist and even down her strong legs. Her thick, dark hair was braided like a crown around her head and woven with golden California poppies. "What?" Imani stopped and gave Mercury a crooked smile.

"You look like a dryad! Like you could step out of a tree, or maybe grow into a tree," said Mercury.

"That's a compliment?" asked Imani.

"That's definitely a compliment."

"Well, then, thanks. What do you need me to do before you start?"

"Just be sure those four buckets are filled with water and sitting at the beginning of the planting rows," she said.

Imani raised her brows. "We're going to add something to that water, aren't we?"

Mercury grinned. "Only those of us who want to."

"Don't even think about leaving me out," Imani said with a cheeky smile before she headed back to the basin.

"Drink all of this water." Gemma returned and handed Marcus a water bottle. "Then, if your leg feels up to it, you can lean on me and I'll take you to the place I got ready for you. Or Mercury can kinda half carry you if your leg hurts."

"You and I can manage just fine, baby girl," said Marcus. He glanced up at Mercury. "Do you think Stella would paint me? All of you look like you're from the same tribe—one I'd like to join."

"I'm sure she would, and she has time because I need to change. I'll let her know you're next."

"Thanks, and thanks again for getting me up here," said Marcus. "Though I may never go down again."

"It was my pleasure, and I wouldn't blame you if you didn't." Mercury smiled over her shoulder at him as she headed to Stella, who had just finished with Georgie.

"Meow! Meow!" Georgie said to Mercury.

"You make an excellent cat," said Mercury.

"Meow! Meow!" Georgie answered and skipped away, playing several trilling notes on her flute.

"That child sounds more like a bird every day," said Stella as Mercury joined her.

"A bird? That's the song she's playing?"

Stella nodded. "Don't you recognize it? Think bird, but *really* big bird."

Recognition hit Mercury. "It's the whistly sounds that big golden eagle who soars around here makes. It took me a couple days to realize those chirps were coming from that large bird."

"Yep. I remember reading somewhere that when you hear an eagle shrieking dangerously in the movies that's really a red-tailed hawk they've dubbed in," said Stella.

"Huh. Well, let's not tell the eagle."

"My lips are sealed."

"You've done an amazing job with the face paint. How *did* you make that clay look like paint?" Mercury asked.

"Remember that mortar and pestle you and Ford teased me about grabbing from the grocery in Mitchell?"

"I do," said Mercury.

"Well, I ground the clay until it was super fine and then slowly mixed water, and that's about it. Once I found the right water to clay ratio it was pretty easy to add more or less clay for different shades," she said.

"Everyone looks great. I'm going to change and then you can paint me and we can start, but Marcus asked if you'd do him first." Mercury waggled her brows suggestively at her best friend and made some soft kissy noises.

Stella stood and smacked her shoulder. "Stop. How old are you?"

"Young enough to still have fun teasing you." Mercury laughed.

Stella tried unsuccessfully to hide a smile. "Go get dressed. I'll *do* Marcus. Now and—perhaps—later." She tossed back her hair, picked up a couple of the bowls holding the clay paints and the cloth she'd been using to wipe her hands and headed toward the basin and Marcus.

Still smiling, Mercury walked the length of the clifftop to the shelter they'd erected. They'd all opted to get dressed atop the cliff so they wouldn't begin the ritual sweaty and dirty from the climb. As Mercury entered the shelter, she pulled off her damp T-shirt and then startled when she realized Karen was in the shadowy rear of the cave-like area.

"Shit! Karen, you scared me." Mercury put her hand over her heart as it pounded in her chest. And then Karen stepped from the shadows and Mercury gasped. "You look amazing!"

Karen smoothed a trembling hand down the tulle skirt and then tugged at the wraparound shirt that hugged her generous curves. "Are you sure? I feel a little silly."

"I've never seen you look so lovely," Mercury said truthfully. "And Stella's face paint is perfection." In the center of Karen's forehead was a slender cross in deep yellow. Stella had painted a heart around it in a diluted version of the rust, so that it was reflective of the soft pink of Karen's outfit. From the heart were bright yellow lines that looked like rays of sunshine blazing across her forehead and even down her cheeks.

Karen lifted a hand to her forehead, but didn't quite touch it. "I have a little mirror from a compact I carry in my purse. I brought it up here but I've been afraid to look. Everyone else appears so magickal, regal even, in their paint." Her voice lowered to a whisper. "I—I didn't want to look and see an old woman who is pretending to be something she's not."

Mercury went to Karen and pulled her into a tight hug. When Mercury stepped back she had to wipe tears from her cheeks. "Look at yourself. If you see what I see, it'll be a beautiful woman who is mature and magnificent."

Karen nodded shakily and Mercury changed into the flowy dress she'd worn the night Ford had waltzed her around the Madras park—the same dress she'd worn when they'd buried him and she'd waltzed on his grave, coaxing wildflowers to grow.

Mercury shook those thoughts away.

When she was dressed she turned and saw Karen staring at her reflection in a little round compact mirror. She touched her face gently and when her eyes lifted to meet Mercury's they were filled with tears.

"I look lovely," said Karen softly.

"Yes, you do. Bring your mirror. I want to see what Stella comes up with for me. Are you ready to dance?" Mercury asked as they left the shelter.

Karen lifted her chin and smiled. "Yes, I believe I am."

23

꒷꒦

M ERCURY WAS GLAD Karen had brought the mirror. As she faced her little group, she held herself proudly, knowing how fierce she looked. Stella had used the rust red to cover her face and eyelids, from the top of the bridge of her nose to her hairline. Below her eyes across her nose and cheeks the rust became green painted in bold lines that looked like spears. Those same spears slashed vertically from the edges of her eyes, as if they were tears made into weapons. More slashing lines were painted from her bottom lip down her chin, neck, and chest—even over the swell of her breasts. But her favorite part of the face paint was the triple moon image Stella had drawn on her forehead in purple so dark it looked black.

"I told you," Stella had said when Mercury studied herself in Karen's little mirror. "*Fierce.*"

Fierce fits, Mercury thought as she raised the little knife she'd brought with her and placed it in one of the four buckets of water that waited at the head of the rows ready for planting. Everyone went silent.

"Merry meet!" Mercury said. She waited, and then in an exaggerated whisper added, "You're supposed to repeat it."

"Merry meet!" responded her friends with some nervous laughter.

"This is going to be a simple ritual that has one purpose. In spell-work, or during Ritual, purpose equals intent, and intent is important. It is what we focus on as we move through Ritual and weave our spell."

Georgie's hand flew up.

Mercury smiled. "Yes, Georgie?"

"What spell are we doing?" asked the little girl.

"Good question. This is a planting ritual and the spellwork is intended to send positive energy to our seeds through the air, the fiery heat of the sun, the water, and the earth herself," explained Mercury. "I would usually cast a circle traditionally, work some spells or a spell, then close the circle and we'd feast and dance. But because this is the first Ritual we've had in our new world I thought I'd change it—make it our own."

"That sounds like a good idea," said Gemma. Then she clamped her hand over her mouth, and through it said, "Sorry, is it okay to speak?"

"Of course." Mercury assured her. "This is *our* Ritual, not *my* Ritual." She paused to see if anyone else wanted to say something before she continued. "So you're all kind of just clumped here between the basin and the rows we need to plant." She grinned at the twins, who sat behind everyone with their drums, just far enough up the side of the basin that they were elevated. Chad hadn't moved from his place closer to the pool. Marcus leaned against a rock in the shade. Badger and Khaleesi rested beside him, and Mercury saw the little white fluff that was Dandy sleeping between Badger's enormous front paws.

Mercury took a moment to give Marcus an appreciative look. Stella had painted dots in saffron from his strong chin in a line, up his face, over his nose, to his brow. She'd highlighted his expressive eyes with the deep rust and used it to make bold infinity circles on his cheeks and neck. *Marcus also looks fierce*, she thought before she continued. "I'd like you to go to the section of rows you've chosen to plant and stand in front of them."

They spread out in front of the rows, so that they were lined up loosely side by side. At the head of each row were little bowls that held the seeds they were to plant. Earlier, they'd decided which crop would go where and noted everything on the paper on which Stella had created a drawing of the large garden and filled in what crop was being planted in each row. They'd discussed the specifics of exactly how each different group of seeds needed to be planted and had pre-chosen which they would plant.

"We're not in a circle, but I'm going to call each of the elements, and when I do we'll turn to face the direction associated with that element. Just follow my lead on that. It's not difficult. But before I begin I'd like to ask Karen to open Ritual with a prayer." Mercury motioned for Karen to join her before them, and then she stepped aside.

"Thank you, Mercury. Please pray with me." Karen clasped her hands and bowed her head. "Sweet, faithful Jesus, I ask that you smile on us this day as, with joy and love, we plant food that will succor our bodies, and we also make merry to succor our spirits.

"What we do today we do to honor the earth and the gifts given to us that will help us survive this new world. We only wish to thrive in peace and prosperity and to live with joy and grateful hearts. In your precious name we pray. Amen."

"Amen," echoed the group.

Karen stepped back to her row and Mercury returned to the head of the group. "And now let's call the elements and continue to bless this planting. First, we turn to the east." Mercury did so, and the group mimicked her. She'd already decided to keep the calling short, so that the words would be remembered and repeated, and she began. "Air is my breath. I call you air." Then Mercury turned to face the south, and the group followed her. "Fire my spirit. I call you fire." She continued turning to face the west, as did the group. "Water is my blood. I call you water." Finally she faced north. "Earth my body. I call you earth."

Then she turned to her friends again and smiled. "The elements are here with us and now we plant." Her gaze went to the twins, who were standing by the drums that were so big they stretched to the boys' waists. "Cayden and Hayden, we're going to chant while we plant. Would you pick up the beat of our chant with your drumbeat?"

"Yes!" the boys shouted together before moving behind the drums, hands on the skins of the instruments, waiting eagerly.

Georgie's hand went up.

"Yes, Georgie?" Mercury asked.

"I can play my flute with one hand while I plant. Is that okay?"

Mercury smiled. "Absolutely. As we plant we're going to chant, which is really just a song. I'll start, but join in with me, please," said Mercury. "And remember, as we plant we focus on sending positive energy through the elements to our seeds. Ready?" She paused and everyone smiled and nodded. "Let's plant!"

Mercury went to the section she'd chosen—squash—picked up the first bowl for the first row, and as she bent to plant and cover the seeds she chanted. "Air is my breath—fire my spirit—water is my blood—earth my body. Air is my breath—fire my spirit—water is my blood—earth my body."

The group joined her, and as their voices blended. they grew more confident, harmonizing, lifting, falling, weaving together over and over. "Air is my breath—fire my spirit—water is my blood—earth my body." The twins picked up the beat of the chant and drumbeats, echoing heartbeats, throbbed around them. One boy's drum held the main beat, sonorous and steady, and the other wove a secondary beat that played with the melody. And then Georgie's flute trilled between the drumbeats, lifting like magickal birdsong.

All the planters were barefoot, and soon Mercury saw Gemma twirl as she stomped her feet in the soil between rows. And then Imani joined her, twirling at the end of one planted row and moving her feet with the drumbeats before she began to plant a new row. Karen was the only one of the planters who didn't move with the music.

Mercury felt the music as if it was inside her body. She was energized and connected to her group—and filled with joy.

When the seeds were planted they were smiling and laughing and sweaty—and they returned to the head of their rows where they'd begun. Mercury went to the bucket of water in which she'd placed her knife and lifted it. They watched as she stepped in front of them again.

"We know that four of us can make plants grow with our blood. Stella." Mercury looked at her best friend, who moved to stand beside her. "Imani." She joined the two of them. "Gemma." The teenager lifted her chin proudly and moved to stand with them. "And me." From the edge of her vision Mercury noticed that Chad suddenly sat up and leaned forward, watching them intently. "We don't know how much blood it takes to grow this many plants, but we're willing to do what we can to help them out." Mercury went to the buckets and the three women followed.

She pressed the blade of the knife against the meaty part of her palm under her thumb, drew a deep breath and then made a long, shallow cut, which immediately began to weep scarlet. Stella took the knife from her as Mercury plunged her hand into the water.

Without hesitation each of the women sliced their palms and dunked their hands in their bucket, swishing them around until the water blushed pink. "Don't forget to use your cut hand to sprinkle the water," she said softly. The three women nodded. Then Mercury smiled up at the children. "We'd like some more of your music."

"Are you going to chant again?" Hayden asked.

"We definitely are, but I want you to start the music first because our ballerina is going to dance." Mercury turned to Karen. As the drumbeats wove the earth's heartbeat around them she said, "Please lead us, Karen. We'll follow you."

Karen smoothed her hands down her skirt and then nodded. She walked past Mercury a little way down the center row. Her back was to the group. Her spine straightened. She raised her arms to form a graceful circle, where her fingers almost touched. And then Karen began to dance with the beat, though Mercury thought that *dance* wasn't the right word for what Karen did. *Float.* That was more like it. Karen swayed and bent, turned and reached, and even leaped. She was a feather, blown by the beating drums, finally set free after a lifetime of being caged, and in her freedom Karen was exquisite.

Mercury, Stella, Imani, and Gemma spread out and followed Karen—joyfully, but not as gracefully—they cupped their bleeding hands through the pinkening water and flung the liquid around them as they danced their way down and up the rows. Mercury began the chant, and the group took it up again. Their dance was uninhibited and filled with the promise of new life—in the seeds they were nurturing and in the world they were creating.

No Ritual has ever been so perfect. Thank you, Goddess. Thank you.

As Mercury twirled and swayed, spun and beat out the rhythm with her feet and hips and arms, she glanced at each of her friends—that core group who had become her family—and saw how radiant they were and how, just for a moment, each of their eyes glowed emerald green. Mercury's gaze was pulled upward, and above the clifftop circled the huge golden eagle as if he had been sent by Mother Earth to show her delight with them.

24

R ITUAL ENDED WITH Mercury happily thanking each element after all the blood-tinged water had been sprinkled over the planted seeds. Then Imani began the siphon on each irrigation hose, and carefully watered the newly sown seeds. There was a lot of laughter as they also used the hoses to rinse off the clay paint. It was inevitable that the dogs got involved, and the clifftop echoed with the sounds of children laughing, dogs playing, and one tiny kitten who seemed to already believe she was a canine.

The group ate dinner together on the clifftop, sitting around the big campfire, sheltered from most of the wind by the jutting rock formations and the expanded tent area. After dinner, Marcus reiterated that he'd be spending at least that night up there, and his young doctor agreed that he needed to rest his leg. It didn't seem to surprise anyone that Stella chose to remain with Marcus.

The group, minus Marcus, Stella, and Badger, made their way slowly down to their original camp before sunset and darkness made the steep path too treacherous to use. Mercury loved the feeling of contentment that permeated the air. Everyone was tired, but a good tired. Even Chad went to bed early. He hadn't said much after Ritual, even though Mercury noticed that his eyes followed Gemma as she helped the children get ready for bed. Gemma spoke to him softly. Mercury couldn't hear what they said, but she was pleased with the girl. She'd stopped puppy-dogging around after Chad, which was a huge relief.

Karen seemed to glow. She'd taken off the skirt just before she'd retired, and spread it across the curved wall of the cave near the head of her sleeping pallet. It looked beautiful and ethereal there, like a three-dimensional painting. Before she went to bed she'd sat up long enough to share a joint and a bottle of wine with Mercury and Imani, and then kissed each woman on the cheek as a good night.

"It was a wonderful Ritual." Imani spoke softly. Dandy, always her shadow, slept curled on her lap. She and Mercury were the only people awake, and both of them were happily exhausted and fading fast.

Mercury sipped the last of her glass of wine. "It was my favorite Ritual ever. And I cannot wait to see what happens with those seeds."

"They will flourish and grow." Imani spoke with no hesitation. "I think we will too."

Mercury nodded and smiled. "I'm thinking that Stella's flourishing already."

Imani's wide smile made her look elfin. "I'm glad for them."

"Ditto, and I want all the details," said Mercury.

"Oh, definitely. She'd better spill the tea when she comes down off that"—Imani paused dramatically and then finished with a mischievous glint in her dark eyes—"*hill*."

Mercury almost snorted wine from her nose. "The first time I saw him I did think he looked like a mountain."

"The brother is large, that's for sure."

"I'm glad he's joined us," said Mercury.

Imani nodded then lowered her voice. "Chad didn't participate today, but he also didn't make any obnoxious comments. Progress?"

"Maybe." Mercury assumed everyone was asleep, but she kept her voice soft too. "But more importantly it seems like Gemma's crush is over. She's still nice to him, but that's it. Just nice and not flirty and giggly like she was at first."

"Yeah, I've noticed. She's a smart girl. I knew she'd figure it out." Imani finished her wine, stood, and stretched. "I'm going to go to my cedar before I fall asleep right here. You staying up?"

"Nope. Getting the Marcus Mountain up the actual mountain did me in, and that didn't even count the dancing."

Imani's impish grin returned. "The dancing was great. The children definitely have a musical gift."

"Let's look for other instruments while we're out and about," said Mercury. "It would be awesome if we had even more music."

"That's a good idea. Night-night. See you in the morning."

"'Night." Sleepily, Mercury gathered their wineglasses and put them in the bucket of water designated for dirty dishes. She banked the fire, and then Khaleesi padded with her to bed.

Mercury's last thought before she fell asleep was about Ford. *You would have loved Ritual. I hope wherever you are you were watching.*

One thought kept Gemma moving forward. *Get home. Get to the cave. It'll be okay if you just get home. You'll be safe. It'll be okay.* She stumbled in the darkness and almost fell, grimacing as her bare foot stepped on another sharp rock. But she made no sound. She wanted him to believe she was still out there—still washing him off of her in the creek. If he knew she was going home he would stop her.

"Gemma!"

From behind her his voice drifted with the shadows and darkness of the night. She didn't hesitate. She didn't try to peer back to see where he was. She just kept moving.

"Gemma!" His voice was farther behind her. He hadn't realized she'd gotten away yet. If he had, he'd make straight for the cave.

Her bare foot, slick with blood from the last rock she'd stepped on, slipped, and she fell again, but Gemma didn't slow down. She could see the glowing coals of the campfire now. She was almost there. Gemma lurched from a jog into a run. Her most sensitive parts hurt. The wetness leaking down her thighs increased. *How much is blood? How much is him?* Gemma shook her head. No. Don't think about it. *Get home. Get to the cave. It'll be okay if you just get home.*

She was cold, which was weird because, even though she'd told him she was going to the creek to wash, she'd not actually done more than step into the water enough to make splashing sounds before she'd snuck away, sprinted up the bank, and then headed for *home.* Back by the creek he'd called her name. "Gemma, what's taking you so long?" he'd said, like he actually believed she was going to come back to him.

He was wrong. Gemma had already left the creek. His voice had been a goad that had forced her from a walk to a jog. If he caught her he'd drag her away with him. He'd told her his plan—take the Jeep because it was faster than the truck and could travel off road better—and head to the cabin he'd hidden at before.

Gemma shivered in disgust as his words came back to her. He'd bragged about the fact that he'd never intended to go back to Condon for his grandma—that the only reason he'd left the cabin was because he'd run out of supplies. Had he not run out of gas, he would have stolen as much as he could from Condon and then left again. Without his grandma. After hearing that, it wasn't a surprise to her when he admitted that over the past couple of days he'd stolen some of their supplies and stashed them where he could easily grab them on his way out. *It's no big deal. They have more than enough.*

How had she ever thought he was cute?

A little sob of relief caught in her throat as she stumbled into the cave. No one was awake. She hadn't expected anyone to be. She stood for a moment by the glowing embers of the fire. *Home.* She'd made it. He couldn't hurt her again now. They wouldn't let him.

Gemma almost sat down to rest. She wanted to curl in on herself. As her arms wrapped around her chest she cringed. Her breasts hurt. She hadn't even noticed that before. She didn't look down; Gemma knew what she'd see and it frightened her. She'd only been wearing the oversized T-shirt she slept in. She hadn't thought anything about following him outside in just the shirt when he'd tapped her shoulder and whispered in her ear to wake up, that he had to tell her something important.

When she moved toward the sleeping area, Gemma's steps were slow. She knew everything would change when she woke them, but she didn't hesitate.

After what he'd done to her everything should change.

Gemma almost went to Mercury first. She was their warrior. But he wasn't there. She'd made it home before he could stop her, and there was no way he'd come to the cave. Not now. Not after what he'd done. So she went to Imani first. She needed a mother more than a warrior.

Gemma wanted to kneel beside Imani and wake her gently, but her body felt so foreign, so sore and wrong, that she just stood there, unable to bend or crouch or kneel—or even speak. She hadn't realized she was crying until she drew a ragged, shuddering breath. Gemma wasn't surprised then when Imani's eyes opened and she sat sleepily, brushing her hair from her face as she looked up at her.

"Gemma? What is it, baby girl?"

"*Help*" was all Gemma could force through her cold lips as sobs shook her body.

"Mercury, wake up."

Her eyes opened immediately, though sleep still clung to Mercury as she peered up at Imani, who was bent over her. "What is it?" She was already pulling on her jeans as Imani answered with one word.

"Gemma."

The way Imani said the girl's name sent a stab of fear through Mercury.

"She's by the fire," Imani continued to whisper in a voice so filled with anger that she seemed to bite the words. "I'm waking Karen, but we have to be quiet. We can't wake the kids."

Mercury nodded and finished pulling on her jeans and boots as she stood. Without another word Imani hurried past her, heading to Karen's pallet. Followed by Khaleesi, Mercury went to the main room of the cave.

When Mercury saw Gemma she wanted to burst into tears. She did not. Gemma was sitting on the log closest to the fire, which was burning with inappropriate cheeriness. Gemma's face was pale and streaked with dirt and tears and snot. Her oversized T-shirt fell off one shoulder, exposing a hand-shaped bruise near her neck that was changing from red to purple. Her bare legs were pressed tightly together, though Mercury could see the streaks of blood and fluids that had leaked to her calves and ankles. Her feet were cut and bruised.

Mercury and Khaleesi went to the teenager. The dog nosed her and licked her face, and then curled beside her, within touching distance. Gemma's hand lowered to slowly pet her. Mercury squatted beside both of them. Very carefully, she put her arms around Gemma, who leaned into her. Her body shivered over and over as Mercury held her. Then Gemma pulled back and wiped her face and nose with her hand.

"He's going to take the Jeep. He has the keys." Gemma's voice was raspy, as if she hadn't spoken in a long time, but she met Mercury's gaze without looking away.

"Where is he?" Mercury asked the question in a low, soft voice, though she wanted to scream her rage.

"I don't know. We were down by the creek, toward the road. We'd walked a ways before h—h—he . . ." Gemma's trembling voice broke off on a sob.

"Will you be okay here for a second?"

Imani answered her. "Karen and I will take care of her. Do what you need to do."

Mercury cupped Gemma's face gently between her hands. "It's going to be okay. I promise." She kissed the girl's forehead and told the pitty, "Stay here with Gemma." Then she grabbed a flashlight and jogged out of the cave.

Mercury didn't need to turn on the flashlight to find her way to the Jeep. The star-filled sky and the moon illuminated everything so well that the trees and rocks cast shadows. She moved quickly and silently, listening intently for even the slightest sound that might betray Chad's presence.

She heard nothing and wasn't surprised. Chad was the kind of person who wasn't used to dealing with consequences. He wouldn't feel any urgency to put as much distance between himself and her as possible. But she wouldn't take chances. He wasn't going to get away.

When she reached the Jeep she opened the hood and pulled the main cables from the battery. Then she flipped off the flashlight and stood very still for a moment, allowing her eyes to acclimate to the night again—and listened. She heard nothing except the usual symphony of insects and frogs, and jogged back to the cave.

Karen was heating water in a bucket over the fire. One of the bags Gemma kept her medical supplies in was open beside the teenager and Imani was pulling from it clean strips of cloth Gemma always had prepared for large bandages. On the log beside Gemma was a fresh T-shirt. Imani dunked one of the strips of cloth in the warm water, wrung it out, and then turned to Gemma.

"Baby girl, can you take off that dirty shirt so that I can see how badly you're hurt and get you cleaned up?"

Gemma nodded shakily and slowly, as if each movement hurt, and she pulled the shirt over her head. She paused for only a moment before she tossed it into the fire. Then she dropped her arms to her sides and exposed her body to them.

What Mercury had thought was dirt on her face were actually bruises. Her lips were swollen and her bottom lip was cut. Her jaw was swelling too, as well as one blackened eye. Her neck was ringed in bruises. Her breasts had red marks on them from where he'd squeezed and sucked. The insides of Gemma's thighs were streaked with blood and fluids down to the pads of her bare and battered feet.

"I'll be quick so you can get dressed," said Imani.

"You don't have to be. I'm not really cold. I just can't stop shivering," said Gemma.

A small sob came from Karen, but she quickly pressed her lips together and wiped her face. Her gaze met Mercury's. "I'll get her a bottle of water if you find the pain pills."

Mercury nodded and squatted by the bag of medicine and bandages.

"We should save those pills for someone who really needs them," said Gemma.

Mercury looked up from the bag. "You are someone who really needs them." She found one of the bottles, popped it open, shook out a couple pills, and gave them to Gemma as Karen opened the water bottle and handed it to her. The teenager gulped them.

"We have chamomile tea. I'm going to brew her some," said Karen.

Mercury took Karen's place, taking the bloody cloths as Imani handed them to her and replacing them with clean cloths newly dunked in the warm water.

"Can you tell us what happened?" Mercury asked.

Gemma had been staring into the fire. Her gaze lifted to Mercury's. She nodded jerkily. "He woke me and whispered that he had something he had to tell me. I thought . . ." Her words trailed off as Karen returned with a pot she'd filled with water and the box of tea.

"Take your time," said Mercury. "If you can't tell us now, it's okay."

Gemma cleared her throat. "No, I want to tell you. I *need* to tell you." She continued. "I thought he was going to say something about the ritual, like that he was sorry he hadn't done any of it. At first he didn't say anything, though, except that he wanted me to walk with him down by the creek. It was like Marcus and Stella—you know, he's been asking her to walk with him every night after dinner. I thought Chad was being sweet like that. He even offered me his arm, like a gentleman." Her expression twisted. "He's not a gentleman. He's a monster."

"We'd walked so far that I finally told him that it probably wasn't a good idea to go much farther. He said just a little more and kept moving me forward until I reminded him that we can't see the green mist very well at night. That stopped him. He started to tell me how hot I looked today and that he knew I'd been dancing for him." Gemma shook her head. "I didn't think he was serious and I kinda laughed and said that I'd been dancing for the seeds and the elements. He said that didn't matter because I'd looked so hot. Then he started kissing me.

"At first I let him. It—it was nice." Her gaze flicked from Imani to Mercury and then Karen, as if she couldn't really meet any of their eyes. Reluctantly she added, "We'd kissed before, but that was it. One time a few days ago he'd started to touch my breast, but Georgie had come running up to us and he stopped. This time he didn't stop and his kisses were different. Hard. They were too hard. He hurt my lips." She touched the cut on her swollen bottom lip. "I told him to stop and he laughed at me, put his hand up under my shirt and kept grabbing my breasts—really hard. His fingernails dug into me. He tried to keep kissing me, but I twisted my face away and told him to stop again.

"He—he said that if I really wanted him to stop I wouldn't have danced like I did today and I wouldn't have just worn that T-shirt to walk with him. He also said that I was asking for it because of the way I kissed him." She paused and looked at Mercury. "He's the first guy I've ever really made out with. I thought he was maybe going to be my boyfriend. I thought we were just having fun. I didn't mean anything by wearing that shirt. I didn't think I did anything wrong."

"You didn't," Mercury said quickly. "You didn't do one single thing wrong. This is not your fault."

"Listen to Mercury," Imani said, touching her unbruised cheek. "Listen to all of us. You did nothing wrong."

"Sweetheart," Karen said as she handed her the mug of steaming herbal tea. "This is not your fault."

Gemma nodded jerkily, sipped the tea, and then continued. "I kept trying to tell him that I didn't mean anything and that he was hurting me. When he wouldn't stop I said I was going to scream. That's when he hit me. I fell and the breath was knocked out of me and everything went all dark.

"The next thing I remember was when he pulled my shirt all the way up, over my breasts. I realized that h——he was trying to shove *it* in me and I started to fight him really hard, but he's so strong that it didn't do anything but make him mad. When I tried to scream he hit me again and there were bright spots in my eyes. I wanted to yell for help, but I couldn't make my voice work. And then I just lay there. He got pissed and grabbed my legs and pulled them up around his waist. He said that I could help him 'cause it wasn't like I was a virgin.

"I couldn't move. He had his hands around my neck and was ramming into me over and over. I thought he was going to kill me." A sob broke from her and her hand was shaking so hard she had to put down the mug of tea. "It hurt so bad. *So bad.*" Another sob shook Gemma's body.

Except for her legs, Imani had finished washing Gemma and she gently helped her into the clean T-shirt. She put her arms around the teenager as she continued to sob, but Gemma straightened soon, wiped her face, picked up her mug, and took several sips.

"Then it was over. He got off me, but he didn't let me go. He put his arm around me and held me against him, like we'd actually just made love. It was so awful." She shuddered. "And he kept talking and talking—about how I belonged to him now—and how it was all going like he'd planned. That's when he told me he'd hidden supplies he'd taken from us when everyone was busy making the bricks and that he was going to wait and take some guns too, but he'd changed his mind and said we needed to leave tonight because Marcus was up on the cliff. He said he hadn't been able to sneak out at night because Marcus would've known and stopped him. So he took the keys to the Jeep and was leaving with me now." She took a few more sips of the tea and her shoulders relaxed as the painkillers began to work.

"How did you get away from him?" Mercury asked.

"I pretended that I thought it was a good idea. He kept talking about how we were going back to that cabin and how we wouldn't run out of gas this time because the Jeep had one of the gas siphons in it. He said a bunch of other stuff, but I wasn't really listening. I was only thinking about getting away."

"Smart girl," Imani murmured. "Brave, smart girl."

Gemma drew in a ragged breath and continued. "I told him that I needed to pee and to wash up in the creek. He laughed and said it was too cold, and I said I didn't mind because I thought I might be bleeding 'cause I'd been a virgin.

"That made him super happy. He actually laughed and hugged me and said something about how cool it was that he'd popped my cherry and that I'd belong to him and only him forever now."

Her lip curled up in a sneer. "I made myself agree with him. Told him he was right, that now I was his. Then he let me go to the creek, but he kept my shoes. It was dark enough that he couldn't see me real well. I went to the creek, but I didn't go in except to kick around and splash some water. Then I ran away as fast as I could." She looked down at her cut and bruised feet. "I didn't think about anything except getting home. Getting here to all of you. I knew if I could do that I'd be okay. He yelled for me, but I didn't look back. I just kept running."

"You did well. Really well," said Mercury. "And you were right. You'll be okay now." Mercury reached into the medical supplies bag and took out two long strips of bandage cloth, which she put in her pocket. Then she went to a corner of the cave that had several shopping bags full of supplies. She took out a bag of zip ties and shoved them in the waist of her jeans. Mercury considered getting the .38, but her gut said she wouldn't need it. She touched Gemma's head gently and said, "I'll be back."

"You're not going to bring him back here, are you?" Gemma's voice edged on hysteria.

Mercury stroked the teenager's hair. "No. You don't need to worry about him ever again." Her gaze went to Karen and then Imani. Both women met her eyes steadily, and in theirs Mercury saw mirrors of her own rage. "Come on, Khaleesi."

25

CHAD WAS PREDICTABLE. Nothing in his short, entitled life had prepared him for Mercury or retribution. As she hid in the shadows not far from the Jeep, she realized that she hadn't needed to disable the vehicle. Chad was in no rush. He was probably still combing the area between the cave and the creek, hoping he'd find Gemma. It was only after he'd given up on taking her with him that he would head to the Jeep and what he thought would be his getaway.

Khaleesi's ears pricked and Mercury knew he was approaching. She watched from her hiding place as Chad slowly made his way to the Jeep. The area where they parked their two vehicles was quite a few yards from the entrance to the cave, where an outcropping of rock created some protection from the weather. He kept throwing furtive looks up at the cave as he crept to the driver's side of the Jeep. He opened the door and then leaned in to switch off the overhead light, which is when Mercury surged from the shadows.

She pressed the door against him, trapping him between the seat and the door. He cried out and tried to push back, but her strength far surpassed his and she easily held him there. He hadn't managed to flip off the light, so Mercury could see the red rage that moved up his neck to suffuse his face.

"You're not going anywhere," said Mercury.

He turned his head. "What the fuck? I'm some kind of prisoner?"

"Not *some kind*." Mercury's voice was low and rough with rage. "You raped Gemma. That makes you our prisoner."

"Rape?" His laugh was brittle. "Is that what she said?"

"That is what you did."

"Bullshit! She's been after me since we met. You saw the way she danced today. In case you don't get it—that was for me. Tonight she proved it by going out with me dressed in nothing but a T-shirt. I didn't do anything she didn't ask for."

Mercury couldn't listen to him for one more moment. She opened the door and grabbed him by the back of his shirt and pulled him away from the Jeep. "Shut up." She threw him down on the rocky ground and stood over him. "Everything you say is a lie. In case you don't get it let me be very clear—we believe Gemma."

Still on the ground his face twisted into a sneer, but Mercury saw fear flash through his eyes. As Khaleesi growled, he surged to his feet, shouting, "Gemma! Gemma! Tell them! Tell them we're together!"

Mercury balled up her fist, stepped forward, and punched him so hard that his head snapped back and he dropped like a rock. She'd never punched anyone before, but was grateful for the lessons her brothers had given her. Her hand hurt like hell, but she hadn't broken any of her fingers. As Khaleesi continued to growl, Mercury rolled him over, took one of the strips of cloth from her pocket, balled it up, and then opened his slack jaws and shoved it into his mouth, muttering, "Gemma does not need to hear your bullshit." She pulled him into a sitting position and used the second strip of cloth to tie around his mouth and secure the gag. She propped him against the side of the Jeep and quickly zip-tied his hands behind his back and his ankles together. Then she bent and threw him over her shoulder like a sack of rotten potatoes.

Khaleesi walked beside her, growling periodically, as Mercury headed down to the creek. There were more trees there, which meant she'd be able to secure him to one. After a few yards she felt him stir. He lifted his head and tried to speak, and then he started bucking and kicking.

"Hold the fuck still or I will drop you and drag you."

He stopped moving, but Mercury could feel his rapid breathing and pounding heartbeat. She came to the first of the sturdy junipers, growing straight and tall near the creek, and dumped him on the ground, ignoring his muffled protests. She fashioned a plastic rope out of the zip ties, grabbed the back of his shirt again, and dragged him to the tree, shoving his back against it. He kept making muffled noises, which she continued to ignore as she secured him to the tree.

When she was done, she stepped back and looked down at him. "I'll finish dealing with you tomorrow." Mercury and Khaleesi walked away, paying no attention to Chad's frantic, muffled cries.

When Mercury returned to the cave, she thought Gemma looked like a baby owl, all wide-eyed and intent.

"I heard him." She spoke softly and her hands still trembled, though she had them wrapped around her mug of tea.

Mercury nodded. "I'm sorry about that. I should've known he'd try to call to you. You won't hear him anymore."

Gemma swallowed audibly. "Did—did you kill him?"

"No, but he can't get away and he will never hurt you again," Mercury said.

Imani was sitting on the log on one side of Gemma. Karen sat close on the other side. Mercury went to Gemma and touched her head again, smoothing her hair. "You're brave and strong and it's going to be okay. We promise." Then she took the flashlight with her and went to the bags where they kept the rest of their precious medical supplies—things they'd confiscated from the pharmacy at the general store in Mitchell, as well as what Doc Hilary had given them when they'd left Timberline. Mercury breathed a sigh of relief when she found the box she thought she'd remembered and carried it back with her to Gemma.

Mercury showed Gemma the box. "Do you know what this is?"

Gemma took the box and read it, nodding. "It's the morning after pill." She looked up at Mercury. "Can I take it?"

"Absolutely, but it's your choice. No one here will make you take it or judge you about whether you do or do not," said Mercury.

Gemma didn't hesitate. She tore open the box, put the pill in her mouth, and downed it with a gulp of tea. Then she looked at Karen and her lip trembled. "I know you probably don't approve, but—"

"I support your choice. Period," said Karen.

"As do I," said Imani.

Gemma breathed out a long, tremulous breath and swayed a little. "I'm really tired now."

"Would you like me to lie down with you until you fall asleep?" asked Imani.

The teenager nodded. "Yes, please. I—I need a mom."

Imani put her arm around Gemma. "Well, you have one."

Karen rested her hand on Gemma's knee. "And another."

"And another," added Mercury.

Imani helped Gemma stand and then slowly they walked back to the sleeping area. Imani held her hand as if she was just a little girl, and Gemma walked so close to her that their arms pressed together.

When they were gone, Mercury went to the pile of kindling that was mounded near the entrance and began picking through it for short juniper boughs and long lengths of sage grass. Behind her she could hear Karen tidying the area and placing the soiled strips of cloth in the water bucket that was over the fire so that they could be boiled clean.

"What did you do with him?" Karen asked.

Mercury took the juniper and grasses and sat by the fire, braiding them tightly together. As she worked she answered Karen. "I punched him to shut him up, then gagged him, bound his hands and feet, and tied him to a tree down by the creek."

"I'm glad you gagged him. When Gemma heard him . . ." Karen paused. She worked her cross between her thumb and forefinger and shook her head. "It was terrible. She cringed and cried and cried."

"I should've gagged him right away."

"You did your best." Karen glanced at the braid. "What are you doing now?"

"I'm going to cleanse myself and make offering to prepare," said Mercury.

"For?"

Mercury looked up from the braiding and met Karen's gaze. "For what must be done. I want to be sure my mind is clear and I'm following the right path."

Karen nodded. "Like when I pray on something, asking for answers."

"Yes, except I believe I already know the answer. I'm going to ask for strength and wisdom to do the right thing," she said.

"You will. I absolutely believe you will do the right thing," said Karen.

"I believe we all will. You, Imani, Stella, and me. I want input from the core four."

Karen's lips lifted only slightly in a sad smile. "The core four. I like that. Is there anything I can do to help?"

"Pray for wisdom and strength. This won't be easy for any of us," said Mercury.

"I will," said Karen.

Mercury finished the braid and went to where they kept the bottles of wine they hadn't yet carried up to the top of the cliff. She chose carefully—a rich, expensive-looking red—and opened it. Then she put a box of matches in her pocket and the same small, sharp knife they'd used in Ritual. She gathered the braid and turned to Karen. "I probably won't be back until after dawn. As soon as it's light enough I'll go up the path and get Stella. I'm going to take Chad up there with me. I want him out of sight when the kids wake up."

Karen nodded. "That's smart. I do not believe I'll be able to go back to sleep. I'm going to stay by the fire and finish cleaning the bandages. As I do I'll pray. I imagine Imani will join me soon."

"Okay, I'll see you after sunrise." Khaleesi remained at her side and Mercury let her feet guide her without consciously willing them, though she wasn't surprised when she found herself at Ford's grave.

First, Mercury stripped off her clothes, leaving them on the flowers that still carpeted the grave. Naked, she picked her way carefully down the bank to the creek. Ignoring the chill of the water, she walked into it until she was submerged to her waist, then she began to wash, splashing water over her body as she thought about the connection she felt to the earth through her bare feet, and how the air passed over her chilled skin and the water cleansed her.

She returned to the grave, picked up the dry braid, and lit it. Mercury blew out the flame and then used her free hand to coax the evergreen-scented smoke over her bare skin as she concentrated on the magickal properties of juniper: cleansing, protection, and warding away evil.

When she was satisfied she was fully cleansed, Mercury dressed, picked up the bottle of wine, and then went to the closest cedar tree. As she poured the wine on the ground, she circled the tree. When the wine was gone, Mercury took out the knife and cut her palm, right beside the pink, healed line from which she'd bled earlier that day. She circled the tree again. Her blood dripped from her palm, mixing with the red wine as both soaked into the earth.

"I give this offering of wine and blood freely to thee, Gaia, my goddess, and your earth. I ask that you continue to guide me on your Path and that you grant me the wisdom to know what should be done with Chad Condon, who has violated our Gemma, as well as the strength to do what must be done. So I have spoken. So mote it be."

Then Mercury returned to the grave and sat cross-legged in the center of it. She grounded herself and gradually slipped into such a deep, meditative state that she did not return fully to herself until the blush of morning registered against her closed eyelids.

Ford had not come to her, but she hadn't called for him. She hadn't thought of him. This was women's business.

She stood and went to the cedar. In a circle around it, where she'd poured libation and given sacrifice, bloomed large white flowers whose stamens and stigmas were bright red, like blood against pale skin. She pressed her palm to the bark of the tree and bowed her head. "Thank you," she murmured, and was sure she felt the bark of the tree expand and contract as it sighed a breath.

With the knife in her hand, Mercury walked resolutely to the place she'd tied Chad. His head slouched forward and he twitched in sleep. Mercury kicked his foot and he startled awake, his head snapping up to stare at her through bleary eyes.

"I'm going to untie you and then you and I are going to walk up to the top of the cliff." He started to shake his head and make noises through the gag, and she held up her hand, cutting him off. "The only choice you have is whether you walk up the path or I drag you."

She bent and cut the plastic rope that bound him as well as the zip tie around his ankles, though she left his hands bound behind him. Then she grabbed the back of his shirt and lifted, so that he scrambled to his feet.

He made some pathetic noises and his eyes kept cutting to the creek.

"Yeah, I get it. You're thirsty. I'm not going to take that gag off until we're up top. Then if you're good I'll let you drink." She pushed him ahead of her and he stumbled toward the camp and the steep path around the side of the cave that led up. At the entrance to the path, he stopped and turned to look at her. "You're going to walk in front of me. If you try anything stupid, I will knock you out and drag you. I will not be gentle. Do you understand?" He made muffled noises. "Just nod."

Chad nodded.

"Good. Get going."

Mercury felt as if it took forever to get up the cliff. She refused to unbind his hands, which meant she had to almost carry him during the steepest parts of the trail, but he finally stumbled over the lip of the path and fell to his knees.

Mercury didn't wait for him to try to stand. By his bound hands she dragged him over to a pile of rope and then quickly secured him to one of the jutting rocks near the cliffside.

He started making more noises, jerking his chin toward the big pool of water. "Just sit there. I'm going to get Stella. Then you can have some water."

Mercury turned to cross the clifftop to the shelter, and their newly planted garden caught her gaze. Young green sprouts covered the rows, jutting up eagerly like children turning their faces to the summer sun. Mercury felt a rush of pride and happiness at what she and the other women had created together—feelings that were a direct contradiction to those foremost within her that day. *Why must it be like this? Why must joy and beauty and the creation of life be tarnished by violation and violence?*

Only the lonely wind answered her turbulent thoughts, but on it she seemed to hear a whisper that said *It doesn't have to be like that . . . it can be better.*

In front of the clifftop shelter the big campfire was just embers, and not far from it was a cozy pallet where Stella was wrapped in Marcus's arms, her head resting on his wide chest. Mercury wished with everything in her that she didn't have to wake her friend, but even as she thought the wish, Stella's blue eyes opened and found her. She sat right away, pushing her hair back from her face.

"What's wrong?" Stella asked.

Marcus woke then. "What's happened?" He said as he sat too.

"Last night Chad raped Gemma."

Stella gasped and all the color drained from her face. Marcus's arm went around her. "I brought him up here, gagged and tied. I want Marcus to watch him while you and I go down and talk to Imani and Karen about what's next."

"This is the bad thing my gut told me would happen if we didn't leave him out there in the desert," Stella said as she pulled on her jeans and boots.

"Next time, no matter what, we follow your gut," said Mercury.

26

GEMMA WAS STILL asleep when Georgie and the twins woke early, as was usual for them. The four women had agreed that they should be honest with the kids, so they carefully explained that Chad had attacked Gemma and that she would be okay, but right now she needed to rest. The children ate their breakfast subdued and silent, and then they got out their fishing gear and all of them, except the still sleeping teenager, went down to the creek.

While Georgie and the twins fished, careful to keep a lookout for the green mist, which often drifted with the morning breeze over the creek, Mercury, Imani, Karen, and Stella moved far enough away from them that they couldn't overhear their discussion, but they could still see the kids.

Mercury was surprised that there wasn't much to debate. The four women were grim, but in agreement.

When they saw Gemma in the entrance to the cave, Mercury, Imani, and Stella went to her while Karen remained to watch the children.

Stella went to Gemma and pulled the teenager into her arms. "You're going to be okay."

"I know," Gemma said as she stepped back and wiped tears from her cheeks, grimacing as she touched her swollen, bruised face. "I'll bet I look terrible."

"You look like a survivor—strong and whole," said Stella, "I'm so proud of you for getting away from him. Like I've said all along, you're one smart kid."

Gemma tried to smile, but her breath hissed as her lip broke open and began to bleed again. Gemma touched it gingerly. "It's a lot harder to heal myself than someone else."

Mercury took a closer look at Gemma. The girl was still bruised, and her lip and eye were swollen, but her eye could've—*should've*—looked worse, and her jaw was also less swollen than it should be. "You're doing a great job," said Mercury. "Sleep will help."

"How does the rest of you feel?" asked Imani as she spooned up some oatmeal for Gemma.

The teenager sat carefully. "Really sore."

Imani nodded. "That's okay. I'm going to make a sitz bath for you a little later. That and sleep will help you continue to heal."

Gemma met Mercury's gaze. "Where is he?"

"Clifftop with Marcus."

"What are you going to do now?" asked Gemma.

"Make sure he never hurts anyone else," said Mercury.

Gemma nodded. "Good. I want to be there. I want to face him."

"Kid, you don't need to do that," said Stella.

"Yes. I do," said Gemma. She ate the last bites of her breakfast, got up carefully, and put her bowl in the dirty dishwater. Then she faced the group. "I'm ready if you are."

Karen chose to remain by the creek with the children. She hugged Gemma and told her how brave she was and told the other three women, "You're doing the right thing. I will pray for all of you." Then Mercury, Stella, Imani, and Gemma began the climb up the cliff. When they were close to the top, Mercury hung back to speak with Gemma.

"I will give him one chance to tell the truth and apologize to you," said Mercury. "But don't expect much. He lied about it last night; I don't think that will change. He'll also blame you. Do not let him mess with your head. You did nothing wrong. You didn't deserve any of this. We *all* believe you. No one blames you. That is the absolute truth."

"Don't worry. I don't expect anything from him, and thank you," said Gemma.

"You don't have to thank me. This is how the world should work. When a man brutalizes a woman, the woman should not be blamed. She should be supported and believed. The consequences are for the attacker and for him alone. We're only doing what's right," said Mercury.

"I don't know what I'd do if you hadn't believed me." Gemma blinked hard to keep the tears welling in her eyes from falling.

"You'll never have to wonder about that," said Stella.

They climbed over the lip of the trail. Marcus was sitting on a rock not far from where Chad was tied. Before she and Stella had gone below, Mercury had taken the gag from his mouth and let him drink his fill. When she retied him, it had been with enough slack in the rope that he could stand. As soon as the women came within his view, Chad struggled to his feet.

"Gemma! You have to tell them it was just a misunderstanding! You're my girlfriend. Tell them." As he spoke Gemma strode toward him with Mercury on one side and Stella and Imani on the other. The closer she got, the more his voice faltered as he took in her bruised and broken face.

Marcus pressed the long branch that was his crutch to the middle of Chad's chest. "Shut. Up." His deep voice rumbled with anger; beside him Badger growled and bared his teeth at Chad. Then Marcus turned to Gemma. His big hand lifted to gently touch her cheek. "I'm sorry this happened to you, baby girl."

Gemma nodded, swallowed hard, and then faced Chad. "*This*"—she pointed to her face—"was not a misunderstanding. When I told you no, you hit me. Twice. You knocked me to the ground and raped me. I am not your girlfriend."

"I didn't mean it. I just wanted you so bad, and you know why."

"Because I saved your life. Because I was nice to you. Because I kissed you. Because I wore a big T-shirt to go on a walk with you. Because you made up in your head that I danced for you. That's crap. Complete crap. But even if it was true, *I told you no!*" Gemma spit the words at him. "My dad said I'd meet guys who are nothing but garbage human beings. I used to think that was mean of him, but he was right. I know because now I've met one. You're a garbage human being, Chad Condon."

"And you're a cock tease!" Chad shouted at her.

Fast as a viper, Mercury moved forward and slapped him so hard he staggered back. "If you say anything like that again I will fucking gag you."

Chad pressed his hand to his cheek and narrowed his eyes at Mercury. "Just take me and drop me off in the desert somewhere. I don't ever want to see any of you again."

"Where did you hide the supplies you stole from us?" Stella asked.

His mean, narrowed eyes cut to Gemma and he opened his mouth, but Mercury snapped. "Say one more shitty word to Gemma and I will gag you and find the supplies myself."

He pressed his lips together and then his shoulders slumped. "It's not like you don't have plenty of food." When no one said anything, he sighed. "Whatever. The stuff is in a backpack not far from where, uh, Gemma and I . . ." His words trailed off.

"Not far from where you raped me," said Gemma. She turned to Mercury. "I can show you where that is."

"Good. Why don't you show Stella and Imani while I finish up with Chad?" said Mercury.

Gemma shook her head. "No. I'm staying."

"As am I," said Stella.

"I'm not going anywhere until we're done here," said Imani. "This isn't just on you, Mercury. It's *our* decision."

"I'm not part of this," said Marcus, "but I want you to know that I'll support whatever you've decided to do with him."

"Good. Then all of you can witness our justice. It is swift. It is final. We don't blame victims and we don't slap the wrists of men who brutalize us. Their lives are *not* more valuable than ours. That part of our old world is fucking dead and gone," said Mercury.

"Hey, wait." Chad's gaze flicked from Mercury to the rest of the group. What he saw there had his voice shifting from bravado to a whine. "What do you think you're going to do?" He looked at Marcus. "Tell them what it's like when a man is teased and teased. It's as much her fault as mine!"

Marcus shook his head. "You think you've acted like a *man*? You're a mean, spoiled boy. You deserve whatever happens to you."

Mercury took two steps so that she stood very close to Chad. She waited until he looked at her and then she caught and held his gaze, and spoke clearly. "Chad Condon, you are a stain on this world. What you did to Gemma is inexcusable. We will not allow you to hurt anyone again. We will not allow you to put our camp and our people in jeopardy." Mercury walked around Chad to where the rope was tied to a rock. She untied it and then returned to him and untied the other end that was secured around his bound hands. Mercury dropped the rope.

"I'll go and I won't come back." He glanced at Gemma, and when she stared back, silent as stone, he shrugged and continued. With a glimpse of freedom, Chad had regained some of his confidence. "It'd be a lot easier to get me back down that path if you untied my hands."

"You're going back down, but you aren't taking the path and I won't need to untie your hands." Mercury grabbed his zip-tied wrists with one hand and the scruff of his shirt with the other and began pulling him toward the edge of the cliff.

"Wait, stop! What are you doing?"

"Serving justice," said Mercury.

He tried to fight, but Mercury's grip was a vise and his struggles only caused him to stumble, so that she dragged him.

"You can't do this! It's not fair!"

"Putting a predator down is more than fair. It's wise." Mercury lifted him, and with one swift, strong motion, threw him off the cliff.

His scream echoed and echoed and then went completely still.

Stella was beside her in a moment. She put her arm around her friend's shoulder and held her tightly. It was only then that Mercury realized she was trembling all over.

Then she lurched from Stella's embrace, bent, and puked and puked. Imani joined them. She patted Mercury's back as Stella held her hair. When she was finally done, she straightened, grimaced, and wiped a hand across her mouth.

Gemma walked to her, hugged her, and then said, "Thank you."

"Ladies, heads up. Look to your twelve o'clock," Marcus called from where he still sat beside the discarded rope.

The women peered into the distance. From the clifftop a stretch of Bear Creek Road was visible. Making their way along the road were five vehicles. Two were trucks and one was a van, but the other two were strange looking, almost like golf carts.

"It's Jenny and the people from Timberline!" said Stella. "Look, those weird things are the Polaris carts they use at the resort."

"Their timing is bad," said Imani.

"Actually, it's not," said Mercury. "If they want to join us they need to know our rules and the consequences of breaking them."

"They're all going to know about what happened to me." Gemma's voice was soft and very, very young.

"You have *nothing* to be embarrassed about or ashamed of," said Stella firmly, taking Gemma's shoulders in her hands so that the teenager looked up at her. "You're a fucking survivor. That's a badge of honor and no damn body is going to make you feel less than that. Not here. Not in our world."

"Exactly," said Imani.

"We've got your back and we always will," said Mercury. "Now let's go greet our friends and see who wants to live in our world, and who will need to keep on moving."

27

✦

"MERCURY!" JENNY JUMPED from her seat in the first Polaris and ran down the road to the Chevy. Mercury was out of the cab and met her as the younger woman flew into her arms, laughing and crying happy tears. "Ohmygod! It's so good to see you! It took us *forever* to get here." She stepped back, wiped tears from her cheeks, and said, "Uh, we are here, right?" Jenny glanced around. "We came to the right place?"

Mercury smiled. "You did, but we're off the road far enough that you have to know we're there to find us."

Doc Hilary joined them, as graceful as a willow bough. She hugged Mercury tightly and waved at Stella, who waited in the cab of the truck. "We made it! It will be so nice to stop traveling and have a home."

Mercury met her gaze. "Well, that's something we'll need to talk about, but first y'all can follow us to camp."

Hillary's smile faltered. "Has something happened? Are we not welcome?"

"Yes, something has happened, but you are very welcome, and if you want to stay you may. It's just that some of you may not want to stay. I'll explain everything at the camp."

Jenny got in the cab of the Chevy with them. She was rumpled and dirty and sweaty—and looked as if she hadn't slept in days.

"It was a tough trip," she said. "We all agreed to avoid highways, and a few of our people, like Marge and Nathan and a twenty-something guy named Jim who's from Bend, know the area well enough that we were able to cut cross-country for almost the whole way, but we had to go slow because of the Polarises. And three times we had to double back or go the wrong direction for almost half a day to avoid the green mist." Jenny shuddered. "At first we stopped at houses to spend the night, but we saw some really awful things and from then on camped outside on top of a hill or cliff, or anything raised. Even then we slept in shifts, keeping a lookout for the mist and for people."

"Did you run into any living people on the way here?" Stella asked.

Jenny shook her head. "Not up close. Only in the distance, and none of them approached us."

"It was a good idea to caravan," said Mercury.

Jenny looked at her. "What's happened?"

Mercury blew out a long breath. "Last night Gemma was raped."

"Oh my god! Is she okay?"

"She's going to be," said Stella.

"Doc Hilary can help her heal. She's been really good at that. The mist did something to her blood more than just the plant growing stuff," said Jenny.

Mercury nodded. "Yeah, Gemma has that too, though she says it's harder to heal herself. It'll be nice to have the doc help her."

"Is that why you said some of us might not want to stay here? Because Gemma was raped?" Jenny asked.

"No. I said that because of what I did to the rapist," said Mercury.

"*We*," Stella corrected. "The four of us made the decision together."

"Well, what—" Jenny began, but Mercury shook her head.

"No, it's better if you find out with everyone else." Then Mercury put her arm around Jenny's shoulders. "I am truly glad to see you."

"I missed you a lot and have so much to tell you." Jenny leaned away enough to study Mercury. "You look different."

"Different how?"

"Stronger. Not like muscle stronger. Wiser stronger," said Jenny.

"I hope you keep thinking that," said Mercury.

"Jenny will. It's not her you need to worry about," said Stella. The two women looked at her. Stella shrugged. "And you don't need to actually worry about anyone who won't stay. That's their decision. Remember that."

"Oh, I will," said Mercury.

There were a total of twenty-three people who made the trip from Timberline. Five of the original Timberline survivors had decided that even though the structure of the lodge was crumbling and the green mist pooled oddly and was more unpredictable the higher the elevation, they felt safe remaining at a place they knew and didn't want to chance the journey. The other two people had slipped into what Doc Hilary described as a catatonic state. They'd withdrawn from the world, stopped eating and drinking, and had died quietly in their sleep. Out of the twenty-three people there were nineteen women, ages ranging from Jenny, who was twenty-five and the youngest, to a woman named Janet, who at fifty-seven was the oldest. The four men were Tyler, the eighteen-year-old who had been working during spring break at Timberline; Marge's partner, Nathan; Keith Carter, who was in his mid-forties; and Jim Butler, who was twenty-seven.

Mercury observed the group as they got slowly out of the well-packed vehicles. Even tired and dirty, they looked to be in pretty good shape. Marge, whose leg had been badly broken during the bombing, still limped, but could walk by herself. Nathan moved carefully, showing that his ribs were not quite healed. A few more people moved stiffly, but all of them studied the cliff and the campsite with bright, eager eyes.

At the group's arrival, the kids, Karen, and Khaleesi came up from the stream. And then, as everyone congregated in front of the cave, Imani and Gemma joined them. Gemma stayed close to Imani, though she held her head high so that her bruises showed clearly. Color flushed her cheeks, but she hugged Doc Hilary tightly and greeted several of the Timberline people warmly.

"I can help soothe your injuries," Hilary told Gemma as she stroked her cheek.

Gemma's cheeks flushed even pinker, but she nodded and whispered, "Thanks."

Stella moved close to Mercury and spoke softly to her. "Your plan is good, and now is the time. Show is better than tell."

Mercury nodded, drew in a deep breath, and then like a diver plunging into deep water, strode to stand before the group of new people.

"In case you don't remember, I'm Mercury. This is Stella, Imani, Karen, and I think you all know our Gemma." She pointed to each person in turn. "And it is my pleasure to introduce to you Georgie and her twin brothers, Cayden and Hayden." The kids waved and the group smiled at them. "Oh, this is Khaleesi." Mercury ruffled the pitty's ears and then pointed at the ball of fluff that sat at Imani's feet studying the crowd with bright, blue, curious eyes. "And this is Dandy."

Several of the women in the group cooed at the kitten, and Mercury waited for them to quit before she spoke again. "Above, on the clifftop where we're working on moving our campsite, are the final new members of our group, Marcus and his German shepherd, Badger. He'd be down here to greet everyone, but his leg is healing from a nasty break and the steep path is still difficult for him."

Mercury spoke to the group as she had the students in her classroom. She made eye contact with them. Her voice carried easily. Her manner was relaxed, though internally she dreaded what was to come.

"We're glad you're here," Mercury continued. "And you are welcome, though we want all of you to understand that there are rules that go with our community and consequences for those who break the rules."

"Who makes the rules?" asked Keith Carter.

"Good question," said Mercury, ignoring his sharp tone. "Our rules are made by Stella, Imani, Karen, and me. There aren't many of them. Basically, those who join our community agree to be compassionate and kind to one another. Our resources will be shared, as will the talents and experience of individuals. We will respect each other's privacy. If there is a dispute over something, you may come to any of the four of us and we'll decide what should be done, but we don't expect that to happen often because of rule number one: we agree to be compassionate and kind to one another. Violence against members of this community will not be tolerated."

"What happens if someone breaks the rules?" asked a thirty-something-looking woman with hair that was fading from pink to blonde.

"What is your name?" asked Mercury with a smile.

"Bree," she said.

"Bree, I'm glad you asked," said Mercury. "As you can all see, Gemma has been hurt. Last night she was raped by a young man whose life she saved just a few days ago. He broke our rules. Please follow me." With Stella by her side, Mercury began walking around the cliff, past the place where they parked the vehicles. The group followed, though she told Khaleesi to stay and so did Imani, Karen, Gemma, and the kids, who remained at camp with the kitten. Mercury didn't speak, and neither did the Timberline group.

Mercury kept walking. She wound around the jutting rocks at the base of the cliff until she spotted the blue shirt Chad had been wearing. An edge of it lifted in the morning breeze like a broken flag. She couldn't see all of him yet, but even from that distance his body lay awkwardly—legs bent in the wrong direction, head twisted, torso flattened. The rocks around him were splattered with blood and gore. Purposefully, she quickened her pace, drawing ahead of the group so that her body blocked their view of the grisly site. As they caught up with her, she said. "This was Chad Condon. The young man who raped Gemma." And she stepped aside.

There were gasps from the group and several women turned their heads, averting their eyes.

After a few silent moments, Doc Hilary said, "This is the consequence of violence against one of your people."

Although she didn't phrase it as a question, Mercury answered. "Yes."

Jenny nodded. "We need new rules for a new world. This makes sense."

Mercury waited to see if anyone else would comment, and when no one did, she spoke into the silence. "I want to be very clear. None of you have to stay here. We will pack supplies for you and if the rest of your group agrees, you may take one of the vehicles that brought you here."

Hilary spoke up. "If people want to leave they absolutely may take one of the vehicles."

Janet asked, "Doc, are you staying?"

Hilary's response came without hesitation. "Oh, yes. Definitely."

"Good," Janet continued. "Because I'm definitely staying."

Though Mercury was surprised by Janet's words, she continued her explanation. "We wish those of you who decide not to stay well. We understand if you don't feel like our community is the right fit for you."

"To add to what Mercury has said, if you leave I urge you not to go to Madras, as there's some scary shit going on down there, but, again, that would be your choice," said Stella.

"Wait, let me get this clear," said Keith. "If anyone disagrees with you, he's going to be thrown off the top of the cliff?"

Mercury met his gaze. She told herself to remain as calm as a still pool of water. When she spoke, her voice was smooth as oil. "No, Keith. As I have already explained, if people have disagreements or disputes they can bring them to one of the four of us and we will help resolve them. Our community is one where we work together to make a safer, better world. If someone, like yourself, can't get along with others—can't show kindness and compassion even during disagreements—you will be told that you must leave, and we will compassionately be sure you have supplies and a shelter to take with you. This"—Mercury pointed over her shoulder at Chad's broken corpse—"is the consequence for rape or any brutalization of one of our people." She looked around the group. "Any other questions?"

"When do we need to make our decision whether to leave or not?" Keith asked.

"Tomorrow," said Mercury. "You're tired and hungry. We'll get your vehicles unloaded, show everyone around, feed you, and make sure you're comfortably settled for the night. If you choose to leave, you may do so after first light in the morning."

"We brought plants," said Jenny. "Lots of growing, thriving veggies."

Stella smiled. "That's fantastic. We have a large garden started on the clifftop. They'll transplant there well." Then her smile included the group. "So, everyone should rest and relax today. Get a good night's sleep. In the morning if you'd like to leave, we'll help you pack a vehicle and see you off. Does that sound fair?"

The group nodded.

"Okay, let's go back and get you settled," said Mercury.

As she walked through the group to return to camp, someone asked, "What are you going to do with his body?"

"Right now, nothing," said Mercury. "Helping to get your group settled is more important."

"We'll bury him pretty soon, though. We have chickens and rabbits, which means we don't want coyotes drawn here," said Stella as she walked beside Mercury.

The silent group followed.

"Don't worry," Stella told Mercury softly. "You did well. The one who needs to leave will, which is a very good thing."

Mercury's brows lifted. "You mean they're not all going to leave. Well, all except Jenny, Hilary, and Janet."

Stella snorted. "Not even maybe, Acorn."

28

Mercury thought it was weird to have so many people around. Not necessarily bad weird, just people-y weird. Khaleesi seemed to agree. When she wasn't shadowing Mercury, she would scramble up the cliff side to hang out with Badger and Marcus, watching silently as the newcomers worked to bring up supplies and erect temporary shelters.

The addition of twenty-three people had them scrambling to set up sleeping areas for everyone, though the core four had expected the newcomers and already had a plan for them.

Those whose injuries kept them from climbing the path to the clifftop would stay in the cave. The children had opted to move up top, which hadn't been a surprise to anyone. Since they'd discovered the path and started readying the clifftop for their permanent home, Georgie, Cayden, and Hayden had been climbing the trail and had quickly proven to be goat-like in their ability to clamber up and down. It seemed the only thing they enjoyed more than scaling the side of the cliff was playing their instruments or fishing.

With the children transplanted up to the top of the cliff, Imani chose to move clifftop, too, which made sense. The kids loved all four women, but Imani was who they looked to first for comfort and a mom hug. In turn, she adored them.

Though Karen practiced the climb up and back every day, she chose to remain in the cave until the cliff homes were completed and everyone moved to the top. She told Mercury that heights made her nervous, but that was something she was working on—along with getting into good physical shape.

Marcus said he was content to remain clifftop and had no intention of attempting that path again until his leg was closer to a hundred percent. Mercury had expected Stella to move her pallet up there with him, but her best friend had just smiled and said, "Hello! You know me. I'm not much for cohabitating. Marcus and I are grownups and can be lovers without being all in each other's business."

They spent that entire first day, until dusk, expanding and erecting tents against the little cave clifftop and making sleeping pallets. They hung what extra fabric they had to partition rooms and give privacy—and Stella added curtains, sheets, and even area rugs to their list of supplies they'd look for during the next trip to Mitchell.

Out of the twenty-three new people, only five chose the cave versus the clifftop to set up their pallets. Even Keith, whose face appeared to be frozen in a permanent frown, said he'd prefer to sleep clifftop. Marge and Nathan, who had the worst of the injuries, Janet, who admitted to hating heights and was an extremely inexperienced hiker, and Jenny and Hilary chose to remain below. Mercury decided to stay in the original camp with Karen and Stella and Gemma.

That first day was hectic. Though Janet, Jenny, and Hilary were the only people who had announced they were staying, everyone worked together to get bedding, tents, and supplies up on the clifftop before dusk made the path up too treacherous. The eight women and Nathan didn't eat dinner with the larger group above. Instead, Mercury, Stella, Jenny, Hilary, and Gemma had carried armloads of supplies up and returned for more to begin the steep trek up again and again until, finally, sunset allowed them to rest. Then they'd washed in the creek and been grateful to retreat to the relative quiet of the cave where Karen, Marge, Nathan, and Janet had prepared a fragrant dinner of fried fish from the creek and boiled potatoes and thick cut tomatoes that the group had brought from Timberline. They opened a couple bottles of precious wine and found places circling around the campfire to eat and then sip wine and pass around a joint.

There was a restful sense of completion that night that Mercury felt in her bones. It wasn't that they didn't still have a lot to do—of course they did. It was more that the feeling was one of coming together, of knowing that those who remained with them after the morning would be of the same mind. They would work together to create a place of safety and community—of family. Mercury felt the tension begin to release from her shoulders as she acclimated herself to the sounds of new voices and shared laughter.

"We don't want to be rude," Marge said as she stood carefully, still favoring her broken leg, and then gave Nathan a hand up. His breath hitched if he moved too quickly or laughed too hard—which was tough because Nathan seemed to find humor in almost everything, which meant several times a day he had to clutch his ribs and breathe slowly to recover—not that the discomfort kept him from laughing again. "It's early and we like the company, but we're really looking forward to a solid night of sleep."

Mercury smiled at the couple. "It's not rude at all. You two rest well."

"We're glad to be here. And we will really be glad to remain here tomorrow," Nathan said, and then they turned to go to the inner area of the cave reserved for sleeping.

"We happy that you've joined us," said Stella.

"They seem like a nice couple," said Karen as she poured herself a little more wine.

"They are," said Jenny. She held out her glass to Karen for a refill.

"As soon as I'm okay again, I'll work on healing Marge's leg and Nathan's ribs the rest of the way," said Gemma. Then her eyes widened and her gaze went quickly to Hilary. "Oh, crap. I didn't mean that to sound disrespectful or offensive. It's not like you did a bad job or anything."

Hilary smiled. "No offense taken at all, honey. Mercury has told me about your incredible healing skills, and I look forward to observing what you do."

Gemma shrugged. "It's not really a skill. It's magick from the green mist. That's all."

"That's not true," said Karen. "Gemma, I've watched you study those medical texts you got from the library. You pore over them and take notes. That's learning a skill."

Stella raised her glass to Karen in agreement. "Exactly. We don't know what the mist is, but what we do know is that it amplifies abilities we already have, which means you were already on your way to being one hell of a healer."

Hilary nodded. "I have to agree with that. As you can all see, my ability to heal physical wounds isn't as powerful as Gemma's."

Absently, Gemma lifted her hand to touch her eye. It was still bruised, but Hilary's touch had gotten rid of all of the swelling. "I feel a lot better everywhere since you worked on me," she said. "And I haven't had a headache or a panic attack all day."

"I'm so glad that I helped. I've discovered that my new powers are more focused on emotional healing and pain relief than the actual knitting of bones and closing of wounds." Hilary took a long pull on the joint Stella had just passed to her, and after she breathed out a cloud of fragrant smoke she added, "That very much mirrors where I was heading with my practice before all of this happened. I was going to focus more on women's mental well-being."

Jenny took the joint from Hilary. "Yeah, we've talked about this a bunch. My blood can't grow plants, but I have a master's in botany and have always been good with plants. I did most of the tending of our gardens in Timberline, and the veggies grew and grew and grew for me."

"My blood doesn't make plants grow either," said Karen. "But I've always been religious. Even *overly* religious." Stella snorted and Karen smiled wryly before she continued. "The mist has granted me the ability to see the spirit world and also to be more discerning with my own spirituality." She met Mercury's gaze across the campfire. "I don't think I told you, but during Ritual when we were all dancing, everything glowed emerald—the ground, the water, us—everything."

"Wait, there's dancing?" Jenny sat up straighter.

"And Ritual?" Hilary asked.

Gemma grinned. "Yeah, it was great." Then her gaze went to the fire and the happiness drained from her face.

Karen reached over and squeezed her hand. "He can never hurt you again."

Gemma wiped away a tear and looked up, lifting her chin. "I know." Her gaze shifted to Mercury. "And I'm glad."

Janet cleared her throat and then said, "My husband used to brutalize me. He took me whenever he felt like it. I was terrified of him. When the bombs dropped we were at Timberline *celebrating*"—she spoke the word as if it tasted sour—"our twentieth wedding anniversary because he loved to ski. It didn't matter that I hated it. Nothing I hated mattered. When the green mist dissolved him into jelly I was relieved, even though this is the first time I've admitted it out loud." She met Mercury's gaze. "I'm glad you threw that guy off the cliff and I'm relieved to live somewhere women are safe from monsters." In the silence that followed her statement, Janet stood. "I wish you all good night." On her way to the back of the cave she stopped beside Gemma and rested her hand on her shoulder for a moment and said, "Now that he's not here—not getting away with hurting you—it'll get better. You'll never forget, but it'll get a lot better."

"Well, that was a surprise," said Stella.

"Janet's okay," said Jenny. "She comes off as gruff. I think that's because that asshole she was married to spent twenty years isolating her and she's awkward, has a hard time making friends, but like she said, she's getting better."

"I'm glad she finally said those things aloud," said Hilary. "I've been working with her and she just took a really big step forward in her healing."

"I think I understand her," said Karen. "My marriage was"—she paused, considering her words—"claustrophobic. I'll pray for her and spend some special time with her."

"That would be lovely," said Hilary. "Oh, and Janet is an extraordinarily skilled seamstress."

"Ooooh! Adding sewing supplies to my list," said Stella.

"What other special skills have your people exhibited?" asked Mercury as Stella passed her a bottle of wine.

"Well, only about half of us were exposed to the mist," said Hilary. "Five of us can grow plants with our blood, and then there are people like Jenny who cannot, but who seem to have had their natural abilities enhanced. Bree, the young women with pink hair, made her living creating pottery. Her blood can grow plants. She's spoken often about feeling compelled to get back to her pottery, and I've wondered what kind of amazing things she'll create when she does."

"Imani will love that," said Gemma.

Stella nodded. "We'll make a kiln up top. Bree can be in charge of that."

Jenny spoke up. "Astrid's blood can't grow plants, but she is the most amazing baker I've ever known. Like magick-level amazing." She glanced at Stella and grinned sheepishly. "No offense."

Stella snorted. "None taken. I'm an excellent cook. So is Marcus, but the more excellent cooks we have the better—and baking is a skill we definitely can use."

"What else?" asked Mercury.

"Tamara." Hilary and Jenny spoke together. Then Hilary continued. "Her blood grows things *and* she knows when the mist is near."

"Always," said Jenny. "She saved our asses multiple times."

"So even after the trip here, none of you have been exposed more than once to the mist?" Mercury asked.

"No. The men, obviously, were not exposed at all, and there are several women who weren't exposed either," said Hilary. "The mist didn't make it down to the men's or women's saunas."

"Or the spa in general." added Jenny. "Remember, that's why Christine, Frances, and Louise weren't exposed."

"That's right. So, we have seven women who weren't exposed at all," said Hilary. "And the rest of us were only exposed once. But your question makes me think that some of your group *have* been exposed more than once."

Mercury nodded. "Imani, Gemma, and I have been exposed twice—though not on purpose. We're trying to avoid getting exposed again. We've seen things. Not just that it kills women who are exposed too long, though we don't know how long too long is, but other things." She paused. Her mouth had gone dry and she had to take a drink of wine before she continued. "I saw strange plant things growing out of the body of a woman who looked like she'd died because of the mist." Mercury shuddered. "We should all avoid it."

"It's such a mystery," said Hilary. She sighed and ran her hands through her long, wavy hair so that it cascaded like a veil down her back. "And I find it fascinating. I have so many questions about it that are unanswered—that will probably always be unanswered."

"I wish we knew how much is *too* much exposure," said Gemma. "I mean, after the second time I breathed it in I got way better at healing people. I wonder what would happen if I was exposed a third time. Would I be a super healer or, well, dead, or a creepy pod person?"

"I wish I knew where it came from," said Karen. "Not because we can do anything about it now, but just because I'm curious."

"I wish I knew what it can do to all people," said Mercury as she stared into the fire.

"I wish I knew what it was doing to my community," said Hilary.

"Your community?" Karen asked.

"Yes, the LGBTQIA+ community."

"Oh. I didn't know you're gay," said Karen.

Hilary's smile was beatific. "I've been out for decades. My wife died in the earthquake that tore apart Timberline." Her smile faded and her eyes went dark with sadness. "I'm active in the community, especially as I focus on women's health issues. I know many trans and nonbinary people. I cannot help but wonder and worry about them. We know the mist kills every man who breathes it in, but does that include our trans sisters? And what of those who identify as nonbinary? Does the mist follow biology or the spirit?"

"The spirit." Stella's voice was firm. She blinked as if waking from a dream and looked from woman to woman around the fire. "That has to be the truth. I didn't think that answer. I *felt* it. The mist isn't simple biology. What it's done to us—the changes it's made—proves that it is *more* than biology. Imani *wished for a deep, raised basin of water to sustain us, and it appeared.*" Stella spoke the words reverently. "That's not earth science; it's earth magick."

Hilary turned to her. Tears pooled in her expressive hazel eyes. "I'm going to believe with you."

Just after dawn the next morning, as Karen brewed coffee, Stella made breakfast and their group had begun waking and stirring for the day when Keith Carter entered the cave. He carried a bedroll under his arm and a bulging backpack strapped behind him.

"Good morning," Karen said brightly. "Would you like some coffee?"

"Only if you have something to pour it in that I can take to go. Marcus and the crew up top already fed me."

"I believe I can find a to-go cup for you," said Karen, and she went to the cooking supplies stacked against the wall.

Mercury stood. "You've chosen to leave?"

He nodded. "I have." Then he shrugged. "Don't really understand why, but it seems I'm the only one."

"I know why," Stella said from where she stood, stirring the oatmeal that bubbled over the fire. "Everyone else is good with women leading. You aren't."

"I can't say you're not honest," said Keith. His gaze went to Hilary. "If I have my choice of the vehicles I'd like one of the Polarises. Might seem a weird pick, but they don't take much gas and they're good cross-country."

"That is absolutely fine. The keys are in it," said Hilary.

"We'll fill your tank and give you a full gas can," said Mercury. "Be careful in that Polaris. With no windows you won't be able to drive through the mist. We've noticed that it acts a lot like water and can lap against a vehicle like waves."

"We made it all the way from Timberline in two of those vehicles without an exposure. I'll be fine." Keith spoke bluntly. He turned his attention to Nathan, who was sitting beside Marge as they sipped coffee. "Nat, you and Marge are welcome to come with me."

Marge snorted a laugh. "Exchange this community and the safety of the cliff for a Polaris and no destination? No thank you."

"Actually, I was talking to your husband," said Keith.

Nathan laughed. "Dude, Marge and I are in agreement. We want to stay. The truth is this isn't the right place for you, but it is for us. Good luck, though. I hope you find somewhere that's a good fit."

Keith nodded sharply before he turned to Stella. "Yesterday you said something about Madras not being a good idea. Can you tell me why?"

"It's run by a woman," was all Stella said.

Keith nodded again. "Got it."

"Any idea where you're going?" asked Nathan.

"I'm thinking south, but I'll cut east of Madras. I've been camping at a place called Summit Lake in Northern California. It's far enough east that what happened to the coast shouldn't affect it and it's not near any major cities or military bases." He shrugged. "I remember seeing some cabins in the area. Think I'll find one of those and make a place for myself."

"Do you need any food supplies?" asked Stella.

"No, Imani gave me plenty of canned goods and even some seeds. My blood won't grow things, but maybe I can coax something to sprout. I would appreciate a hunting rifle and a fishing pole, if you can spare either."

"We can do that," said Mercury. "Gemma, would you get Keith a fishing pole and a couple hooks and some lures?"

"Sure!" Gemma headed outside the cave where they stored several poles and the fishing gear.

Mercury went quickly to the cache of weapons they hadn't moved clifftop yet. She got a .22 and a box of shells. "Do you know how to use this?" She asked Keith as she handed him the weapon and ammunition.

He made a derisive noise in the back of his throat, and then when Mercury continued to silently wait for a real answer he said, "Yeah. I'm a hunter."

"Here you go." Gemma gave Keith a fishing pole and a little plastic bag with some tackle.

Mercury eyed the bag, making sure Gemma hadn't been over enthusiastic in sharing with him, which she had not been.

Keith checked the .22 to be sure it wasn't loaded, engaged the safety, and then tucked it, the box of ammunition, and the fishing supplies in his bedroll.

Karen gave him a paper cup filled with coffee. "I wish you all the best," she said. "I shall add you to my prayers."

"Thank you, ma'am," said Keith as he hefted his bedroll and the fishing pole. He looked around the group. "I won't tell anyone where you are. I'm not like that. Just because I don't want to stay doesn't mean I'm holding a grudge against you or yours."

Mercury's smile was sardonic. "There's nothing for you to grudge about. Goodbye, Keith, and remember to cover your tracks when you reach the road."

"Will do." He waved and left the cave.

It wasn't long before they heard the Polaris and saw the trail of dust that caught in the wind and feathered behind him.

29

❦

"WHY ARE YOU going to that fucking little nowhere town again?"
Eva put a fist on her hip and tapped her stiletto boot against
the road. She and Al were standing in front of the hotel. It was not even
noon yet, but the day was already warm and so bright that Al couldn't
see her eyes through her mirrored sunglasses.

"You said you want more green bloods, right?" His voice was always
calm when he spoke to Eva, especially when she was pissed. That wasn't
because he attempted to soothe her or any such bullshit. She could act
like a screeching harpy for all he cared, but since his resurrection, Al
didn't worry about the crap that used to drive him crazy. Before, he had
to be sure everyone knew he was the man in charge. Now he *knew* he
could take charge any time he felt like it. He simply didn't feel like it. Yet.
And Eva was more pleasant to be around when she wasn't screeching.

"Yes, of course I want more green bloods," she said. "Their blood
lets us grow anything. Have you seen the banana tree grove in the park?
Do you know how much blood it takes for banana trees to thrive in
Oregon?"

"I'd guess quite a bit," said Al.

"Obviously, which is why I'm doubly annoyed that fucking Martina
and her green blood managed to slip away last night. I need more green
bloods, not less. But what the hell does that have to do with your obsession with Mitchell?"

"Remember those pain in the ass teachers we talked about before?" Al put his own shades on and took the keys to his favorite bike from his pocket as Eva nodded impatiently. "They're all green bloods."

Eva frowned. "One of them isn't—the fat, old one. Her blood was tested when they were here."

"I don't know that one, but I'm sure the two I do know are green bloods." *The bitch told me they were right before they killed me,* Al added to himself. He hadn't told Eva that part of his story. He may never tell her. "I know they've returned to Mitchell. I think they will again, and I have a score to settle with those two, so it's a win-win for us if I grab them."

"Fine, but I'd rather have them alive. I prefer multiple uses for them versus a single use," said Eva. "And after losing Martina, I've decided to set up a holding cell area for problematic green bloods so that I can keep using them without taking the chance they escape or talk enough shit to the other women to cause issues."

"Okay with me."

Eva whipped off her sunglasses and rolled her eyes. "Then take a fucking SUV. How the hell do you think you'll get at least two living women who do *not* want to come with you back here on a motorcycle?"

For a moment Al's temper flared, and it was all he could do to keep from slapping Eva so hard she fell off those stilettos she loved so much.

Then he drew a deep breath and thought of the cool darkness of shadows and the deep strength within the earth. He understood both, and Eva understood almost nothing. Yes, someday soon he was going to have to put her in her place, but not now. Not today.

He smiled. "The air conditioning will feel good. You're right. I'll take an SUV. Where will you be in a couple hours or so? I'll meet you."

"Actually, you and I are going in the same general direction today. I did a sweep a couple weeks ago or so north of Mitchell. More little nothing towns."

Al nodded. "You mean like Mayville, Fossil, and Condon—around there?"

"Yes."

"I know the area," he said.

"When I went through there before we got a decent haul of stuff from Condon, but the other towns had too much green mist for us to stop. There probably won't be any living people there and since the mist hung around so long, it's likely that the stores haven't been raided. So I'm going to take three of the SUVs. Wes's buddy Pete Davis, you know, the guy with the wonky eye?"

He nodded again. "Yeah. Ugly guy."

Eva curled her scarlet lips. "Definitely. But Wes said Pete was a big camper." She shuddered. "Such a disgusting hobby. Anyway, he knows all the back roads around that area. Says there're a bunch of campsites. I'm taking two SUVs to fill with what we find in the stores and a third to fill with any green bloods who are camping. I mean, they definitely need saving."

"Oh, for sure. Where do you want to meet?"

"South of Fossil, where highway 19 and 218 intersect in about three hours. That'll give you plenty of time to get to Mitchell, collect any teachers you might find, and then join me. I'll have already swept a bunch of those shitty little side roads for campers and anyone hiding out there. Then we can head into Fossil together," she said.

"Sounds good to me." He put the keys to the bike back into his pocket and went to gas up an SUV. Who knew? Today might be his lucky day—and a *very* unlucky day for a couple teachers.

"I really wish you'd let me go with you," said Gemma.

"Kid," Stella sighed. "I already told you that we'd take you with us in a heartbeat if you were a hundred percent, but you've healed three people in three days—Marge, Nathan, and Marcus."

Gemma's frown turned into a grin. "Even though Marcus didn't want to let me."

Stella mirrored her grin. "Even though."

"And you did a damn good job healing all three," said Mercury. "But it's taken a lot out of you. You're limping and acting like your ribs are sore."

"That'll go away," insisted Gemma.

"Yeah, and after it goes away you can definitely come on a supply run with us, but until then you need to stay in camp, rest, and recover," said Stella.

"But I've been going back and forth to the Painted Hills for clay, and that's been perfectly fine." Gemma's voice was unusually whiny.

"We stopped that yesterday when we noticed the limp and the dark circles under your eyes," said Mercury. They'd already explained all of this to Gemma twice, but Mercury got it. The mist had given Gemma an incredible gift, and that was beginning to set her apart from the group. Not their original group. It was the Timberline people who treated her as if she was more goddess than human—and Mercury understood how uncomfortable that kind of adoration could be. "Honey, this is going to be a super fast trip. Stella says we need the rafts, so we're grabbing the rafts, a few other random supplies, and then we're coming right back. We promise that next time we'll take you."

"As long as my gut doesn't tell me no," said Stella.

"Yes, that," agreed Mercury.

"Can I come next time too?" Georgie said as she rushed up to them. The little girl bounced on her toes in excitement. "I'd really, *really* like to go."

Stella smiled. "How about next time we make it a special girls' trip? There's a cute little shop in Mitchell I'll bet you two would like. It's where we found Karen's pretty skirt. We'll go there. Is it a deal?"

"Deal!" Georgie said enthusiastically.

"Deal," Gemma echoed with less enthusiasm.

"Okay, then, it's a date," said Mercury. "We'll see you guys real soon."

In the side mirror, Mercury watched the girls disappear. Georgie was already chasing after something that skittered across the hot ground, probably a lizard, but Gemma just stood there, staring at the departing truck.

"Gemma's pissed," said Mercury.

"She'll get over it," said Stella. "My gut is telling me very clearly that we need those rafts and the life jackets pronto, and common sense is telling me that Gemma needs to stay in camp until she's not limping and acting like she has broken ribs."

"Well, at least that should also mean neither of us is going to get hurt," said Mercury.

Stella's head cocked to the side and then she smiled. "Still no change in my gut. You and I are definitely going to be just fine today."

"Does your gut say we can get those rocking chairs?" Mercury asked hopefully.

"Well, as long as there's room, my gut says that's just fine." She glanced at her friend. "How are your dreams?"

Mercury sighed. "He hasn't been in them since the Timberline people showed up, but Stella, I swear I can feel him. Not while I'm just walking around, or schlepping stuff up the cliff or whatever. It's only when I'm daydreaming or at that place between awake and asleep. Then, even though he hasn't been in my dreams recently, I can tell he's still around."

Stella tapped the steering wheel contemplatively. "Maybe you should *accidentally* fall asleep again out by the creek around dusk."

"That's actually not a bad idea. Dusk is the cutoff for people coming and going from the clifftop and everyone down below should be inside by the fire eating dinner. If he's not coming to me because too many people are around, that would fix that problem."

"Just tell me when you're going to do it. I don't want you actually sleeping out there and chance getting caught in a bank of mist being blown around at night," said Stella. "I'll give you until it's dark and then come get you."

"Look for him when you come to wake me. I'd feel a lot better about it if you saw him too." Mercury turned to smile at Stella. "And now can we talk about Marcus? It feels like forever since we've been alone and I need details. Just how good a lover is the mountain?"

Stella's smile was wide and satisfied. "*Verrrry* good."

"You know I need way more details than that," said Mercury. "Get specific. *Verrrry* specific."

"You know I don't kiss and tell," Stella said with a wide grin.

"That is an outright lie. Spill. All. The. Tea."

"Well, since you insist. He is—" Stella's words broke off as she stopped the truck.

"What the hell?"

They'd come to where Bridge Creek Road fed into highway 26. Stella pointed off road to her left. The barren land dipped, and the low area was filled with an emerald river. Just above the river something metallic glinted in the bright morning sunlight. "Is that the roof of a Polaris?"

Mercury squinted. "Oh, hell, I think it is." She glanced around. "Do you see Keith?"

"Nope, not from here." She sighed. "The ground's pretty flat over there until that low spot. I think I can drive close enough to look *without* getting in the mist."

"Let's just get close enough to see if he's in the Polaris. If not, we'll know to look for him on the way to Mitchell." As Stella steered the truck off the road, Mercury added, "But no heroics. Keith chose to leave."

"Yeah, and he also chose to take the Polaris instead of a truck or that van, even after he was warned not to," said Stella.

The closer they got to the low spot, the more Mercury thought that it must be one of the many runoff streams that only held water during the rainy season. It hadn't rained for more than a week, so it was dry and Mercury could see why someone cutting cross-country might think it was a good idea to use it as a primitive road—especially if that someone was arrogant or foolish enough to believe he could either outrun or outsmart the mist.

They reached the area where the mist gathered and washed up the sides of the little gulley. The wind was lazy that morning, and the mist mirrored that, moving sluggishly. It reminded Mercury of taffy being pulled as it curled and swirled in long, mesmerizing cables of green. Stella drove parallel with it until they reached the roof of the Polaris. Gracefully, like slow-motion waves, the green lifted for a moment to expose the Polaris and what was left of Keith.

"Oh, shit." Stella turned the wheel and accelerated toward the road. "Nope, he didn't walk away from that."

"We'll need to come back and get the Polaris," said Mercury. "After a windy day." She glanced at Stella. "Did you know that was going to happen?"

"I knew it was a mistake for him to leave, but that it was the best thing for our community if he did, which is why I didn't try to talk him out of it," said Stella.

"I don't think anyone could have talked him out of it," said Mercury. "And I'm glad Marge and Nathan weren't with him."

"Ditto, Acorn."

It wasn't that Gemma didn't like the Timberline people. Actually, she liked them a lot. It was just that they looked at her in such a weird way. She didn't think that they were being all gossipy about her, but every time she joined a group of them working in the garden or making bricks, their easy, friendly talking stopped like she was a walking mute switch.

She didn't really blame them. It was crazy that she could heal people. Sure, Doc Hilary could too, but Hilary was an *actual* doctor, and she couldn't do all that Gemma could. She couldn't make bones come back together and bullet wounds heal and snake bites . . .

No. She was not going to think about him.

Gemma kicked a rock and sighed. She didn't want to go inside the cave and rest. And she *absolutely* didn't want to go to the clifftop where everyone except Karen and Janet were either working in the garden or making a gazillion adobe bricks.

The kids were fishing, as usual, with Karen and Janet watching them. Gemma sighed again. She was glad that it seemed that Karen and Janet were becoming best friends, but they were *so boring*.

She could take a book down to the creek and read, but her mind felt too restless. All of the bunnies and chickies had been moved to the clifftop, so she couldn't even feed or take care of them. Even Khaleesi, Badger, and Dandy were nowhere to be seen. She really wished she had a pet of her own.

Then an idea came to Gemma and she stopped shuffling her feet in the dirt outside the cave. They'd just moved the bunnies and chickies to the clifftop that day, and with Mercury off on a supply run there's no way anyone else would have carried all of the bags of feed up there for them.

Gemma hurried into the cave and went to the niche that held the animal food. Bingo! There were still bags of rabbit pellets, and shoved behind them were a couple big bags of something called Purina goat chow. Gemma grinned. She grabbed one of the plastic bags they'd hoarded and poured a bunch of the goat chow pellets into it.

"Whatcha doing?"

Gemma spun around. "Georgie! You scared the crap outta me!"

Georgie's face fell. "Sorry."

"That's okay, just make some noise next time."

Georgie scuffed her feet around and then repeated. "So, whatcha doing?"

"Nothing," said Gemma as she finished scooping the pellets into the bag.

"Yes, huh. You're doing *something*." The little girl studied her with bright, intelligent eyes. "And I want to do something too. I'm tired of fishing. Cayden and Hayden love it, but fish are real slimy and I don't love that."

Gemma considered her options. When Georgie got something in her head, she would not let it go. Plus, Georgie looked like she was as bored as Gemma. And anyway, they really weren't doing anything wrong. Mercury and Stella had said she couldn't go with them on a supply run—that she needed to rest. Well, she wasn't going on a supply run and she wasn't climbing up and down the cliff. She'd be driving and that was just sitting, which was also resting.

"Okay, I'll tell you what I'm doing and you can even come with me, but I want it to be a surprise for everyone, so I'm going to tell Karen and Janet a little white lie," Gemma fabricated quickly. It would be a cool surprise if she could pull it off, so the little white lie wouldn't matter at all.

"I can keep a secret," Georgie said, suddenly sounding a lot older than almost eleven. "Sometimes I keep secrets from the twins because I don't want them to be scared."

Gemma nodded. "Yeah, that's like what I'm doing today. I want to surprise everyone, but also I wouldn't want Karen or Janet to worry."

"That's smart. I can help you. So, what are we doing?"

"Hey, Karen!" Gemma called from the bank of the creek down to where Karen and Janet were sitting on a weather-whitened log with their bare feet just touching the water while the boys fished several yards upstream from them.

Karen turned, shielded her eyes, and smiled up at Gemma. "Honey, do you need something?"

"No, I just wanted you to know that I'm taking the Polaris and going to the hills for more clay. Georgie's coming with me. We won't be gone long."

"Okay, be careful. And you know if you see any green mist in the way—"

"I know," Gemma interrupted. "I'll turn around and come right back."

"That's right. See you two soon." Karen and Janet waved.

Beside her, Georgie waved back at them before skipping beside her to the Polaris. Gemma had already put the bag of goat chow in the back seat, so they climbed in. The little vehicle started easily and they headed out.

Gemma already felt better. She was doing something—something fun! Georgie was humming a song and pretending that her hand was flying as she held it out of the windowless Polaris.

They covered their tracks and turned left on Bear Creek Road, and then left again when they came to Bridge Creek Road.

"I remember seeing goats off this road a little way down here." Gemma told Georgie. "It was getting dark then, but I memorized the place because there were three trees that surrounded a big rock not far off the road. The goats were hanging out looking for grass and stuff."

Georgie sat up straighter and peered out of the Polaris. "Do you think we'll see them from the road?"

"Maybe not, but there are a bunch of dirt roads, really just big paths, that campers use. I know 'cause my mom and dad used to take me out here and our truck could cut across the country on the roads. Like that one up there. See it?"

Georgie nodded. "Yep! Are we gonna drive on it?"

"I'll wait and find one farther down this road. The goats weren't this close, and since I don't see any of them, there's no reason to go off the road yet, but keep on the lookout for three trees around a big, flat rock."

"Okie dokie."

Gemma drove on for about another half an hour and was just wondering if she'd really remembered correctly when Georgie pointed. "Look! Look! Is that it?"

Gemma grinned. "It is! Okay, now, be on the lookout for goats and I'll take us off road the next time I see a decent path." It wasn't long before she found a narrow dirt road that snaked off to her left. Carefully, Gemma turned the Polaris onto it and headed into the countryside.

It seemed she drove for a really long time, but she really wasn't that far from the road when Georgie squealed. "Goats! I see them!"

A rush of happiness flooded Gemma. She was going to be able to surprise Mercury and Stella and everyone! She stopped the Polaris a good distance from the goats, who had raised their heads to watch the vehicle.

"We don't want to scare them," said Gemma as she got out of the Polaris and took the bag of feed from the back seat.

"We'll be really quiet and calm," Georgie whispered from beside her.

"Yeah," Gemma spoke softly too. She just realized she hadn't brought any ropes or even leashes, but that didn't really matter. It would take forever to get back if she had to lead goats from the side of the Polaris. "Okay, this first visit all we're going to do is start getting them used to us. We'll get as close as we can, and then put out the food."

"But can we keep some in our hands just in case they come close enough that we can feed them?"

"That's a good idea. We can start taming them and then one day, really soon, I'll get one of the trucks and you and I can come out here with ropes and lead them to the bed of the truck. We can put them in the truck and then take them back to camp," said Gemma.

"Do you think we can lift them into the truck? We're not strong like Mercury, and they look big," said Georgie.

"We can't lift them, but they like to jump, so we'll just put the feed in the back of the truck," said Gemma.

Georgie grinned. "And they'll jump right in!"

"Yep, they will." They were pretty close to the goats by then—close enough to see that they were eating sage grass that grew under a line of junipers that dotted the edge of a deep ravine. Gemma grinned and whispered. "Hey, look at that drop-off. Goats are good climbers, but if we're slow and careful and don't scare them I'll bet we can get pretty close."

"That's a great idea," Georgie whispered. "They're gonna be tame as puppies by the time we bring the truck to get them."

"That's the idea." Slowly, Gemma and Georgie crept toward to cluster of goats. Every time they lifted their heads the two girls would pause until the goats relaxed and began to eat again.

They got closer and closer—so close that Gemma motioned to Georgie to take a handful of feed so that they could offer it to the goats. Every bit of Gemma's attention was focused on the animals. They were spread out along the edge of the ravine eating grass that grew in the shade under the junipers. She counted ten of them. Three were babies, and so, so cute! Two others had giant bellies that had to mean they were pregnant, and there was one boy goat with big, curved horns and a long beard who kinda scared her, but she thought he was a pretty brown and white color.

The ravine behind the goats was a lot steeper than it had looked from a distance, and Gemma was glad. The goats had moved along it a little, but they stayed under the trees and didn't really seem like they were trying to get away from the girls. Actually, they were pretty much ignoring them. Gemma and Georgie were approaching from the left. To the right of where the herd was grazing the land sloped up to a rocky hill that the goats could probably climb pretty easily, but it was bare, with no trees or wildflowers or even much sage grass, so the animals were reluctant to leave the ravine edge—which was fine with Gemma.

They finally got close enough that Gemma decided to pour out the feed. They were only a couple yards away from the little herd by then, and when the pellets rained from the bag, every goat lifted its head. Not in a scared way, but in a very curious goat way.

Gemma took Georgie's arm and moved back a few steps, whispering low, "Stay really still."

Georgie seemed to hold her breath as she nodded.

It didn't take long for one of the mommy goats, with a baby by her side, to trot to the pile of pellets, which started a goat stampede. Gemma had to suppress the urge to cheer as they jostled for the food. She looked at Georgie, who stared up at her with big, expectant eyes. She winked and pointed her chin at the goats. And then, with Georgie at her side, she walked very, *very* slowly toward the herd, hands with the feed cupped in them held out.

They came right up to them! The goats actually trotted to Gemma and Georgie. Their warm, wet lips and quick, licking tongues felt funny on her palm as they ate every morsel of food. Georgie giggled as a baby butted up to her. Gemma thought they were the cutest things she'd ever seen and had to stop herself from laughing happily when they let her pet them.

And then everything changed.

The goats heard them first. Their heads shot up and they took some nervous steps back. The girls followed. Gemma had no idea what was going on until the engine noise came to her. The herd sprinted away, up the rocky hill and out of sight, as three big black SUVs roared toward them.

CHAPTER

30

❧

"GOD, IT'S DISMAL out here," Eva muttered to herself as she stared at the dry, barren land around them. They'd been bumping around off road, sweeping back and forth across the land north of Mitchell and south of Fossil, basically burning time and, annoyingly, fuel, and not finding shit except some gun-toting white trash camping in the middle of nowhere. Eva had glimpsed a few women cowering behind the men holding the guns, and quickly decided they weren't worth the risk of getting shot.

"Wes, take the next thing that looks more like a road and let's head up to Fossil." If Al wasn't there yet, they'd go into the town without him. He could catch the hell up. She hated few things as much as when a man wasted her time, and his ridiculous obsession with Mitchell was definitely a waste of her time.

"Yes, ma'am," said Wes. "I remember a decent road that should be close. One of those with creek in its name. Did some camping around here too. It's not far from the Painted Hills and—"

"Wes, I do not care. Just find the damn road." She interrupted his boring drivel.

"Yes, ma'am," Wes said again. And that was all he said.

Eva smiled. He was so much more accommodating since her lovely swarm had killed what's-his-name in Sunriver. She should kill someone every once in a while in front of her men. Apparently, that was the key to keeping them in line.

Well, except for Al. He hadn't changed how he acted toward her at all. Not after she started growing her swarm within her and not after he watched her kill with them. He still entertained her with his ideas and he fucked her. She liked the way he fucked her. Her ruby lips turned up at the corners. She liked it, even though he refused to kiss her. Not that she blamed him.

Eva wondered, not for the first time, where his leeches went when they fucked. She'd expected to see them, which she'd had mixed feelings about. They didn't disgust her and she definitely wasn't afraid of them. She snorted a small laugh. His leeches were full of blood. Her swarm drank blood. If they got in her way, or out of line, the swarm would drain them to little black husks. But Eva hadn't had to drain them, or even see them attached to his skin, where she was sure they usually were. She'd seen him naked. Several times. And no leeches. *They must absorb into his skin—or maybe they enter him through* . . . She shuddered. That thought did disgust her.

"Ma'am, I see some goats up there by that ravine on our right," said Wes.

Thoughts of Al Rutland evaporated instantly as Eva sat up and looked out the window to their right. Sure enough, there was a nice-sized herd of goats clustered together under a line of trees by a ravine.

"We brought rope, correct?" Eva asked.

"We did," said Wes.

"Hum, you think you could catch a few, tie their legs, put down the back seats, and shove them in there? We'd only need a male and a couple females. They breed like rabbits. We can put them in one of the other SUVs, and the rest of us can go on to Fossil," said Eva.

"Yeah, they're not very big. And they're decent eating."

"Spare me the commentary. Let's just get them and move on," said Eva. Then something else caught her eye and she rolled down her window so the tint wouldn't interfere with her vision. "Well, well, well—there are two people out there with them. Good. We can use a couple goat herders. Let's grab them and bring them along as well." *I hope they're green bloods*, thought Eva.

As they got closer the goats took off, which annoyed the hell out of Eva, but they shouldn't be too difficult to round up. And her annoyance was tempered when she saw that the goat herders were, indeed, women—or rather girls.

Eva pulled up beside the girls. The other two SUVs parked behind her. "Let me handle this. We need to see if there are more people around here somewhere, but if I tell you to grab them—grab them."

"Yes, ma'am."

Eva put on her best smile and got out of the SUV. She made her way toward the girls over the hard-packed, rocky ground, glad she'd changed from her favorite stilettos to the cowboy boots she'd taken to wearing on her forays into the country.

"Well, hello there!" She beamed at the girls, who stood so close together that their arms touched. "We didn't expect to see anyone out here, especially not two lovely young ladies. Are both of you okay?"

"We're fine," said the teenager, the older of the two.

"Just feeding our goats," added the younger one.

Eva widened her eyes. "Oooh! They're yours? That's exciting. We could really use some goats in my town, and girls who know how to handle them. What are your names?"

"Georgie," said the young one.

The older one hesitated and then said, "Gemma. Who are you?"

"How foolish of me. I completely forgot to introduce myself. I'm Eva Cruz, mayor of a beautiful city called Madras. Do you know it?"

The teenager's face paled and little Georgie stepped closer to her. *They definitely know something*, thought Eva.

"Not really," said the teenager. "Well, we gotta get back home. Nice to meet you." The girl took Georgie's hand and backed away a few feet.

"Home? We can take you home. That's no problem," said Eva.

"That's okay. We left our Polaris a little way from here by the road." The teenager took a couple more nervous steps back.

"Hey, wait. We're out here looking for people. I've made Madras a sanctuary city. It's safe there. We have plenty of food and generators for electricity—we even have a festival every week with barbecues and dancing." Eva smiled as she spoke. "How about you show us where you live and we'll talk with your parents? I'll bet they'll be happy to hear about a place where they can be safe."

"No, thank you," said the teenager.

Eva's gaze flicked to Wes, and she nodded almost imperceptibly. He turned and said something too low for her to hear to Tate and Christopher, who'd gotten out of the other SUVs, and then the three men began to slowly spread out, cutting off the girls' retreat. With the ravine so close at their backs, and the men on either side of them, Eva felt confident enough to begin walking forward.

"I think we should let the adults in your home decide that. They might want to come to Madras," said Eva.

"No, they don't! They've already been there and know bad people—" the little girl began, but was cut off by the teenager.

"Look, we already said we don't want to go with you, so just leave us alone." She stepped back, taking Georgie with her.

Eva held her hands out innocently. "Hey, I'm only trying to help."

"We don't need your help," insisted the teenager.

Fucking teenagers. I didn't like them when I was a teenager, and now I remember why. Mouthy little assholes.

"I don't think you can speak for your parents," said Eva.

"I one hundred percent know they won't go with you," said Gemma. "So, seriously, just leave us alone." Then she whispered something to Georgie.

Eva sighed. "Fine. We'll do it the hard way." She glanced at Wes. "Put them in the SUV."

"Now!" Gemma shouted. She dropped Georgie's hand and the little girl sprinted to a large juniper that perched close to the edge of the ravine as the teenager took off in the opposite direction.

"Don't let that kid climb that tree!" Eva shouted at Wes, who ran after Georgie, who was already scrambling up the sticky, prickly tree.

"Come here, kid," said Wes. He reached up and yanked on Georgie's shirt, and the little girl lost her handhold, tumbling down.

"Leave her alone!" Gemma rushed at Wes. She'd picked up an arm-sized branch and hit him across the back with it.

"Ouch! Fuck!" Wes turned and tried to grab the branch from her, but the teenager danced backward as she held the branch like a baseball bat.

"Georgie, get up that tree," Gemma told the girl, though she didn't take her attention from Wes.

"Tate, grab the kid. Wes and Christopher, grab the teenager. She's a fucking *child*. How much damage can she do with a fucking stick?" Hands on her hips, Eva shook her head and silently bemoaned the fact that most men were absolutely useless.

Georgie climbed like a monkey and was almost out of reach when Tate snagged her ankle and jerked, causing her to scream and tumble to the ground, where she lay gasping for breath. He picked her up and carried her like she was a sack of grain as she kicked ineffectively and started to cry.

"Georgie!" Gemma shouted and tried to get past Wes and Christopher, but the men closed on her, easily ducking away from her swings.

They kept moving closer to her so that she had to back away from them. Her wild eyes darted to Georgie. Then Wes moved too fast for her and he grabbed the branch, twisting it from her hand. Christopher lunged forward, reaching for her arm, which had Gemma scrambling backward—to the lip of the ravine, where the loose, rocky ground gave way beneath her.

The girl's arms flailed as she tried to regain her balance. Both men rushed to grab her, and one even managed to take hold of her shirt, but it ripped as Gemma fell back into the ravine.

"Gemma!" the little girl screamed the name as Tate shoved her into an SUV.

Eva joined the two men. She shook her head. "Well, you two fucked that up." Carefully, she picked her way to the edge and looked down. The girl hadn't fallen all the way to the bottom, but was lying on a rocky outcrop about twenty or so feet below. Her arm was twisted in an awkward position. Her face was turned away from Eva, but she could see the pool of red that was expanding from under her head. Eva sighed. "She's either dead or will be soon enough. Let's not waste any more time. The damn goats are gone anyway. We need to get to Fossil."

Christopher asked. "Ma'am, want me and Tate to take the kid back to Madras?"

"It's Tate and me—and no. Why would you do that? She's one small girl. She's not going to take up enough room to be an issue," said Eva. When he just shuffled his feet, she sighed. "What?"

"She's going to cry and shit like that," he said.

"Do you know nothing about children?" Eva shook her head and answered her own question. "No, you don't. Come with me and I'll show you how to handle children."

Eva marched to the second black SUV. Georgie was inside the vehicle in the back seat; her cries and screams echoed around them as she pounded on the tightly closed window. Tate stood outside, the key fob in his hand. He'd locked the doors and looked like he'd rather enter a nest of snakes than the SUV.

Eva took the fob from him, unlocked and then opened the door. "Shut up," she told the kid, who looked up at her, red-faced but silent. "Listen up because I do not repeat myself. You're going to sit here, with your seat belt on and your mouth shut. You're not going to scream or whine. If you cry you will do so quietly. If you do not, Tate will stop the SUV and gag you so that you cannot make one damn sound. Do you understand?"

Shakily, Georgie nodded.

"Say it. Say I understand."

"I—I underst—stand," Georgie stammered through tears. Then she wiped a hand across her snotty face and asked, "Is Gemma dead?"

"Yes. Be good or you will end up like her. Put on your seat belt." Georgie did as she was told. "Excellent. You and I will get along just fine as long as you do what you're told." Then she closed the door and handed Tate the key fob. Her glacier blue gaze took in all three men. "*That* is how you deal with children. You only use threats that you'll follow through with, so if the kid does not shut up, gag her. Got it?"

The men nodded.

"Good, let's get to Fossil."

31

꙳

MERCURY AND STELLA loaded the rafts first and tucked all of the life jackets around them. Then they drove the short way to the furniture store and managed to cram five of the rocking chairs into the bed of the truck, as well as three little kid-sized rockers.

"Hey, when the cliff houses are done do you think we can come back and get some of these bed frames?" asked Mercury as she gazed wistfully at the rows of beds and comfy mattresses.

"I don't see why not. They'd have to be small, like the twin-sized ones, but that would be really nice," said Stella.

"Sleeping on a bed sounds incredibly good," said Mercury.

"You know what else sounds incredibly good? More wine." Stella looked at her friend. "I hate to say this, but after the addition of the Timberline folks, I think it is now reaching the desperate wine hour." Both women looked back down Main Street to where the pub sat—filled with dead people, dog feces, and wine.

"Well, shit," said Mercury.

"I know, right?"

"We knew this time would come, and I'm with you," said Mercury as they got in the truck and Stella retraced their path through the body and vehicle obstacles. "I've definitely done my part in depleting our wine. But they brought more wine from Timberline. My sore back muscles specifically remember carrying several cases to the clifftop."

"Yeah." Stella passed the pub and swung the truck around so that it was pointed out of town the way they'd come. "But add a bunch more wine drinkers and those bottles are going to go fast, especially while we're rocking up there on that clifftop watching the sunset."

Mercury smiled. "Sounds glorious, doesn't it?"

"It does. We could wait until we're closer to running out of wine and then come back to raid the pub, but do we really want to take the chance that someone else beats us to it?" Stella put the truck in neutral and raised her brow.

"No, hell no. We're here. Let's go in, grab all the bottles, and get out."

Stella nodded. "There are table busing tubs behind the bar."

"Good. Pile them full of the wine and I'll carry them to the truck. Are you ready?"

"Hell no, but yes," said Stella.

As usual for their forays into town, Stella left the truck running in neutral and engaged the emergency brake. Mercury grabbed a rock from the side of the road. "I'll prop the door open with this. That might help." Stella opened the door wide, Mercury stuck the rock in front of it, and they entered the dark pub.

Mercury gagged. "This is so disgusting."

"This helps." Stella pulled the collar of her T-shirt up so that it covered her nose. "And don't look at them. That helps too."

Mercury pulled her tee up over her nose, averted her eyes, and followed Stella behind the bar, where they emptied the bus tubs and started filling them with bottles of mediocre wine, as well as hard liquor and some excellent craft beer.

Mercury had carried four tubs of booze to the truck and managed to wedge them under and around the rocking chairs. She was hurrying up the stairs to tell Stella that she could only fit one more tub when Stella was suddenly in the doorway, clutching a half-filled tub in her arms.

"We gotta go. *Now*," she said, and thrust the tub at Mercury.

Mercury didn't spend time asking why or what for. She took the tub from Stella. Her friend raced around the truck and got behind the wheel. Mercury stowed the tub in the bed, secured the last tie down, closed the tailgate, and was jogging to the cab when the sound of an engine approaching could be heard over the truck's idling.

"Get in! Get in!" Stella shouted.

Mercury wrenched the door open and slid inside. Before she'd even closed the door, Stella floored the accelerator. The truck's tires squealed and bottles clinked as they raced up Main Street. Mercury swiveled around so she could stare out of the back window. She saw the big, black SUV, and knew when the driver saw them because the vehicle accelerated.

"Go faster!" Mercury said.

The truck fishtailed as Stella wrenched the wheel, steering around the stalled vehicles. They bumped and squished over bodies, and the truck slid and skidded as the SUV gained on them. The windows were tinted, so it was difficult to see inside, but Mercury caught a glimpse of the driver—a man whose only feature she could see clearly was his blond hair.

"There's a guy driving the SUV. He's gaining on us," Mercury panted.

"Fuck! Shit! This is as fast as I can go!"

They were out of downtown and Stella was able to floor it, but the shiny new SUV roared behind them, eating the ground between them. "He's going to fucking catch us!" Mercury quickly got into the glove box and pulled the .38 from the holster. Then she swiveled around again to stare at the black vehicle.

"It's bad," said Stella as she gripped the wheel and coaxed the old truck to go faster. "Mercury, if he catches us, shoot. Do not hesitate. Whoever is in that truck is dangerous."

"Got it." She wiped her sweaty palm on her jeans and gripped the weapon as she watched the vehicle draw closer and closer.

A figure, moving so fast that he blurred, raced from the barren land that flanked the highway. He ran straight at the SUV.

"Oh, shit!" Mercury cried as the man tucked his shoulder and rammed into the passenger's side of the moving vehicle. The SUV spun around in the center of the road like it was a dreidel, then it tipped, fell over on its side, and continued to spin.

The man stood off the side of the road. As the truck roared away from the wreck their eyes met. Mercury truly saw him—saw *all* of him. Then his body blurred with superhuman speed and from the place he'd stood a huge golden eagle lifted into the cerulean sky, arrowing to the northeast.

"What the fuck happened?" Stella kept her gaze on the road as, tires squealing, she steered around sinkholes and debris.

Mercury continued to stare and took several breaths as she tried to process what she'd seen.

"Mercury! What the fuck?"

She shook herself and turned back around in her seat. Mercury put away the .38 and cleared her throat as she faced Stella. "It was Ford."

"What!" Stella glanced in the rearview mirror again. "I don't see anything back there except the SUV on its side."

"That's because he's gone. He came from out there." Her shaking hand gestured at the land off the left side of the road. "Moving so fast I couldn't really see him, he rammed the side of the SUV."

"Rammed it? Like you mean with his body?"

"Yeah, with his shoulder. Like Superman would have." Mercury drew in a long breath and let it out slowly before she continued. "While the SUV was spinning he stood there—on the side of the road—looking right at me. It was him, Stella. I saw him clearly. He has horns and hooves and fur from his waist down. Then his face changed, like he'd heard something, and he took off. I know it's insane, but he turned into a golden eagle and flew into the sky."

"You're serious?"

"Absolutely."

"Holy fucking shit. Where is he now?" Stella kept glancing in her rearview mirror.

"I don't know. Before he left our eyes met. He smiled and kinda dipped his head."

"With horns," Stella said.

"Yeah, with horns. Like a goat's or ram's. He dipped his head and smiled, like he was saying *you're welcome*, and then his expression changed and he flew away."

"As an eagle."

"Yes. A very big eagle. That's what I saw." Mercury brushed back her hair. Her hands were still shaking, so she clasped them together in her lap. "He saved us."

"Again," said Stella. "Acorn, it's pretty obvious that Ford's a lot more than a ghost. You're going to have to figure out a way to tell him that he can come home. It's okay. We'll accept him."

"But will we? Will all of us? There are a lot more of us than just the core four and some kids now."

"Marcus would accept him."

"Yeah, but how about someone like Janet? Or Nathan? Or even Marge? The core four—we've seen things, experienced things the others haven't. The rest of the people aren't like us," said Mercury.

Stella was silent for a few minutes while Mercury's heartbeat slowed and her body stopped trembling. Then her friend said, "They're going to accept him."

"Is that a for sure feeling?"

Stella nodded slowly. "It's for sure. It's just not a right away feeling."

"What's that mean?"

"It means to give it time. When I focused on Ford returning to us, I got a very strong sense that it will happen in the right time and not to rush it. Meanwhile you need to see him and find out exactly what's happened to him." She glanced at Mercury. "Like, does he *want* to rejoin our camp? What's with the horns and hooves, and can he really turn into a bird?"

"He's also bigger than he used to be. And, um, more muscular," Mercury added softly.

"That sounds interesting. I approve of big men." Her lips quirked up.

"He's big, and not just because he now has hooves. He's, um, naked. Like I could see all of his chest and arms and . . ."

"And?" Stella's blonde brow went up.

Mercury smiled. "And he definitely has an eight pack."

"Nice," Stella said.

"And then there's that other question for him." Stella glanced at her and Mercury continued, "Like, why aren't you dead?"

32

F OSSIL WAS A bust. Mist haunted it like a gang of emerald ghosts had taken up permanent residence. Eva did manage to break into several houses on the edge of town. They took all the coffee, any booze, knives, tools, and siphoned gas from every vehicle they found, but the town itself was impossible—though Eva did contemplate driving herself in and taking a look around. But Al had said she needed to limit her exposure, and he was the only man she knew who had come out of the exposure alive and with some pretty impressive powers, so she heeded his warning. Instead, she and the three men pulled under some scrubby trees south of the town just off the highway, took out the lunch Amber had meticulously packed for them, which included an excellent bottle of white wine for Eva that was iced to perfection, and they ate while Eva gave Al time to get his ass there.

The kid was quiet. She wouldn't eat, but Eva didn't give a shit about that. As long as she wasn't whining or screaming, Eva was satisfied. Eva planned on seeing how much information she could get from the kid— like it had been obvious that at least the teenager was aware that Madras wasn't exactly as Eva presented it. How could that be? Eva sighed and poured a little more wine and nibbled at an excellent plate of cheese, fruit, and crackers. She'd interrogate the kid, but not until she was done with lunch.

Eva was just dabbing strawberry juice from her lips and returning the wine to the cooler when Al rejoined them. His SUV looked terrible and sounded worse. She hurried to him as he stopped it in the middle of the highway. The left passenger's door was dented badly, like something had T-boned it. The other side of the vehicle didn't look much better, and Al had one hell of a time wrenching the door open. When he climbed out she noticed the cut on the left side of his forehead. It had stopped bleeding, but his face was bruised and dried blood caked his hair and shirt.

Seeing him injured made Eva's stomach feel queasy, which surprised her. He amused her. He'd helped her find her powers, and he was a good fuck—but she hadn't realized she actually cared about him until that moment.

"Al! My god! What happened?" She touched the side of his head and he winced. Before he could even answer she called over her shoulder. "Wes, bring me the first aid kit." Then she turned back to Al and took his arm. "Come over to my SUV. It's shady there. I'll clean up that cut and I have wine."

He went with her. "Wine sounds good. And what happened is bizarre as hell."

Now Eva was doubly interested. If Al, the man who was perfectly fine with sentient leeches and her swarm of mosquitoes, called something bizarre it must *really* be wild.

He sat on the folding chair Eva hadn't yet put away. "Well, pour him a glass of wine," she told Wes after he'd handed her the first aid kit and then just stood there like the idiot he was.

Wes hastily poured the wine and gave it to Al, who began to tell the story as Eva cleaned the nasty cut on his face. When he got to the part about the guy with horns and hooves, Eva's hands stilled and she stepped back to study him, wondering if the knock on his head had scrambled his brain.

Al met her gaze and snorted a laugh. "Yes, I'm in my right mind. Not only did I see the guy, but I recognized him."

"I didn't know you knew a satyr," she said.

"I didn't know I knew one until today either." He glanced at Wes, Tate, and Christopher and told them, "Give us some privacy."

As always, they looked to Eva, who nodded and said, "Pull his SUV off the road and check it over. If it's too messed up we'll siphon the gas dry and leave it here."

When they'd walked away, Al continued. "I haven't told you how I came to be changed by the mist."

"No, you haven't."

He nodded at the bottle of wine. "It's probably best if you poured yourself a glass."

Her brows went up, but she filled her glass, sipped, and nodded for him to continue.

"I was exposed the day the bombs hit, but only a little. It gave me a nosebleed."

"After the mist, men with nosebleeds always die, it just takes them longer," said Eva between sips.

"Yeah, well, I didn't get a chance to test that theory. Something else killed me. That's also one of the reasons I am, as you put it, obsessed with those teachers. I went to Mitchell and found two of the teachers, Mercury and Stella, scavenging with a Mexican named Oxford. The wetback tried to double-cross me and I shot him, but before he died he'd pushed both of us into a bank of mist. And then that bitch, Mercury, shot me. I died in the mist. The next thing I knew I started to wake up. It didn't happen fast, but when I was finally *me* again I was alive, but changed."

"The leeches," said Eva.

"Yeah, and some other things. The way I can move in shadow and fade into the night. That kind of stuff," said Al.

"What does that have to do with today?"

"The women in the truck I was chasing were Mercury and Stella. And the man—the guy with the horns and hooves who ran into the SUV—that was the Mexican."

"Are you sure?"

"Positive. It shouldn't be a surprise. He and I died basically the same way, shot and then we sucked in the mist with our dying breaths. It changed us." Al took a long drink from the wineglass.

"That's fascinating. So you said this Mexican, who looks like a satyr, rammed your SUV?" Eva's gaze went to the damaged vehicle. Wes had pulled it off the highway and the three men were walking around it, surveying the damage, but Eva could clearly see a massive shoulder-shaped dent in the passenger's door.

"Yeah."

"Were you driving when it happened?" She shot the question at him.

He nodded. "Yeah, I was following the teachers' truck and gaining on them."

"Following them on the highway?"

He nodded again. "He came out of nowhere, so damn fast, and rammed me. The SUV spun, lost balance, and then tipped over on its side."

Eva's gaze returned to Al. "If it was tipped over, how did you get it up?"

He smiled. "The Mexican isn't the only one with extra strength." Then his smile faded. "But I don't think I can move like him. He was *fast*. I had to have been going almost eighty." A movement from the front of the SUV that was parked behind Eva's vehicle caught Al's eye. "Who the hell is that?"

Eva followed his gaze. The girl was sitting on the ground, tied to the front bumper of the SUV. There was a paper cup full of water and an uneaten sandwich on a dirty napkin beside her.

"Her name is Georgie. We found her and some other kid, a teenager, back there a ways." Eva gestured to the southwest. "They were with a herd of goats. Their people, whoever the hell they are, know something about me. We tried to grab both of them, but the teenager fell off the side of a ravine." She shrugged. "The damn goats bolted too."

"Know something about you, huh?" He paused. "Wait, was the teenager a girl?"

Eva nodded. "Yeah, her name was—"

"Gemma." Al spoke the word before she could.

"How do you know that?"

"Because she was with those fucking teachers the first time I met them. The second time I could tell that there were people packed into the back of their old truck, but they had a camper shell on and that bitch Mercury was shooting at me, so I didn't get a good look at her. I'm not surprised they collected some kids. All teachers are annoying bleeding hearts." He looked from Georgie back to Eva. "You don't like kids, do you?"

"If I liked kids that one would be over here playing house with me instead of tied up by the SUV. If I liked kids I could probably have coaxed her into talking to me, but I have zero patience for snot-nosed brats." She shrugged. "I should've left her out there to rot with the teenager."

"Oh, no no no. I'm very glad you didn't." Al downed the rest of his wine, stood, and went to the girl. Eva followed with her glass in hand. He crouched in front of the girl, whose face was still blotchy from crying. She was dirty, her hair was a tangled mess, and it smelled like she'd peed herself. Eva thought she was exceedingly unattractive, but Al's voice was charming when he spoke, and his smile actually looked genuine. "So, Eva tells me your name is Georgie. My name is Al." Eva saw something flash in the girl's eyes, but she didn't speak. Al continued. "I think we know some of the same people—Mercury and Stella."

The girl's eyes widened at their names. *Damn, he's right. Those fucking teachers definitely get around.*

"Are Mercury and Stella with your mommy and daddy?" Al asked.

"No," Georgie said. "Mommy and Daddy are dead." Her gaze flicked behind Al at Eva. "And she's a bad lady."

"Well, she's no lady, that's for sure, but that's not necessarily an insult," said Al with a laugh. "So, where are Mercury and Stella? We'll take you back to them."

The girl studied him. "I don't know how to get home from here."

"What if we drove back to where Eva found you? Could you find home if we did that?"

She shook her head quickly, defiantly. "No. I don't know how to get home. Gemma knew, not me." Her bottom lip quivered then, but she didn't cry.

"Are Stella and Mercury in a town? If you know the name of a town we can get you back to them," said Al.

The girl's eyes slid away and she nodded slowly. "Yeah, C—Condon." She stumbled over the name. "I think that's what it's called."

"How long have you been there?" Eva asked.

The girl's gaze lifted to Eva and narrowed with dislike. "A long time. We went there after we left your stupid town because you're stupid and hateful."

Eva's laugh was humorless. "Little girl, I could care less about your opinion of my town or me."

Georgie just stared at her.

"If you live in Condon, then why were you and Gemma out there by yourselves?" Al asked.

Georgie hesitated, obviously trying to figure out what she should or shouldn't say. Finally she answered in bursts of words, like they broke from her almost against her will. "We were taming the goats. It was supposed to be a surprise. We shouldn't have been all by ourselves."

"Thanks for talking with me, Georgie," said Al. "You should drink that water and eat something. It'll make you feel better."

"The only thing that will make me feel better is Gemma," said Georgie.

"Well, kid, tough luck with that. Your friend is dead." Al stood and motioned for Eva to follow him out of earshot of the girl.

"She's lying," said Eva. "I went to Condon a day or so after those teachers escaped from Madras. They definitely weren't there."

"Oh, she's not going to tell us where they are."

"Hey, I'm all for leaving her on the side of the road. That brat would cause me all sorts of headaches if I brought her back to Madras. Since she won't tell us where her people are, she's no good to us. We could do a quick experiment with her—find some mist and see how many times I can dunk her in it before she changes or dies or whatever. What do you think?" Eva asked.

"I think she's more valuable alive," said Al. "And she doesn't have to tell us where her people are. How did she and Gemma get to the goats?"

"The teenager said they had a Polaris, but I didn't see it, though I can't say I was looking."

Al nodded. "Yeah, their camp has to be close to the goat site. All we have to do is take her back to where you found her, let her *escape*, and then watch from a distance. She's either going to lead us to her people, or her people will find her."

Eva flashed her sexiest smile at him. "Well, well, you are full of good ideas, aren't you? I think it's fair to say that Mercury and Stella have probably collected a nice group of people—hopefully, all green bloods."

"You don't want their kind in Madras. You think that little girl would be trouble? Add a few liberal teachers and their kind. Fuck no. That would mess up your town," he said.

"Hum, you're probably right. Then why bother following the girl, or even taking her back where she was? Might as well leave her here."

"Remember the part about the Mexican pushing me into the mist and Mercury shooting me?" His blue eyes went dark sapphire as he spoke.

"Revenge. I get that." Eva nodded approvingly.

"I like to think of it as vengeance, but whatever. They killed me. They need to be killed. And I also need to figure out what the fuck is going on with that reborn Mexican."

"Puerto Rican," Eva corrected.

"What?"

"The man with them. The one who pushed you into the mist. I remember Amber telling me that he's Puerto Rican," said Eva.

Al shrugged. "Whatever. They all look the same."

Eva joined his laughter as she finished her glass of wine.

It was an easy decision to abandon the wrecked SUV. They quickly siphoned gas from it, then Al joined Eva and sipped more wine as Wes backtracked to the spot where they'd found Georgie. The girl rode in the other vehicle, with Tate and Christopher following in the third SUV.

"Here's what we're going to do," said Al as they left the road and bumped cross-country toward the ravine. "We're going to let her believe she escapes."

Eva raised a brow and opened the second bottle of chilled white wine. "Do tell."

"We'll pretend to go after the goats." He gestured to the little herd that had returned to graze along the ridge. "I'll tie her to the bumper again, loose enough so that she can get away. I'll play the good guy and whisper to her that she should run while I have you distracted."

"You think she's really going to go for that?" Eva asked.

Al laughed. "Of course she will. What is she, eight or nine? She's a child. Right now she's only thinking about going home."

"Good point. Should we leave Tate or Christopher to follow her?"

"No. I don't want them fucking this up. I'll do it. After the girl takes off, just leave me one of the SUVs. I'll trail her on foot until I know the general area they're camped in, and then I'll drive back to Madras. We can figure out together how to move forward from there."

Eva sipped her wine and then nodded. "That sounds reasonable. Just be careful. You don't want to be on foot out here after dark."

Al grinned. "Oh, the darkness isn't a problem for me."

Wes stopped the SUV close to the ridge, causing the goats to scatter. Christopher pulled up behind them and Al got out, meeting Tate as he was leading the girl by the rope tied around her hands to the front of the vehicle.

"I'll take her from here. Eva wants you and Tate to help Wes gather that herd," said Al.

Christopher's gaze went over Al's shoulder to Eva and at her nod he handed the rope to Al. "Here you go."

Al took the little girl around to the front of the SUV. He squatted down and looped the end of it loosely around the bumper. Georgie's gaze went to his. Al lifted a finger to his lips, soundlessly telling her to be quiet. Then he whispered. "I'll keep them busy chasing the goats and you run away as fast as you can. Got it?"

She nodded vigorously. Al smiled, stood, and headed back to Eva.

33

As Stella pulled the truck up to the campsite, Imani rushed out to them, cutting them off before they could park properly. She was holding a rifle and had a box of shells tucked under her arm. Mercury's gaze went to the place where they kept their vehicles. All of them were missing. "What the hell?"

"Bad. This is bad," said Stella.

Mercury opened the door and Imani spoke quickly. "It's Gemma and Georgie. They're gone. They took a Polaris. Gemma told Karen they were going to get more clay from the Painted Hills. That was right after you two left this morning. When they didn't come back, Karen came and got me. I went to the hills. They weren't there. People in both trucks and the van have been out looking for them for hours. There's no sign of them or the Polaris."

"Fuck," Mercury said.

"Have you just looked between here and the hills?" asked Stella.

Imani nodded. "Yeah, and beyond the parking area we usually go to, deeper into the hills. Still nothing."

Stella turned to Mercury. "You know something."

"What?" Mercury ran a hand through her hair. "I don't know shit. Gemma was supposed to stay here and rest!"

"No. Yes." Stella blew out a long breath and began again. "What I mean is you know something about Gemma the rest of us don't. Think,

Mercury. Gemma has talked to you about something that's a clue to where she and Georgie went."

Imani and Stella stared at her as Mercury went back over conversations she'd had with Gemma. *I said we'd take her and Georgie to Mitchell, but we were there, and they wouldn't follow us like that. Hell, even if they had we'd have seen them. No, it has to be something else. Something that's not the Painted Hills or in that direction, but something close . . .*

"That's it! Goats!" Mercury clapped her hands. "Gemma and I saw goats on our way back from Condon, remember? Not far from here, off that little dirt road that led to those campers with the guns. Gemma named it Gun People Lane."

"Oh no! They could've grabbed the girls," said Imani.

"Get in." Mercury scooted over and Imani jumped into the cab beside her and closed the door. "Stella, you know where I'm talking about?"

Stella nodded as she quickly turned the truck around and headed out. "Yeah, it's a gravel road just a few miles north off Bridge Creek Road."

The women braced themselves as Stella accelerated quickly. "I'm not stopping to cover our tracks," said Stella as they roared from the dirt onto the road. "We don't have time."

"It's that bad?" Imani asked.

Stella just nodded. Her grip on the wheel had turned her knuckles white. She shifted the truck into gear and floored it.

"I should've kept a closer eye on her. I knew she was struggling," said Imani.

"It's not your fault," said Mercury. "She asked us to take her with us and we said no."

"I didn't think she'd take off," said Stella. "I keep forgetting how young she is."

"She's gone through so much," said Imani as she wiped a tear from her cheek.

"We're going to find her," said Stella.

Mercury turned to look at her. "You know that?"

Stella nodded, but said nothing else.

"Shit," said Mercury.

"Is she dead?" Imani voice was brittle.

"No," said Stella.

But when she said nothing more, Mercury knew in her gut that no was really *no, not yet*.

Speed propelled them off Bridge Creek Road onto the gravel road Gemma appropriately called Gun People Lane. They threw up a contrail of dust behind them as Stella struggled to keep up speed and not lose control.

They'd driven a few miles when she began to slow.

"What's going on? Do you see something?" Mercury asked as she and Imani scanned the land around them.

"Not yet, but I feel something. Keep looking. To the left," Stella said.

"There!" Imani pointed ahead of them to the left of the gravel road.

Mercury followed her finger and shock zapped through her body as Stella left the road.

"Ohmygod," Imani gasped. "What is that? It has Gemma!"

He carried Gemma cradled in his arms like she was an infant. He was moving quickly, holding her tightly against him, obviously trying to keep her limp body from being jostled any more than necessary. When he saw them his head lifted and he slowed to a jog, changed direction so that he would meet them, and then he slowed to a walk.

Stella accelerated as Mercury spoke in a calm voice that didn't reflect the sea of emotions that flooded her. "Not an it. A he. Imani, that's Ford."

"What!" Imani's gaze snapped to her.

"It's okay," said Stella. "He's still one of the good guys."

"I don't understand," said Imani.

"We don't really understand either," said Mercury.

Stella slid to a stop a few yards from Ford. She put the truck in neutral and then got out. Mercury got out of the cab and without any hesitation walked to Ford. Stella followed with Imani, but more slowly.

Mercury tried to think of something to say as she approached him, but he was quicker.

"I think Gemma's shoulder is dislocated, but that's not the worst of it. She has a head wound. It's still bleeding. She was conscious only for a moment. She cried out for Georgie—said *run*. Is Georgie missing too?"

Ford's voice was almost exactly the same. A little deeper, but it still had that hint of his heritage in a soft accent. His eyes were also the same distinctive amber color—kind and unflinching as she stared at him.

"Yes, Georgie is missing too," said Stella from behind her. "Wasn't she with Gemma?"

"No. Gemma had fallen down a ravine. I scented Georgie, but could not find her trail. There were tracks from three large vehicles near where I found Gemma."

"Someone took her," Imani said. Then she cleared her throat and added. "Hello, Ford."

He dipped his head and said, "Hello, Imani."

Mercury dropped her gaze from Ford to Gemma. Her chalky face was blood-smeared and her hair was matted with fresh and dried blood. Her right shoulder looked wrong. Gemma's eyes were closed and her lashes were dusky against her pale skin. She was very, very still.

"Can you save her?" Mercury blurted.

Ford shook his head sadly. His long, dark hair moved around his bare shoulders. The ram's horns that curled back from above his temples were ebony and glistened in the afternoon sunlight. "I do not have that power, but the doctor with you does. She can save Gemma. Be sure she knows that."

He stepped forward and Mercury felt Imani move back, though Stella did not. Ford placed Gemma gently in Mercury's arms. She was shocked at how lifeless the teenager's body felt, and her stomach tightened with dread. She looked up at Ford.

"Will you come back to camp with us?"

The corners of his lips lifted in the hint of a smile. "Not today, Bellota." His gaze went from her to Stella. "Is that not right, Seer?"

Stella nodded. "That's right."

"We need to talk," said Mercury.

"Come to my grave. Tonight. After dark," he said.

"You—you know where we buried you?" The words came out before Mercury could think to stop them.

"I do. Thank you for the flowers. And the dance. Next time you will not dance alone."

Mercury felt heat rise in her face. "Can you find Georgie?"

"I will try," said Ford.

Then he turned and sprinted away, and as he reached the line of trees that flanked the ridge his body blurred and became a golden eagle that soared, arrow-like, into the sky.

"She needs a CAT scan. She needs a hospital." Doc Hilary spoke softly as she studied Gemma's head wound. "I know she is concussed. I know her brain's swelling. But that is all I know."

They'd made a pallet for Gemma near the central fire in the middle of the main cave room. It was late afternoon and still light outside, but they'd added candles and had flashlights ready in case Hilary needed the light. Ford had been right. Gemma's shoulder was dislocated—something that was easily fixed because Gemma had not regained consciousness.

As the hours passed and Gemma didn't stir at all, Doc Hilary had become more and more agitated, which was very apparent, as she was usually a bastion of serenity.

The cave was quiet. The only people there were Mercury, Stella, Karen, and Hilary. Gemma had healed Marge and Nathan well enough that they'd been able to climb the path, but at that moment they were part of the search and rescue squad out looking for Georgie in Timberline's van. Marcus and Badger were in his Jeep searching, as were Jenny and Tyler in one truck and Tamara, the young woman with the ability to sense the mist, and Imani in another. Karen prayed quietly as she kept strong tea brewed. Mercury paced and Stella watched Hilary. Khaleesi lay quietly out of the way, her muzzle resting on her paws. Curled beside the pitty was little Dandy, who gravitated to her when Imani was out of her sight.

"You can heal her."

From where Hilary knelt beside Gemma, she looked up at Stella. "I've tried. That's how I know it's a traumatic brain injury. I can't reach her mind. I can't heal it because of the physical injury." She wiped a hand across her brow. "Her brain is swelling and there is nothing I can do about that."

"But there is." Mercury joined Stella.

Hilary visibly deflated. "No. I don't have Gemma's powers. Mine have manifested differently."

"That doesn't mean you can't heal her," said Stella. "Do you believe that I have been gifted with knowing things?"

"I do," said Hilary.

"Then listen to me. Everything within me is telling me that you can heal her—that *only* you can heal her. If she'd been shot you probably couldn't, or if she'd broken her neck or had any other fatal injury except one that affects her brain you probably couldn't. But you've been gifted with the ability to heal minds—to soothe pain and anxiety, loss and hurt. You can do this."

Hilary clasped her hands together and studied Gemma. "I could if I was able to reach her, but that's the problem. I don't have the ability to reach an unconscious mind. I found that out when I lost the catatonic patients at Timberline. They retreated within and I could not find them."

"But it's different with Gemma because she wants to come back. She's only withdrawn because she's been hurt; she hasn't retreated on purpose," said Mercury.

Hilary continued to study Gemma. "No, she hasn't. In Gemma's case if there was some way the wound could be healed, just enough to allow her consciousness to resurface, then I could probably help her heal herself."

"I know you can do this," insisted Stella.

"Doc, if Stella says you can do it then I know you can," said Mercury.

"You have the ability," said Karen from across the campfire. "What I've learned from my own gift is that you must find the power and the confidence within to access it."

Hilary stared at Karen, and then her downcast expression lightened. Her gaze went to Mercury. "When we got here you told us to keep watch for the green mist by the creek. Could you go out and see if you can find any there now? The closer the better. Jostling her around is very bad."

"But—" Mercury began but Stella cut her off.

"Whatever Hilary says to do we should do."

"That's good enough for me." Mercury jogged out of the cave and down to the creek. That day the breeze was typical, which meant it blew regularly from the northwest, gently lifting her hair. She went to the bank and looked upstream to the right. She saw no mist. She turned her face into the breeze. The afternoon had shifted to evening and she had to shade her eyes from the sinking sun as she peered downstream. A veil of mist hovered, moving lazily with the breeze, several yards away. The dying rays of the sun gilded it so that it glistened chartreuse. "Gotcha!"

Mercury sprinted back to the cave. "The mist is over the creek not far downstream. It's drifting this way with the wind."

"I'll need your help and your trust," said Hilary.

"You have both," said Mercury.

"Carry Gemma as close to the path of the mist as possible. I'll take her from there."

"Gemma has already been exposed twice," said Karen. "We don't know what another exposure will do to her."

"I understand that," said Hilary. "But I can tell you for sure if something doesn't change, Gemma's brain will keep swelling. It's a major injury. If she wasn't so young and healthy, she would already be dead."

"What are her odds if we do nothing?" asked Mercury.

"I give her less than a ten percent chance of survival—and if she does survive she may very well be badly impaired," Hilary said. "I don't know if this helps, but Gemma won't go into that mist by herself. I'll be with her. As long as I'm conscious I'm going to concentrate on the mist washing the injury from her, and when I regain consciousness my first thoughts will be on Gemma—on reaching her and guiding her back so that she can heal."

Everyone looked at Stella. "It's a good plan."

Mercury lifted Gemma. She felt so slight in her arms that it made her stomach ache. Unconscious she looked much younger than sixteen. Treading carefully, she carried Gemma down to the bank of the creek, with Hilary walking beside them. Stella and Karen followed silently. Mercury turned left, into the northwest wind, and picked her way slowly along the rocky bank as she headed to the glowing blanket of mist that hovered near the surface of the water as the breeze blew it toward them.

"Stop here," Hilary said. Then she moved to the edge of the water in a spot where the bank was more sand and clay than rock. She took off her shoes and pulled up her long broom skirt, exposing her slim calves as she slid her feet into the creek. She lifted her arms. "Put her on my lap so that her back is to me and her head rests against my chest."

Mercury did so. They'd taken off Gemma's dirty, bloody clothes and put on one of the oversized T-shirts the teenager liked to wear to bed, so her legs and feet were already bare. They rested against the doc's, partially in the water. Gemma's head lolled back and Hilary shifted her position until her cheek was pressed against Gemma's bandaged temple. Then she looked up at the three women. "You can't stay here. The mist is coming. Wait out of the way. Don't come back until all of it is gone."

"You can do this," said Stella.

"We believe in you," said Mercury.

"I will pray that you find the strength you need," added Karen.

They didn't walk back along the bank the way they'd come. They didn't have time. The mist was too close. It flowed toward them like a second creek, with crests of diaphanous waves undulating in the wind. The women climbed to the highest part of the bank and turned in time to watch the tide of chartreuse engulf Gemma and Hilary.

Instantly the breeze died. Everything went still. Even the sound of the evening insects quieted. The only voice in the twilight was Karen's as she whispered a fervent prayer and rubbed her crucifix between her thumb and forefinger.

The mist did not move.

"I hate this," said Mercury. "Should I go down there? I could hold my breath and probably drag them back away from that stuff before I have to breathe in."

Stella put her hand on Mercury's shoulder. "Remember what he said. Hilary can do this. She's the only one who can."

Mercury nodded. They hadn't told the others about Ford. It had been a decision the three of them—Mercury, Stella, and Imani—had made. Everyone's focus needed to be on Gemma and Georgie. And Ford had agreed that it wasn't the right time for him to return to them. Yet. Mercury could not stop glancing at the western horizon. Twilight was a sapphire curtain closing on daylight. *Come to my grave. Tonight. After dark.* His words shivered through her mind.

"Look," Karen spoke softly as she pointed.

From the unmoving layer of floating green all along both sides of the bank wildflowers had begun to sprout. They spread below in brilliant shades of yellow and purple, red and white—like someone had thrown a handful of magickal glitter among the grasses.

Mercury's stomach roiled. "Oh, goddess! Is Gemma bleeding out?" She took several steps forward, peering down at the water. "Do you see any blood?" She turned impatiently to Stella. "I can't just stand here. I have to go down there and get them. I have to help."

"No. You have to let Hilary do what she needs to do. Stay here, Acorn," said Stella firmly.

Then the sound of crickets and frogs sang once again in the twilight. The breeze lifted Stella's thick blonde hair, blowing a curling strand across her face, and she smiled. "It's moving again."

Mercury turned to the creek to see that the mist was wafting with the renewed breeze. It swirled and eddied almost playfully. Together the three women hurried back along the bank, not descending yet as the mist was still too close below. As they came to the spot they'd left Gemma and Hilary the last tendrils of green were curling away. They paused only long enough for them to blow past and then the three women slid down the bank.

They lay together, half in, half out of the water. Even though her eyes were closed, Hilary's arms still held Gemma. Wildflowers carpeted the area around them. Hilary's skirt, the yellow of bright, new honeycomb, moved gracefully with the creek so that it appeared as if they were in the center of a huge flower whose petals were opening.

Mercury got to them first. She went to her knees, checking Hilary's throat for a pulse. It was there, strong and steady. When Mercury lifted her fingers to check Gemma, they shook. The teenager looked so pale, so young, so vulnerable. Mercury let go the breath she hadn't realized she'd been holding when she felt the warmth of Gemma's skin and the unfaltering beat of her heart.

Gemma's eyelids fluttered and opened at the same time Hilary drew a deep breath and coughed. Gemma's gaze found Mercury immediately.

"Georgie." Her voice was a croak. "They took her."

Stella and Karen crouched beside them, supporting Hilary's shoulders to help them sit.

"Carefully," Hilary said, her voice sounding normal. "Gemma shouldn't be moved too abruptly."

"Georgie." Gemma insisted.

Mercury nodded. "We know. We're out looking for her."

Gemma tried to get up, but groaned, and her hands went to her head.

"You were hurt badly," said Karen. "You have to be careful."

"Kid, you know we have the Georgie thing handled," said Stella. She touched Gemma's cheek. "We almost lost you."

"I'm so sorry," Gemma whispered.

"It's okay," said Stella. "Everything is going to be okay now."

"Mercury, please carry Gemma carefully back to the cave," said Hilary. Then she smiled up at Stella and Karen. "I'll follow if you two will help me. I'm feeling good, but shaky."

Mercury put one arm under Gemma's legs and the other behind her back, and easily lifted her, cradling her close. She was incredibly relieved to feel life back in the teenager's body, even though she was pale and grimaced with pain every time Mercury jostled her.

"I have to tell you something," Gemma spoke softly as Mercury slowly carried her along the bank, tracing the path of newly formed wildflowers.

"It can wait," said Mercury.

"No. It's about Ford. I—I don't know if I was delirious or what, but I really think I saw him. Actually, he saved me."

Mercury smiled down at her. "You weren't delirious."

Gemma's eyes widened. "Seriously?"

"Seriously, but only Stella and Imani know. He's out looking for Georgie right now, which is the only reason I'm not completely freaking out," said Mercury.

"Um, Mercury. I think I was delirious because, um, in my dream or whatever he had horns and from the waist down he was covered with fur. To his *hooves*."

"Again, you weren't delirious."

"Holy crap," said Gemma.

"Yeah."

"I see why you haven't told anyone else yet," whispered Gemma.

They came up over the bank at the fishing place near the cave to see that everyone except Imani and Tamara had returned, which was no surprise to Mercury. She'd warned them all to get back by dusk because the green mist was too easy to stumble into in the dark, but with Tamara's gift of knowing the location of the mist and Imani's connection with Georgie, Mercury expected the two of them to be gone all night. When the returning searchers saw Gemma, their somber expressions shifted to smiles. Badger trotted to Mercury and nosed Gemma gently. She grinned down at him and ruffled his ears.

Hilary shook off Karen and Stella's help. She hovered close by Gemma as she spoke with uncharacteristic sternness to the group. "Gemma needs quiet. I know you all care about her, and the best way for you to help is to allow her the peace she needs to heal."

Marcus nodded, his deep voice resonating around them. "We should all go up the path right now, before it gets too dark and is dangerous. Baby girl does not need us nosing around her tonight." He smiled at Gemma. "I'm glad you're back with us."

"Me too," said Gemma.

"With me, Badge," commanded Marcus and the big shepherd gave Gemma's hand a quick lick before he and the rest of the group followed Marcus to the path.

"No one found Georgie," said Gemma as Mercury gently placed her back on the pallet they'd made for her by the fire.

"They will," said Stella. Then her face broke into a wide grin and she repeated, "*They will!*"

"Praise Jesus," Karen murmured.

"Did you just get that feeling?" Mercury asked.

Stella nodded and wiped a hand across her brow. "Just now. I couldn't get an answer before and it was worrying the hell outta me, but I've got it now. She's coming home and she's okay."

Quietly, Gemma began to cry.

Hilary put her arms around the teenager. "Ssh, honey, ssh. All is well," she soothed.

Out of the slate-colored twilight four headlights beamed as two vehicles headed slowly toward them. Gemma tried to stand.

"No," said Hilary sharply. "You stay put."

"I'll get a bedroll for you to lean on if that's okay with the doctor," said Karen.

"Yes, she can sit or recline. No standing. I don't want her to exert herself in any way," said Hilary. "And she needs liquids." She turned her fierce gaze back to Gemma. "Do not get up. I'm going to my herb bag to choose what to brew for you."

Gemma lifted a shaky hand to the bandage wrapped around her head. "I'll be good. Promise."

Mercury couldn't wait. She headed outside and around to their parking area with Stella by her side. Tamara was driving the Polaris and Imani was behind the wheel of the truck. Mercury could just see the top of Georgie's head, pressed as close to Imani as possible. As soon as the truck stopped, Georgie burst out of the door and raced to Mercury, clutching her around her legs as she sobbed.

"Is Gemma dead?"

Mercury squatted down and wiped the little girl's face with the end of her shirt. The child was a mess—filthy, pale, and smelling of urine. "No, honey. She is not. Gemma is awake and going to be just fine."

"Oh, thank god," said Imani, who was hurrying up to them with Tamara.

Mercury stood and took Georgie's hand, but before she turned to go to the cave, the unsmiling expressions on Tamara and Imani's faces stopped her.

"What is it?"

"Eva Cruz and her goons grabbed Georgie and caused Gemma to fall over that ravine," said Imani. "And then they were joined by Al Rutland."

"What!" Stella gasped.

Georgie nodded vigorously. "He even told me his name, and he's the one who let me go. He kept that mean woman and the awful men busy while I ran away."

"Oh shit," said Stella.

"There's more," said Imani.

"And, apparently, it's not as crazy as it sounds," Tamara said.

"Oh, they're talking about Ford. Did you know he's kinda like a goat now?" Georgie asked Mercury in a matter-of-fact voice. "He has horns and everything. Like a big daddy goat."

"You saw Ford?" Mercury felt numb.

Georgie nodded again. "Yep. That's how Imani and Tamara found me. When I got away I ran as fast as I could all the way back to where Gemma and I left the Polaris." She paused. Her face fell and her little shoulders went up like a sparrow's wings as her chin tucked down. "We're really sorry. We were just trying to surprise you with the goats. And we fed them, *by our hands*." She spoke the last words as if she'd whispered *abracadabra* and made a flock of rabbits appear. Then she continued with a big grin. "So I got to the Polaris and was trying really hard to remember how Georgie turned it on and made it go. I was super scared 'cause I knew that bad woman and those men would be chasing me, but I couldn't figure it out, especially 'cause I couldn't really reach the pedals.

"And then Ford was there. At first I was kinda scared 'cause he's different and a lot bigger, but he called me *pequeña dama*, and he still has the same smile. He told me it'd be okay, that he'd never hurt me. Plus, his horns are really cool. He even let me touch them. And then he made the Polaris go and drove it straight to where Imani and Tamara were coming down the road. Now can I go see Gemma?"

"Yes, honey, but let's not tell anyone else about Ford, okay?" said Mercury.

Georgie nodded solemnly. "I won't because they might be scared and Ford really isn't scary at all."

Mercury smiled. "Exactly."

"I'll take you to see Georgie and then help you get cleaned up," said Tamara. "I think Mercury and Stella and Imani need a moment anyway." She gave them each a pointed look before taking Georgie's hand and heading to the cave.

"Ford saves the day again," said Stella. "And holy fucking shit, Al Rutland is alive."

Imani nodded. "Ford and I talked while Tamara was hiding in the truck totally freaked out and Georgie was trying to tell her it was okay. He said that Al followed Georgie. That he was watching us. It's why it took us so long to get Georgie back here."

"You didn't head straight back," Mercury said.

"No. We went quite a ways in the opposite direction. Ford said he'd try to distract Rutland, so we hoped he bought us enough time that he didn't see us circle back," said Imani.

"Doesn't matter," said Stella. "When he doesn't find us in the direction you went he'll start sweeping the area. Eventually he'll see something that'll bring him in this direction. There are too many of us to hide."

"Was he changed too?" asked Mercury.

Imani shook her head. "Not according to Georgie. She described him as a pretty man. I asked her a bunch of questions, specifically if he had horns and hooves like Ford. That made her laugh. She said no. As far as she could see he looked totally normal."

"Which means a lot better than when he died," said Stella. "He was skeletal and had that nasty bloody nose."

"Why the hell is he back?" Mercury spoke more to herself than her friends.

"He's the Destroyer. That's why he's back," said Imani.

34

&

MORE THAN ANYTHING, Al Rutland hated losing, so as he jogged through the twilight back to where the SUV waited for him, he seethed with anger. His friends knew it. They writhed against his skin as if seeking the enemy that had pissed him off.

"That fucking enemy can't be reached." He ground the words between his clenched teeth and glared up at the sky.

That Mexican. Al huffed and mentally corrected to Puerto Rican. "Whatever. They're all the same," he muttered. Not only did he have inhuman strength, horns, and hooves, but the bastard turned into a goddamned *eagle* and swooped and attacked and fucking forced him to cower under a bunch of sticky junipers until the woman had taken the kid and they were gone. The damn bird hadn't stopped dive-bombing him until the sun set. Being outside after dark didn't scare Al, though. He was powerful at night, attuned to its deep shadows. Al moved liquidly among them. His keen senses warned him when the mist was near and he easily circumvented it. He would have found the night enjoyable had the circumstances been different.

As it was, he hated every moment of it.

The SUV was where it was supposed to be. Al was glad that Eva hadn't waited, but returned to Madras with the men. It took an enormous amount of control for him to tolerate her shit, and that night he was definitely not in the mood. Were she there, sneering her disdain, he'd have to shake off the compliant façade he put on around her and shut her the fuck up.

His mood lifted slightly when he saw she'd left him the cooler and some wine floating in the melting ice, which he opened and drank straight from the bottle, draining half of it before he felt calm enough to head the SUV back to Madras.

The day had given him a lot to consider. From the seemingly innocent chats he'd had with the kid, he'd discovered a lot. The teachers had a settlement somewhere close. And despite her dirty, rumpled appearance, the kid had been in good shape, which meant they were doing well.

The kid was cocky, even though she'd been scared. Al didn't know a lot about children, but he knew people well enough to believe that the kid's cockiness meant she felt sure of herself, empowered as the woke idiots would say. The child wouldn't feel like that had she been with a group struggling to barely survive.

He hadn't recognized the two women who had found the kid and the wetback, though he remembered the idiot that had let that teenager kneecap him not long after the bombs hit, saying they'd added a colored woman to their group, and she'd been one of the two who had found the kid.

Al wondered how many people were in Mercury's group now—not because he was worried. There was no way those women would ever be as ruthless as he was. He only wondered out of curiosity. Hell, the more the better, especially if they were, as Eva called them, green bloods.

His only true concern was the man. He was strong and fast, Al knew that. And he had the ability to shape shift. Al snorted as he drove. It was something right out of one of those over-the-top fantasy series people used to like to binge.

What the hell had been his name? Al thought back. Oxford. That was it. Oxford, and then something else that was wetback like García or Díaz . . . that was it. Oxford Díaz.

Briefly he thought about Mexico and Puerto Rico and hoped the bombs had reduced them to rubble.

Díaz could prove problematic. He'd interfered with Al twice today. He was probably in charge of the teachers, but that really just meant he'd have to take Díaz out before the rest of them would fall.

Al's lips lifted in a fierce grin. Díaz might actually make his vengeance easier. Once he got rid of him—killed him for good in front of the women—they'd crumble.

What was the old adage? That vengeance was best served cold? Al didn't believe that. He believed at any temperature vengeance was tasty.

Mercury made her way quietly to Ford's grave. It was dark, so she took one of the lanterns they'd confiscated from the Mitchell general store with her. It was supposed to serve the dual purpose as light and mosquito repellant, so the flickering flame cast delicately moving shadows around her while it perfumed the air with citronella, evoking memories of warm Oklahoma evenings.

Ford wasn't there, so Mercury put the lantern down at the head of the grave mound that was still covered with flowers. Khaleesi had followed her, and the pitty was busy snuffling around the base of the junipers, looking for rabbits. Mercury was just beginning to think he wouldn't show—that maybe he was still distracting Al from finding them—when Khaleesi raised her head and stared out into the darkness beyond the lantern's reach. She growled low in her throat and her hackles lifted.

Shit! I should've thought about this. He must seem bizarre and threatening to Khaleesi. Mercury was moving toward the dog to take hold of her collar when Khaleesi's demeanor changed. Her ears pricked, hackles relaxed, and her tail began wagging so fast that it made her butt dance. Mercury turned and there he was, moving into the lamplight.

Her breath caught. He was Cernunnos, magnificent in the rawness of his masculine power. Tall and broad-shouldered, his dark, silver-streaked hair was long and sleek. From behind his temples thick ebony horns grew, curving back and tapering to points. They caught the light from the wind-dancing flame and glistened like jewels. His chest was bare and smooth, free of hair so that nothing hid the definition of his muscles.

Mercury's eyes traveled down to his waist, where his skin changed to a dark pelt that looked soft and thick. Before he'd worn nothing, but she saw that now he was wearing jeans that had been cut off like shorts midway down his thick thighs. Her gaze dropped all the way to his hooves. They were the same smooth ebony as his horns.

Khaleesi barked happily and trotted to him. Ford squatted and ruffled her ears, petting her as he smiled and murmured endearments. When he stood she lay by his hooves, occasionally sniffing them with doggy interest. His eyes found Mercury's. They were as they had been before he'd died, the color of amber resin, and they flashed in the dim light.

"Hello, Bellota." His deep voice made a caress of the words.

"Are you a satyr?" Mercury blurted and felt her face flame with heat.

He smiled. "I do not know. I've never met a satyr, have you?"

A small, semi-hysterical laugh slipped from her lips. She cleared her throat. "Um, no. Until now I didn't think they existed. Or at least not in this world."

His smile widened. "I believe *this* world is not the same as our old one."

"That's for fucking sure," she said.

He laughed. "What I can tell you is that in this form I feel more truly *me* than I have ever been—more comfortable within my skin than before." Ford paused and then added, "Have you thought about how it makes you feel?"

"It?" she asked.

"Your strength. Your ability to bring forth life with your blood."

Mercury opened her mouth to answer, but hesitated. She *hadn't* thought about it, not like that, and when she did, the realization was less of a surprise than she might have imagined. "I feel good. Whole. True to myself."

"Exactly," he said. "That is what I mean by feeling more authentic than ever before. It is good to see you, here, when you are fully awake."

"So you really did come to my dreams."

"Not exactly. I came to the place where you are between awake and asleep. It is there I visited you, held you, kissed you." His amber eyes captured hers. "Do you fear me, Bellota?"

"No," she answered quickly and then shook her head and repeated. "No."

He did not move toward her, but held open his arms. "Will you come to me, or is it too soon?"

She closed the distance between them and wrapped her arms around him as he welcomed her into his embrace. She pressed her cheek into his chest and breathed deeply of his scent—pine, sweat, and the earth. "I don't know how you're back, but I'm so glad you are."

He stroked her hair and kissed the top of her head. "I do not know how I came back either, but I do know why." She shifted in his arms enough so that she could look up at him. "I am here because the earth needs me. I am here because you and your new world order need me."

"Why is Rutland back too? The description that Georgie gave us indicated he hasn't changed. Well, except what she described was more like how he must have looked before the bombs."

"Balance and free will. The earth herself has changed, has awakened for the first time since the ancients lost their belief in her and the rest of the old gods. Do you remember when you led me through the mini Ostara ritual in Madras?"

She smiled. "I'll never forget it."

"Neither shall I. You said that the Lord of the Forest represents the positive masculinity of the woods, the very earth."

Mercury nodded. "Of course. It's part of my Pagan belief system."

"I am that positive representation, but if there is a positive there must be a negative for balance. Al Rutland is that negative, as is Eva Cruz—they chose their paths with free will. They embrace the negative and find power through it. Neither may readily show their changes to the world as do I, but believe me, Bellota, both have been drastically altered. They are vile people who can call to them things that lurk in shadow. My hope is that they do not realize the extent of their powers yet, but do not ever underestimate them."

Mercury shivered and his arms tightened around her. "They're going to come against us, aren't they?"

Ford nodded.

"What the hell should we do?"

"You could run, find a more distant place to live, but I can assure you that evil waits everywhere and the only thing that stops darkness—"

"Is light," she finished for him. "I don't want to run. We've already made a home here."

"The earth has, indeed, given you what you need to do more than just survive. Here you will thrive. I agree that you should not leave those gifts behind," he said.

"Then we prepare to fight to keep our home and our lives," said Mercury.

"You have already made a good start. The cliff dwellings will do much to keep you safe."

Mercury chewed her lip and nodded as she thought. Then she said, "We all need to move clifftop before they'll be ready, though."

"I agree. Especially as you have crops planted, shelter, and an excellent water source."

Her brows went up. "You know about all of that?"

He smiled. "I have been watching, Bellota."

A jolt of understand shocked through her. "The eagle! The one that circled us during the planting ritual. That was you."

"It was." His expression darkened. "I was also there when you carried out the sentence on the one who brutalized Gemma. Forgive me. I should have stopped him."

"I've been finding it hard to forgive myself for not watching him more closely. Stella knew from the beginning that he was bad news." She studied Ford. "What do you mean you should have stopped him? Were you there that night?"

"No!" he almost shouted, and then lowered his voice. "Had I been there he would not have hurt Gemma. I did not know then that I can be connected to others, and not just you. I didn't understand that until today."

"What do you mean?"

"I've been connected to you since I awakened. I can feel you. I know when you're happy or sad or frightened. I also can find you, though I don't know how far that ability extends. That's what happened today as you were leaving Mitchell. I felt your fear when the SUV began chasing you. I followed that fear and found you. It was as I was standing there, watching you depart, that I felt Gemma. I believe it was because I wished I could return to camp with you, and that led me to think about the others—Stella, Imani, Karen, Gemma, and the children. When I remembered Gemma my mind was filled with her fear, and then Georgie's fear also hit me—hers was mixed with panic."

"Then you followed the feeling and saved Gemma," said Mercury.

"I wish I could have saved Georgie her ordeal," he added.

"But had you saved her we might not have known about Rutland."

He nodded. "That is true. I hadn't looked at who was driving the SUV that chased you. I simply reacted to your fear and the danger you were in."

"So we need to prepare. Do you have any idea how long it'll be until they come for us?"

He shrugged his wide shoulders. "Rutland did not follow Imani back to camp. I made sure of that. But now he knows you cannot be far from where they left Georgie. He'll search and eventually find you."

"We'll work fast, but it'll take at least two days to get everything moved and enough shelters made up there to hold everyone," Mercury said. "Plus, Doc Hilary, the doctor from Timberline, says Gemma shouldn't climb that steep path for at least a couple days."

"She will heal. Our Gemma has gained more power from the mist," Ford said.

"Do you know how often we can expose ourselves to the mist before it will be bad for us?" Mercury asked.

Ford shook his head, causing his dark horns to gleam as they caught the flame. "That question is impossible to answer. The mist reveals and enhances what we are beneath the surface—our spirits, our consciousness, us at our most authentic with all else stripped away. Who is to say that it would be *bad* to have more and more of that revealed?"

"But eventually it kills. We've even seen it in women."

"Does it kill or does it just reveal life in a different form?"

"Before I knew you were real and had returned, I would have said it kills. Now I'm not so sure, but I am sure I'd rather not find out—or at least not right now." She rested her hands against his chest. "Will it change you more?"

"No. I am still male, so it is dangerous for me to enter the mist."

Mercury felt sick. "It would kill you?"

"Or change me even further so that, perhaps, neither of us would recognize me," he said softly.

"Then please avoid the mist."

"For you, Bellota, anything," he said.

She stared up into his eyes. With him so close she could feel his magick. It was like how she used to know a thunderstorm was rolling into Tulsa over the prairie—electric, powerful, familiar. He amazed her. "Can you shape shift into other things besides the eagle?"

He smiled. "I believe so, but I have not tried more than just that one form. The eagle serves me well." His hand lifted to caress her cheek. "When you see him you will know I am close, watching over you."

"I wish you could come back to camp with me."

"I want to be accepted by your people, and that will take time," he said. "For now I am happy you have accepted me."

Her hands moved up his chest to his shoulders. "I'll always accept you. I promise."

Ford bent and kissed her. It started soft—questioning—and as Mercury answered the question by pressing herself to him, molding her body to his, Ford deepened the kiss. Their tongues met. His taste was as intoxicating as his scent. His bare skin was hot and slick against her and Mercury wanted to pull off her shirt and kick out of her jeans so that there were no barriers between them.

But then she felt his insistent hardness against her stomach and an image of his cloven hooves and the fur pelt that covered him from his waist down flashed through her mind and her desire faltered. Not because she didn't want him. Not because she was afraid of him. Because of the strangeness of him. *What would his penis look like? What would it be like to be made love to by Pan? Or a satyr? Or Bacchus, the Roman god who was sometimes pictured goat-like from the waist down? Would he be too rough? Would she hate it? Love it? Be grossed out by it? Be obsessed with it?* Mercury's mind whirred with doubts and questions.

Slowly, gently, Ford's lips left hers. He smiled down at her. "You need time."

"I need time," she agreed.

"And you shall have it," he said. "I will be close, watching for Rutland. If you have need of me, call and I will know it."

"Will you meet me here again tomorrow night?"

He cupped her face in his hands and just before his lips touched hers in farewell he whispered, "I will, Bellota."

35

Their work began at dawn. Everyone was busy and Mercury decided that she was truly glad the Timberline people had joined her, and not just because she loved having Jenny back. It was nice to share the workload, which was divided up according to people's interests and talents. There was no whining or complaining. The entire group was of a single mind—make their home as safe as possible as quickly as possible and get ready to defend it.

One group of people, led by Tyler, who had a surprising amount of experience at fishing, blew up the three rafts and created a space by the creek to dock them along with the mound of life jackets they'd brought back from Mitchell.

Mercury carried the rocking chairs to the clifftop, which was absolutely worth the effort when the kids squealed in happiness over their special chairs, and the adults grinned and couldn't wait to take turns rocking and looking out at the horizon.

Jenny led the tending of the huge garden that teemed with life. All of the seeds took root and grew at a remarkable rate. Every plant that had been transplanted from the basement grow station at Timberline to the clifftop garden survived—including a dozen very healthy cannabis plants.

Astrid, the woman whose special power was baking, soon proved that she was generally excellent at all types of cooking. Marcus knew how to build something amazing called a Dakota fire hole, which was basically a way to bake things underground, and with the help of Jim and Nathan they dug three of them. Even with the stress of not knowing when Rutland, Eva, and their minions might show up, dinner started to be something the entire group looked forward to as Stella, Marcus, and Astrid put their heads together and created mouthwatering dishes.

By lunch that first day, Mercury decided that she had almost turned into a pack mule. She didn't mind, though. As she thought more and more about the conversation she'd had with Ford the night before, Mercury embraced her new strength. She was glad that she was able to climb the steep, narrow path much more quickly than anyone else, even when she was loaded with supplies. And she was usually loaded with supplies.

It was astounding how many things they'd already accumulated. Unlike the old world, they threw nothing away. Items as simple as a plastic grocery sack, a ripped T-shirt, or an empty tin of tuna were repurposed and carefully inventoried and stored.

Most of that first day, after the girls returned, was spent dividing up jobs. By dinner everyone was tired and hungry but satisfied. The adobe brickmaking went a lot faster with the extra people. Imani finished building a ladder with an actual rail so that climbing down from the clifftop to the site of the first adobe homes was a lot less frightening. That afternoon she began laying the first bricks.

Except for the .38 and two .22s, they'd moved all of the guns and ammunition to the clifftop. During the daylight, that bothered Mercury, and she considered bringing down more of the weapons, just until they could all move up top, but the truth was that of the few of them still in the original camp, only she and Stella were decently proficient with firearms. Mercury knew all too well that guns in the hands of those who hadn't been properly trained to use them were worse than useless—they were dangerous.

There was still not enough shelter on the clifftop for everyone. Hilary insisted Gemma rest at least one more day before Mercury would help her climb the steep trail, and then she'd be like Marcus before his leg was fully healed—she'd stay clifftop until Hilary released her for normal activities.

That night just Mercury, Stella, Gemma, Karen, and Janet remained below in the original camp. After the boisterous day, Mercury was glad that there were just a few of them. Karen and Janet went to bed shortly after dusk, leaving the three women sitting around the campfire.

"Are you going to go see Ford?" Gemma asked.

Mercury's brows raised, surprised at the question.

"What?" Gemma laughed. "You two are a thing—even with the horns and hooves."

"Yes, I'm going to meet him in just a little while. I wanted to finish my wine first," said Mercury.

Stella snorted. "Wanted or needed?"

"Both, I think," said Mercury. She looked at Gemma. "Hey, how are you feeling after your third exposure to the mist?"

"Good, but I discovered something this evening while I was down at the creek washing the rest of the dried blood and yuck from my hair." Her hand went to her head, where she fingered the healing wound carefully. She'd been able to go without the bandage because the wound had not just stopped bleeding, but was scabbed over.

"What'd you learn, kid?" Stella asked as she blew out a cloud of fragrant smoke and passed the joint to Mercury.

"My blood makes dead plants live again," she said.

"That is an excellent skill," said Stella.

"That's what I thought," said Gemma. "I'd gone out to where the creek is about up to my shoulders and was washing my hair. It turned the water around me kinda bloody and a dead branch floated by—real close. You know the current is pretty slow over to the right around the curve by Ford's grave."

Mercury and Stella nodded.

Gemma continued. "Well, the old branch floated around me before it drifted downstream, and when it went through my blood all of a sudden I saw green leaves sprouting on it. I thought maybe it hadn't really been dead. I mean, a potato isn't really dead when we sprout it. Seeds aren't dead, etcetera."

"Right," Mercury said.

"Then what?" Stella asked.

"I thought I'd test it out and see if maybe I can actually make dead things grow. So I stopped rinsing my hair and went to the bank. People have tromped a bunch of the plants around the banks we use a lot, and that's a good bathing place, so some of those flowers that grew along the bank after yesterday had gotten smushed. One was totally dead—like shriveled up. The flower didn't have any petals and the stem was wilted and brown. I took my wet hair and wrung it out on the flower and when the pink-ish water hit it, it popped up. The stem and leaves were green and there were new petals on it."

"That's amazing," said Mercury.

"Would you guys think it super weird if next time someone gets hurt I try a little bloody water on their wound?" Gemma asked hesitantly.

"I think it sounds logical," said Stella.

"Me too. We've been given our gifts for a reason," said Mercury. "We should be sure we understand them as best we can and use them for the good of others."

"Well put, Acorn," said Stella.

"And as soon as this Al thing is settled, we're going to go corral those goats," said Mercury.

"Seriously?" Gemma's face lit up.

"Seriously. Stella will make us cheese," said Mercury as she stood and returned the joint to her best friend. "I'm going to go see Ford."

"Hey, tell him I said thanks for rescuing me," said Gemma.

"I will."

"I'll wait up for you," said Stella.

"You don't need to," Mercury told her.

Stella lifted a blonde brow. "Are you kidding? I want *all* the details."

"What makes you think there will be any details to give?" Mercury asked.

"Do not question your seer," Stella said, intoning the words like she was part of an ancient Greek chorus.

Mercury took the lantern and went out into the night with Khaleesi at her side and Gemma's giggles fading on the cool evening breeze.

That night Ford was there before her. Khaleesi rushed ahead, with yips and wags, and his deep chuckle greeted Mercury when she caught up with the pitty. Ford was sitting on his grave, leaning his back against a cedar tree, petting the very exuberant Khaleesi. He looked up when her lantern light reached them and smiled.

"Hello, Bellota." His voice was as warm as his gaze on her.

"Hi." She sat beside him and he put his arm around her. Khaleesi licked his face one more time and then padded to the bottom of the carpet of flowers, circled three times, and curled up, her eyes already closing.

Ford bent and nuzzled Mercury's neck, gently kissing the sensitive skin there. As she shivered he said, "You smell like weed and wine."

She laughed a little breathlessly. "My two favorites."

His laughter was warm against her neck as he kissed her again before straightening and tucking her more securely beside him. "The camp has been busy today."

"Yeah, and there's still a lot more to do, but we do have most of the supplies lugged up the cliff and Imani has started to construct the first adobe house."

"That is exciting," he said with a smile.

"The bricks are beautiful," she told him. "I'm glad we took the time to get clay from the Painted Hills. Stella's helping Imani arrange the bricks so that they create mosaics. She says some will just be colorful patterns, but eventually she wants to make pictures, like of wildflowers and animals and even some images of the old goddesses and gods."

He nodded. "They will like that."

Mercury shifted so that she could look up at him. "Do you talk with them?"

"Talk isn't the right word, but I can feel them—their pleasure and displeasure." He met her gaze. "You can feel them too. You acknowledged them long before I did. They know you, Bellota, and you know them."

"Gaia," she said the name of her patron goddess softly.

"Yes, especially Gaia."

Mercury felt an incredible sense of joy build within her. Growing up in Oklahoma, the heart of the Bible belt and the intolerance bred there, it had been difficult to openly show her Pagan faith—especially when she was younger and less confident. She'd never been able to be open about it in her classroom. Religious freedom in the Oklahoma public school system had been a joke. If a teacher wasn't a conservative Christian, then that teacher either hid her beliefs or was admonished and even fired for them. So, to hear that her goddess, the one she'd loved and honored for decades and who she could now worship openly without fear of losing her job or being thought of as sinful or less than, *knew her* and had known her all this time made her bright with happiness.

"I did not mean to make you cry." Ford wiped away a tear that tracked down her cheek.

She sniffed and shook her head. "They're happy tears. They're tears of freedom and validation."

"I'm glad." Ford paused and then said, "Rutland searched for you today, though he did not get uncomfortably close."

Mercury sighed. "I hope we have a few more days until he finds us. Gemma still isn't a hundred percent and the temporary shelter clifftop needs to be expanded to fit the five of us."

"Work quickly. He will find you."

"Do you know what will happen?" Mercury asked quietly.

"I have no such powers, but Rutland will eventually find you. That is common sense. He's filled with anger and violence, and you, Stella, and your people have become his target."

"You think Eva Cruz will join him in coming after us?"

"As long as it serves her, yes, she will join Rutland in his attack on you, and I imagine she believes it will be a benefit to collect more women whose blood makes plants grow."

"Not to mention our weapons and food and the rest of our supplies." Mercury shivered again and Ford tightened his grip on her.

"But they will not come tonight. Tonight is for us," he said.

Mercury moved out of his arms long enough to turn and lean across his lap. She lifted her arms to his shoulders. "Then let's enjoy the time we have." She pulled him to her. She was the initiator, the aggressor, and Mercury kissed him with the heat of her desire that had been building all day.

He responded in kind, chasing her tongue with his and pulling her body to his. Mercury needed to get closer, to feel more of him, and she straddled him, exploring the width and strength of his shoulders and chest as their kisses deepened.

She felt his hardness against her core, and her need for him consumed her, chasing away the last of her trepidation. Mercury stood and stepped back, but only far enough so that he could watch as she pulled off her shirt. She wore nothing under it and his amber eyes devoured her. Then she kicked off her cowboy boots, unzipped and shimmied slowly, seductively out of her jeans before she stepped from the pool of her clothes to stand naked before him.

"I would worship your body if you allow it." His voice was husky.

"I will, but I want to see all of you too," Mercury said.

Ford stood, towering over her. With a single motion he took the clothes from his body, releasing the fullness of his lust. He stood very still while Mercury studied him. "One word—stop or no—and I will cease touching you. I will not be angry, my Bellota. I will understand and honor you and your wishes. Always."

The warm light of the lantern's flame suddenly blazed, as if it was a Beltane fire. Ford looked like he had stepped from the pages of mythology. He was the Green Man, Lord of the Forest, and Cernunnos all in one, but he was also Oxford Díaz, the man she had begun to love and who had been taken from her too soon. And now he was back, and she too was more than she had once been. They fitted together as perfectly as they did in their new world.

With no hesitation she went to him and wrapped her arms around his shoulders as she pressed her body to his. "I never want you to stop touching me."

And Ford didn't. He worshipped her and the night was filled with the music of their joining as if the earth herself rejoiced.

CHAPTER

36

Ironically, it was Díaz who led Al to find the teachers' camp. Al spent a good part of one day searching, taking side roads and cutting cross-country on his bike, all the while looking for signs, tracks, anything that would show that a campsite was near, and had been frustrated as hell when he didn't find anything. Yeah, they had to be fairly close to the ravine where they'd found the kids, but that didn't mean there wasn't a lot of area to search—and much of it was rough, filled with canyons and cliffs, ravines and plateaus, with many, *many* places a small group could hide.

Then he'd looked up, and when he saw it, realized what it meant, he kept glancing up.

The golden eagle gave them away. It circled one area all that day, and it wasn't tough for Rutland to put two and two together and figure out what he'd find at the center of that aerial circle.

Al was careful not to get too close. He didn't want Díaz to know he was on to them. Instead, he kept a surreptitious eye on the eagle, using it to narrow his search parameters. The bird didn't deviate. Whenever it took wing, which was frequently during that long day, it stayed in the same area—continually circling and watching.

Al knew the area well enough. He hadn't been a big camper, but he'd grown up on his family's hops farm in north central Oregon and had spent his teenage years exploring the land—mostly to find places for keg parties. He'd been a rural Oregon high school sports hero, excelling in everything from track to football, which meant he was a god at his school and had a nice-sized pack of followers. Back then he did some serious partying. Al smiled in remembrance. He was still a god, and one a lot more powerful than a high school jock.

He took those memories of exploring the country, and using his newly keen senses, figured that the eagle was circling a campsite somewhere in the heart of the Painted Hills and John Day Fossil Beds. They'd have to settle near a clean water source, and he remembered a couple creeks that flowed through that area, as well as the Painted Hills Reservoir. That was when he got out the map Eva had given him to help with his search. With a little more studying of the eagle and figuring, he ruled out the reservoir. That was too far to the north. There were two creeks that ran through the hills and the fossil beds, Bear Creek to the west and Bridge Creek to the east. Because the girls had been found to the east, he put his money on their settlement being somewhere off Bridge Creek.

With the area narrowed down to the creek, he knew he could easily find them, though he drove around aimlessly until dusk threatened before returning to Madras. Al wanted to lull Díaz and his group into believing he had no idea where they were.

It wasn't difficult to talk Eva into his plan. Al only needed a few men—Wes, Tate, and Christopher and their guns should be enough to take the women, especially after he got rid of Díaz. The men hadn't liked it. They were afraid to head out before it was fully light, but they were more afraid of what Eva would do to them if they refused. Al appreciated Eva's control over them; it was one of the reasons he didn't do away with her. He was used to leading men through intimidation and fear, and she did an excellent job of it. Al also knew that maintaining that level of control over others, especially men, was tedious. So why not let her shoulder that responsibility as he reaped the rewards?

Before the sun lightened the eastern horizon the next morning, Al drove the lead SUV north from Madras, followed by two more big, black vehicles. Wes drove one and Tate and Christopher caravanned behind them in the third. Eva had insisted they take three vehicles. At the very least she wanted the bodies of the green bloods brought to her for fertilizer, and she hoped that their camp would also have supplies Madras could use.

Al didn't give a shit about any of that. He wanted Díaz dead—permanently—and the women to know that they were at his mercy. If that meant he'd have to kill them too, he would, but Al was hoping he'd get to have some fun with them, or at least Mercury, before he had to do anything too permanent.

As the sky lightened from deep sapphire to a blush of pink and coral, they reached the creek and the bridge under which it flowed. Al parked and motioned for the men to wait for him as he walked to the bridge. From a distance it'd looked like the earthquakes had shaken a tree across the entrance to the bridge, but when he reached it, Al smiled. It'd been staged to keep people out. He knew the campsite wasn't to the southeast, so it had to be northwest and somewhere close enough to the creek that they felt the need to stop people from following the road.

Well, they wouldn't follow the road. They'd follow the creek.

He returned to the SUV, pulled off the road, and drove along the creek far enough to be out of sight from the road with the other two vehicles following. There he stashed the SUVs under junipers, not wanting their engine noise to warn the camp and also not wanting them to be easily spotted from the sky.

"We're going to leave the SUVs here," he told the three men. "Bring the guns. We'll follow the creek until we find them."

Wes looked nervously around them. The sun hadn't cleared the horizon yet, and everything was still cast in the murky, undersea dimness of predawn. "The mist likes to hang out around low creeks like this. Maybe we should wait until there's more light."

"You know how Eva has control over the swarm?" Al asked the question in a friendly voice.

Wes shrugged. "Yeah."

Al's voice hardened. "I have control of more than just a swarm. I can also see in the dark better than the three of you put together. Stay close to me and quiet and I won't let you stumble into the damn mist. Or would you rather I give you a demonstration of my *extra* abilities?"

"We'll follow," said Wes as Tate and Christopher nodded in quick jerks of their heads.

"Good. Don't speak." Al turned his back to them and began following the creek into the heart of the preserve.

Mercury didn't think even an apocalypse would ever change her dislike of mornings, and as she lay in her bedroll listening to the bright laughter and chatter of the twins, Georgie and Imani—who had come down from the cliff early to have breakfast with and then escort Gemma up top—she allowed herself to fantasize for a moment about the possibility that maybe one day when they were settled in their adobe homes, she could sleep in.

Khaleesi whined from her place curled beside Mercury. "Okay, yes, we can go see the kids and you can go clifftop and play with Badger." She sat, kissed the pitty on her nose, and pulled on her clothes and boots as the dog trotted ahead of her into the front of the cave.

Yawning and moving with less enthusiasm, Mercury followed. She looked around the campfire circle. Everyone was eating breakfast, and as her dad would've said, was bright-eyed and bushy-tailed.

"Mercury!" Cayden rushed to her and hugged her around her waist.

She ruffled his already standing-up hair and smiled. "Good morning, Cayden." Her grin included his twin, who was sitting beside Imani. At her feet little Dandy batted at Khaleesi's whiskers as the dog licked her. "Morning, Hayden and everyone."

"Did we wake you?" Stella, a dedicated morning person, asked with mock innocence.

"Coffee," said Mercury. "Please."

Stella laughed softly and handed her a steaming cup. "Already poured you some as soon as I saw Khaleesi."

"Thanks." She took a couple careful sips as she sat beside Stella. It was nice to just relax and listen to the kids' bubbly voices and take in the homey scent of cooking oatmeal. Khaleesi and Dandy started playing a game of tag, which had the children giggling because of how funny it was to see tiny Dandy chasing the pitty around the cave.

Mercury was tired, but so, so content. The night before with Ford still glittered with magick whenever she thought about it—and she thought about it a lot.

Stella leaned into her and said softly. "I haven't seen that smile on your face in a long time."

"I almost don't want to say it." Mercury kept her voice low. "But I'm happy."

Stella nodded. "Ditto, my friend."

"It feels like tempting the Fates to be so content."

"I think it's wise to snatch happiness whenever we can," Stella whispered. "If it's balance you're worried about, we already know there are bad guys looming. That'll tip the scales back to the *oh shit* level we're used to soon enough."

Her words reminded Mercury of what Ford had said about balance and free will, and she decided that was her cue to get busy. She handed Stella her empty coffee cup. "I'm going to use the facilities, brush my teeth, and then just let me have one more cup and I'll be ready to help Gemma up to the clifftop."

"Yea!" said Georgie from where she perched on the other side of Imani's log.

"No giant rush," said Gemma, who was sitting near Stella. "You can eat first."

"Janet and I added raisins and brown sugar to the oatmeal today," said Karen as she stirred the big pot that rested on a couple flat rocks that held it suspended over the glowing coals from the fire.

"That sounds great," said Mercury.

"Mercury! Mercury! Have you peed clifftop yet?" Cayden asked as he danced around her with joyful little boy energy.

"No, I don't think I have," she said.

"It's really awesome," said Georgie.

"Yeah, you can see *forever* from the potties up there," said Hayden as Cayden nodded his head in vigorous agreement.

"I'll look forward to it. Be right back."

Feeling less grumpy, Mercury visited the latrines and then went down to the creek to brush her teeth. Even though it was only midmorning, the sun was brilliant in a cloudless sky, already heating the high desert, and the breeze from the creek felt refreshingly cool. She looked downstream, noting the green mist that spread over the water and was being pushed sluggishly toward their area, though that was not unusual.

The mist followed a loose pattern. The wind was able to move it faster the hotter the days grew. It tended to cling to low spots, especially when night cooled the air, so it wasn't out of the ordinary for it to drift lazily past as it hugged the cooled air over the creek, or even to wash against the far side of the cliff, sometimes until almost noon and again after dusk. Their group knew to be on the lookout for it, and if they used the clifftop path early they watched for green. When they fished early everyone was on alert for it until the sun had heated the air enough to allow the wind to blow it easily away.

Mercury yawned and stretched and thought about how nice it would be to wake clifftop where the mist couldn't reach. She turned and began to meander to the cave, her mind again wandering back to the night before. She smiled. They'd made love twice. The first time they'd come together hot and fast and almost desperate. The second had been the opposite. It was Ford's tenderness the second time that remained with her. The passion had been great—heady and exciting—but it was his compassion and the intimacy it evoked that had truly moved her and lingered long after he'd said good night and disappeared into the darkness.

As if her thoughts had conjured him, the eagle dived and landed like a spear before her. There was a burst of light that blurred her sight, and then Ford was suddenly there, in the bright, midmorning sun, standing in front of her. She grinned and stepped toward him, but his urgent words had her body freezing and her stomach roiling.

"Rutland approaches. Three men come with him, up the creek from the road. They all have guns. They'll be here in minutes."

"Fuck! The kids are all down here—Georgie, Cayden, and Hayden."

"They can climb fast. Get them up the path. Now!"

"Stella and Imani can probably move quickly enough to go with them, but Karen's down here and so is Janet, another older woman who isn't good at climbing—plus Gemma. There's no way she'll be able to move fast enough." She glanced at the creek. "We have a plan B, though. Rafts are down at the creek, beached there and ready with life jackets. We can get away in them, but the green mist is over the water."

"I've seen the boats. I know where they are, and I can cut a path for you through the mist," said Ford. "Tell the kids to get clifftop with Stella and Imani. Everyone else needs to go to the rafts. Including you, Bellota, and bring a gun. I'll meet you at the creek."

Mercury didn't take time to reply. She sprinted to the cave.

Mercury rushed inside speaking urgently. "Rutland is coming with three armed men. Imani, Stella, take the kids. Get them clifftop. Now."

"But—" Stella began.

"No time," Mercury cut her off. "Go! Ford's going to help with the rest."

"Let's go!" Imani said, picking up Dandy and shooing the kids in front of her.

"Khaleesi, go with Stella," Mercury told the pitty as she rushed to the ledge where they kept the weapons and grabbed a loaded .22.

"Should we take guns?" Stella paused at the mouth of the cave long enough to ask.

"No, they'll slow you down. Just get clifftop. There are plenty of weapons up there. Ford and I won't let them follow you."

"I love you. Be safe," Stella said before she hurried after Imani and the kids.

Karen was standing by the fire, rubbing her crucifix between her thumb and forefinger. "Ford?" she asked in a shaky voice.

Mercury opened a box of shells and shoved a handful into her jeans pocket, and then she faced Karen, Janet, and Gemma. "We only have a few minutes, so I'm going to be fast. Karen, Ford's back, but he's changed."

Karen paled. "Back? From the dead?"

"Yes. And he's going to look scary to you, but please trust me. Trust him. He's not Satan. I give you my word."

"Satan?" Janet gasped.

"Mercury's telling you the truth. Ford carried me from that ravine. He also saved Georgie. But he looks different," said Gemma.

"Satan?" Janet repeated.

"He has horns and hooves," said Mercury. "But he's still him."

"Oh, Lord!" said Karen.

Mercury put a hand on Karen's shoulder. "You know the world is different than it used to be. You've already witnessed those differences and you've accepted them, especially the ones that have happened here." Gently, Mercury touched Karen's chest, just above her heart. "Do the same with Ford. Accept him. Let him help you—let him help us. The alternative is Al Rutland."

Karen swallowed hard. "No. Not Rutland." She took Janet's hand. "It's going to be okay."

"Let's go." Mercury led them from the cave, moving as fast as she could without hurting Gemma. The teenager's color was still off and she'd admitted the night before to episodes of dizziness and headaches, which Doc Hilary had said was perfectly normal and more evidence that she shouldn't exert herself.

Mercury glanced back at Gemma in time to see her misstep on a rock and sway like her balance was way off. Mercury moved to her quickly and wrapped an arm around the teenager's waist, partially carrying, partially guiding her the rest of the way to the spot on the creek bank where the rafts were beached.

Ford stood there. He'd punctured two of the three rafts and was standing near the third, life jackets in his arms.

"Oh, sweet Jesus!" Karen blurted.

He smiled. "Hello, Karen."

"No. I don't think I can do this," said Janet.

"I promise I will not harm you—any of you—ever," said Ford.

"I believe you." Gemma's voice was weak, but she smiled and said, "Hi there, Ford."

"Glad you're better," Ford said as Mercury guided Gemma to him. "Put this on. Fast." He handed the teenager and Mercury each a life jacket and then held the other two out for Karen and Janet.

Karen grasped Janet's hand and spoke firmly. "I know this man. We can trust him." And led her to Ford.

Both women stared wide-eyed at him, but took the life jackets and put them on as Ford dragged the raft from where it was beached out onto the creek.

"You first, Gemma." Mercury put the rifle down on one of the deflated boats and with her arm still firmly around Gemma's waist, waded out into the water while Ford held the raft stable.

"But there's mist upstream," said Gemma as Mercury lifted her into the raft.

"It'll be okay. I'll help with that," said Ford.

"Karen, Janet, come on." Mercury held her hand out for the two women. They shot Ford fearful looks, but took Mercury's hand and clambered awkwardly into the raft.

"Now you, Bellota," said Ford.

But before Mercury could get into the raft, Imani, Stella, and the kids rushed down the bank to them. Imani still carried Dandy and Khaleesi ran by Stella's side.

"Green mist on the trail. We can't get the boys past it, not even on our shoulders," said Stella. Then her gaze went to the two deflated rafts. "Oh, shit."

Mercury looked at Ford. "Can you really keep the mist away from us?"

"I can part it so that you may slip through," he said.

"Okay then. Here's the plan." As she spoke Mercury tossed life jackets to Stella and Imani. "Put these on." Then she hurriedly helped the twins and Georgie into their own jackets. "Kids, get in the raft."

Mercury carried Cayden on one hip and Hayden on the other out to the boat.

"Whoa!" Cayden said. "Ford has horns and stuff!"

"Hello, boys," said Ford with a quick smile.

"Cool!" said Hayden.

"That's all it will hold," said Ford, keeping the raft steady.

"I know. That's why the rest of us are going to swim beside it."

"I'm not a very strong swimmer," said Imani.

"That's what your life jacket is for, plus there's that rope that circles the raft and dangles down the sides. We can hold on to it and float with the raft," said Mercury. She grabbed the rifle. "Come on." Without waiting, she waded back to Ford and the little boat. Imani handed Georgie the kitten. "She's scared. Keep a tight hold on her."

Georgie nodded somberly. Then Stella moved to one side of the raft. Imani was on the opposite side. Mercury handed the rifle to Gemma, as well as the extra shells she took from her pocket. "You good with this?"

Gemma said, "You showed me how and I practiced. I can shoot it and I can hit things."

"Be careful. The safety is off." Then she stood with Ford at the end of the raft. "Now what?" she asked him.

"You, Stella, and Imani take hold of the rope. I'm going to push you, hard, to the center of the creek. When I let go the current will catch you and it'll take you toward the mist. I'll get there first and part it. Just keep going. When it's safe to return I'll find you."

"But you can't let the mist get near you," said Mercury.

"I won't. Go!"

"Khaleesi, come on!" Mercury said as she and the other two women sank down into the water and Ford began pushing the raft out into the deep center of the creek. Khaleesi was a strong swimmer, used to traversing the creek with Badger, and she paddled eagerly out to Mercury as Ford gave the raft an enormous push to the center of the creek. The current caught it and began carrying it downstream, closer and closer to the blanket of green that drifted toward them.

She didn't look back, but she heard Ford surging from the creek. Janet gasped and Georgie said, "Wow! Ford can run faster than Mercury now!"

The raft spun and suddenly Mercury was half swimming, half holding on to the rope alongside the front of it. She could see Ford race past them along the bank toward the mist. When he was almost at the green, he slid down the bank and dived into the creek, swimming powerfully until the midway point of the creek, where he stopped to tread water directly in the path of the raft.

Mercury's stomach heaved as the mist wafted ever closer to him—to them—and then Ford drew in a deep breath, so deep that even the mist responded, eddying toward him. With a sound like a dragon breathing fire, Ford loosed his breath, blowing into the mist.

The blanket of green parted, leaving a tunnel of clean air through its center.

"Whoa!" said the twins.

"So awesome," said Georgie.

Ford breathed in another huge breath and sent it out to the mist again, keeping the tunnel of clear air open.

The sound of a gunshot shattered the morning from behind them and Mercury heard a bullet splinter a cedar along the bank. She turned in the water to see Al Rutland standing by the deflated rafts, aiming his rifle at them.

Then a deafening shot cracked from the boat as Gemma fired back at him. Rutland ducked down behind a rock. They'd almost reached the tunnel through the mist. Ford drew in one last deep breath, blew, and then his head disappeared under the water as the raft floated over him and entered the tunnel.

They drifted through an oasis of clear air, but green surrounded them. Khaleesi paddled close beside Mercury, who told her what a good girl she was and encouraged the dog to stay near.

Another gunshot cracked and Gemma shot again, causing Rutland to take cover.

"Dandy! No!" Georgie cried and then she screamed as the kitten, panicked by the gunfire, clawed from her arms and jumped on the slick, round edge of the raft. She couldn't find a hold. With a pitiful cry, the kitten fell into the creek not far from where Imani clung to the little boat.

"Imani, don't—" Mercury called, but her friend didn't seem to hear her. She let go of her hold on the raft and began struggling toward where the kitten had surfaced and was meowing in panic, barely remaining afloat.

Imani reached the kitten, who scrambled onto the shoulder of her life jacket and clung there, digging in her little claws, shivering and meowing pitifully.

"Imani, the mist! Get back here!" Mercury shouted.

Imani glanced to the side. She had floated within a couple feet of the eddying green. Her dark eyes widened and she began stroking the water, kicking hard as she tried to catch the raft.

But the boat was fully caught by the current and moving ever quicker. As it sped through the cleared air, the tunnel began to lose shape and close behind it, covering Imani and the kitten like an emerald wave.

"Imani!" Georgie screamed.

"Ford!" Mercury couldn't see him, but he had to be near. "Help Imani!"

From the distance more gunshots reverberated, and Mercury realized they weren't coming just from behind them. They were coming from above them. Her people knew they were in trouble and were trying to help!

Abruptly the green that had been staining the sunlight chartreuse cleared and they were through the mist. The tunnel closed completely and the green continued to drift with the breeze as the raft pulled farther and farther away from it.

Where was Imani? She had to be unconscious! Had she drifted to the shore? Rutland could capture her. Where was Ford? Had he surfaced within the mist? *I should go back. I should help Imani.*

"Mercury Elizabeth Rhodes, you stay with this boat." Stella swam to the front of the raft. Still holding onto the rope, she looked across the rounded bow at her. "Trust Ford. He won't let Rutland get her."

Mercury nodded quickly, but kept staring behind them at the departing mist. Then Mercury glimpsed orange and Imani popped from the wafting wall of green. She was unconscious, but her head was held out of the water by her life jacket, to which little Dandy clung, crying plaintively.

"Imani!" The twins shouted through their tears.

She kept drifting toward them and Mercury realized Imani was moving *faster* than the current, as if something under the water was driving her forward. As she neared them, Mercury could see flashes of orange and scarlet just below the surface of the crystal creek. She blinked water from her eyes and stared. It was a salmon—the largest one she'd ever seen. *I didn't even know they got that big!* Its powerful tail whipped back and forth as it used its head like a battering ram and pushed Imani's limp form to them. From the raft Karen reached out and snagged her life jacket.

"Got her!" Karen said and then Janet plucked the kitten from her precarious perch and cradled her, holding the shivering baby close.

Mercury was still watching the huge salmon. It swam a tight circle around her, almost teasingly, and then headed to the shallow water closer to the bank. Through a flash of water-muted light, Ford surfaced where the mighty salmon had been, shaking his long, wet hair from his face. He stood to his waist in the creek and smiled victoriously at Mercury before he climbed the bank, crouched, and in an explosion of light a golden eagle took wing and speared the sky.

"Oh, my dear sweet Jesus!" The words burst from Karen.

"I have never!" Janet said.

Across the water Mercury and Stella shared a smile.

37

A L RAN. HE was glad for his preternatural speed, though he could've moved faster had it been night and he could slip from shadow to shadow. Still, he easily outdistanced Wes, Tate, and that idiot Christopher. Most importantly he outdistanced the green mist. He gritted his teeth with anger, baring them as if he could rip out his enemy's throat. Al fervently wished he could.

And perhaps eventually he would. Al was far from defeated.

Everything had started so well. They'd followed the creek and about midmorning he started to see signs that someone—actually, by the look of the bank a group of someones—had been frequenting the area. He'd ordered the three men to slow and stay behind him as he slipped forward, using scrub, cedar trees, and clumps of grasses as camouflage. He scented cooking food first, and then the women and children. He tasted the air several more times and his brows lifted. Yes, he could definitely pick out the odors of a dog and a cat. He remembered the pit bull that had been with the teachers in Mitchell and the kitten his little friends had been draining. Al smiled.

As they crept closer to the origins of the scents, they drew nearer to a large hill. The top was shaved in steep layers. He barely glanced up, though. The bottom of the cliff was all that interested him. It looked as if someone had carved a rough triangle at its base, splitting it open so that it was cave-like.

This is where you've been hiding! It was a good camp. They'd had to hike several hours from the road to find it. Al stopped and studied the area. There must be at least a dozen people plus the teachers and the kids, as the ground showed evidence of being trod on by many feet and there were so many scents he couldn't sift through them all. He could just see within the cave, where a fire flickered inside a well-built fire pit. Over the pit was a cooking tripod. Just outside the front of the cave there was a large, round grill and a neatly stacked pile of firewood. *This is almost too easy*, Al had thought. *Like shooting fish in a barrel.*

Then he'd realized that he saw not one person. He tested the air, glad it was blowing from the northwest to him. He could still smell them, but their scents had scattered, which was no big deal. He could track them easier than a bloodhound.

He turned to whisper to the men behind him. "They've left the cave. A few of them are going around the right side of the cliff. A few more are somewhere in front of us near the creek." He paused and sniffed again several times, not giving a shit that the men stared at him with expressions that ranged from shock to disgust. "The woman I want most is by the creek. Stay close. Watch the rocks along the bank. They're slick. Do not make any noise. When we get closer, you three head to the camp. I'll take care of the group at the creek."

He didn't wait for their nods, but moved forward along the bank, close to the water. He could hear them now. Not their words, but the timbre of their voices—urgent, scared. They knew he was there. Probably that fucking bird had told them, though he'd tried to stay under cover of the trees as much as possible.

Oh, well. The bird-goat-man wouldn't be around much longer anyway.

And then the wind changed. The second group, the one with the dog and—he paused and scented the air again—Stella, had joined the first group at the creek.

Al picked up the pace. He knew the men were lagging behind, but he didn't care. He had a rifle. He could take care of business until they caught up. He remembered the .38 that bitch had pulled on him. Twice. The second time she'd killed him with it. He slowed a little, careful to use the trees and scrub along the bank to remain hidden as much as possible, until he rounded a curve in the creek and there they were! They'd loaded into a raft and were floating down the middle of the creek, heading directly into a bank of green, but as Al watched, Díaz blew a hole in the fucking mist before he disappeared under the water!

Al would have to move, climb the bank, and get away from the creek before that shit reached him, but he needed to stop them. He'd just clip a couple of the women. They'd panic. He'd run around the mist and ambush them as they came out of it downstream.

He lifted his rifle and fired. He hadn't aimed for Mercury. He couldn't even tell which one she was; he'd just randomly shot at one of the two old women sitting like terrified hens in the rear of the raft.

He missed and cursed under his breath. He could almost hear his father's admonishing voice in his head: *A real man hunts—a real man is a better shot than you.* A gunshot cracked through the air and a bullet whizzed by him. Al shook off the past and ducked behind some cover.

He popped up quickly. The raft had entered the odd tunnel-like hole in the mist. He aimed to fire and as he did he saw that damn teenager, Gemma, pointing a rifle at him. He shot and ducked again in one movement, missing the raft and everyone on it.

Then the mist closed after the raft. He looked behind him as the men jogged up, panting. He gave their lazy asses no time to rest.

"Forget the camp. They're all with the raft. Follow me. We need to get around the green shit. Then shoot at the raft. We'll punch holes in it and fish them out of the water."

He sprinted up the bank and began running parallel to the creek when suddenly two more gunshots rang out, though they weren't coming from the creek. He ducked behind a tree and looked up. High above, from the edge of the cliff, he could just make out a line of people, rifles in hand, pointing down at them.

"What the fuck!"

"Now what?" Wes shouted from where he crouched behind a big rock.

"We run. Fast. Get around the mist and stay under the cover of the trees. They won't be able to get a clear shot," Al said.

"Good for you maybe," said Christopher. He'd tucked himself into a ball behind a whitened log.

"Yeah," said Tate. "We're not as fast as you are."

Al opened his mouth to tell the guy to grow a pair, but a strange sound from the creek drew his attention. He stared, incredulous, at the giant eagle that hovered over the creek, directly above the blanket of green. It beat its enormous wings down at the mist, and as it did so, the green was driven from the water. It no longer drifted lazily on the morning wind, but surged directly toward them, a tidal wave of death.

"I'm fucking outta here!" Wes broke first. He stood and sprinted back the way they'd come, with Christopher and Tate following close behind.

Al stood and sighted at the eagle, but a shot from above had him ducking again and another beat of the bird's wings flooded the bank with green. As it washed against his shoes he had no choice. Rutland turned and ran after the men, who he easily caught and passed.

He'd thought that they'd regroup out of sight of the cliff, but the fucking eagle was relentless. It followed them, beating the mist with its massive wings and keeping it at their heels. Christopher tripped and went down. He got up right away, but was limping.

"Wes, Tate, Al! Someone help me!"

Al didn't even glance back. He wasn't a fool. He heard Christopher's shriek and then a gurgle as the man became jelly.

"Better hurry the fuck up!" Al shouted. But it did no good. The eagle kept driving the mist at them. Only Al remained ahead of it. Only Al had the preternatural strength that allowed him to run for miles and miles, though after several miles he was well and truly fucking tired of the whole thing.

Ahead of him he saw that he was coming to a little stand of junipers that grew tightly grouped together. He darted to it, entered the stand, turned, and lifted his rifle. The eagle still hovered over the mist, fanning it with his great wings, driving it forward. Al barely had time to sight before he fired. He shouted victoriously as the bullet clipped the bird's wing.

Rutland didn't wait. He raced from the junipers, made it to an SUV, and sped away before the fucking bird could recover and come after him.

But Rutland didn't head south to Madras. No, he wasn't going to slink back to Eva with his tail between his legs and have to explain that he'd lost her three best men to a fucking bird. No. Al Rutland was far from defeated. Instead of backtracking he headed northwest to a little town named Pine Grove and a group of men who used to call him Boss Man.

38

M ERCURY DIDN'T KNOW how far they drifted, but eventually the sounds of gunfire either faded or stopped. Khaleesi hadn't been able to keep up with the raft, so Mercury encouraged her to go to shore, and the pitty padded along it after them, keeping the raft within sight.

"I think we can go to shore now," Stella said through chattering teeth.

"Good, I don't think I can stay out here much longer," said Mercury as she shivered. She glanced back at Imani, who had regained consciousness, but was silent and ashen and barely clung to the raft's rope.

There were paddles lashed to the inside of the raft, and the little boys did their best to move them out of the center of the creek and the swiftly moving current, while Mercury and Stella kicked and kicked. Finally, they were in shallow enough water to stand and they dragged the raft close enough to shore that everyone could get out, and then Mercury beached it.

Mercury, Stella, and Imani wanted to collapse, but Gemma wouldn't let them. "Hypothermia," she said. "You three keep moving. Walk along the bank. Strip off at least those wet shirts and lay them on big rocks that are in the full sun." She pulled off her T-shirt and handed it to Mercury so that she stood there in her sports bra. "Dry as well as you can with this."

Karen helped Imani peel off her sodden shirt and then took off her own cardigan and wrapped her in it.

"Are you okay?" Gemma went to Imani too, studying her closely.

Imani nodded. "I will be."

Georgie approached her hesitantly. "I'm really sorry."

Imani smiled and touched the little girl's cheek. "It wasn't your fault. Dandy was scared, that's all. And we're all okay now."

"Here, sweetheart." Janet handed the exhausted kitten to Georgie, who cradled her carefully in her arms. "I think she wants to sleep close to you."

Georgie perked up and sat on a log holding Dandy, with Khaleesi keeping watch.

By the time their clothes were dry and they'd stopped shivering, Mercury was seriously considering beginning the long walk back to camp, but before she could ask Stella what she thought, she saw the golden eagle approaching low in the sky. He was flying awkwardly. One wing looked strange, like he couldn't fully extend it. The huge bird landed clumsily not far from them. Light blazed, and while Khaleesi barked in happy greeting, Ford walked to them, clutching his bleeding right arm to his body as his hooves clattered on the rocky bank.

Mercury hurried to him. "You're hurt! Come over here and sit down."

"Rutland got away," he said as he sat heavily on a boulder. "It was my fault. I was too focused on driving the mist at him. I should have been paying more attention. He got a shot off." Ford looked down at the scarlet ridge that cut across the outside of his powerful bicep. It was weeping blood down his arm.

"That looks like it hurts," Stella said as she joined them.

Then Gemma pushed past Mercury and Stella to study his arm. "This needs stitches," she said.

He smiled at her. "It is not the first time you've had to sew me up."

"Well, this time I don't have anything with me to fix you," said Gemma. "And it'll take hours of walking to get back to camp. *Unless* you fly back ahead of us and have Doc Hilary fix you."

"I don't think I should fly anymore right now. The wound is worse in my eagle form, and I prefer Doc Gemma," said Ford with a slight smile. "It's really just a scratch."

"You don't want to get an infection," said Karen. She watched him with bright, curious eyes. "Antibiotics are going to be in short supply soon."

"I'll keep that in mind," said Ford. His gaze went to the woman who stood a little behind Karen. "I'm Oxford Díaz. My friends call me Ford."

"J—Janet. That's my name," she stuttered.

"It's nice to meet you," said Ford.

"Okay, here's what I'm going to do," said Gemma, who had been studying the wound. "I'll heal you enough so that you don't have to worry about infection, and if you suddenly have to fly it won't be so hard on you. Hold still. It'll only take a sec." She lifted her hands to press them over his wound, but Ford quickly stood and stepped away from her.

"No, Gemma. I will not take any energy from you, not after you have so recently been badly wounded. It's a scratch; I will be fine," he repeated.

Gemma put her hands on her hips, frowned at him, and opened her mouth to chastise him when Stella said, "Try your new thing. That doesn't take energy from you, correct?"

"Hey, I didn't even think of that! And you're right. That doesn't make me hurt or tired at all," said Gemma.

"What new thing?" asked Imani.

"Does anyone have a knife or anything sharp?" Gemma asked.

Hayden nodded and pulled a folding pocketknife from the pocket of his jeans. "Marcus told me that it's smart to always have a knife."

"Marcus is very wise," said Stella.

"Will someone please tell me what is going on?" Imani insisted.

Gemma smiled at her. "After my third time in the mist I found out that my blood can make dead plants come back to life."

"Cool!" said Cayden.

"Interesting," said Ford. "And now you'll bleed on me?"

Gemma chewed her lip for a moment before she answered. "Before, my blood was diluted with water and the water got on a dead plant, making it live again. So I'm thinking that maybe it'll also heal you. I'm not sure what to dilute it with, though."

"I think you should just let a few drops fall on his wound," said Mercury. "Yeah, it sounds gross and not even very sanitary, but weirder things have happened to us."

"Yeah," said Georgie. "Like Ford being a bird *and* a goat."

"Yes, exactly like that," said Ford with a grin.

Gemma went to the creek, washed the knife and her palm, then she returned to Ford. "Ready?" she asked him.

"Whenever you are," he said.

Gemma pressed the sharp little blade against the meaty part of her palm under her thumb and made a narrow cut. She wiped the blade on her jeans and returned it to Hayden and squeezed the wound until it was beaded with scarlet. Then she turned her palm over and let several drops of blood drip onto the long laceration. When she was done, she returned to the creek and washed her hand. By the time she returned to Ford, she'd stopped bleeding and her cut was healing.

"Let's wait a few minutes and see what'll happen," said Mercury.

"I don't mind resting for a little while," said Ford. "But it is safe to return and we need to start back soon. The walk will be long."

Then Cayden and Hayden were clambering around Ford. "Hey, Ford! Can I touch your horns?" Asked one of the twins. "Yeah, me too!" said the other.

Laughingly, Ford dipped his head and they giggled as they touched the curved ebony points.

"Ford?" Georgie said. "Did I say thank you for saving me?"

"You did, *niñita*."

"Did I?" Gemma asked softly. Carefully she hugged Ford from his uninjured side. "Thank you."

"We should all thank you," said Imani.

"There is no need. It is my great pleasure to protect you." He glanced down at the rifle that rested against another rock nearby. "Though you do a good job of taking care of yourselves." His kind face broke into a wide smile as his gaze moved to his arm. "You did it, Gemma!"

Gemma hurried to his wounded arm, which had stopped bleeding and, miraculously, begun to scab. She released a long sigh of relief. "That looks good. How's it feel?"

"Much improved." Ford stood. "I definitely feel well enough to walk back."

"The raft?" Stella asked.

"We can get it with the truck," said Mercury. "Let's go home." She took Ford's hand and they began walking along the bank. She looked up at him. "You said it's safe. Do you mean for good?"

From beside Mercury, Stella spoke up. "No. As long as Rutland is out there and knows where we are, we won't be safe." She looked around Mercury to Ford and added, "It's time for you to rejoin us now. Come home for good, Ford."

He squeezed Mercury's hand and nodded. "Yes."

"Yippee!" Behind them the kids cheered and Khaleesi barked.

It was evening by the time they reached camp. Jenny and Doc Hilary rushed out to greet them, but stopped abruptly when they saw Ford. Mercury stepped forward, still holding his hand.

"Jenny, Doc Hilary, this is Oxford Díaz, but his friends call him Ford. We met him just after we found the kids outside Madras. He was part of our group and then he was taken from us, and now he's back. It's a long story, but what's important is that he's one of the good guys." She looked up at him and met his eyes as she finished. "And I love him."

Marcus came out of the cave with Badger by his side. The big shepherd pricked his ears at Ford and then padded to him, tail wagging as Ford bent to pet him.

"Huh," said Marcus. "Whoever you are, if Badger says you're okay, then you're okay."

Ford smiled. "Call me Ford."

"Marcus." He held out his hand for Ford to shake.

Hilary was studying Ford closely. "Looks like you have a healing wound. I'd like to take a look at it, but we've moved all the medical supplies to the clifftop." Her gaze went to Mercury. "Actually, we've moved everything we could carry. We've set up another shelter. We didn't think it'd be a good idea for anyone to stay down here."

"You're right about that," said Mercury. "And Ford's wound was made by a bullet during the camp attack, but Gemma healed it."

Doc gave Gemma an appreciative look. "Well done. Are you okay?"

Gemma fidgeted. "Yeah. It didn't hurt me to heal him. I, um, have a new way of doing that."

Hilary's brows shot up. "I want to hear all about that."

"Is there anything else we need from down here?" Stella asked.

"There are a couple big SUVs parked by the bridge over the creek," said Ford.

Imani spoke up. "We don't need more vehicles. We should siphon the gas and then disable them."

Stella nodded. "Yeah, the day isn't far off when we'll be permanently out of gas." She glanced at the horizon. "It's almost dark. It feels to me like we can wait until morning to take care of that, though."

"Did those men get away?" asked Hilary.

"Their leader did," said Ford. "The mist took the other three."

Hilary's eyes widened. "The eagle. Did you have something to do with the eagle that was driving the mist at them?"

"Yes," said Ford.

"That's how he got shot," said Georgie.

"I think we'd all like to hear that story, but we should get up the path before it's any darker," said Hilary.

"Agreed." Mercury jerked her chin toward the cave opening behind them. "Do you need me to carry anything heavy up there with us?"

"It can wait," said Stella. "Rutland isn't coming back tonight or tomorrow."

"But he *is* coming back," said Ford.

As they headed to the path up to the top of the cliff, Imani drew Mercury to the side. "I'm going to follow you a little later."

"But it'll be dark soon." Mercury didn't like how quiet Imani had been, nor did she like how pallid she still looked.

"I won't have any trouble climbing the path after dark," said Imani.

"Are you really okay?"

Imani nodded slowly. "I am, but I'm also changed."

"Can you describe it?" asked Mercury.

"Let me go to the cedar. I think I can get answers there," she said.

"Would you like me to come with you? I'm pretty sure I can climb the path in the dark too."

Imani shook her head. "This is something I have to figure out myself."

Impulsively, Mercury hugged her as she said, "Remember that you're not alone in this. We've all been changed. We've all be uncomfortable with those changes. We're here for you. We love you."

"Thank you," Imani murmured before she headed away from the cave toward the ancient cedar who stood watch over the creek.

Mercury shouldn't have been surprised at how easily the group accepted Ford. As Stella reminded her, he just needed to be introduced at the right time, and the right time was that night. As soon as they understood that he was the eagle that had chased the bad guys away, he was bombarded with questions about what it feels like to fly, which he answered with seemingly endless patience and a sense of humor while Hilary examined his wound and declared it healing beautifully. And then Georgie mentioned that he'd also turned into a salmon, and that let loose another tide of questions.

Mercury sat contentedly beside Ford as the night lengthened. With the increased number of people on the clifftop and no need to try to hide their campfires, they'd created three more fire pits, around which logs and an occasional rocking chair had been situated. At first Mercury observed the people carefully. From her tenure of high school teaching she was well aware of the cliques that could spring up, weed-like, and choke out a healthy group dynamic. But it didn't take long for her to realize she had nothing to worry about. People flowed from campfire to campfire as conversations shifted. The children and pets had a great time moving from one group to another, talking, laughing, and basically being more carefree than they had been since the bombs hit. Every time someone added a log to one of the fires, sparks flitted into the sky like lightning bugs hovering over them and blessing them with tiny specks of magick. Even though the danger of Rutland was real and shadowed their future, Mercury was content. The people fitted well together, and she was so glad to have Ford beside her that she could pretend, at least for that one night, that everything would be okay.

Gradually, people called good nights, banked all the fires except the main one, and departed for their sleeping areas, most of which were just tents that backed to the jutting teeth-like rocks that created the small cave-like structure at the end of the flat clifftop area. There was a lot more wind on the top of the cliff, and the tarps and tents flapped continually in the breeze, but the fire was warm and they had all survived—and Mercury was filled with gratitude.

When Imani finally rejoined them, only Mercury, Ford, Stella, Marcus, and Karen were still awake. Badger and Khaleesi were curled together beside the fire with little Dandy sleeping on the shepherd's front paws. Just before Imani stepped within the circle of light made by the fire, Mercury had glanced at Karen, surprised that she was still with them as she usually excused herself not long after dusk. That night she'd remained, which Mercury had thought was because she was fascinated by Ford, but when Imani rejoined them the older woman stood and went to her with a glass of wine in hand.

"Come, you must be cold and tired. Sit with me by the fire. I saved you some dinner," said Karen, guiding Imani to one of the log chairs that circled the main campfire.

"I'll take the wine, but I'm not hungry," said Imani. She sat beside Karen and sipped the wine. The kitten had woken at the sound of her voice and trotted sleepily to her. Imani scooped her up so the baby could sleep in her lap. Then she cleared her throat. "Mercury, remember when you told me that you thought you used to feel the elm by your condo breathe?"

"Yes."

Imani met her gaze. "You were right. And trees don't just breathe. They feel. They watch. They love and grieve and experience joy. I know because Grandmother Cedar let me join her. Mercury, I went *within* her. It—it was like she absorbed me, though I also remained myself and apart from her." Imani's dark eyes implored Mercury to believe her. "They knew. The trees knew our old world was coming to an end—and not just the trees. They're all woven together, the trees, flowers, grasses—all the plants. And the animals too, especially the wild animals. Even the creek has a type of sentience. They *all* knew it was ending."

"I believe you," said Mercury.

"They are filled with spirit." Karen's voice was gentle, hesitant.

"Go on," Stella encouraged from where she sat beside Marcus not far from Mercury and Ford. "Say the rest of it."

Karen nodded. "I will try." Her forefinger and thumb found her crucifix. She rubbed it as she continued. "I've felt it more and more, especially after the planting ritual. It's a sense of acceptance, of watching and approval that I get from this." She pressed her palm to the ground.

"It frightened you at first," said Imani.

"Yes," Karen nodded. "Many of our changes frightened me." Her gaze went to Ford where he lounged with Mercury tucked under his arm. "Ford, you would have terrified me just a week ago."

"I am glad I no longer frighten you," he said.

"What changed?" Marcus asked Karen.

"A verse from Matthew refused to leave me. It echoed around and around in my mind, especially when I was overwhelmed or frightened. Jesus commanded us: *Thou shalt love thy neighbor as thyself.* It's a command that too many of my fellow Christians ignore; I was guilty of that once too.

"The verse wouldn't leave my mind, so I began to think that maybe my Lord was trying to tell me something—that He was speaking of loving more than just our human neighbors. It was then that I realized He could have also been referring to the world around us and that we should care for the earth and her plants and animals with kindness and compassion." Karen folded her hands on her lap. "The more I considered it, the more it made sense."

"And that allowed you to accept that there is more to our world than what normal eyes can see," said Stella.

"Exactly," said Karen.

"I'm glad it has helped you find peace," said Marcus. He and Stella sat so close their legs touched, and as he spoke she wove her fingers with his. Mercury thought the way Stella looked at him had decades of heartache fading from her face until her light shined bright with youthful expectation again.

"It is a great gift, the ability to reach the spirits that exist within our world," said Ford.

"Yes," said Karen. "It has made my life richer than I ever believed it could be."

Stella leaned forward. "Imani, there was more to what Grandmother Cedar showed you."

"There was, but I'm still processing it." Her brow furrowed and she shook her head slowly as she stroked the sleeping kitten. "I know it's me, that I'm not used to feeling connected to the world in this way. It's wonderful but overwhelming."

"That's completely understandable," said Mercury. "I just have super strength and that's taken some getting used to."

"But don't take too long to process," said Stella. "There's a battle coming and we need all the information we can glean to win it."

Imani released a long breath and smiled shakily. "So, no pressure."

"Oh, lots of pressure." Stella laughed. "But we believe in you."

"You'll figure it out," said Mercury.

"And we'll be right here with you when you need us," said Karen.

Imani nodded and wiped a tear from her cheek. "You're good apocalypse partners."

"The best!" Mercury lifted her wineglass.

"The best!" They all raised their glasses and joined her in the toast.

The star-filled sky above them glistened, jewel-like, as if the Goddess of Night had draped her headdress of stars over the clifftop as a sign that she looked down on them and smiled.

CHAPTER

39

❧

I T WAS MIDMORNING the day after the failed attack on the teachers when Rutland halted the caravan he'd led to Madras. The guards around the perimeter of the city had let him through and assured him the mayor was still at the hotel. Al thought how nice it would be if Eva rushed out and threw her arms around him in relief and welcome, but that was just a pipe dream. In reality, Eva did rush out of the hotel. She was beautiful as always, but unsmiling. Her heels tap-tapped on the broken asphalt of the circle drive as he got out of the big black SUV, motioning for the rest of his group to remain on their bikes or in their vehicles.

"Where in the hell have you been all night?" Eva glanced behind him and then shot another question at him. "And where are my vehicles and men?"

"Yes, I'm fine, thank you for asking," said Al sarcastically. "Forget the SUVs and the men—though the Expeditions are a bigger loss than Wes and Tate and Christopher." He gestured at the line of motorcycles and various other vehicles. "I've replaced them with better models—of men, not vehicles."

"I don't see the teachers," said Eva.

"No. They proved to be typically problematic," said Al. "But I have a solution for that." He glanced behind Eva as Amber came out of the hotel. "Have Amber find rooms for our new people while you and I talk."

Eva raised a perfect blonde brow. "How many new people?"

"Fifty-two men and ten women. All ten are green bloods who know to keep their mouths shut and do what they're told. They'll probably be a good influence on some of the women in this town." He nodded to the first of the vehicles behind him.

Al watched with open curiosity as Eva's gaze went to them. The windows were down and their tired faces could clearly be seen. They were etched with defeat. Their eyes were dull—their expressions blank. Some had bruises on their jaws or puffy black eyes.

"I recognize their type," said Eva.

"Type?" Al asked, intrigued. He'd wondered if Eva would feel pity for them. "What type are they?"

"Weak. Defeated. Powerless. They've given up, probably even before the bombs dropped." The only expression in her cold blue eyes was disdain. "They're as different from me as a spider from a moth caught in her web."

Al chuckled. "You never fail to say the most interesting, heartless things."

"Heartless? If that's what you want to call the truth." She gestured at the men watching them from the caravan. "So the women know how to act. What about the men? Do they also know how to keep their mouths shut and do as they're told?"

Al shrugged. "Depends on who's telling them what to do." He shouted over his shoulder at the man on the first motorcycle behind the SUV. "Hoyt, this is Amber." Al nodded at the redhead. "She'll show everyone where they can settle."

Amber didn't move until Eva nodded. "Go ahead. Take the men to the school. It's almost empty. Take the women to the green blood housing." Her gaze went to Al. "And you come with me."

Before he followed her he called back to Hoyt. "Unpack your crap, but keep your weapons locked and loaded. We have business to take care of."

"Today, Boss Man?" Hoyt asked.

"No. It's too late today, but soon. Just don't get too comfortable."

"Will do," he replied.

Eva shook her head. "You're not exaggerating at all?"

Al smirked. "Why would I do that? Come with me when we take out the teacher settlement. You'll see his horns and hooves and you'll probably also see him shift into an eagle—that is, if I really just nicked his wing. It pissed me off that I had to rush the shot, but now I'm glad about it. You'll be able to see for yourself."

Eva tapped the arm of the plush leather velvet chair in the sitting room off her bedroom suite. "It might be interesting for us to capture him without killing him. His powers could come in very handy."

"Díaz is not going to use his powers for us," said Al.

"Don't be so sure. Perhaps he just needs the right motivation. He's attached to those teachers. That was obvious when they were here. I heard that he seemed especially interested in one of them."

Al nodded. "Mercury."

"Well then, that's easy enough. We don't kill Mercury. We hold her as *motivation* for him to work for us," said Eva.

Al noticed Eva's more frequent use of the words *we* and *us* and decided everything was going according to plan. He might not have to kill Eva Cruz. He'd never wanted to. She was sexy, a whore in bed, and she ruled Madras with a well-manicured iron fist. She cared for the stupid minutiae of governing, about which he didn't give a shit. They made a good team—until they didn't, and when that happened, *if* that happened, he'd take care of her and assume full control of Madras. He'd have to keep Amber around, though, to deal with the minutiae.

"Are you listening to me?"

The razor edge of Eva's voice pulled his attention back to her. "Sorry. Just thinking."

"I said, when are we taking out the teachers?"

"Soon. Very soon," said Al.

"But how are you going to do that? They have that clifftop defense. The teachers are a pain in the ass, but they're not stupid. They will guard any routes up to them."

Al's smile was slow and knowing. "My new additions to Madras come with a surprise for those teachers and their supposedly impenetrable cliff. You'll see."

Then Al reached for her. She opened to him willingly. *I truly hope I don't have to kill you . . .* was his last coherent thought as lust usurped everything else.

Mercury stood, and in her best teacher voice, she projected over the hum of conversations as the group finished breakfast. "I'd like your attention, please."

They went silent.

"Thank you. You need to know that Rutland and his people are returning. They will want to draw us out and capture us or pick us off," said Mercury.

Jim Butler, who had been working closely with Imani on the adobe homes and had proven to be an excellent builder, waved his hand, and Stella nodded for him to speak. "Do you know why they won't leave us alone?"

Stella, who sat beside Mercury, stood. "We've had several run-ins with Al Rutland. He's mean." She glanced at Ford, who sat on Mercury's other side. He nodded slightly, giving her permission. "He killed Ford." Then she looked at Mercury. "Tell them the rest."

Mercury sighed. "Rutland killed Ford and then I killed him. But right before both of them died they breathed in the green mist."

"So do you think that means he can shift like Ford?" asked Marcus.

"I believe if he could he would have when I drove him from here with the green mist," said Ford. "But do not underestimate him. The mist changed him. Those changes are just less obvious than mine."

"It doesn't surprise me that his are hidden," said Stella. "He's a manipulator and a liar—a dangerous man who only cares about himself. It makes sense someone like that hides who he really is."

"And what we know from Georgie and Gemma is that he's joined forces with Eva Cruz, the mayor of Madras," continued Mercury.

Jenny spoke up from her seat beside Tyler, with whom Mercury noticed she spent *a lot* of time. "You told us before Keith left not to go to Madras, and we know that y'all didn't stay there. Why not?"

Karen stood and joined Mercury and Stella. "Eva Cruz is a monster. She pretends to be a good person, a good leader, and instead she traps people in Madras. If anyone causes problems, like insists they want to leave, she has them killed. I know. Mercury and I witnessed it."

"What we saw made us think Cruz is keeping those of us whose blood makes plants grow prisoner in her town," said Mercury.

"And that's what we can expect to happen if she captures any of us," said Stella.

"I can vouch for that as well," said Marcus. "Cruz's group came to Condon. They were slick as snails, talking about how Madras is a sanctuary city—a utopia. Almost everyone believed her and went with them." He shook his head. "I had an itchy feeling about them. The same feeling I get whenever I'm in danger. I didn't believe them, though they weren't overly interested in me. They wanted women and the women wanted to believe her, so they did."

Ford nodded. "That's what we saw while we were there. People want to believe her. They want to be safe. So they look the other way and ignore signs of her cruelty."

"We're not telling you this to scare you." Mercury looked around the group as she spoke, meeting gazes. Her voice carried, but she was calm, unhurried. "We're telling you so we can prepare and so you know what we're up against."

"Do we have any idea how many or what kind of weapons they have?" asked Marcus.

"We've seen that they have guns and plenty of gas and vehicles," said Mercury.

"And they don't mind hurting kids," said Gemma.

Janet raised a shaking hand and said, "But they can't get up here, correct?"

"Correct. They cannot," said Stella. "There is one way up and that's our single file only path. We can definitely stop them from getting clifftop."

"We have plenty of food and water up here," said Mercury. "We'll be okay." *A siege would be awful, though,* she thought as she studied the group. *How will our people react to armed men surrounding us indefinitely? And what's going to happen when we run out of ammunition? Are we going to throw rocks at them to keep them from getting up here?* No, she wouldn't think about that now. "It's important that we don't get lax about our defenses. We may not see them at first. It would be like Cruz to hide out and snatch us one at a time as we go down to the original camp."

"We should get everything we need today and not leave clifftop until this thing with Rutland and Cruz is settled," said Marcus.

"Agreed," said Mercury.

"How much time do you think we have before they attack full on?" asked Doc Hilary.

"Not long. Cruz might want to play a long game and, like Mercury said, lay traps for us, but Al Rutland is not the kind of man who takes failure well. He's driven by anger and greed. He's pissed at us and he's seen our camp. Besides capturing us, he'll want what we have—our supplies and even our settlement," said Stella.

"Also, he underestimated us before and only brought three men with him and limited firepower. He won't make that mistake again," said Mercury.

"What can we do to get ready?" asked Marge.

"You've already done most of it," said Mercury. "We have almost everything moved. We'll bring the rest of it up this morning. Ford saw that Rutland left two SUVs by the bridge. We'll siphon the gas from them this morning and disable them."

"We should bring all the gas cans up here," said Marcus. "I can make Molotov cocktails with them."

"Good," said Mercury. "While we're down there we'll take the keys and batteries out of our vehicles. They can replace the batteries and probably know how to hotwire them, but all of that takes time."

"Not to mention that we can move the vehicles to where anyone messing with them will be seen, and shot, from up here," added Marcus.

From the corner of her vision Mercury noticed that Imani flinched at Marcus's statement. She smiled reassurance to her friend, but she looked quickly away.

Stella was saying, "And then we wait. Safely. Patiently. And continue to build our adobe homes in the sky."

"I have a suggestion," said Marcus.

"Go for it," said Stella with a warm smile.

"What do you think about moving around some of the large rocks up here to the edge of the cliff to use as barriers against gunfire? I couldn't see what kind of weapons they had, but assault weapons would be bad for us."

"They carried hunting rifles," said Ford. "I can retrieve three of them from their bodies."

Marcus nodded. "If they have scopes for those rifles and someone who is prior service—"

"Like you?" Stella said.

"Like me." Marcus's teeth flashed. "If they have anyone who is experienced with firearms enough to be decent shots and they have scopes, we'd be in serious danger of being shot."

"Oh, Lord!" Karen gasped. "I—I'd assumed we were completely safe up here."

"We'll make it as safe as possible," said Marcus.

"Let's all be aware. If we spot strangers we stay under cover," said Mercury. Her gaze found Imani again, who sat silently beside Karen. "Let's continue to make bricks, but I don't think it's wise for you to work out there on the cliffside for a while." She nodded toward the edge of the cliff.

"That makes sense. And it'll be nice to get ahead in the brickmaking," said Imani.

Mercury thought her friend looked less pale today, but she was still unusually quiet. She made a mental note to seek her out later and ask what was wrong. "After we get everything up here and the vehicles taken care of, Marcus and I will give everyone refreshers on how to handle the guns."

Marcus nodded. "That's wise. Also, we should place weapons and ammo behind the rock barricades. We know where we need to focus our attention—the path up here and all along there." He pointed to the cliffside that faced out away from the mountain that hugged the back of their settlement and from which the waterfall flowed. "Unless Ford says he thinks they can scale the back of that." Marcus jerked his chin at the mountain.

"No, we're protected from that side. It's too sheer," said Ford.

"But wait. Those big rocks are very heavy," said Janet, wringing her hands. "How can we move them?"

Mercury looked from Marcus to Ford, and her face broke into a smile. "Oh, I think the three of us have that handled."

40

THEY CAME FROM the west the next evening.

As the sun dropped toward the horizon, the line of men crept forward, hoping to remain unseen by those blinded on the clifftop by the brilliant yellow light.

But it's damn difficult to blind a golden eagle.

Ford's shrill cries warned them, and the sound of gunshots as the invaders tried to knock him out of the sky was also a giveaway.

"I don't think they're very smart," said Stella as she and Mercury stepped away from the cliffside and moved to the center of the vast, flat area on which they'd settled. Khaleesi trotted at Mercury's side as their people rushed from more vulnerable positions across the clifftop to join them.

"They're mean smart," Mercury said. "We can't forget that just because they do seemingly stupid stuff like shoot at Ford and completely blow anything that might be left of their surprise attack, that doesn't mean they're not cunning."

"True," Ford said as he caught up with them. He brushed his long, tangled hair from his face as they pushed through the group so that they stood in its center. Everyone pressed around them, quiet and attentive.

"How many of them did you see?" Mercury asked Ford.

"I counted about fifty." As a whole, the group gasped.

"That's a lot more than us!" said Georgie, and her brothers nodded vigorously beside her. She held Dandy tightly in her arms. She and the twins were pressed against Imani, their eyes wide and frightened.

"Hey," Marcus squatted in front of them. "You know Badger and I were soldiers, right?" The shepherd went to the boys and sat close to them so that their small hands could stroke his thick fur. The kids nodded, though they still looked terrified. "So let me tell you something about war. Where we are gives us a big advantage over anyone who would try to hurt us from down there. No matter how many bad guys there are, it doesn't matter because they can only get up here one at a time."

"So we're safe?" Cayden asked.

"As long as we stay up here, yes," Marcus assured them.

"But they do have guns," added Mercury. "So stay away from the side of the cliff."

Marcus stood and ruffled the boys' hair. "I've been considering it, and the safest places for the kids and anyone who is not actively return-ing fire is back there, within the shelter. Those teeth-like rocks form a protective barrier." He nodded to the far end of the cliff. "Also it's safe around the pond and garden. They're far enough from the vulnerable edge, though they're close to the entrance to the path." His gaze met Mercury's. "From now on someone who is armed should always be sta-tioned at the mouth of that path."

"Agreed," said Mercury.

"Okay, good," said Hilary. "So we can still work the garden. That's a relief."

"And the shelter is safe," said Stella.

As she spoke those words, gunfire erupted from below. It zinged off the barricade boulders and had everyone ducking. Several people cried out, and Janet burst into tears as they ran from the center of the clifftop area to the far side where the mountain tucked against it. There they cowered, huddled close to each other.

"Hey!" Mercury shouted above the noise, drawing their attention. "We're okay. They're not going to get up here. Remember that. Gemma, Karen, Janet, and Hilary—please take the kids to the shelter." She cast her eyes around the group. "If you feel comfortable with your ability to use firearms, be careful, but make your way to one of the barrier stations with weapons. Jim, I know you're a good shot. Would you man the mouth of the path?"

"Absolutely." Jim crouched as he jogged across the clifftop to the one entrance and the rifle waiting there.

More shots split the morning, followed by sounds of bullets chipping rock. "Okay, get to the shelter," said Mercury. "Stay safe. We'll keep you apprised as we can."

"I'll read to everyone!" said Gemma with forced brightness.

Imani knelt in front of the children. "Go with Gemma and Karen. I need to stay out here with Mercury."

"But what if something happens to you?" Georgie's lip quivered as she spoke.

Imani kissed her cheek. "Nothing will happen to me because I'm going to be very careful." She stood. "You must be careful too, so that we'll all be safe."

"Badge, go with the kids," Marcus told the big shepherd.

"Gemma, grab Khaleesi's collar and be sure she stays with you in the shelter," said Mercury.

"Will do," said Gemma.

"Come on, everyone," said Hilary with a smile. "It's time to start lunch anyway. And today we'll cook while Gemma reads us stories."

The children, faces pale and grim, nodded bravely, and then as a group they sprinted for the shelter, hugging the back of the clifftop.

Ford, Marcus, Stella, and Imani remained with Mercury. "Let's go check out this shitshow," she said. "Ready?" As the gunfire paused, Mercury sprinted across the clifftop, running to the largest rock barricade, which was about halfway along the lip of the cliff. They'd just made it there when Al Rutland's voice boomed over a crackly bullhorn.

"Hello the cliff! Let's talk."

Stella snorted. "He thinks that's all it'll take to get us to file down there like fucking sheep?"

"Hello? We got a white flag waving down here!" Al shouted.

Mercury peeked around the boulder barricade. She could see the forms of men just inside the trees that ran along the creek. When she shifted her gaze she spotted several more men crouched behind the vehicles they'd moved to the front of the original campsite the day before.

Between the creek and the vehicles, Al Rutland stood with a bullhorn in his hand, looking up.

"Eva's there, just inside the tree line. Do you see her?" Beside her, Ford pointed.

Mercury nodded. "I'm not surprised she's with him."

"Neither am I," said Stella. With Marcus, she peered carefully around their barricade down at the camp. "Those two make a great couple."

"Mercury! We want to talk to you!" Al insisted.

"He thinks you're going to go down there," said Marcus. "I know we keep saying to remember that he's not stupid, but that's pretty fucking stupid."

"Mercury doesn't have to go down there to talk with him," said Imani. She was pressed against the rock barrier and the only one of them who wasn't looking down.

Mercury ducked back behind the barrier. "What do you mean?"

"Use your super strength," said Imani. "It intensified everything about you physically. You have no idea how easy your voice lifts and carries when you speak to the group. Concentrate on it and shout down at him. He'll hear you."

Stella shrugged. "Imani has a point. You're loud, even when you don't really try to be."

"Well, here goes." Mercury cleared her throat and peeked around the barrier again. *"What do you want, Rutland?"* Mercury's voice shocked her. It reverberated around them, blasting down the cliff. She watched Al take an automatic step back and pause before he lifted the bullhorn to his mouth again.

"Your surrender, of course," Rutland said.

"That's never going to happen. Go away. Leave us alone and we'll show you the same respect."

"But we don't want you to leave us alone," said Al. "We want you to join us."

"Not interested."

"We're not asking. We're insisting," continued Al.

"You're wasting your time. We're not coming down. Ever."

"Oh, I think you will," said Al. "Think about this and then get back to me." Rutland moved back into the tree line and a man took his place. He lifted a monstrosity of an assault rifle, aimed, and fired up at them.

"Get down!" shouted Marcus. He and Ford hurled themselves on top of Stella, Mercury, and Imani as the something hit the cliff, just to the right and below their barricade. It shook the ground around them and hurled rock and debris through the air. "Get back! Now!" Marcus grabbed Stella and Imani, almost dragging them with him as he sprinted away from the cliffside. Mercury and Ford raced with them. As they ran Mercury shouted at the others who were spread out along the cliff's edge behind other barriers. "Get to the shelter!"

Then from the end of the cliff where the only entrance was located, Jim cried out and fired several shots, one after another.

"Jim! Are you okay?" Mercury called.

"Yeah, but two of theirs aren't," Jim replied. "I'm staying here. No one's getting past me."

"We'll relieve you soon," shouted Marcus.

"What the fuck was that thing they fired at us?" Stella asked Marcus.

"It looked like an old grenade launcher, one of the under barrel ones, like an M203. Military started using them in the late sixties, during the Vietnam War," he said. "Dangerous as hell but not as bad as a bazooka. It's less accurate and not as powerful. Thank all the gods."

"But still bad," said Mercury.

He nodded somberly. "Still very bad. Of course, a lot depends on how much ammo they have for it. With plenty they can tear us up. With only a few shells they can still do a lot of harm."

"Tell me what the shells look like and I can fly down there and see how many they have," said Ford.

"No!" Mercury told him. "That's what they want. They will shoot you out of the sky."

"I agree with Mercury," said Stella.

"Okay, so we need to stretch out along the clifftop and start picking them off," Mercury said. "I know I'll be able to take several of them out. Marcus, you can hit them from here too, right?"

Before he could respond, Imani's voice cut between them. "No. That is not how we should do this. Not if we want to win. Not if we want our world to actually change."

Stella said. "You've figured it out, haven't you?"

"I have." Imani nodded and Mercury realized the healthy, fawn color was back in her cheeks, and her dark eyes were bright and clear of the shadows that had been dimming them.

"Tell us," Mercury said. "We want our new world. We'll listen and do what must be done."

"You're not going to like it," said Imani.

"It can't be worse than having Al Rutland lob grenades at us," said Mercury.

"Not worse than," Imani said with a quirk of her lips. "But definitely more frightening." As Imani explained what she had come to understand through Grandmother Cedar and her connection with the land, Mercury agreed. It was, indeed, frightening . . .

41

It didn't take long to get ready. Imani's plan, though terrifying, was simple. The weapons and all the ammunition they had were already spread out along the cliff at barricade points and at the entrance to the path down. It was a quick thing to pile them together, even as periodic gunshots snapped around them.

They built up the campfires. Twilight approached, and the breeze had cooled and increased. It whipped the flames, sending sparks up into the sapphire sky.

It was a simple thing to rinse five buckets and fill them with fresh water from the pool. They placed the buckets in a line along the cliff, one right next to the other. Beside each bucket of water rested a knife that occasionally caught the reflection of a flickering flame so that silver winked across the cliff.

The group stood along the mountainside that pressed against their cliff. They were silent, but their hands were linked. Mercury faced them. On her right stood Stella, Imani, Karen, and Gemma. Ford was on her left.

"Your intention is in the verse Imani taught you. Don't be afraid. Chant it with us. Remember that you're not alone. *We're* not alone. The earth herself is with us," said Mercury.

"The elements are with us," said Imani.

"The plants are with us," said Stella.

"The animals are with us," added Gemma.

"The spirits are with us," finished Karen.

Hilary spoke from the center of the chain of people. "We're not afraid."

Marcus stood beside Hilary. His wide smile was aimed at Stella, but Mercury felt its warmth as he said, "We're all with you. We believe in this. We believe in you."

"Ready?" Mercury asked the women to her right.

"Yes," they answered together.

"Ready?" Mercury looked to her left.

Ford nodded. "Ready."

"Let's change the world." Mercury turned and with her friends and her lover beside her, strode to the cliff's edge. She moved so that she could peer over the battered barricade and shouted. *"Rutland! We have something for you."* She saw the shadows within the tree line stir, but didn't wait to watch him step from them.

Mercury bent and picked up an armful of guns from the pile behind her and tossed them over the edge of the cliff. Stella, Imani, Karen, and Gemma joined her. They threw every handgun, every rifle, and every box of ammunition over the cliff. They could hear them clatter against the jagged rocks below.

When they were done and all the weapons were gone, Mercury looked down at Rutland. He lifted the bullhorn.

"Wise choice. We accept your surrender. Come down slowly," he said.

"As usual, Al, you are unable to grasp the point. Let's see if we can help with that." Mercury turned, lifted her hand and dropped it.

The twins sat behind their drums. Georgie stood beside them with her flute. The children, the dogs, and the kitten remained within the safety of the rock teeth shelter at the end of the cliff, and as Mercury signaled the boys began a heartbeat rhythm. The sonorous sound echoed easily across and down the cliff, joined by Georgie's flute that wove between beats, creating an ancient tapestry of sound.

Mercury began to sing the mantra in time with the drumbeats. *"The air the fire the water the earth awake, awake, awake, awake. The air the fire the water the earth awake, awake, awake, awake."*

As they moved to stand beside the water-filled buckets, Stella, Imani, Karen, and Gemma joined her, singing. "The air the fire the water the earth awake, awake, awake, awake."

In time, as if they'd rehearsed for this moment all their lives, each of the five lifted a knife and slashed it across the skin of her wrist. Together they plunged the wounds into the water while Ford's deep voice joined their song.

"The air the fire the water the earth awake, awake, awake, awake."

"Mercury! I'll count to three. If your people haven't started down we'll get the fucking grenade launcher out again!"

Al's voice sounded very distant as the women picked up their buckets and walked to the lip of the cliff. Behind them their people sang.

"The air the fire the water the earth awake, awake, awake, awake."

"I claim the Warrior gifts you have given me, mighty Gaia," Mercury said. "So I have spoken; so mote it be." Mercury poured the bloody water from her bucket so that it rained down the side of the cliff.

"I claim the gift of Sight that you have given me, Divine Feminine," said Stella. "So I have spoken; so mote it be." Stella poured her scarlet-stained water over the side of the cliff.

"One!" Al shouted.

"I claim the gift of the Mystic that Mother Earth has given me," said Imani. "So I have spoken; so mote it be." She lifted her bucket and poured the tinted water down the cliffside.

"Two!" Al continued.

"I claim the gift of Healer that the old gods have given me. So I have spoken; so mote it be," said Gemma. With a fierce smile she tossed the water over the edge of the cliff.

"And I joyously claim the gift of Spirit, my Lord Jesus, and that which is His beloved earth has given me. So I have spoken; so mote it be—amen," Karen said as she poured her bloodstained water over the cliff.

Behind them the group continued to sing the awakening chant.

Mercury moved to the very edge of the cliff and her friends joined her. They clasped hands and Ford completed the chain by taking her hand in his. She raised her arms and they all lifted theirs with her. As blood spattered from their wrists down around them she spoke, and her words soared over the drums and chants. *"We have turned from the destruction of man to embrace nature, and we ask, Lady of the Woods and Streams, Hills, and Land—and Lord of the Forest and Mountains, Oceans, and Plains—that you protect and keep us as long as we honor this pact with you. So we have spoken; so mote it be. The air the fire the water the earth awake, awake, awake, awake!"*

"Three!" Al's voice was filled with rage. "Three! Three! Fucking three! Hoyt, get your ass over here and light them up!"

Mercury continued the chant as she and her people gazed down. Twilight had softened the land around them, so when the man with the grenade launcher joined Rutland it seemed he did so gracefully, as if in a dream. He lifted the weapon and sighted. Stella's hand tightened on hers, but none of them balked. They remained, straight and proud, and in full view of those below.

The instant before Hoyt pressed the trigger the earth beneath his feet slashed open and from it burst a vine, black as night. Thorns covered it as, snake-like, it slithered around Hoyt. The man shrieked and dropped the weapon as it tightened and pierced his body with hundreds of razor-edged needles.

There were more shouts and shrieks as the earth all around the base of the cliff split open and more of the inky vines sprang from it. They didn't simply form a barrier before the camp, they encircled the attackers, spearing them in place.

At the same moment the night breeze changed. It howled like a banshee, and as it swept into camp, green mist—thick as water—came with it.

Some of the men threw down their weapons and ran, but the vines were relentless. They cleaved the earth, cutting off their retreat. The men the thorns did not spear drowned in the tidal wave of green.

Mercury saw Eva Cruz burst from the tree line. She didn't try to escape as the men had. She sprinted to Al, who had backed away from the impaled body of his man. He was caught between the widening wall of thorns and the mist that shadowed it and the camp.

When Eva reached Al, he turned and stared up at Mercury.

"I will not end like this!" His voice blasted at her. He turned to say something to Eva, who nodded. As he ran toward the bottom of the cliff, Eva Cruz spread wide her arms. Even from the clifftop Mercury was able to see her draw in an enormous breath, so deep that her chest expanded grotesquely, like a boa constructor unhinging its jaw so that it could swallow its prey. Then her head fell back and she pursed her lips and exhaled through them.

The sound of a gale wind roared and from Cruz's scarlet lips came forth a swarm of insects. Their movement in the air beat at the mist, keeping it from engulfing her. The dark cloud of insects obscured her, then as the swarm encased her body Eva became visible again. She was covered with insects so that she hummed and undulated with millions of wings. Arms still outstretched, Eva's body lifted and ascended toward them.

"What in the holy fuck is that?" Stella asked, still clutching Mercury's hand.

"An abomination," said Ford. "As is that." He gestured down and the women peered over the side of the cliff to see Rutland crawling his way up the cliff. He moved in an inchworm-like motion, as if his hands and feet had suckers that attached to the rock.

The group moved back from the cliff's edge, and as Eva dropped from the sky to land lightly in the center of the clifftop, the music and chanting died. Someone screamed. All Mercury could do was stare. The horror before her froze her mind.

Mosquitoes covered Cruz. They filled her hair so that it swayed, Medusa-like. Her mouth was a scarlet slash in a sea of swarming bodies. Her eyes glowed neon blue with rage. *"You think you can defeat me?"* Manically, she began to laugh and from her open mouth poured more insects. The multitude arrowed out across the cliff, attacking Mercury and her small group.

Mercury tried to swat at them, but they filled the air around her, choking her, blinding her. She was going to drown in them!

Stella's voice cut through her panic. "Mercury! Get to the garden. The citronella! Pull the citronella, marigolds, lavender. Bring them back here. *Run!*"

Her words thawed Mercury's frozen mind. Blindly, she turned away from the cliff's edge and sprinted. Her impossible speed cleared the insects from her vision and she raced to the garden, charging through rows of half-grown vegetables, to the separate area where Stella had planted the herb garden and framed it in insect-repelling plants. Mercury tore handfuls of them. Clutching the plants close to her body, she ran back to where her friends, her family, were staggering and falling and shrieking as the swarm began to devour them.

She didn't need Stella to tell her what to do. Mercury knew. She dropped the bundle of plants at her feet and with her fingernails tore open the healing laceration she'd so recently made across her wrist. She held her arm over the clump of plants. Her blood spurted, hot and thick. When they were coated with scarlet, Mercury picked them up and raced toward the thing that was Eva Cruz. She dropped her shoulder and plowed into Cruz, knocking her off her feet. Mercury stood over her and released the bundle of blood-soaked plants onto her.

"*Grow!*" Mercury commanded.

The plants responded instantly. They shivered and twitched, and then they began to grow, spreading like ivy all over Cruz's body. The pungent scent of citronella mingled with the distinctively straw-like odor of marigolds and the calming, earthy smell of lavender.

The swarm reacted first. It began to die, and not just the mosquitoes on Eva's body. All around them mosquitoes dropped to the ground like grains of toxic rice, writhing. Eva began to shriek. The plants continued to cover her, trapping her against the ground. Mercury stared as lavender sealed Cruz's mouth. Citronella covered and filled her nose. And marigolds bloomed where there had been blue eyes, neon with hatred. Then Eva Cruz's body was pulled down into the earth, absorbed like rain, and every mosquito incubated within her dissolved into nothingness.

"*What. Have. You. Done!*"

As one, Mercury and her friends turned to see Al Rutland slither over the lip of the cliff. His body was covered with fat leeches. Their skins glistened darkly in the firelight. He stood, but his movement was liquid, more like a cobra lifting to strike than a man.

"Keep him busy." Imani whispered to her before she raced away toward the clifftop shelter.

Rutland didn't notice Imani. He only had eyes for Mercury.

He took a rolling step forward. His body rippled as if more of the leeches waited impatiently, just below his skin.

"You shouldn't have killed her." Rutland's voice had changed. There was a quality to it that reminded Mercury of stagnant water, deep wells, and things that crawled in shadow and reveled in darkness. "You will pay for that."

"You're beaten, Rutland. Leave now and save yourself," said Mercury.

"And why would I do that? The fun is just beginning," he sneered. "I'll still have you, but only after you've watched me kill your people."

Every time he spoke, every time he opened his mouth, Mercury could see the moist, black bodies of more leeches pressed against his cheeks and clinging to the roof of his mouth. She tasted bile and focused on his eyes.

Screams came from the people who were still in the shadows across the clifftop, clustered against the mountain that rose at their backs. Mercury's gaze went to them. Leeches crawled from the ground, dropped from the wall behind them, slithered from every shadow on the cliff. There were hundreds of them, thousands; they were huge and fast—an extension of Rutland's rage and madness—and they surged over her people, fastening to them, feeding on them.

Then Imani was back. She ran up behind Rutland. She carried a twenty-pound bag slung over her shoulder and shouted. "Ford, hold him!"

Rutland didn't even turn. He just flicked his wrist and leeches dropped from his body and streamed toward Imani. She ignored them and kept approaching.

Ford closed the space between himself and Al in an instant. With a grimace of revulsion, he grabbed the front of Al's shirt, catching several leeches in his powerful hands, and shoved him backward. Rutland laughed. As he fell to his back Al grasped Ford's wrists, pulling him down with him.

Ford was on top of Rutland, almost like a lover, and the leeches spread from Al's body to Ford. They covered him and attached to his skin in a feeding frenzy.

"Yes!" Al said. "Yes, my friends! Glut yourselves! Feed! Feed!"

Mercury was already moving to Ford. Stella, Karen, and Gemma were beside her. She tried to pull the leeches from Ford's body, but as the group in the shadows had discovered, they had anchored themselves to the skin, as if they'd been welded to their victims. They would not release.

And then the leeches were crawling up Mercury's legs. Beside her, Karen shrieked and Gemma stumbled back, crying and pulling at the horrible black things.

"Mercury." Imani's voice was utterly calm.

Mercury met her gaze. Leeches crawled up Imani's body, but she ignored them. Her gaze and her voice were serene.

"Open his mouth," Imani said as she took the bag from her shoulder and pulled the drawstring that held it closed.

When Mercury saw what was within, she understood. She, too, ignored the things that were boring into her body. She shut out her friends' cries for help and Ford's groans of pain. She went to Al's head and dropped to her knees beside him.

"Begging will not work, but I do enjoy seeing you on your knees. Perhaps I'll wait a day or two before I kill you," said Al.

"Ford, don't let him get up," Mercury said.

Ford turned his head. His face was covered with leeches, but he nodded, dropped his forehead to Al's chest, and used his whole body to trap him against the ground.

Mercury reached for Al's jaw. His eyes narrowed and he tried to twist his head away from her, but Ford had him pinned and Mercury's preternatural strength was too much for him. Mercury caged Rutland's jaw and pressed her fingers into it so that his mouth was forced open. Leeches glinted in the saliva, their heads lifted, seeking her.

"You did this to yourself," Mercury said. "You chose this. Others may also choose evil, but it's over for you. Reap what you've sown. So mote it be." She pried his mouth open as far as it would go, and then Imani lifted the sack and poured the salt into his maw.

Rutland's body writhed. He gagged and choked, but Ford kept him pinned to the earth, Mercury continued to hold his mouth open, and Imani poured and poured.

The shrieks that filled the night changed. Mercury's people no longer cried in pain. Instead, the leeches gagged and writhed and shrieked, mirrors of the thing she and Imani and Ford held captive. The fat creatures fell from the bodies they had been devouring, and as Al Rutland's face began to dissolve so, too, did they, until they and Rutland were no more than dark, putrid stains on the earth.

At that moment the sky opened and rain, cool and sweet, began to fall, washing away every blemish left by Rutland and his creatures.

42

T HE NEXT MORNING the only evidence left of the incredible events of
the night before was the wall of thorns that surrounded their campsite. As the sun lifted above the eastern horizon with peacock feathers
of color and light, the wall of thorns changed from ebony to emerald so
bright and brilliant that it gleamed.

There were no guns anywhere. Nor were there any bodies left. It
seemed the earth had absorbed everything—weapons, ammunition, and
men.

The wall of thorns was huge. It created a generous circle around their
encampment, encasing much of the creek as well as the entire cliff and,
as Ford reported after he'd taken to the air, the mountainous area that
backed it.

That morning the only people who ventured down to the original
campsite were Mercury, Stella, Karen, and Imani. Gemma remained
clifftop to help Doc Hilary care for those who had been injured the
night before—though the two healers assured the group that everyone
would survive.

Slowly, the women, the core four, walked the camp. Almost as
though her feet had a will of their own, Mercury found herself heading
for Grandma Cedar. When she reached the tree, she wasn't surprised
that Stella, Karen, and Imani had joined her. As one, the four women

pressed their palms against her rough bark. Mercury breathed deeply of the familiar scent of her bark and boughs.

"Thank you," Mercury whispered.

"We love you," Imani said softly.

"We honor you," said Stella.

"We see your spirit and are blessed by it," Karen said reverently.

The four women smiled. Mercury's heart was filled with gratitude. Her gaze touched each of their faces. *My family. My sisters.*

Not far from the cedar, the wall of thorns grew, thick and dark. Imani walked to it and they followed her. When Imani reached the wall she drew in a deep breath and said, "If I'm wrong, Mercury is going to have to carry me up to Gemma to be healed."

"Wait! What the—" Mercury began too late because Imani walked directly into the wall of thorns.

Karen gasped and a little shriek escaped Stella.

But Imani wasn't skewered or cut into bloody strips. With the sound of a woman's sigh, the thorn wall opened for her. Imani walked through, turned, smiled, and then walked back to them. The thorn wall closed behind her as if it had never parted.

"What the hell was that?" Stella asked.

Imani touched the emerald vine softly, caressingly, as she answered. "She understands intent. We aren't prisoners here. We may come and go freely. I believe anyone may cross through the barrier if their intention is good."

"But if it's evil?" Mercury asked.

"Shish kebab," said Imani.

"Fuckin' A right!" said Stella with a laugh.

"It took a long time to create that barrier," said Karen.

"Generations," agreed Imani.

"Mankind, and I do mean *man*kind, began this apocalypse, and the earth herself has finished it—is healing it. We will try to always live in a way which honors that," said Mercury.

"Yes." The other three women spoke that single word together.

"Um, hello?" A woman's voice came tentatively from the other side of the wall of thorns.

Mercury moved closer to the wall. "Hello," she called back.

"I can hear you, but I can't see you," said the woman.

Stella stood beside Mercury. "Who are you?"

"My name is Martina. I escaped from a place called Madras a few days ago. This might sound crazy, but I believe I was drawn here."

Karen joined the other three women. In a clear, strong voice she said, "Martina, walk into the wall of thorns."

Again, the sound of a woman's sigh filled the space around them as the wall rippled and opened to expose a young woman who led a gray mare through the opening to them. As she joined the women, Martina smiled and then turned to watch the wall close behind her. "Wow," she said reverently. "That's amazing." She faced the four women. "I would very much like to join you."

"Welcome, Martina," said Stella.

"Martina, I'm Karen. Come with me. I'll show you our home and explain, well, everything."

Still smiling and staring around her as if entranced, Martina led her horse and followed Karen.

"I have a feeling Martina isn't the last person who is going to be drawn here," said Imani.

"You're right about that," said Stella.

"What now?" Imani asked quietly.

Mercury grinned. "Now we build our city in the sky and live in peace and gratitude."

"Do you think there will be more bad guys?" Imani asked.

"There will always be more bad guys," said Stella as she hooked her arm through Mercury's. "But that just means we need to live loudly and joyfully to balance it. Right, Acorn?"

"Absolutely," said Mercury as they followed Karen and the two new members of their family.

Linked forever by love and laughter and light, the core four made their way to the family that awaited and the wondrous life that opened before them, glistening magickally with promise as a magnificent golden eagle soared above, ever vigilant.

ACKNOWLEDGMENTS

THANK YOU TO my wonderful agent, Rebecca Scherer, who is always in my corner.

I very much appreciate my team at Crooked Lane—special XXXs and OOOs to my longtime editor and friend, Tara Gavin. It was lovely to work with you again! And THIS COVER IS SO FABULOUS! Thank you, Team Cast!

A big thanks to my chemistry teacher brother, Brad Cast, for his help with explaining the molecular makeup of gases and how altitude and weather can change their behaviors. Any science mistakes are mine and not his (though I'd love to blame him!).

I appreciate the supportive help of Emily Suvada. Your ability to makes sense out of chaos is astounding and wonderful!

And thank you to my awesome nephew, Dr. Keithen Cast, for medical info about setting nasty bone breaks.